CONSTRUCT

Book I of The Chronicler Saga

by Luke Matthews

Developmental Editor
Annetta Ribken
www.wordwebbing.com

Copy Editor
Jennifer Wingard
www.theindependentpen.com

Cover Artist
Carmen Sinek
www.toomanylayers.com

CONSTRUCT
Book I of The Chronicler Saga

Published by Luke Matthews
Seattle, WA

First Paperback Edition: February 2015

10 9 8 7 6 5 4 3 2 1

ISBN: 978-0-9906508-2-9

www.chroniclersaga.com

For Christina—

Without you, there would be nothing to write for.

Chapter One

Images crashed into him, lifting him and roiling like the drag of storm-swelled surf, like memories but somehow foreign. Amidst the turmoil, some few stood out, splitting through the morass of pseudo-remembrances, plastering against his waking mind.

Cold eyes bore into his, so close he can see nothing else. Their color could be grey or blue, but reflect a silver sheen in the dim light. The voice coming from beneath them is little more than a whisper, forming words laced with malice. "You made it too easy, canner. You denied me my challenge, and I can't abide boredom."

Fingers press against his chest, and coldness rushes into his core. Blue light floods his sight and extinguishes as fast as it came, leaving only darkness. Numbness replaces the cold, and his hearing falters. In his last moments, the distant murmur of conversation echoes somewhere above him, a second voice chilling him even through the spreading numb. "There's too much. They'll figure it out, and we're out of time here."

"Then burn it. Burn it to the ground."

He lay paralyzed in the coagulating gore, unable to tear his eyes from the grisly

scene. *Her name eludes him, but her face...he can't forget her face. Where has he seen her before? What had she looked like alive? Memories of fleeing this place dance at the edges of his consciousness. What drew him back? His limbs betray him, stripped of real strength.*

A noise pulls his attention, someone at the door. Thoughts of the consequences of being found here begin to erode his paralysis. His fingers twitch. Knocks at the door become more insistent, the urgent calls of the men outside unintelligible. Willing himself mobile, he manages to roll, still burdened with agonizing weakness. As he gains his feet, knocks transform into crashes, and the door bursts inward.

Raising his hands to protest his innocence, his voice fails. Something strikes his shoulder, a ripple of weakness crashing through to his feet, driving him to his knees. Fires of hatred burn bright in their eyes as they continue hitting him, each impact sapping his energy—his life—away.

His face comes to rest in a cool, sticky pool of drying blood. Again he sees her face, her eyes still pleading with him for help, just as they had in the last moments of her life. Another strike; everything is gone.

The pleasant scent of wood-fire drew him back to consciousness. It reminded him of some far-off place, a distant memory he couldn't quite grasp. When his vision returned, he couldn't focus, the jumble before him a confusion of flotsam. Disorienting weakness hindered his movement, and a weight bore down on him that was not his own.

An arm lay across his chest, disappearing under the heavy form of a downed bookshelf. The hand at its end was supple and young with fingers bearing scars of light burns, like someone who works with wax or molten glass. A pair of silver rings, together forming the image of two winged serpents locked in mortal combat, wrapped the middle two fingers. The cuff of a simple tunic was buttoned tight around the wrist. Past the cuff, the white cotton changed, sewn or dyed with a random pattern.

The hand on his chest was nothing like his own. Softer and more delicate, it bore an extra finger opposing its thumb than the three that adorned his. His own hand was worked metal of burnt orange, like armor of copper or bronze, but his fingers moved with a subtlety an armored glove would not allow. Searching for any memories that would help him discern where—or what—he was, he found only a yawning void. Even his own name eluded him.

He turned his head to take in his surroundings. Clutter dominated the small room, tables and shelves overflowing with books, parchment, glass vials, small dishes, and unfamiliar tools. Haphazard piles of items littered the floor. One of the worktables had been upturned, its contents a shattered mess beside it. Something obscured the tops of the bookcases at the room's periphery. The ceiling itself roiled as though insubstantial, more gaseous than solid. Panic strummed a discordant note, shocking his senses back to focus with a terrible realization: The building was on fire.

Smoke poured down the walls. Flames licked at the borders of the room, the crickle-crackle of dry leaves crumbled in calloused hands. He sensed the heat. His vision dimmed and his head thumped back to the wooden floor. Strength receded from him like a wave, then crashed back to wash away the weakness. Fear took over. *I have to get out of here.*

Scrambling to free himself he found his left arm useless, offering no leverage. With what strength he could muster, he managed a roll. The dead man's hand slid away from his chest and landed behind him with an unexpected *slap* on the wooden floor. A still-expanding pool of fresh blood seeped from beneath the bookcase. The pattern on the sleeve was not dye after all.

A wave of sorrow and targetless remorse cut through his confusion. Was he a victim or an assailant? He shook away the thought—answers were for later. Fumbling the serpent rings from the dead man's hand, he found they were connected in a single unit fitting over both fingers. Maybe it would help him identify this person and discover his own identity.

His immobile arm thudded against his body as he rose, swinging from a crippled shoulder. He balanced above his feet, his stance weak. His movements were jerky and stiff; his joints creaked like a warped door on rusty hinges.

The fallen bookcase blocked access to the room's only door. Hooking the fingers of his good hand under the blockage, he widened his stance and pulled with every ounce of might he could gather. A subtle shift but nothing useful, the movement due more to the softness of the support beneath than the result of his efforts. *Damn this broken limb! With two good arms I could make a solid effort at it. But like this...*

The floor floated and bucked beneath him as he swooned again and pitched forward to his knees. Tipped onto his good right hand, his defective left thunked hard on the wooden floor. The serpent ring skittered out of his grip. A haze slid in around his mind like the incoming tide, draining him, drowning him. He retrieved the dropped ring, clinging to the idea that it was important.

He powered back to his feet. A heavy cloak hung on the wall near an upturned worktable. Fumbling it around his shoulders, he dropped the serpent ring into an interior pocket and donned the hood, clutching the cloak closed at the neck. Not much protection against fire, but there weren't any other options.

A tendril of the ever-lowering smoke caught his attention, twisting downward to slink away between the bookcases at the rear of the room. He lunged for the corner, probing the fingers of his right hand between the shelves, looking for anything leading to the opening that pulled at the smoke. When nothing obvious presented itself, he grabbed the edge of the corner bookcase and pulled.

It moved.

The bookcase did not fall as he expected, but swung outward on hidden hinges. Planting his foot against the neighboring support, he heaved. The effort produced an opening just wide enough to see into.

Behind the bookcase stood a small chamber, no more than three feet to a side, with a low, angled ceiling and no doors or windows. Over his shoulder, the door had caught fire, hungry flames licking upward. Tentacles of heat writhed across the ceiling to consume the books on the top shelves opposite. The wood-fire smell now carried the sweet scent of cooking meat as the tumbled bookcase began to burn and its prisoner along with it.

Inside the corner chamber, the smoke settled, drawn between the cracks in the chamber floor. He pushed inside, splintering the old wood on the backside of the bookcase with his metal shoulder. One of the floorboards ended short of the rest. Near the board's end, metal glinted through a split in the wood. The split hinged open to reveal a large ring beneath... *A trap door!*

A loud crash startled him as the walls and supports of the room, engulfed in ravenous flame, began to collapse. He lurched up, spreading his feet off his glorious escape door. Grasping the iron ring, he gave as mighty a yank as he could muster and... nothing. The tide of weakness betrayed him and the iron ring held fast, the wood of the false floor barely creaking under the feeble pull.

The inferno clawed at his back as he moved in for another try. Shelves fell to the floor as their supports burned. Glass melted atop worktables that had become elevated pools of fire. Glowing embers of paper swirled in the superheated air of the oven-room. Flames touched at his face as the moving bookcase caught. He flinched away and dropped into a crouch.

Gripping the ring tight, he uncoiled his legs and back. With a creaking sigh, the trapdoor swung upward. Elated at his success, he braced himself over the open space. The darkness beneath gave no hint to where he would end up. *Couldn't be worse than here.*

Even so, he hesitated, looking one last time back to the burning room into which he had been born. He felt distant, spying the flames through a looking glass, and his thoughts fell into a murky weariness. Slipping downward, he dropped into the inky blackness below. The trap door slammed shut as the room above collapsed into flaming debris.

The Chronicler Saga

Chapter Two

Colton sat astride his horse under what passed for an eave, on the driest piece of dirt he could find in the little grassland village. With a subtle shift of the reins, he sidled his horse closer to the building, hoping to move out of the nagging drizzle leaking from the blanket of grey overhead. It was mid-afternoon and already darkening, the failing light compounded by autumn rainclouds. In spite of the dimness of the afternoon, bright golden-orange light danced along the alley wall, not from any sun peeking through, but from the raging inferno devouring a building across the street.

A fire of this magnitude in one building was a danger to the whole village, which consisted of perhaps twenty buildings all told. The humid air and light rain offered only marginal help, so most of the villagers formed a fire brigade. Attempts to douse the fire itself had been for naught, so now they worked to prevent it from spreading to nearby buildings. Colton's partner sat a few strides ahead of him, watching it all with morbid amusement.

"Shame," the man said without turning back toward Colton. "I rather liked Ferron."

"You don't like anybody, Bales." Colton replied. "We should go. We can come back in the morning, but we shouldn't just stand around."

Colton pulled the reins, and his horse backed away. The mouth of the alley grew smaller, closing around the edges of the blaze until it framed a small, bright rectangle of flickering orange and red with Bales silhouetted in the middle. Colton exited the opposite end, and the despicable coldness of the grassland drizzle sneaked down his neck. He lifted his collar and turned away, hoping Bales would follow.

Colton shielded his eyes from the flat, bright light of morning as he woke; the tattered curtains in the inn room had been left open. He sat upright, rubbing his eyes with the heels of his hands. A deep breath brought with it the musty smell of the old room, mingled with a wisp of the morning air and the faint scent of sugared oatmeal from the tavern downstairs. He rested his elbows on his thighs, hands still covering his bleary eyes.

Standing up was more of a chore than it had been in years past. His back ached from the lumpy bed, his road-weary knees and hips cracked as he applied pressure to them. Rolling the ache out of his left shoulder drew a muffled grunt from him as the joint complained. Numbness was slowly replaced by the prickles of returning bloodflow as he shook his hand back to life.

The morning sun hung only a finger's width above the mountains. The washbasin below the window had been freshened, surely not by Bales, and Colton marveled at how tired he must have been for a maidservant to make it in and out of the room while he still slept. He splashed some of the tepid water on his face and washed his hands, drying off with a towel laid out on the table beside the basin. He dressed in his riding clothes and pulled on his wide leather belt, running his thumb over the shallow relief adorning the bronze buckle.

His hands moved around his belt, checking each of the pouches hanging at intervals around his waist. Satisfied everything was in order, he slipped his weathered tricorne from the bed post and settled it on his head. Stepping to the door, he paused and closed his eyes, taking in several long breaths. Between the seemingly endless nature of their mission and Bales's disagreeable temperament, Colton had grown weary.

With one hand on the door, he drew a small glass vial from a pouch at his belt. Pale blue light played in a tendril of fog within the small container. Colton uncorked the vial, placed it to his lips, and drew the light into himself. It washed away some measure of weariness, and he set out with a deep, numb breath, pausing at the top of the stairs.

The large central firepit in the nearly empty tavern still carried a small flame and red embers. Chairs stood upside-down on the few scattered tables. A hefty barmaid in a utilitarian blouse worked behind the bar, wiping down mugs with a green wool rag.

A tavern boy knelt before the bar, dunking a scrub brush in a washbucket to his side and attempting to erase a series of black and grey scuffs from the floor. The tavern had been empty most of the night, allowing Colton and Bales to drink in peace. After the sky darkened, the tired and doleful lot of ranch-hands and dirt farmers who'd been engaged with the fire across town filtered in, drinking and eating in somber silence, saving revelry for happier times. Colton welcomed the quiet atmosphere.

Colton spotted Bales near the front door, munching on a handful of *farls*. His partner's hands emerged from the worn sleeves of his waistcoat like cave denizens, jittering as they worked to shell another nut. As Colton descended the stairs toward the main floor, Bales stood, grabbing his riding coat. He tossed the remaining *farls* into the pile of shells at his feet, drawing a look of contempt from the tavern boy and barmaid in the process. As Bales crossed the bar, clods of mud dislodged from the sides of his boots to scatter across the newly scrubbed floor.

Bales worked his tongue around his gums, evidently clearing some detritus left behind by his morning snack. He swiped his dark hair away from his face before donning his own hat. "Nice of you to join us!" he said to Colton, in a tone too cheery to be genuine. "Can we be on our way?"

Colton was used to this kind of reaction from Bales, but that never meant he enjoyed it. After every job, his partner—an inadequate description of their relationship—was coiled like a spring, desperate to move to the next task in their ongoing assignment. "Every moment you think of me as lazy, Bales, is a moment I find you over-eager."

"Be that as it may, it's time to go." Bales raised his voice, to no one in particular. "It's time to put this smelly little washbasin of a town behind us." The barmaid's face wrinkled as though she'd just gotten a whiff of sour milk.

"We have local business to attend to, Bales, so lengthen your nerves."

"My nerves are long enough, Colton," the last words came out thick and black. "But they're strapped to thinning patience. Let's. Go."

Bales turned on his heels and flicked his coat downward as he donned it, knocking over the washbucket in the process. The tavern boy looked up from the gray puddle around his knees and began to protest, but held his tongue as Colton passed him by. Bales swung the doors outward and exited to the street without thought for his partner, who caught the swinging doors with upraised hands.

"Will ye be needin' the room another night?" The barmaid peered over the bar, her knuckles white around the dirty mug in her hand.

"Even need wouldn't make me stay here another night." Colton said as he exited.

Chapter Three

The drop from the burning room ended in cold water, where he lost consciousness. He awoke submerged, face down, with no idea how long he'd been there. Some sense described his surroundings in the pitch-black cave, feeling every curve of the smooth rock walls, where the stream wound through the stone floor, guiding him toward the way out. Soon, daylight filtered back into his sight and led him to a chamber open to the sky.

Climbing out of the cave mouth was a chore with only one working arm. A rope-and-slat ladder to one side of the deep hole looked sturdy enough, but attempting to climb it snapped the ropes and brought the ladder clattering down on his head. The climb was treacherous, but he found enough handholds and footing to make it up to open air. At the edge of the opening was a calm pool fed by a small stream that ambled down into the grove from the higher foothills.

With no sign of his memory returning, he tried to parse out the things he knew from the things he didn't. Basics were still present—the names of objects and colors, how to walk and balance, language, mathematics. And yet, in all that basic knowledge, what images he could discern felt out of place. None of the names that cropped up in the jumble of his thoughts rang familiar, and certainly none felt true enough to be his own. More disturbing to him than not remembering who he

11

was, though, was not remembering *what* he was.

He obsessed over this thought as he studied his one working hand. His fingers moved with strength and grace, and could bend almost as far backwards as forward. His feet had no toes but were segmented from ankle to tip, the bottoms made of a wood-like substance as hard as stone. His entire foot could curl almost completely down onto itself to provide him with sure footing and balance, certainly a help in climbing out of the cave.

The rest of his body was a collection of metal plates in varying hues of gold and orange and brown, held in place by rivets whose tops were worn almost flat with time. Some were stained green with age, but he found almost no signs of rust. Certain sections—his shoulders near his neck, his right outer thigh, and the lower sides of his torso—were built of the stone-wood material. All his joints moved freely from his toes to his neck, save for the damaged arm, but he couldn't quite see *how* his joints articulated. At times, inflexible metal parts seemed to shift and twist to make movement possible, and any actual joints that existed were well hidden beneath the metal.

None of that matters if I don't know what or who I am. Somewhere, in all these plates and rivets and joints, must be some sort of clue. As he contorted himself to scan the less accessible parts of his form, the sun peeked over the horizon, glinting off of the metal of his upper back. He caught the reflection in the water below and saw something dark on the backside of his shoulder.

Brushing away the dirt that had settled into the crevices was difficult, but the light began to pick up as the sun rose, and in the reflection he saw what lay beneath: letters. The engraving was old and worn and almost unreadable, but he could make out a few shapes in the reflection; an S and an A together, what looked like an M, at least what he could see of it, a large gap of nothing followed by most of an L, the rest unreadable.

No matter how many times he tried to make a word, the letters didn't quite work out, and the spaces in between were too worn to be read. Was it a name? *Samuel?* He rolled the word over in his head, searching for familiarity, but found none. *Maybe if I say it out loud?*

"Samuel." His own voice surprised him. A smooth, resonant

sound…natural. He had expected something grating or metallic, but it was measured and even rather pleasant. "Samuel," he repeated. Still no familiarity, no pang of recognition, no sudden flash of memory.

"I guess it's as good a name as any," Samuel said.

The Chronicler Saga

Chapter Four

Colton followed Bales across the small town to the remains of the burned-out building. The pace was faster than Colton would have liked. Avoiding excess attention was paramount, and enough was directed at them just for being outsiders. They cut down an alleyway between two low buildings, emerging across the street from where the rubble was being tended to by an old man in the boots and breeches of a farmer. Colton stepped up his pace and caught Bales by the shoulder.

"Let me handle this," he said. Bales gave him an exasperated look. "You're too wound up. Just hover around the side and do your thing. I'll go talk to the old man."

"Weh' thanker vereh much, sur." Ah, Bales's sarcasm. "I jes go ovur here an' do's as I'm told."

Colton tightened his grip, just enough to hurt. "Yes. You will. Or else we'll end up in a repeat of Tam, and neither of us can afford that right now."

Colton could smell stale beer mixed with *farls* on Bales's breath as he leaned in close. "Don't forget who's in charge here," Bales said.

Colton's eyes narrowed and he set his jaw, a convincing look for his partner's benefit even though he knew that Bales's perceived authority was spurious. "Don't you forget it was your mistake that required my presence in the first place. Let's just go take a look so we

15

can get out of this pit."

Bales backed off, and the two of them headed toward the smoldering ashes. The old man sifted the rubble with a shovel, dousing any still-glowing embers with water from a nearby bucket and prodding still-standing timbers to test their strength. The old man looked up from his work and leaned on his shovel, eyeing Colton and Bales as they approached.

"Can I he'p you boys with suh'm?" the old man said.

"Many thanks, sir," Colton replied. "We came by to see the results." His tone was amiable, with just the right note of somberness. "Rode into town last night just as this was dyin' down. What happened?"

The old man glanced at Bales as he strode around to the side of the building, then looked over his shoulder at the twisted pile of beams and shingles. "Dunno, really. Man that run this place's name was Ferron. An alchemist, always work'n on suh'm." He turned back to Colton. "Been set up here a few years now. Did repairs, little smithin', worked on constructs if anyone had 'em need workin' on. Place jes started up a'blazin' last night, not much warnin'."

Colton stepped forward, sifting the front of his boot through some of the ash on the street-side of the lot. "What a shame. Anyone hurt?"

The old man nodded. "Found some bones back inna back, look like prolly Ferron's." He shook his head.

Bales had worked his way toward the back and was kneeling just outside the perimeter. Colton could see his eyes were closed, but to a passerby he probably looked like he was staring at the building's remains, trying to find something beneath. He'd have already begun, and Colton needed to give him a little time. "No one else, though?"

"Not unless you count a construct o' two." Colton's ears perked up. "Bits an' parts of a couple of 'em inner, prolly drop-offs."

"Drop-offs?" Colton asked.

"Ain't many folks round here got money o' skills to have a construct." The old man shifted his weight off of the shovel and turned, talking while he poked, and peered over his shoulder to where Bales had knelt. "Most o' Ferron's construct repairin' business came from merchants. They drop broke 'uns off here on one way, an' pick 'em up onna way back. *Drop offs*. What's he doin'?" He turned back to Colton, pointing his thumb back at Bales.

"Bound to be some upset merchants coming back through your town soon," Colton deflected. Bales was dead still. How long would this take? "Do you know how many were in there?"

"Can't say fer sure yet. 'Least two, best I kin tell. Lots o' piles o' parts and stuff back in there, but the fire was so hot as to melt the metal, so's nothin' much left, now. Don't really know how that happens, unless Ferron's gettin' inta some alchemy he shouldn't."

Colton pressed his palms to his back just above his hips and arched, stretching out soreness. "I've seen a few fires do that. Usually takes a little something extra, but it's not uncommon."

The old man was staring at Bales. "Uncommon 'round here, it is." He turned back. "What's he doin'?"

Colton leaned and looked at his partner, who had just opened his eyes and was beginning to stand up. "I don't know, honestly. He has a weird fascination with fire, and he likes to study remains like this." He leaned toward the old man, friendly, and lowered his voice. "You ask me, it's a little off, but do you mind if he roots around a little? I never know what he sees in these things, but I have to ride with him for at least another few days and I'll hear about it the whole way if he doesn't get the chance."

"Ain't no hair off my feet. Let him root all he wants."

"Thank you much, sir." He clapped an amiable hand on the old man's shoulder. "I do appreciate it."

"Ya find anything valuable, it comes to me for takin' to the sheriff. Just 'member that, a'ight?"

Colton nodded and skirted around the old man. Bales looked up at him and shook his head. Colton nodded and tilted a hand toward the ruins, and Bales stepped into the middle of the rubble, around piles of unrecognizable remains, then leaned down and scooped up a handful of ashes. With his hand to his nose he inhaled, then let the ashes sift between his open fingers.

"Anything?" Colton asked as he approached.

"Nothing, as expected." Bales made to look like he was searching the rubble, but was looking past it out into the grassland. "Nothing for at least fifty miles in all directions. Nothing got out."

"I hope you're right."

"Have I ever been wrong?"

Colton shrugged, looking around in the room where he stood. He guessed this was the front area of the shop, where customers would come to do business. Along the opposite wall was a blackened heap of half-melted metal. In the shape, Colton could make out what used to be a hand and part of a face.

Bales had made his way toward the back of the shop, where there was more wood and timbers, enough to prevent much digging. As Colton joined him, he pointed into the pile. Jutting out from beneath the black latticework he spied a skull turned on its side facing away from them. The bones of an arm reached out into the room, searching for something it would never find. Bales directed Colton's gaze to the rear corner past the body, where he saw another melted form slumped against what might have been a bookcase, jutting up from a hardened pool of metallic slag. "Good enough?" Bales's eagerness set Colton's teeth together.

"Good enough," he agreed.

Bales turned without a word and tromped out of the ashes back toward his horse.

Chapter Five

Samuel bound up his dead arm with torn strips of his cloak's lining, and sat on a rock outcrop at the edge of the cave mouth peering down on the town. The village's palette of tans and browns was marred at its closest edge by a fierce wound of black and gray that still contributed tendrils of colorless smoke to the morning haze. Just after dawn, two travelers came to question an old man tending the ruin and sift through the rubble themselves. They were as out of place in the village as a bear at the dinner table, clothed head to toe in dark leather and capped with hats whose brims had been folded to form three points.

Samuel's anxiety spiked as their search neared his escape route, but they never found the trap door. The shorter of the two seemed anxious to leave, the other more staid and calm. When they completed their search they mounted their horses, already packed for long travel. The town sat on a crossroads of sorts, a place where three well-traveled paths converged in the tall grass. The westerly track on which Mr. Anxious and his friend left headed off into the grassland opposite Samuel's perch, over a low rise in the distance and away from the north-south road.

I could sit here all damned day, Samuel thought. *I just need to pick a direction.* He took a step to the south and hesitated, noting the western road's slight southerly bend. Samuel knew nothing of the two investigators, but the fact that they spent the morning searching the ruins of a building where he almost died tickled his intuition, and he didn't feel like running afoul of them anytime soon, so he set off to the north.

Samuel's thoughts drifted through his void of memory, trying to distinguish what he knew from what he didn't. Deductive reasoning remained intact, at least at some level. Based on the temperature and position of the suns it was likely the end of autumn, heading into winter. A few plains flowers still showed their petals, opening to the small shafts of sunlight that touched them through the cloud-mottled sky. He knew the high mountains stood to the east and the small, distant range stood to the west, with the vast, grassy plain between. He knew words like *forest* and *road* and *grass*, and could even identify the types of foliage surrounding him. He was positive if he were to run across an animal, he'd be able to identify that, as well.

Yet his own name escaped him so he made one up. Although there were flashes of others of his kind in his erratic memories, he couldn't hazard a guess about his race. The metals which composed his skin— *shell?*—were familiar, but the fluidity of his movement and the nature of his construction remained a mystery. The most frightening gap in his knowledge was that he didn't know who he could trust.

At best, the person who set fire to that building didn't care that he was trapped within; at worst, that person knew for sure and wanted him there. He was grateful his instinct and sense of self-preservation had stuck around through whatever trauma scrambled his memory, allowing him to escape at least with his life. Was it life, really? A walking structure of metal and stone and wood, riveted together and powered by wonder and worry and fear.

The grass parted and he stepped out onto the northern road, sinking slightly into the hard-packed earth that shed no dust after the night's rainfall. The path would, for a time, give him a direction and a purpose as simple as *follow the road*. The last of the visible travelers was already past him toward town, and the road rose out of the plain to begin a long but gentle climb. Maybe it was best to just walk and think.

Daylight passed beneath Samuel's notice; the suns—Big Sister and Little

Blue, he recalled—falling low in the eastern sky ever closer to the tall mountains. Samuel encountered only one other in his long walk, a grumbling old farmer with an empty, mule-drawn cart. "Ganna!" the little man kept snarling at the mule, who'd nicker and bray in response, and occasionally take a few steps forward. Samuel called over to the farmer between his arguments with the mule and received a dismissive grunt from below the brim of a worn straw hat. The man had no interest in conversation and moved along without a second glance.

Samuel continued northward as the suns were pulled over the horizon, the sunset first igniting the eastern sky with brilliant oranges and then, for the few moments after Big Sister had gone to bed but Little Blue stayed out to play, a cool blue-gray hue took over, casting eerie shadows in the grass. After a few moments, Little Blue's light failed, and the last fleeting moments of day chased the siblings over the mountains. Stars twinkled to life across the wide-open sky, and deep blue twilight faded down to the black void of night.

The day's travel had not brought even a hint of exhaustion, thirst, or hunger. He wondered about his need for food or water, or if his kind had other means of nourishment if any was even necessary. There had been little dust or wind to aggravate his joints and a blessed lack of rain, although he could see a darkness in the far distance to the west that hinted of some in the near future. The cloak provided ample protection, but were the elements even much of a concern? He felt no urge to stop or camp, no desire to rest or relax, and he found the fading of the sunlight had not dampened his sight to the degree he thought it might. In the cavern beneath the town, in utter blackness with not even a hint of light, he could not see but instead sensed. In the nighttime starlight, however, his sight remained sharp but colorless.

In a world drained of color, the grass took on a ghostly grey against the almost stark black-and-white of the distant trees. Starlight danced in glowing halos along the tops of anything that broke the surface of the sea of grass. Rock outcrops glistened as though wet, scrubs glittered in the light breeze, and solitary trees shone with angelic brilliance. Steps before the top of a long rise he turned back, taking in the valley and distant mountains. Looking out across the open plain was like standing atop an oceanside cliff as moonlight danced along the tops of waves. Wind rustled the leaves and grass around him, and he nodded a silent goodbye to the crossroads village, now so far behind.

The road flattened as he crested the ridge, running level for some time and curving around a hill to the east, the tree line in the distance. The bulk of the forest stood as a black wall edged in radiant silver in his darksight, the grass giving way to more and more underbrush closer to the trees. After cresting the hill he picked up his pace, spurred on not only by the easier terrain but the allure of the looming forest.

He wasn't sure how long night had been upon him when he turned the bend in the road. The tree line ahead was closer than he expected, and now flickered with an orange glow that brought him to a halt. After taking a moment to adjust, he found the splash of color in the otherwise gray-toned image was the result of a series of campfires.

A pair of fires flared in his vision, and light from several more reflected not only off the trees, but from the sides of a clutch of wagons on the northwest side of the road. They appeared to be less than an hour's walk away, a distance Samuel thought he could cover in half that time judging by his almost unnerving excitement. Was it anticipation, or fear, or a mix of both?

Before he knew it, Samuel closed in on the caravan, turning away from the road to approach them through the grass. A small flurry of activity within the camp signified he'd been spotted. Torchlight moved about near the collection of wagons, and a party of six moved away from their confines to intercept him. Two flanked wide to his left and one to the right, while the remaining three took position between Samuel and their camp. The apparent leader of the group, tall and broad shouldered, sporting a thick black beard but no mustache, stepped forward into his path.

"Good evening, stranger." His voice was forceful and deep. "Odd time to be walking so far out in the plains, eh? What's your business tonight?"

Samuel stopped, taking note of the positions of the men surrounding him. They were agitated, and he had no wish to cause a confrontation. His cloak still hung tight about his shoulders and his face was couched in the deep shadow beneath the hood, which also hid the glow of his eyes. These men would find out soon enough he was not like them. Samuel took stock of his situation and decided being forthright was the least dangerous option. With his good hand, he shook off his hood.

"I'm in need of assistance," he said, freeing his broken shoulder from beneath his cloak. "If any among you can"—*What would be the proper word?*—"repair me, I have a rather grave injury." He gestured to his sling and broken shoulder.

The black-bearded man halted his approach, and the others tensed. "Where is your master, construct?" The tone was tinged with accusation. "You should know the mandate by now."

Construct. Samuel let the word float in the air for a moment, absorbing the man's name for Samuel's kind. A full grasp of the term's meaning would come with time, and he filed it away as the first helpful knowledge gained since his awakening. The mention of a master had Samuel contemplating his response.

"Well, construct?" the man pressed.

"I...I don't know." How much should he reveal? "I came to consciousness with a broken limb and no master to be found." The image of the blood-spattered hand and the serpent ring came to him, but he thought better of mentioning it. "I've spoken to none that could identify a master, and so I've been...walking." Would appealing to their charity have any effect? "Please, sir, if repairs are possible, I'd be grateful."

Two men moved up to flank Black Beard, a short man with flame red hair muttering something Samuel could not make out. Black Beard nodded and the redhead started back toward the camp at a trot. "Grateful, is it?" he said with a mirthless smirk. "You speak more completely than constructs I've known. Your master must be generous."

Black Beard regarded Samuel for a long moment, narrowed his eyes, and took in a slow, shallow breath. His jaw clenched, then his mouth opened, but no words came out. The men to either side stared at Samuel, their muscles taut.

"Sir, I don't know what happened to my master," Samuel said, trying to break the tension rather than increase it. It seemed like some improvisation was in order. "I...I was...left for repairs at a shop down in the valley," he gestured in the direction from which he had come, "but something happened." Samuel hoped the big man would not bite on his intentional vagueness.

Black Beard's shoulders rose in a breath and relaxed, but his hand had dropped to the hilt of a weapon at his side. "We've heard a few tales from travelers of an incident in Winston." The statement hung in the air, half-question, half-accusation.

Behind Black Beard the red-haired man emerged from the camp accompanied by a portly older gentleman who followed him with a gait something between a trot and a waddle. "I know there was a fire, but I know nothing more," Samuel offered. "It consumed the shop where I'd been left before the shopkeeper could finish his duties. By the time I awoke, it was too late to help." The hefty man was close now, beads of sweat running down his brow as he neared the group.

Black Beard tensed again. "And why should I believe it wasn't you who started the fire and are now fleeing?"

"Don't be ridiculous, Hartings," the portly man interjected. His voice had a nasal quality and registered half an octave above normal. "You shouldn't wear your prejudices out in the open."

"It's out here on its own, Taeman. It says it doesn't even know who its master is." Hartings said, never taking his eyes off of Samuel.

Taeman looked contemplative, then spoke to Samuel: "What do you remember, construct?"

Care was needed with this response. "As I told this man," Samuel gestured to Hartings, "I awoke in the town in the valley—Winston?—with a broken shoulder and no memory." All true, but where would truth lead him with these two?

"And so you just walked?" Hartings snorted.

Taeman scoffed at the bearded man and stepped in front of him. "And you have no memories, you say?"

Telling them about the few fragmented visions he did have would garner no benefit here. "No, sir, I do not."

Taeman relaxed and turned to Hartings. "There is nothing to be suspicious of here," he said. "He must have been in for a wipe, which would explain the lack of memory. The process was interrupted by the fire, and he became disoriented. That's all."

Taeman approached Samuel and placed a hand on his good shoulder. The rest of the group started, expecting something that never occurred. "Come, my friend," Taeman said to Samuel. "Let me take a look at you in better light and see what help I can offer."

What looked like a random arrangement of wagons from a distance turned out to be a calculated pattern. No two wagons were far enough apart for a horse to fit between, and each gap was blocked by heavy barrels and guards were posted. Taeman led Samuel through the one opening in the pattern, just wide enough for a man's shoulders, flanked inside by four armed men.

Samuel counted sixteen wagons. Although they were of similar design, each was unique in some way. Many appeared to be vending carts as well as freight haulers, some even painted with bright signs or lettering for their businesses. A bright green wagon bore the name *Welcock's Wares*, and another more subdued one read *Chamberlain's Staples of Food and Home*.

Hartings and his crew dispersed into the camp, which managed to look larger on the inside than it did from the outside. Some entered wagons, some curled up in bedrolls, and others took guard posts. Taeman led Samuel to the rear of the camp, where he saw a group of what he presumed were other constructs milling about Taeman's wagon, which bore the words *Taeman Bolls, Artificer Extraordinaire* in ostentatious gold script on the side. Taeman pointed to a barrel and gestured for Samuel to sit.

The other constructs were simpler in design, lacking Samuel's bulk or complexity. Their movements were stiff as they performed laborious tasks around the camp. Taeman climbed up the steps into the back of his wagon as Samuel watched them in rapt fascination. These were the first other beings of his kind he'd seen in—by his reckoning—his entire life. Their mere existence lifted a great weight from his mind.

Taeman emerged and made his awkward way down the stairs, carrying a large leather bundle and several strange looking implements. These he set on a barrel next to Samuel, and rolled the leather bundle out on the ground. He removed Samuel's cloak, folding it and laying it across yet another barrel. Samuel hoped he had not felt the serpent ring in the pocket; that was a series of questions he was not yet prepared to answer.

"Let's take a look, shall we?" Taeman reached up and untied Samuel's makeshift sling, allowing his damaged arm to swing free. His

25

examination of the mangled shoulder was sprinkled with the occasional *Hm.* or *Right!* as he poked at the damaged metal.

Taeman sat back. "Well, my friend, it's not the best news in the world." He rolled the leather bundle back up and placed it on the barrel atop his other instruments. "The joint is damaged, as is the junction beneath. This is preventing flow from your core to the limb, which is why your arm won't move." *Flow?* "Unfortunately, I'm not sure I can repair it with my road gear."

Samuel felt his first pang of disappointment. "Why is that, sir?" he asked.

"You are a bit of an old chap," Taeman replied. "That joint is well-constructed but rather complex. It looks like you were built before several of the newest design simplifications were made. Normally that would mean an *easier* repair, but all my travelling equipment is geared toward newer constructs."

Samuel's shoulders slumped and he sat forward on his good elbow, letting his bad arm hang at his side. To have his hopes dashed was more devastating than he'd expected.

"I'll tell you what, though," Taeman continued, "You're lucky I was able to call off the hounds out there, what with all the paranoia right now."

"What do you mean?" Samuel asked.

"Oh, right…the wipe," Taeman said. "I guess you wouldn't know, would you?" Taeman leaned forward and began to examine the shoulder again. "Lone constructs aren't much trusted these days, not after the murder of the Queen Consort."

"The Queen Consort?" Samuel said. The pleading eyes of the dead woman resurfaced in his vision. Was that why her face was so familiar?

"Aye, yes," Taeman replied. "And by a construct, no less." He shook his head and walked around behind Samuel, grabbing the upper part of his broken arm and moving it around, taking stock of the shoulder's movement. "First time in who knows how long a construct visited violence on someone of its own accord. But that was a long way from here."

Samuel wasn't sure what to think. Could he have killed someone? Could that be why his memories were erased? Taeman released the broken arm and moved to Samuel's other side, examining his good shoulder and running his fingers along the crevices between his shoulder plates. His hand gave an almost imperceptible stutter as it brushed across the stamped letters, but Samuel caught the momentary hitch.

"Something wrong?" he asked.

"No, no, no," Taeman said with a pause. "N-nothing to worry about."

Chapter Six

Taeman gathered up his gear and tossed it into his wagon, muttered something about speaking with a colleague about Samuel's shoulder, and waddle-trotted off into the encampment. The artificer's other constructs were still attending to their tasks, oblivious to their surroundings or to Samuel. He stood and walked over to the one brushing the mule.

"Hello!" he said, trying to sound cheery. The construct tilted its head upward toward Samuel, its face a blank shape of copper so unlike his own, with only indentations where eyes would normally be, a feature that felt oddly disconcerting. The construct's other features were simpler in design than Samuel's; large sections of metal with little segmentation and simple, exposed joints.

Without a word, the worker construct turned back to its task. Samuel regarded the others, disappointed at the lack of interaction. He ran a hand over his head, noting the exposed rivets and features that these simpler constructs lacked. All of them seemed to have the same featureless faces and simplistic body designs save one, which had just finished packing a pair of saddlebags. Its face bore more details, including eyes and a mouth-slit similar to Samuel's. It also seemed more weathered, showing signs of wear and the discoloration of age on its metal frame. Perhaps he'd have better luck with that one.

Samuel greeted the saddlebag-packer in similar fashion, and

received the same blank look and dismissal. He tapped its shoulder, to which it turned and offered a longer look. "Hello!" Samuel repeated, but to no avail. It was clear this being's edict was simplistic, and Samuel had neither been identified as a threat nor an objective.

"You won't get any delightful conversation out of this lot, friend." Samuel turned toward the new voice. A man in a long cloak revealed himself, stepping out from between two carts. He moved forward and sat on a large trunk, close enough to speak low and be heard but still a respectable distance away.

Samuel backed up and took his original seat, regarding the newcomer. "How do I know you're my friend?" he asked.

The man pulled back his hood to reveal a slender, handsome face, framed by dark, shoulder-length hair that flowed down into his open hood. His eyes were deep walnut, his skin dark, unblemished olive.

"You don't," he replied. "But I am no friend of the waddling peddler over there…" he gestured toward where Taeman had wandered behind another merchant's wagon, "and I have no interest in seeing him grow richer through theft of independence."

Theft of independence. "I'm not sure what you mean," Samuel said. He did, in fact, know what the man meant.

"Oh, come on," The man said, producing both an apple and a small knife from beneath his cloak. "It is clear enough you're more clever than your contemporaries here," he gestured with his apple to the drones around him, "and it is curious to me you don't know your own master." He sliced off a small piece of apple and took a bite, watching for Samuel's response.

"It seems to me," Samuel said, watching the man, "I am not the only clever one. What information do you seek from me?"

"I seek no information." His response came between chews. "But only to provide some. That man over there"—a nod of the head and more chewing—"does not have your best interests in mind. Taeman has never thought of anyone's best interests but his own." He finished his first bite of apple and took the rest of the segment, freeing his blade to begin another slice.

"You see these lumbering heaps?" He gestured with his apple slice to the other constructs. "Not all constructs live this way. Not all *must* live this way. And not all of them were obtained through honorable means."

"And how do you know the truth of these statements?" Samuel asked.

With a smirk, the man shook his head. "By your own admission, you could be the living embodiment of the idiom *born yesterday*. I know the truth because I've been around this caravan more often than I, or they, would probably like. Taeman's a hustler, through to the bone. The man's a talented artificer, but if there's an honest bone anywhere in his body, he's likely removed it and replaced it with bronze."

A bite of apple. "I've been to cities teeming with constructs, and in those cities, there are some as intelligent and communicative as you are. Not like these…"—a dismissive wave—"beasts of burden." Samuel felt his excitement rise at the prospect, but didn't speak his mind. "These things are masterless hulks, bound to Taeman by a tether—just something to keep them around until he can sell them for more than it took for him to steal them."

"Stolen?" Samuel asked, genuinely surprised. "These constructs are stolen?"

"Fortunately found, Taeman would say." He sliced off another apple piece and ate it, looking almost as though he was using the flavor to overpower the disdain that escaped his lips. "Constructs needn't be dumbed down, and in fact they can be much more helpful if they're not. Constructs generally aren't harmful, and the more intelligent they are, the more useful." He took a few small bites out of the remaining apple core, then tossed the remains under the nearest wagon.

"But if these boys were to remember how they were acquired, they might be more trouble for Taeman than they're worth. So he flushes them. Rids them of knowledge and intelligence, even of learned traits or common sense. Then he re-acquaints them to the world by filling their cores with menial skills until he can foist them off onto someone who wants to put the energy into making them whole again."

Samuel lowered his head and mulled the idea over. "How do you know I'm not harmful? I was just told the story of the Queen Consort's murder by a masterless construct."

The man smirked. "I can guarantee you the construct was not masterless, and was not acting of its own accord. But it's a good story, I guess. A good way to wrap up the crime in a neat little bow. Plus, breeding the sort of attitudes you saw in Hartings and his thugs today makes Taeman's behavior look all the more altruistic."

Samuel had only just awoke and, although his memories were lost, he had no desire to lose the remainder of his thoughts. Could he trust this cloaked informant, though? How was he to know that this one was any better than Taeman himself?

"I can tell you're thinking about it, wondering if I speak true," he said, as though reading Samuel's thoughts. "I don't have any way to make you trust me, not really. This is a judgment call for you. I'll tell you now, though, you'd be better off leaving before he's able to do any real work on you. Get out of here and head north to Morrelton. Plenty of artificers there can help you out, and are honest, longstanding businessmen rather than caravanning con artists. I'll leave you with this, though: have you heard him stutter?"

That got Samuel's attention, and he raised his gaze to the man in the cloak.

"Ah, you have, then," he said, leaning forward before standing up. He stepped back beside the cart from behind which he had emerged, but paused before leaving. "He stutters when he gets excited. He's learned to disguise it for smaller scores, but when he's faced with something big, he hasn't quite gotten the hang of hiding it yet. There must be something about you…something he thinks can make him a lot of money." He looked over toward where Taeman had gone.

"What do you have to gain from all this?" Samuel asked, still scanning the other end of the encampment for the artificer. The cloaked man chuckled. Samuel turned his head to follow up, but he was gone.

His decision was made: any chance of retaining his independence outweighed even the slight possibility of losing it. He scooped up his makeshift sling, throwing it over his neck and arranging his crippled arm into it the best he could, then grabbed his cloak, feeling for the serpent ring. With a glance around the camp, he took note of the guard posts and their direction. Most of the guards faced outward and toward the road, with only one man atop his cart taking watch to the rear.

Taeman was still nowhere in sight, and the rest of the camp's inhabitants were asleep or otherwise engaged. He moved to the rear of the circle and slipped between Taeman's wagon and a large blue and yellow cart that read *Eagle Talon Armory*, crouching in the shadow with the wagons between himself and the low firelight. Atop the armory wagon was a high platform upon which sat this evening's guard who, although still sitting upright, snored into his own chest.

Samuel discovered he was not one to waste an opportunity, and he slipped out into the plain. He was capable of more stealth than even he imagined, and was well away from the caravan in less time than he expected. Not too far from the encampment, the land dipped into a shallow gully, just deep enough for Samuel to stay hidden from view as he moved northward.

The land rose away to the north, and every so often Samuel glanced back at the camp to ensure his exit had not yet been noticed. He moved around back of a small rise, then ascended and lay down facing the camp to watch for trouble. He thought, perhaps, he could outrun any of their guards if they tried to pursue, but he'd hoped his departure would not raise that degree of alarm.

At the eastern edge of the camp Taeman emerged from one of the larger covered wagons, followed by Hartings and another older man, a slender gentleman in a simple, distinguished robe. The artificer, still talking to the older man, turned to walk toward where Samuel had been seated. Recognition of the situation dawned, and Taeman broke into an exasperated waddle, searching. His wagon rocked back and forth with his emphatic movements as he entered, and after a moment he stomped back down his stairs to his camp, cursing. He flung something he was holding into the dirt, and kicked the barrel upon which Samuel had sat, with obvious regret.

"That's an awful lot of vitriol from a man who was just trying to help someone out, wouldn't you say?" The cloaked man's voice startled Samuel. "Those are the actions of a man who just lost a prize, not a patient."

"I'll have to admit I agree with you," Samuel replied, betraying none of the surprise he felt. "And he's not raising the guards or making a fuss with the others about my absence." He turned to the man in the cloak. "You've done right by me once tonight, but I don't yet know why. The least you can give me now is your name?"

The man smiled, but kept his eyes on the camp. "Kaleb. My name's Kaleb. Very nice to make your acquaintance…?"

"Samuel."

Kaleb tilted his head, an amused look on his face. "How…mundane." He turned his gaze back toward the camp, where Taeman now sat on his barrel, massaging his sore foot. Kaleb backed up and rose. "We should probably get going."

Samuel nodded, his attention still on Taeman. The artificer turned, shouting off into the caravan, and was soon joined by a boy who came at his beckon. Samuel reached back and tapped the ground where Kaleb had been laying. "Hold on for a moment," he said.

The boy who stood before Taeman looked to be in his mid-teens, with the solid build of a farmhand. He swiped a mop of shaggy blond hair out of his face as Taeman gestured emphatically and limped up into his wagon. Kaleb returned to his perch and the two of them watched.

After a few moments, Taeman returned and began jabbering at the boy, but neither Samuel nor Kaleb could hear what was being said. Taeman waved a letter of some sort in the boy's face and handed it to him, wagging a finger as though imparting some stern instruction. The boy spoke and Taeman snatched the letter from his hand, stuffing it into an inner pocket of the boy's vest. He shook a coin purse in the boy's face and shoved that into his opposite pocket.

After a pause, Taeman threw up his hands in a shooing motion, and the boy scurried off into the camp. A few moments later he emerged on the road side of the caravan, galloping away on horseback, toward Winston.

"That can't be good," Kaleb said.

"I think you're right," Samuel replied. "It's time for us to go."

Chapter Seven

The pair left the caravan behind and moved northeast along the road. They kept it in sight but stayed off of the main path until a bend took them around a foothill to the east, out of sight of Taeman, Hartings, and their band of merchants.

A question had been milling around in Samuel's mind, and after several hours of walking in silence he asked, "What did you mean by mundane?"

Kaleb laughed, the first sound he'd made in quite some time. "All the intelligent constructs I've known—not the kind like Taeman had, but the ones who really know who they are—have absurd given names," he said. "These aren't always the names they're known by, but if you ask one, it'll be the first name they give. When I was a child, my parents had a construct. We always called him Cass, and for the longest time that's the only name we knew. When I got older, I asked Cass if that was his given name, and he said no. His given name was Cassaemalen. And that's one of the simpler names I've heard. Is Samuel short for something?"

"No, it's just my name," Samuel replied. "I don't know if I had another before I awoke, but that is my name now."

"Fair enough," Kaleb replied. He paused, shaking his cloak free of his shoulders as he walked. His clothing was close fitting but not tight, and he wore a long dagger in a sheath at his hip. "Is it true, what Taeman said to Hartings back near the camp? That you chose your direction because you were disoriented?"

Samuel had no reason to distrust Kaleb, but had no reason to trust him either, and wasn't ready to reveal the full truth just yet. "Not entirely, no. My choice was random, for the most part, but it was still a choice. It was not just disoriented wandering."

"And you have no master to speak of?" Kaleb asked, raking his hair away from his eyes. "No draw to anyone? No link?"

"I honestly don't know," Samuel said. "I don't feel connected to anyone or anything, and I don't know of or remember any master whom I might serve."

"So you're an incon," Kaleb said.

Another new word. Samuel felt, at some point, he had known this word but couldn't place its meaning. He looked at Kaleb with a questioning tilt to his head.

"It's dumb, to be honest." Kaleb said. "It's a simple shortening of *independent construct*. It means a construct is not bound to a particular master, either physically or by ownership. In some places incons are outlawed, and since the Queen Consort's death, there has been an overwhelming amount of suspicion regarding incons."

Samuel nodded. "In truth, I don't know if that's what I am or not. Maybe I have a master. Maybe I'm linked to someone and I just don't know how to identify it."

"Now you're just spouting the excuses Taeman made up for you," Kaleb replied. "If you were linked, you'd know it. It's undeniable and unmistakable."

"How can you be so sure?"

"That's how links are designed, Samuel." Kaleb said, hiking up the straps of his travel sack on his shoulders. "The whole point is both control and ownership. Ensuring the creation remains subservient to its creator. There are entire sects that believe constructs to be an abomination already, even with links in place."

If what Kaleb had said was true, then protecting his own independence was even more important to Samuel now than it was back in the merchant camp. "If I am what you claim, I'm in even more danger than I may have realized. How can I even get into Morrelton?"

Kaleb tipped his head back and forth, as though formulating an idea. "I can cover you there," he said. "I can pose as your owner, taking you into town for repairs. We'll say..." he paused, rubbing his fingers over his mouth. "We'll say you were hauling some building materials for me and took a long fall that crushed your shoulder. How did you get damaged, anyway?"

"Another mystery. It was like this when I woke up."

Kaleb shook his head. "Where in the Vells did you come from?"

"I wish I knew."

They walked in silence. After a while, Kaleb began to drop behind, unable to hold to Samuel's pace. At one point, Samuel heard him stumble and turned to see Kaleb had fallen even further behind than Samuel realized. He looked exhausted.

"Samuel, I need to stop," Kaleb said. I know you can keep moving, but I haven't slept in almost two days."

Samuel experienced a moment of unexpected indecision. As much as he appreciated Kaleb's help back at the caravan, his trustworthiness still had not been proven. If the world were as dangerous for an incon as Kaleb had made out, maybe this was a chance for Samuel to take his leave.

As though reading his thoughts, Kaleb spoke. "Look, I know you have no reason to trust me, but I can help you in Morrelton." He moved to a large rock at the roadside and sat, lowering his head in exhaustion. "I'll get you to an artificer who can help you with your repairs. If you still don't trust me, we can part ways there and you can have a nice life."

The offer seemed genuine, and Samuel couldn't deny the benefit of having Kaleb as a companion, if he stayed true to his word. "I don't even know why you're helping me, Kaleb."

Kaleb smiled in his disarming way. "I'm intrigued by you, Sammy."

"Samuel."

Kaleb raised his hands in a mollifying gesture. "I don't know who or what you are, but there's something about you that feels interesting. Important."

"Don't you have your own life to attend to?" Samuel said, not wanting to forget the decision at hand.

"Honestly?" Kaleb leaned backward, stretching his back muscles, to the sound of several pops and creaks. "Not really. This is kind of what I do. I prefer not to take root in any one place for long. I've been all up and down this region and I was starting to get bored until I met you. I want to see where your story takes you."

Samuel wasn't sure if this explanation helped to build any trust, but at least it was reasonable. His decision was made, but he felt the need to reinforce his feelings with Kaleb. "If you betray me, I'll kill you." He wasn't even sure if he was capable of killing, but he was hoping the simplicity of the statement would carry the desired intimidation.

"I have no doubt," Kaleb said.

Chapter Eight

Kaleb opened his bleary eyes to a shaft of sunlight breaking through the tree limbs onto his face, and judged he had slept a little less than four hours. They had camped a short distance from the road, tucking themselves into the tree line. It was just after dawn, and soon there would be traffic on the road, Kaleb and Samuel included.

The morning felt colder than the night, but perhaps that was just the adrenaline wearing off. Sleeping on the ground always leeched some of the heat from Kaleb's bones, even through his wool cloak. The hulk of a construct he'd thrown in with sat against a nearby tree, facing the road and keeping watch. At any time during the night, Samuel could have left him there. Something about this construct struck him different than all he'd known before and, although he couldn't put a finger on just what it was, he felt something strange and special and frightening.

Kaleb always fed off of that feeling. He always preferred not knowing over knowing, the thrill and mystery of what comes next. It had been a long time since he'd been still for long, and even that stint wasn't of his own accord, strictly speaking. In spite of all his travel and adventure, he'd begun to feel bored. *Not anymore. This one's got a ring to it.*

Samuel turned his head to his waking companion, standing and shaking out his own cloak. "Can we get on the move?"

39

Was he anxious? Yet another trait of this construct that defied his kind. Of the constructs Kaleb had known, many were well-experienced—some almost a hundred years old—but none had been as gifted at simulating emotion as Samuel. Or was it something more? He'd encountered constructs who'd learned how to imitate emotional responses, and were even adept at understanding when those responses were warranted. With Samuel it felt different, genuine. *But that's impossible, right?*

Kaleb stood and shook the leaves and needles from his cloak, smoothing it out and pulling it tight around his shoulders as a shiver ran through him. He took a step and felt a twinge in his left thigh; he must have slept on a rock during the night. The knot in his leg groaned at him and he winced. Not the prime way to start a day of walking.

"Yeah, we can get on the road," Kaleb said, shaking out his left leg. "On foot, Morrelton is a few days northeast of us, at *my* speed. If we come across an opportunity to acquire a horse, we could cut that shorter."

Samuel pulled the hood of his cloak up over his head. "I'll leave that to you. I'm in no need of a mount," he said, as he turned and headed toward the road. Kaleb limped behind, unable to tell if Samuel's comment was an attempt at deadpan humor, or just plain deadpan. Everything about this construct bucked the norm—speech patterns, movements, mannerisms…the fact that he even *had* mannerisms. Even his walk was more fluid and natural than most he'd known, not the heavy, clomping gait of the rest.

Kaleb finally caught up, dreading the pace he knew Samuel would set. "Hey, slow down a bit." His conditioned response to constructs stopped him short of cracking a joke about not being a machine. In his experience, a sense of humor was something constructs failed even to emulate, much less actually possess. With Samuel, though, this was something he would have to test. Samuel slowed, but only a little, moving forward with purpose.

"How much do you know about this town Morrelton?" the construct asked.

"A bit," was Kaleb's noncommittal reply. "I've been through there quite a few times. It's surprisingly large for its location, tucked back into the woods in the foothills. Its origins lie in iron and copper mining, but it's become a sort of haven for artificers."

Samuel might have seemed contemplative, if he'd stopped walking for even a moment. "How much do you know about constructs?"

The question struck Kaleb as odd, a construct asking about its own kind. Even after a full wipe, constructs usually retained that sort of information. "My family owned a couple when I was younger. They were mostly caretakers in my father's house. That's why I suggested we head to Morrelton, actually. An artificer there apprenticed under the man who built one of our family constructs. I've known him for quite some time."

Kaleb wasn't sure whether he heard, or merely projected, Samuel's grunt in response, but that grunt was the last thing Samuel said for most of the day. The road wound along the hills, creeping closer to the mountains. Thin clouds leeched the color from the sky, casting the world in cold and grey, but at least it was bright and dry. As the day wore on, the trees around them crept closer to the road, until they were no longer traveling near the forest but through it.

Kaleb spent most of his life walking, but the pace Samuel set was relentless and constant, even for him. As the road began to ascend into the foothills the pace didn't slow, and Kaleb's stamina began to ebb. There had been little to no discussion at the beginning of the day, and toward the end Kaleb was too exhausted to walk and talk at the same time. Kaleb could only convince Samuel to take a break if it was absolutely necessary, which extended only to gathering water and urinating.

This might have been the least prepared Kaleb had ever been for a journey. They lucked upon another small merchant caravan toward the middle of the day, where Kaleb was able to acquire some provisions: water for his waterskin, a few bread rolls, a block of cheese, and some dried meat. The trip to Morrelton was short, so he didn't need much, but he wasn't sure how much sway he'd have with Samuel over the next few days, so he stocked up.

When nighttime descended, Samuel agreed to settle down and camp. Kaleb built a fire. The darkness brought with it a chill breeze and an unwelcome temperature drop. Samuel seemed uncomfortable and had asked if the fire would draw unwanted attention, but Kaleb assured him this trade route was traveled enough that small fires and encampments were commonplace and no one would even turn an eye. Besides, most everyone chose to travel during the daytime and camp at night, so it was unlikely anyone would even come across their camp. In spite of this, Samuel seemed to keep a fair distance from the fire itself, leaning against a tree just at the edge of its ring of light.

Once their modest fire was self-sufficient and Kaleb gathered enough fuel to keep it for the night, he tore off a hunk of bread and began picking at it by the fireside. "So," he said, "you really don't remember anything beyond a couple of days ago?"

Samuel turned away from watching the road and shifted against the tree to face the fire. The firelight danced in coppery reflections about his face, cut by the low blue-green luminance of his eyes. "Nothing," he replied. "There are moments when I think I'm remembering something. But nothing that seems real. Nothing useful."

Kaleb marveled at the description, but didn't let it show. Memory wipes for a construct were not unheard of, but they were not commonplace. If there was a change of ownership for a construct, many, unlike Taeman, felt their experience was important to their value. Loyalty was rarely an issue with constructs if a link was instituted, so memories carried more benefit than detriment. "Sounds like an incomplete memory purge of some sort. You've obviously retained some knowledge; your language is complete and you know more than just basics, so there's something going on inside." He pulled out his knife and sliced off a small bit of cheese, which he paired with some bread and popped into his mouth.

"As we walked," Samuel continued, "I've searched inside me for any sort of feelings," Kaleb started at the use of the word and forced himself to continue chewing, "or experiences that could help me understand where I came from, but I'm finding nothing."

Kaleb swallowed and shook his head. "I'm not even sure where to start, Samuel." This wasn't like any purge he'd ever seen. To build up this much knowledge in a construct after a purge would take months or even years, and an artificer with greater skill than any he knew. The way Samuel acted, the things he said, the way he spoke… These were things built of experience, not teaching or implanting. Samuel's mind was not wiped, it was *repressed*. "Atherton may be able to help. If nothing else, he can get that arm working again, and then we can try to figure out who you are."

Samuel turned back toward the road. "I hope you're right. Good night, Kaleb." It was apparent Kaleb had begun to earn Samuel's trust. A certain amount of satisfaction came with that knowledge, but it was also unsettling.

Kaleb finished his last bit of bread, tossed another small hunk of wood on the campfire, and curled up in his cloak.

As the morning light broke, a chill wind rustled the tops of the tall evergreens but did not penetrate to the lower branches. The forest huddled together like a group of refugees trudging ever northward. Shafts of light peeked through the trees from the roadside, filled and made solid by the low mist that lingered amongst the branches.

Samuel peered through the trees at his new traveling partner, still curled up next to the embers of last night's fire, burrowed into his cloak on a bed of evergreen needles and leaves on the forest floor. A thin wisp of smoke curled upward from the makeshift fire pit, dissipating into the morning fog. Movement in the branches above Kaleb caught Samuel's eye, and he spotted a squirrel silently making its way across the branches, its long bushy tail and tufted ears twitching all the while.

Kaleb's sleep had been restless and it was clear his dreams were unpleasant. As the fire died down and moonlight took over, Samuel had spied a rise not too far from their camp, and took advantage of Kaleb's dreaming to slip away into the forest. He sat against the stump of a long-dead ironwood tree on the back side of the rise, out of sight of his companion but able to keep a watchful eye.

Samuel watched as Kaleb stirred. After several yawns and awkward stretches, he rubbed the sleep from his eyes and sat upright, looking around between bleary blinks. His shoulders tensed. This was the moment for which Samuel had waited. How would his newfound acquaintance react to abandonment? Any number of scenarios had crossed Samuel's mind as he watched Kaleb sleep that night.

"Samuel?" he said without raising his voice. He tipped his hood onto his back and tilted his head, listening. When he didn't hear anything, he looked around again and repeated "Samuel?" this time a bit louder.

In that moment of realization, Kaleb's shoulders slumped and he just sat, seeming to mull over his next action. For a long while he didn't move, his crestfallen features alternating between confusion and frustration. His lips moved in silent discussion, evidently arguing with himself. A shake of the head, a conclusion, and then his eyes closed and he took a deep breath before standing and brushing off his cloak. He stamped out the last few embers of the fire and buried it, setting out on his way. Samuel continued to spy on him through the trees as he reached the road, and was surprised to see him locked in a moment of indecision before turning south—back the way they had come.

Samuel had seen this moment a hundred times in his head, Kaleb's reactions running the gamut from angry to scared to elated. The most common conclusion saw Kaleb tossing about in a fury, angry at his lost treasure. Kaleb's actual reaction was the one Samuel was least prepared for: genuine disappointment. Kaleb's dejected posture and silent contemplation had come as a surprise, but it came with the information Samuel needed: he wasn't a treasure, or a hostage, or a pawn. Although he might not yet be able to take Kaleb at face value, Kaleb's reaction meant he was acting out of trust, and perhaps his story of seeking adventure was somewhere close to the truth.

Samuel rose from his perch and worked his way toward the road, a bit north of where Kaleb exited the forest. Once he reached the hardpack of the main road, he headed south at a good clip to catch up with his new traveling companion. He rounded a bend and saw Kaleb ahead, well on his way down the road, and called after him. "You're going the wrong way, you know."

Kaleb stopped and looked over his shoulder, his brow raised in surprise and then creased with anger. He stood rooted to the road, staring at Samuel before speaking. "What was that, Samuel?" he yelled, storming back in Samuel's direction. "I thought you just left me behind! What, exactly, were you thinking?"

Samuel waited as Kaleb approached and stopped about ten feet away. "I had to know," was all he said.

"Had to know what?" Kaleb's hackles were still up, and his voice raised but not yelling. "What exactly did you need to know that you couldn't just ask me, huh? I laid down on that ground on the trust you weren't planning on sleeping, or at least that I wasn't just exposed out there alone. Do you know what it feels like to wake up alone in the middle of the woods?" A pause. "No, of course you don't. You're only three days old. Well, what did your stupid stunt tell you?"

"I was worried you might just be stealing me from Taeman."

"Worried? Samuel, you shouldn't even be able to worry!" A further retort jangled behind his still-angry eyes, but nothing seemed to bounce close to his mouth. His jaw clenched and unclenched and his mouth opened and closed several times before he set off northward in a huff. He approached too close to Samuel with the clear intent to thump him with his shoulder. When he contacted Samuel's metal frame he bounced sideways, knocking himself off balance in the process. He regained his balance and narrowed his eyes at Samuel before tromping northward with a low "Let's go."

For the first time, Samuel lamented his inability to smirk.

The Chronicler Saga

Chapter Nine

Kaleb maintained a healthy pace on their second day of walking, fueled by anger and a petulant need to stay in front of Samuel as long as possible. Samuel let him have his fury while it held out; the trick was ultimately harmless and, in Samuel's mind, necessary. He hoped Kaleb would see that sooner rather than later, or this was going to be an even longer trip than it needed to be.

Samuel observed the cold of the day in Kaleb's misty breaths. In some way Samuel knew it was cold, but couldn't identify the source of that knowledge. He had no nerves to sense the temperature, no hairs to stand on end, no skin on which to get goosebumps, and no breath to expel fog into the autumn chill. He was learning these things about himself faster than he'd expected, but realized even he wasn't sure what his expectations should have been.

Amidst all this new knowledge, though, something still felt odd to him, perhaps even *wrong*. He moved well in this metal body, which felt so familiar and at the same time alien. It was as though some part of him felt trapped in this shell rather than at home inside it, but that feeling was giving way to the wonder of discovery. As frightening as this experience was, a twinge of enjoyment was starting to dance around the edges of Samuel's anxiety.

Kaleb's reactions told him the emotions he was feeling were out of place, if not outright impossible. To Samuel, though, every emotion felt genuine. There was no thought or calculation behind it, no imitation. His excitement simply happened and filled up everything inside him. Something in him expected the fear to be overwhelming—it almost paralyzed him as he was parting ways with Taeman—but even the excitement was staggering. The gamut of emotions he ran through on the previous night, reactions to nothing more than speculative inferences, had given him a bitter taste of the less palatable side of his feelings. When the time came for true anger or despair, would he be able to withstand it?

Samuel pushed the question out of his mind. There were too many others that needed answering, and for the first time, he allowed himself a glimmer of hope. The artificer in Morrelton could handle his most pressing problem—his shoulder—but what other questions might this Atherton fellow be able to answer for him? Would he know how old Samuel was? Or perhaps even the artificer who'd made him? With Morrelton being so close to Winston, this man might even have insight on Samuel's true owner, if one even existed. He adjusted his lame arm in the makeshift sling, which at once focused all of his desire on being made physically whole again.

The shadows of the forest grew long as daylight faded into orange-grey twilight. Soon the suns would dip out of view and there would be no sky to keep the road lit for travel. Evergreen boughs leaned in over the forest road from both sides now as the northern forest grew older and taller. At times it felt as though they walked through a tunnel, a man-made corridor through the ancient trees and thinning underbrush. As the light faded the feeling of enclosure deepened, both ominous and sheltering. The twilight faded to a flat grey dark at the beginning of night. They would set up camp soon, and Samuel wondered if Kaleb had settled enough to even communicate that desire to him.

As it turned out, Kaleb had something to say after all. "I don't feel like trudging into the night for long," he said, "but I think we're close to a good spot I've used as a camp in the past." He turned and kept walking without waiting for Samuel's response, so Samuel kept pace and held his patience.

A short time later Kaleb slowed and moved off into the trees, motioning for Samuel to follow. The ground dipped away from the road, and Samuel saw the camp Kaleb had described in the base of a hollow between two large trees. Flecks of an old fire pit dotted the forest floor beneath a newly fallen blanket of needles. A downed tree formed a barrier on the back side of the camp and served as an effective windbreak. Samuel could see why Kaleb would want to camp here, especially if the night proved to be as chilly as the evening air hinted. Kaleb dug out the old fire pit and re-collected the stones for its perimeter. Samuel moved off into the nearby forest to collect firewood and kindling without prompting, hoping a healthy load of firewood would engender some goodwill and make for friendlier travel tomorrow.

In no time at all they had a nice campfire and were as sheltered from the elements as one could be without a tent or lean-to. Samuel sat, leaning against the fallen tree while Kaleb worked through part of his store of bread and cheese. The night breeze through the treetops gave their campsite the air of being planted among a crowd of whispering gossips. The chill stayed high with the breeze, never descending to disturb their little sanctuary.

It was quite some time after they had stopped before Kaleb spoke. "It has been unfair of me to treat you as I have today." He paused, seeming to wait for a response Samuel did not give. "In truth, I have little to be upset over. Your desire to understand my motives was justified, and I'd have likely done something similar in your place."

Samuel wasn't sure how to respond. Telling Kaleb his reaction had been entertaining was likely the wrong path, but the desire was still there. "I went into it expecting your ire." He said, looking at his own feet. "You have nothing to apologize for, unless you allow it to continue."

Kaleb smiled and shook his head. He tore off another small piece of bread crust and popped it into his mouth. "If I'm being honest," he said between chews, "I think I was more upset because I didn't know it was something you were capable of."

Samuel raised his head. "Another thing about me that's not like other constructs, I take it?"

Kaleb shook his head with a small chuckle, and broke off a small piece of cheese. "Samuel, nothing about you is what I'd expect of your kind." He paired the cheese with another hunk of bread and ate it. "You're more intelligent, more reasoned, and more...I don't know, personable than any other construct. It's more nuance than I've ever seen an artificer produce. It's fascinating."

Samuel mulled this over. His own observations had led him down this path, but his experience was, of course, very limited. Hearing someone affirm his suppositions went a long way toward acceptance of his situation, if not understanding. "Maybe I'm not all construct," he ventured.

Kaleb's brow crinkled. "What do you mean?"

Pressing forward with the truth had worked out for Samuel so far, so he decided to try it again. "When I awoke, there was a body in the room with me. On top of me, basically. What if..." he trailed off, not sure how to continue.

Kaleb laughed, which frustrated Samuel. Kaleb seemed to sense his irritation and cut it off. "Whatever you're thinking, it's fanciful but not possible," he said. "That engine of yours stores *khet*, not souls." He wasn't laughing anymore, but he was still smiling.

"Maybe they're one and the same," Samuel retorted.

Kaleb shifted, leaning back on his elbows. "I can't believe I'm about to have a philosophical debate with a three-day-old." He shook his head. "*Khet* is our living energy—the living energy of all things—and although it is a part of us, one's soul is more than just energy. Our souls are the sum of our being, everything we are, from birth to death, and informed by everything we experience in life. A soul can't be trapped or transferred or held; when the body dies the soul...well, that's another debate entirely. Sorry, my friend, but constructs don't have souls, regardless of who that soul might have originally belonged to."

"How else do you explain everything you see in me, then?"

Kaleb seemed to ponder the question for quite some time. "Look, I don't have a good answer for that, Samuel." He shook his head, leaning forward onto his crossed legs. "Whatever's going on with you is complex, that's clear enough. I just can't believe you've somehow got someone's soul bouncing around in that metal casing of yours."

It was Samuel's turn to ponder. He looked up through the evergreen boughs at the night sky but saw only darkness. The overcast day had faded to a starless night that would soon descend into fog. Another question surfaced in Samuel's head and he decided not to be shy in the asking.

"You mentioned my engine earlier," Samuel said. "There are many things coming back to me as we walk, but there are still gaps I can't seem to fill, and one of those gaps is knowledge of my own kind." He let it hang without specifying a question.

"Constructs all have a core," Kaleb started, seeming to understand where Samuel was leading. "It's referred to by any number of names, but I've always heard it called an engine or a core. It's the thing that runs you, energizes you, and enlivens you. In most constructs it is nothing more than a polished stone or crystal, about this big." He held up a fist. "An artificer will spend days energizing the stone, very carefully saturating it with gathered *khet* to shape it for its use. Some stones work better than others; some never work at all. Those copper work mules you saw back at Taeman's camp were likely constructed with low-grade cores and may not even last very long." There was another pause as Kaleb continued his evening meal.

"The process is more of an art than anything else. I've seen an artificer spend a week saturating a core, only to have it remain nothing more than a stone. Or worse, have one break mid-process and explode. It's very delicate work and requires a certain talent. That's why even though there are many artificers who can build a construct, there are comparatively few people capable of creating a usable core."

Samuel was sure he knew the answer to his next question, but asked it anyway. "And what happens if a construct's core is damaged, or destroyed?"

Kaleb took a moment to respond, looking as though he was trying to work out a way to soften his next sentence. "Then the construct is destroyed. Irrevocably." Apparently he hadn't found a way. "Everything that construct was is gone—from the initial knowledge seeded by the artificer to every bit of experience the construct has ever known. Every piece of knowledge, information, and experience that makes up a construct resides in their core."

Samuel sat in silence, letting the words drift into the air amongst the sparks from the campfire. In an absentminded gesture his hand had risen to his chest, and he stared into the firelight, letting the weight and importance of Kaleb's words sink in. His next question was quiet and sounded almost childlike. "Is it easy to do?"

Kaleb raked his hair back from his eyes and raised an eyebrow. "Destroying a core?"

Samuel nodded.

"As easy as breaking any other rock," Kaleb said. "Infusing an engine doesn't grant it any strength or hardness. By its very nature, *khet* is nothing more than an ephemeral force. Storing it in a rock just makes a very pretty and useful rock."

As Kaleb talked, Samuel felt a new feeling creeping into the corners of his mind: fear of his own mortality. All someone would have to do is find his core and break it, and no more Samuel. The idea was as terrifying to him as death must be to any person but, if what Kaleb said about constructs having no souls were true, he couldn't even comfort himself with the idea of an afterlife. Destroy his core and he would simply be…gone.

It was as though Kaleb could sense his discomfort. "Hey, don't go digging your own mind into a hole so soon out of the womb, okay? Most artificers understand the relative fragility of their cores and shield them inside the construct's shell. Not doing so is more than just lazy, it's irresponsible. Like I said before, cracking a core isn't a pretty sight. When I was a kid, my uncle told me a story of a poorly built construct getting knocked over by a carriage in Venel and taking out half a block when his core broke." Kaleb shook his head, as though realizing his tack wasn't doing much to placate Samuel.

"It just doesn't happen. Even without shielding, a core is still a rock, and pretty damned durable. And if it makes you feel any better, your frame is an old one, and could probably take a dive off of a cliff without having to worry about your core." Kaleb smirked, dropping his eyes and shaking his head. "Look at me—*comforting* a construct. Never in my life."

Samuel's entire world felt like a mass of uncertainty, amidst which the concept of his own death had never surfaced. Understanding his own mortality was nearly overwhelming. He was positive Kaleb's mind might break at the idea of a construct contemplating the nature of his own existence, so he just let it drop.

"Thank you, Kaleb," Samuel said. "I'm sure that won't be the last of my questions, but thank you for answering. You should get some sleep."

Kaleb nodded and paused, shaking his head with another little smirk before pulling his cloak around his shoulders and lying down to sleep.

That night ran long for Samuel. Fog settled into the forest, swirling between the trees and creeping lower as the fire died to embers. Samuel was at once grateful and saddened that although he could perceive the chill in the night air, he could not feel it the same way Kaleb could. His thoughts alternated between intellectual contemplation of his mortality and irrational fear of losing his tenuous hold on what life he had. For a moment, he was jealous of Kaleb's vitality; at least he had proof of life and the argument for a soul. While Samuel might not know his creator's name, he knew some artificer, somewhere could claim the title.

Just as the cold night seemed interminable, the overcast western sky grew lighter and morning approached. As the light crept through the clouds and filtered into the fog through the trees, the sky blazed a bright white, leeching much of the color from the world. The fog remained so thick Samuel couldn't even make out the surface of the road from their camp.

It wasn't long before Kaleb awoke, shivering in the chill morning air and wiping a layer of dew from his face. He insisted on building back up the fire for a bit before beginning that day's journey, "to pour some warmth back into my muscles," as he put it. Kaleb warmed some bread and dried meat for his breakfast before snuffing out the dying flames and burying it so they could be on their way.

Their morning route was devoid of other travelers, but Kaleb said this was normal for this part of the forest at this time of year. Later in winter, he said, the colder weather and more frequent fog were perfect conditions for ambushes in this part of the forest, which was known as Bandit's Run. Kaleb mused that some of the Morrelton town guard tried to pass off the name as Bandits Run sans the apostrophe, "because none of 'em would dare stand up to a Morrelton escort," they'd proclaim. Their walk was bandit free, and by noon the wind swooped down to chase away the fog. As the road wound further into the forest it crept upwards, deeper into the foothills at the northern edge of the mountains.

"Smell that?" Kaleb said as they rounded a long bend.

Samuel nodded, having noticed a shift in the breeze and new aromas carried along with it. The scents of wood fires and cooking food now wafted through the forest, as well as a sharp, tangy smell. "What is that?" he asked.

"There are a great many artificers in Morrelton," Kaleb replied. "The town's location gives it access not only to an almost inexhaustible supply of usable *khet*, but also to the raw ores and minerals used to make constructs." Kaleb took a quick sniff and cringed at what he encountered. "That tangy smell is a combination of the by-products from the smelters in town and the adepts saturating cores. When we're in town, you'll be able to separate those smells from each other." He wrinkled his nose again. "But neither is very pleasant."

Samuel heard the constant rush of a nearby stream, perhaps even large enough to be called a river, ahead of them and into the woods on their right. Kaleb looked up the road to the top of the rise they were climbing, and quickened his pace.

"Come on, Samuel." Kaleb said with a grin. "We're almost there!"

Samuel sped up to match as they trotted up the incline. The road took one more bend before cresting, and as they reached the top of the small hill, the forest town revealed itself. He slowed to a stop, marveling at the small artificer's city that lay before them. Morrelton.

Chapter Ten

Grey clouds seeped the same miserable drizzle they'd been riding through for so long Colton struggled to remember the last time he'd seen a sunny day. A side benefit was that it kept Bales in just foul enough a mood to keep him quiet—a trade-off Colton was willing to accept. The road to Cinth was busy with merchants and farmers trudging along in the same dolorous silence.

Not long out of Winston, Colton heard the loud clop of a horse at gallop behind them in the rain. They slid to the side and allowed the rider to pass, Colton shaking his head at the stupidity. In weather like this, puddles that seemed shallow could conceal deep potholes or muddy bogs, and a horse at gallop could break a leg and throw its rider. The rain might be miserable, but rushing wasn't worth a broken neck.

They crested a slight rise at a canter a few days out from Winston and the city came into view, a dark brown pile of debris on the blank horizon of the plainsland. It would remain in view almost a full day before they'd enter it, but the sight of civilization was enough to make Colton antsy. Time seemed to fly beneath his notice, and they approached the outskirts just as the afternoon light was failing.

Cinth's skyline was dominated by a central castle building that served as the governmental seat for the surrounding plains towns as well as the residence of whomever was the current regent. Outside the castle's walled courtyards, though, Cinth was a disorganized collection of squat buildings, very few higher than two or three stories. The streets were devoid any sort of pattern, continuations of open lanes that once ran between tents and huts. Cinth lacked a defensible wall, so it sprawled into the surrounding plain as though simply spilled there.

Darker clouds rolled overhead and pissed a harsher rain, painting the flat tan of the plains with deep browns and yellows. Colton pulled up his tall collar and hunkered beneath his tricorne as he passed the first small houses that marked the entrance to Cinth. Bales spurred his horse to a trot, and Colton followed suit.

Their destination, a dive tavern called the Roc's Feather, sat at the edge of the Barrels District. Although the Barrels District was famous for the exaggerated idea it held a tavern on every block, it was not the sort of place suited for well-meaning revelry, instead catering to rowdies and drunkards and populated by all manner of cutpurses, tramps, and disreputable characters. The perfect place for Colton and Bales to handle their business.

The city drowned in the autumn storm, but the going was easier since the rain had driven most folks indoors. As they passed further into the city proper, taller buildings loomed over any idiot still out in the wet. Colton's nostrils were assaulted by the reek of stale beer and garbage, and a lone prostitute stood drenched by the storm glaring at them from the mouth of an alley, her gaze more challenge than invitation.

They dismounted near a hitching post beneath a large wooden sign in the shape of a feather, coated in peeling red paint that had faded to a dark, brownish maroon. The sign was mounted dead center over the front door and funneled a constant stream of rainwater onto the cobblestones. Neither of them bothered to avoid the waterfall as they entered.

The interior of the Roc's Feather made the autumn thunderstorm seem cheery by comparison. With no central fire pit and only a few meager oil lamps providing light, the main tavern area was dark enough one had to squint to see beyond the bar. Support beams dipped from the low ceiling, making the large room feel cramped. They stood still as the door closed, water streaming off the shoulders of their riding coats. Bales removed his hat and made a point of shaking off the excess water onto a table of patrons. The lot of them began to stand, but sat back down and returned to their drinks when Colton nudged their minds into forgetfulness.

"Not now, Bales." Colton admonished his partner. "I'm tired, so leave them be."

Bales snorted and headed toward the bar. Colton tossed his hat onto a hook by the door and pulled open his tall collar, running a hand over the lower half of his face. After a moment of discussion with the stout bartender, Bales waved Colton over.

"Seems ol' Pelk here has some news for us." Bales said. Colton turned to the stocky barman, who paused his task of removing straw from a clutch of new clay mugs.

"Someone here ta' see ye." Pelk croaked, his deep voice like sandpaper across the back of Colton's neck.

Colton raised an eyebrow but didn't speak. Pelk nodded to a booth in the front corner of the tavern, but to Colton it looked empty. He turned back to Pelk. "How do you know they're here for me?"

"Taeman sent 'im, looks like." Pelk said. "Got a letter for ye, wit' the merchant's seal. His message to me was he was 'put in harm's way.'"

Colton and Bales shared an inquisitive look. "What did the letter say?"

Pelk shrugged. "Wouldn't let me touch it. Only showed me the seal." As they turned toward the booth, Pelk stopped them.

"I don't suppose," the bartender hesitated, "you'd just let 'im deliver his message and then let 'im be, eh?" he asked.

Colton turned a disdainful eye on Pelk. "What business is it of yours?" he said.

Pelk blanched. "None. I just don't—"

"Seem to know when to keep your mouth shut." Bales interjected.

Colton shook his head. "You've never found cause to poke your head up at the wrong time before, Pelk," he said. "How about we keep it that way?" The bartender turned back to his task. The two men headed toward the booth. Bales sped up but Colton caught his arm, settling him a half-step behind to a grumbling protest.

As they approached, Colton saw a pair of young hands wrapped around a clay mug of coffee. The boy raised his face when they reached the edge of the table, deep blue eyes framed by a mop of shaggy blonde hair, his cheeks still swimming just beneath a layer of road dirt. Colton wondered how a messenger from Taeman's caravan would've reached Cinth before them, then remembered back to the harried rider outside of Winston.

"I'm told you have a message for me?" Colton said, keeping his voice calm and endearing, oozing charisma.

The boy hesitated, then took a deep breath and puffed up. "How do I know it's you I'm to give it to?" As usual, a derisive scoff escaped Bales's lips.

Colton obliged by rolling up his left sleeve to show the boy the inside of his forearm. Tattooed there was a family crest, a shield bearing the silhouetted image of a bird with wings spread upward, behind a dagger with a serpentine blade. At the bottom of the shield was a ribbon into which the word *Harms* was scribed in flowing script. "My name's Colton Harms. I'm told that has some bearing on the message you were given by Taeman, does it not?"

The boy visibly relaxed and gestured for the two of them to sit. Once they were seated, he reached into his riding coat and produced a small folded parchment bearing a brown wax seal and handed it over. His eyes gave a nervous flick over to Bales.

"What's your name?" Colton asked.

"T-Torran." The boy said, taking another sip of his coffee.

"Introduce yourself, Bales." Colton said. Bales still did not speak, preferring instead a lazy, predatory grin.

Torran shook his eyes back to Colton. "I'm glad to finally understand what Taeman's message meant. Wasn't too keen on being put in danger."

Colton ignored him and cracked the seal, unfolding the letter and reading the rushed handwriting that terminated in the fat merchant's signature, a gaudy scrawl laden with the weight of his inadequacies. After a moment to let what was written there sink in, he read it a second time. He took a deep breath and set the letter down.

"You missed one, Bales." His voice had gone ice cold.

It took a moment for the comment to register with Bales, whose eyes shot to the letter with contempt. "That's impossible. Where?"

"Winston." Colton replied.

"Bullshit. There was nothing for fifty miles in any direction from that mudhole." Angry, he slid around closer to Torran, leaning in to menace him. The boy's nose wrinkled at Bales's breath and he recoiled on reflex. "What did Taeman tell you?" Bales said, deadly quiet.

Colton stepped in, placing a hand on Bales's shoulder and settling him back. "Now, now." He floated a half-smile at Torran. "Let's not kill the messenger."

Bales turned, still defiant. "It's a load of shit, and you know it. I haven't missed one yet, in all the time we've worked together. There's a lie here somewhere." He turned his malice back toward Torran. "And I'm going to figure it out."

"We'll figure it out," Colton placated Bales, whose eyes never left Torran. "Looks like we've got some work to do." He jabbed a thumb over towards Torran. "This one can tag along and help us out here in Cinth, before we head back." A look of confused fear swept over the boy's face.

Bales's countenance softened a little bit and he leaned back in the booth, a disturbing smile creeping across his jaw. Colton stared into Torran's eyes, and the boy's muscles went taut. Colton leaned back. "You don't mind joining us, do you?"

Torran's mouth fell open and a rush of air exited his lungs, but what emerged was barely noise, and nothing like language. He sat back and, in a jerky motion, raised an arm to the top of the booth, leaning like he was having a light conversation with old friends. His head shivered and shook, and tears streamed down his face. Colton smiled.

Bales leered. "Glad to have you on board." When a pitiful moan was all Torran could manage, Bales laughed like he'd just been told the funniest joke he'd heard in years.

Colton saw Pelk approach the table. "Please, sir," the bartender said, his tone meek, "I would ask that ye remand the boy into my care. There be no need for him to accompany ye."

Colton swung a dangerous glare into the bartender, who stepped back as though struck. "Mind your own business," Colton spat. Pelk's face slackened as his body went stiff, and he turned and walked away with no further argument. Colton looked back to Torran. "Now, there wouldn't be anything else you're not telling us, is there?"

Torran's eyes closed and squeezed out more tears, a gurgling whimper escaping his throat. His tremulous hand reached once more into his riding coat and handed over a small felt pouch. Colton dangled the coin purse between two fingers and jingled it by his ear. "Ah, that Taeman's a good man sometimes." He said, false wistfulness in his voice. "You didn't think he was paying *you* this much just to deliver a letter, did you?"

The boy shuddered, and Colton's smile vanished. "Stop clamoring around in there." Torran's inhuman scream careened through the tavern. The other patrons started at the sound and gaped in their direction when the boy's head hit the table, unconscious. No one found the courage to challenge the glares from Colton and Bales.

After only a few seconds, Torran sat up of his own accord, and grabbed a napkin to wipe his face. It took him a moment before he looked around at the customers, all still staring at him with expressions ranging from concern to contempt. Colton reached his hand into the boy's field of view and snapped his fingers, and everyone in the bar turned back to whatever it was they had been doing like nothing was amiss. He touched Torran's jaw and drew his eyes back.

"You'll come with us," Colton said, his tone matter-of-fact. "You'll help us, and maybe I'll let you go. Just remember this: With no chains, no cages, and no weapons, you will stay with me as long as I will it. You'll never know what happened just now, and no one here will ever remember." He leaned in closer, his eyes intense. "I can take everything from you whenever I choose. It's up to you how long you have before that choice must be made."

Chapter Eleven

Looking upon the town of Morrelton, the phrase *like nothing I've ever seen before* crossed Samuel's mind, but he realized how foolish that thought was in his situation. Morrelton was a fair sight larger than Winston, and woven into the fabric of the forest almost like it had grown there. Low buildings built of rich woods blended into the foliage, taking shape in the least obtrusive ways for the surrounding trees. A central lane, flanked on both sides by tall evergreens, crossed a wide wooden bridge some distance into town. Amongst the buildings, plants of all kinds were allowed to flourish, giving the town natural beauty less like a place people had carved out and more like a sanctuary the forest had allowed them to share.

Shops of all kinds lined the main street, and the town bustled with activity. Amid the clamor, Samuel noted a construct for every four people, the ratio even higher where hard labor was involved. All moved and conversed freely, some following masters or even families, and some looked to be out on their own. Variations in size and style were as wide amongst constructs as amongst people. Seeing his kin lifted the weight of loneliness and renewed his hope of finding out who and what he might be.

Kaleb led the two of them down the main road and over the bridge. As Samuel examined one peculiar building that wrapped around and between two ancient oak trees, he heard Kaleb mutter a curse.

Ahead in the road, three men cut a determined path toward them. A tall, slender man with dark hair and a heavy moustache led the way. Of the two that followed him, Samuel only had time to take note of one of them, a giant of a man who stood close to seven feet high, with cut granite muscles below the sheen of his bald head. When the trio reached Kaleb, their mustachioed leader held up a hand to stop Kaleb, doing a double-take when Samuel stopped as well.

"I have to ask what you're doing in Morrelton, Kaleb," the man with the mustache said, forcing an amiable tone.

"I just have some business with Atherton, Berek," Kaleb replied, matching Berek's tone, exasperated. "You know, you don't need to do this every time I come into town."

"Of course I do."

Kaleb shook his head. "Look...I'll be in and out. I picked up this construct out near Corville, but he's got a bum arm." Kaleb turned over his shoulder at Samuel and snapped his fingers in his face. "Karesthetinil, show the man your arm."

Samuel stood transfixed for a moment, less out of confusion and more of amusement. Kaleb snapped his fingers two more times and made a twirling motion with his hand; *come on, get on with it*. Samuel shrugged off his cloak, showing his damaged shoulder and the makeshift sling that held his arm in place. Berek stepped forward for a better look.

"If you were already in Corville, why didn't you just take it to Vermada?" Berek asked as he stepped back in front of his thugs. Samuel's gaze drifted back to the giant goon behind Berek.

"Vermada? Would *you* trust Vermada, Berek? That woman would just as soon stall-wipe him and claim a faulty core as fix him, and then try to buy him off me at a loss. Besides, you know Atherton and I have a history. He owes me one."

Berek raised an eyebrow and the two thugs exchanged a skeptical look. "Owes *you* one? I have a hard time believing..."

"You'd have a hard time accepting anything I say." Kaleb cut him off. "Look, I just want to get my business done and be on my way. Do you have any reason to keep me any longer?"

Berek inhaled, agitated by the rebuff. "I suppose not." he said through gritted teeth. He leaned in close to Kaleb's face. "I'll be watching you. You know I have eyes in this town, and they'll all be on you."

"Well, I hope not," Kaleb said. "You have a job to do, after all, and it wouldn't do you well to pour all your attention into li'l ol' me." Kaleb stepped aside and walked around the three of them. "Come on, Kares, let's go get you fixed up."

Samuel was still staring at the giant but was pulled back to reality by another series of snaps. "Kares! *Now!*" Kaleb spit. He made his way around the rowdies and fell in step behind Kaleb, readjusting his cloak.

"Karesthetinil?" Samuel asked, after they were out of earshot.

"Sorry, it was all I could come up with on the fly," Kaleb replied. "That's actually the name of the personal construct of the regent of Cinth. We're lucky Berek didn't pick up on that or we might be in more trouble."

"Who is he?" Samuel asked.

"Second in command of the town guard," Kaleb replied. "The smaller of his goons is Seba, and the bald ogre behind him was Cort. Not the most pleasant of people, Cort and Seba, but Berek's a good man just trying to do his job."

Samuel followed as Kaleb turned a corner following an alleyway that was more forest path than an actual street, winding a twisting route between a series of odd shaped buildings. "Why did he have occasion to stop you?" Samuel finally asked.

Kaleb stopped and turned. He looked up at Samuel and took a deep breath. "Look… You'll probably run into that with me every so often," he said, "because I'm not the most popular person in the world. Town watchmen have a problem with wandering types like me. They don't trust anyone who won't put down roots and believe travelers and outsiders are the primary sources of disturbances in their little towns. Berek's no different."

Kaleb turned and continued along his way. "That," he said, "and he caught me in bed with his sister."

Samuel laughed with the deep resonance of a baritone woodwind instrument that seemed to vibrate from within his chest. Kaleb stopped dead in his tracks and turned, looking incredulous. Samuel continued laughing, then began walking to catch up with Kaleb. Kaleb laughed a little himself, shaking his head as Samuel's laughter died down.

"Will wonders never cease," Kaleb said.

"What now?"

"Never in my life have I heard a construct laugh. I'm not sure whether or not I thought it was possible, but I never thought it would sound so…genuine." Kaleb looked up at Samuel. "You are an intriguing mystery, my friend."

"You needn't tell me that, Kaleb," Samuel replied. "I don't even know my real name." He knew his facial structure wasn't capable of a smile, but he hoped Kaleb could perceive one there anyway.

At a fork in their winding path, Kaleb led them right, then left at the next. The way widened and buildings were spaced further apart, giving way to more and more trees. They hadn't quite reached the edge of town when Kaleb stopped in front of a two-story shop building with a simple wooden sign over the large oak door that read only: *Atherton, Artificer*. Kaleb grabbed the heavy iron knocker and thunked it down three times.

A slot opened up just above the knocker and two eyes peered out, first taking stock of Samuel then moving to Kaleb. The eyes widened and the slot closed; locks and bolts slid free in muffled clicks. "Kaleb!" The heavy door swung inward and a boy rushed out and almost knocked Kaleb over with his embrace.

Kaleb laughed and returned the hug. "Nice to see you, too, Michael." Michael stepped back and clapped Kaleb on the shoulders. He stood a few inches less than six feet tall and still carried an awkwardness about him, but his upper body was powerful, although not overly thick. His crop of ashy brown hair fell about his face and covered his ears, but only just. If he'd needed to shave, it didn't show, and his eyes were bright and enthusiastic.

"Michael," Kaleb said, "I'd like you to meet Samuel." Samuel was surprised at the use of his real name, but did not betray his feelings as he held out his hand to Michael.

Michael took his hand and, without a word, turned it palm up and began examining it. He held Samuel's wrist and began tracing the lines of the plates and joints in his hand with his fingers. Samuel looked up at Kaleb, who sensed his confusion and made a gesture that said *just let him be*. Michael turned his arm over again, examining the back of his wrist and his arm up to the elbow. He didn't even look up when he began to speak.

"The craftsmanship is amazing!" he said, clearly excited. "I mean, he's gotta be ancient! The joints are old-style flex segments with protective plates. Nobody builds constructs like this anymore." He turned back to Kaleb. "Where'd you get him?"

"Michael?" Kaleb gestured toward Samuel.

"Oh!" Michael turned and shook his head, as if to clear it. "I'm sorry, Samuel. It's very nice to meet you. I'm Michael, Atherton's protégé." He offered a quick and shallow bow. "I get a little caught up when I see a new style of construct sometimes. I apologize."

"No harm done, Michael," Samuel said. "It's nice to meet you, too."

Michael paused, tilting his head ever so slightly, then turned toward the door. "Come in! Come in!" he said to the both of them, and headed back inside. Kaleb gestured for Samuel to follow and fell in step behind him, shutting the door as they entered.

The shop was larger than Samuel expected and quite cluttered. Floor to ceiling shelves covered the walls, every shelf filled with the staples of Atherton's trade. The majority housed raw materials, everything from stones to blocks and planks of different colored wood to sheets of various metals. In one corner hung an array of implements, across from which were stacks and shelves of limbs and parts of constructs, topped by an entire shelf of heads in various states of completion. Next to this area stood a completed shell, as tall as Samuel but not as bulky, and not yet active. This section of the room was eerie to Samuel, and he had to look away.

What had seemed, at first, to be jumbled clutter was, in reality, meticulously organized. Although every shelf was filled—sometimes overfull—and there were stacks of raw materials on the floor, Samuel noticed everything had its place. There wasn't a speck of dust in the entire room.

At the rear, heavy hinges supported a large door of solid iron. To its right sat an L-shaped bench behind a large table, looking almost like a booth in a tavern. On the left side of the door were two heavy stone slabs laid out in the same configuration as the benches they opposed. Michael gestured for Samuel to have a seat on one of these slabs, and Kaleb took a seat next to him.

"I'll go get Atherton," Michael said, his smile beaming. He turned a heavy latch on the iron door and leaned into it, pushing it open with some effort. Its hinges produced an echoing creak and he stepped through, latching it again from the other side with a loud *clang*.

"That seems excessive," Samuel said, gesturing to the door.

"Remember what I told you about what happens when a core cracks?" Kaleb said. Samuel nodded. "A lot of artificer's workshops are armored—from the inside. It's mostly to protect customers who happen to be in the building in case…something goes wrong."

Samuel nodded his understanding. He thought back to his birthing chamber in Winston, noting it was not armored in this way. "Are all artificer's shops built like this?" Kaleb knew very little of Samuel's origins, so Samuel hoped the question would come across innocuous.

"No, not by far," Kaleb replied. "A lot of artificers can't afford this kind of modification. The smaller shops that focus on repairs don't always need this kind of protection either, since they usually won't be going anywhere near a construct's core." He chuckled. "Atherton's skill with constructs makes him the least likely to make a mistake, yet it draws a client base that demands these sorts of protections."

"How long have you known him?"

Kaleb took a long breath. "A long time. Atherton was our family's artificer," he said. "Not like a private contract, or anything, but my father knew him and trusted his work. I met him a few times as a kid, but didn't get to know him until I was out on my own. I worked for him for a short time, doing a lot of the same things I'm sure he has Michael doing, but I had neither the talent nor the patience for his line of work. I wanted to be *out there*, not tied down to any one place."

Kaleb seemed in a nostalgic and amiable mood, and Samuel had a great many questions to ask, but they were both distracted by the creak of the iron hinges as Michael returned. An older man followed close behind, the sleeves of his brown shirt rolled up to the elbows, his arms covered in grime. Wispy grey hair stood out from his head, escaping from beneath the strap of a pair of large, leather-rimmed goggles. Craggy wrinkles around his mouth and forehead told the story of his long life. The removal of the goggles revealed hard eyes buried in a stern visage.

"Atherton!" Kaleb said, standing to greet the old man. Samuel stood as well.

Atherton shook Kaleb's hand, but his austere posture remained. "To what do we owe the pleasure of this visit?" His voice was gravelly and carried an authoritarian air.

Kaleb stepped aside and gestured to Samuel. "This is Samuel. He's got a bit of a problem, and I knew no one better to go to than you." Kaleb turned. "Show him your shoulder..."

Samuel unpinned his cloak and turned his damaged arm toward Atherton. The artificer removed Samuel's sling and grabbed the lifeless arm, turning and twisting and running his fingers over the disfigured plates where the arm joined Samuel's torso. Partway through his silent examination, he spoke to Kaleb without diverting his attention.

"It's fixable," he said. "It may take as much as two or three days to fashion the appropriate parts, but correcting the flow and getting the arm working won't be a problem." He paused, casting a critical eye on Kaleb. "Where did you happen upon this one?"

"Along the way, just outside Winston." Samuel was again surprised by Kaleb's honest approach. "He had come into Taeman's possession and I...acquired him." This time, his words had been carefully chosen.

Atherton raised an eyebrow, but didn't question. "Well, better in the possession of any slump, than herded by that cretin," Atherton said, his voice low. He paused, then: "Can you afford this repair, young man?"

Kaleb nodded. "I have business in town, after which I'll be able to afford it." He smiled. "As long as you don't try to overcharge me."

Atherton scoffed and shot Kaleb a look. Samuel couldn't tell if the look was genuine disdain at the audacity of Kaleb's comment, or an attempt to play along with the joke. Samuel wrote it off as the latter. "You know my fees, young man. I'll expect payment on delivery."

"You got it," Kaleb said, smiling. He turned to Samuel. "You're in the hands of the best artificer I know, my friend."

Atherton stepped aside and conversed with Michael, who then broke away and approached Samuel. "Come on, I'll take you back to the workshop." Samuel looked toward Kaleb, who nodded a *go ahead*, so

Samuel let Michael lead him through the large iron door into the back area of the artificer's shop.

In the smaller workshop, the organization of the front area gave way to a more cluttered arrangement. Workbenches filled the room's periphery, separated into several stations, each with its own array of tools and focused purpose. Surfaces strewn with parts of deconstructed constructs in the midst of repairs again gave Samuel a disquieted feeling. In the corner nearest the door, several complete or nearly complete constructs, either stood or sat on the floor, but none of them were active.

Samuel noticed the entirety of the small room was encased in metal. Most of the walls were covered in iron sheeting, but in some parts the iron gave way to copper or bronze or even steel. Even the ceiling was armored, the metal plates held up by extra-heavy beams that made the ceiling feel lower than it actually was.

Michael led Samuel to another stone bench along one wall and gestured for him to sit, then moved away to one of the workbenches, rifling through a stack of papers until he found what he needed. Samuel could hear Atherton and Kaleb talking outside the door, but couldn't make out what they said.

"Where are you from, Samuel?" Michael asked, scratching something down with a pencil.

Samuel wasn't sure how to answer. "Winston, I would say."

"How long have you been active?" he asked, his tone oddly clinical.

"Four days," Samuel replied. Michael stopped writing and looked at him quizzically. "I don't have any recollection prior to four days ago."

"All right," Michael said, shaking his head and returning to his writing. "Complete wipe, I guess," he mumbled as he wrote.

"What are you writing?" Samuel asked.

"Filling out an invoice," Michael said, still not looking up. "Part of my duties as Atherton's apprentice is doing all his paperwork and bookkeeping." He smiled. "Good thing, though. This whole place'd fall apart if the old man was doing it for himself." He set down his pencil, then came back over to Samuel.

"You're very inquisitive for a construct," he said. "You're not like other constructs Atherton works on, or I've seen around."

"I've been told that a lot recently," Samuel replied in a good-natured tone. "I'm not too sure what's going on. I'm hoping Atherton might be able to help figure out where I came from. Before four days ago, I mean."

Michael sat down next to him, looking up into his eyes. "You're fascinating, you know," he said.

"How so?"

"I don't know. Just...different. I feel like I could sit here and talk with you like an old pal." He shifted his position. "You feel more...real than other constructs, you know? I don't know, maybe I'm just being foolish."

Samuel found he rather liked Michael. He was young and intelligent, and carried himself well. "You're not being foolish. I'm glad to know I'm different. I'm very curious to know why I'm different, but glad nonetheless."

"You really don't remember anything past four days ago?" Michael asked.

"No," Samuel replied. "Not a thing."

"That's just...strange." Michael said. "Even if someone had wiped your core, they'd normally leave a base behind—something worked into your core before you were activated. A construct should be able to tell when they were activated no matter what someone has done to their core. I mean, you're clearly more than four days old, so why can't you remember when you were activated?"

Samuel thought about it, but didn't respond. The silence hung about them for a moment before he spoke. "How long have you been Atherton's apprentice, Michael?"

"Quite a while," he said. "I did odd jobs and errands for him when I was a little kid, and he took me on as an apprentice when he felt I was old enough."

"I think he made a good choice," Samuel said.

Michael gave him an odd look, but then replaced it with a smile. "Thanks." He looked like he was about to continue, but Kaleb entered the room.

"Go talk to Atherton," he said to Michael, nodding back toward the door.

Michael got up and headed out, grabbing the invoice along the way. He turned back and said, "I'll talk to you more later, Samuel," then stepped out of the room.

Kaleb sat down next to Samuel. "What do you think of the place?" he said.

Samuel looked around the room again, taking note of the large table in the center which, at the moment, was tilted up at a steep angle. He looked closer and saw the pedestal upon which it stood hinged, allowing the table to be brought down flat. The bottom was edged with a shelf where a construct could stand in its upright position and be lowered for repairs.

"It's a shop," Samuel said simply, and Kaleb laughed.

"Thank you for that astute observation, professor," he said. "Atherton and Michael will take good care of you, and get that shoulder back in working order. They might even be able to help identify where you came from. Atherton's knowledge of construct history is pretty deep. He might even be able to tell you who built you."

This made Samuel feel hopeful, but he was still hung up on an earlier statement. "What do you mean, they'll take good care of me? Are you going somewhere?"

Kaleb nodded. "Since I'm in town, I have some business to attend to. If all goes as planned, it'll only take me a day or so, but I might not be back for a couple of days."

"What sort of business?" Samuel asked.

Kaleb lowered his head and took a breath. "My own," he said. "Don't press this one, Samuel. It doesn't much concern you, and I don't really want to talk about it, okay?"

"All right," Samuel replied. He was having trouble containing his curiosity at this point, but he wanted to respect Kaleb's wishes. Something about his tone worried Samuel, though.

"Look, ask Atherton whatever you want. I've told him the basics of your situation, and he will help however he can. You can trust him. Michael, too."

"I like Michael," Samuel said.

Kaleb smiled. "Yeah, he's a good kid. Atherton picked well with that one. He's gonna be a damned fine artificer one day. Really smart."

Kaleb stood. "One thing, though…Atherton doesn't have any sort of quarters for constructs. I'm not sure how you'll feel about it, but he'll probably just leave you in here overnight."

Samuel wasn't thrilled with the idea of spending the night alone in this shop. It reminded him a bit too much of the burning room in Winston, and the deactivated constructs in the corner unsettled him. "It's not my first choice, but I'll go with it."

"You'll be fine." He turned toward the door, but stopped and looked back at Samuel. "I'll be back soon. Hopefully Atherton can help you out." He paused and nodded, almost to himself, then left.

The Chronicler Saga

Chapter Twelve

Before long, trepidation set in. Samuel had grown used to Kaleb's company over the last several days and with that company had grown trust. Even so, the things Kaleb would not say nagged at Samuel. He just wanted the next couple of days over with. He wasn't given time to let his mind wander as Atherton and Michael joined him in the workroom.

"Come, come, Samuel," Atherton said. "Let me take a closer look at you." He waved Samuel over to the angled table. "Step onto the platform."

Samuel did as he was asked and leaned back against the surface of the table. Michael moved around to his left and turned a crank connected to the pedestal, tilting the table until he lay flat on his back and his head and limbs sank into indentations in the wood. For the first time, he noticed straps at intervals on the table designed to hold a construct in place. The idea of being strapped down, even for his own benefit, did not sit well.

Samuel turned his head as much as the indentations allowed but couldn't see much besides Atherton moving around to his broken shoulder, his goggles lowered. Atherton wheeled over a small table with a box of instruments and a writing pad. At first he worked on Samuel's shoulder with his fingers, tracing every dent and bend, taking note of every detail. The continued examination felt like an eternity of being measured and prodded while the artificer took notes. After some time, Samuel heard Michael speak. "What kind is he? Where was he built?"

Atherton's only reply was to shush the boy and continue his examination. He rarely spoke, and when he did it was to himself, mumbling notes or calculations. Time crawled by for Samuel until Atherton stood, waving Michael over. Michael turned the table's crank, returning Samuel upright.

"Sir, might I ask what you've discovered?" Samuel asked.

Atherton gave him an odd look that was only amplified by his goggles, which now sported a magnifying glass over one eye. He shook his head and pulled the goggles off, as if he was only just realizing he was still wearing them. "You are a mystery, now, aren't you? Expressing genuine concern over my examinations." He lowered his eyes and shook his head, scratching at one earlobe. "I've encountered many who were adept at affecting an air of concern, but never one who was so wholly convincing."

Samuel wasn't sure how to reply, so he made his best attempt. "To the best of my knowledge, sir, this is not an affectation. My concern, I think, is well-founded."

"Well, to that, my concerned construct, I say the repairs are not the most complicated I've dealt with, nor the simplest. Getting your arm back in working order should be a simple affair, but reconstructing your shoulder so it works properly might not be so easy."

"And why not?" Samuel asked, trying to sound more inquisitive than exasperated.

Atherton sat on a stool next to his workbench and placed a hand on his chin. "Because you are very old indeed. I've not seen artificery the likes of yours in a great while. The very construction of your shoulder joint is"—a hint of a smile touched his lips—"sublimely complex. It will be a challenge, but one for which I am prepared."

Samuel felt relieved, eager for the work to be finished and to have two usable hands. "When can we begin?" he asked. "If restoring the use of my arm is a simple procedure, can we take care of that now?"

"Not yet," Atherton said, turning back to his workbench and replacing his goggles with a pair of thin-framed glasses. "I could restore flow to your arm, but the moment you tried to move it you could do more severe damage to that shoulder of yours. No, tonight I will begin fashioning what parts I can, and we'll take care of both problems in one fell-swoop tomorrow afternoon." He turned back to Samuel and peered at him over his glasses. "Will that suit you?"

Samuel nodded, more than a little disappointed.

"Good," Atherton replied. He turned back to his workbench without a word, leaving Samuel to his own devices.

Samuel puttered around the front shop area, examining the shelves full of materials and trying to decide what to do with his time. Michael had been sent on an errand, and with Atherton buried in a workbench and Kaleb off to who-knows-where, he was left with no one to talk to. As he walked around, he could not help but be drawn back to the corner where the half-complete constructs sat beneath the shelf of detached heads.

As he approached the dismembered limbs, he found himself less and less disturbed by them, seeing them now as mannequins or broken toys where before he had seen them as fallen brethren. The most complete form in the bunch was a headless torso with one arm and one opposing leg, which produced a short, dull, hollow ring when Samuel rapped it with his knuckle.

Above the partial construct was a deep shelf upon which were laid an array of upper limbs. Everything from complete arms to hands alone to solitary fingers were stacked in as organized a way as possible. Samuel picked up a hand from the top of the stack and peered inside the wrist, to find it hollow but for a light support structure. He wiggled the fingers and replaced the hand on the shelf.

The top shelf held his mind in rapture, some four feet long and bearing a row of seven construct heads. All similar in size, their faces and structures could not have been more varied. Some had wide, round eyes where others bore thin slits. One had no mouth at all, yet one had what appeared to be an articulated jaw. None of them had noses, however— this seemed to be a unifying design to all the constructs he had seen so far.

One head in particular caught his attention; its eyes were similar to his own but the rest of its face was much more angular, all sharp edges and menacing features. The mouth was turned down into a semblance of a scowl, and two rows of rivets ran diagonally from the corners of its mouth and met at around back of its bronze domed skull. From the back of the head where the rivets met to the middle of the forehead ran a thick metal fin, a sharpened edge along its top, a hand's width tall at its uppermost point. The whole of the head was dinged and battered, indicating it had served its construct for a great many years.

He held the head in his one good hand, supporting it just behind the jawline. "I wonder what happened to you," Samuel said to the skull. "What was your name? Where did you come from?"

Samuel couldn't help himself. *"I'm from the same place you are!"* Samuel said, lending his voice to the skull as he tipped it up and down with the cadence of his words.

"Do you think we were friends, once?" he asked the head.

"Of course we were!" The skull tilted back. *"Of course, all these people will tell you constructs don't have friends…"*

"True enough." Samuel said. "I guess I'm the only one."

"Well, make that two of us, then!"

A snort from the other side of the room startled Samuel out of his conversation, and he flinched in surprise. Michael was standing near the front entrance, shuddering with laughter. Samuel replaced the head on the shelf and took a step back. "Sorry you had to see that," he said. "Do you think it's possible for a construct to go insane?"

Michael wiped tears from his eyes and reined himself in. "Oh, wow, Samuel. That might be one of the strangest things I've ever seen. And never in my life have I—"

"Seen a construct get startled?" he asked, cutting Michael off. "I know, I've heard this one before." He felt the snip in his voice and regretted directing it at Michael. He took a seat on the granite bench. "I'm sorry. I don't mean it to seem like I'm upset with you."

Michael was still smiling, shaking his head as he approached and sat down on the other arm of the bench, leaning against the wall. "Don't be. You have no idea how exciting it is for me to see a construct that behaves like you. When old farts like Atherton are talking about how different you are, you know something's going on. I only hope I can help you figure it out."

"I appreciate that, Michael." He paused, trying to think of how to phrase what he wanted to say. "Truly. It's not an act or a calculated response."

"You know," Michael replied, "somehow I know that. I just...know it." He smiled. "And don't worry about Atherton's predictions on your repairs. They won't be that difficult. He's always overly conservative when he gives out estimates, to keep expectations in check."

Samuel nodded. In truth, that did make him feel a little better.

Michael leaned forward, putting his elbows on his knees to support his weight. "Are you frightened? To figure it all out, I mean?"

Samuel leaned back. "Not even a little bit. I just want to know, so I can figure out what to do next. I feel like I'm stuck in a void until I can put this one thing behind me and move on with whatever comes next."

"Well, let's start by getting that arm moving again. That's gotta be annoying."

"You have no idea."

"Actually, I do," Michael replied. "When I was younger, I was cleaning the shelves in here and a stack of legs came tumbling down onto me and broke my right arm. I was in a splint and a sling for a month."

"Okay, then," Samuel said. "Maybe you do know how I feel." He paused, searching for a question. "Michael, I know you're just an apprentice right now, but can you tell me anything about where I might have come from?"

Michael took a deep breath and looked Samuel over, evoking Atherton's manner now that he was in examination mode. "Well, I can't pin it down for certain, but I'd put down good money you were constructed in one of the southern cities...maybe Padorean or Balefor. You've had a lot of replacements over time, though." He leaned in and pointed to plates on Samuel's upper leg and the side of his torso. "These two look to be somewhat recent, probably within the last year. And I can tell you're very old...I'd say over a hundred years. I've seen more recent constructs that kind of look the same style as you from those cities, but simpler, more streamlined. You...You're an antique."

Samuel and Michael conversed for quite some time. Samuel learned about the southern cities and the constructs that dwelled there. Michael told him in the metropolis of Balefor, constructs were not as common any more as they were in Morrelton, and were only found in the most affluent households. "Many regulations and restrictions govern construct ownership," Michael said, "and even more on their creation." Smaller artificers left the city and set out for other, more amiable places, not long after the time Michael believed Samuel to have been created. Their conversation then meandered to other topics, like how Michael was enjoying his apprenticeship, how he came to know Atherton, and how both of them knew Kaleb.

"I see the way Atherton looks at Kaleb when he comes around," Michael said, turning his eyes to the floor. "Every once in a while, I see the old man shake his head when Kaleb leaves, or make other little gestures. I think he's disappointed, like he feels Kaleb could've done something better with himself. Now, Kaleb only comes around once in a long while. This is the first time we've seen him in months." Michael leaned forward onto his knees again. "Sometimes I wonder if I can ever live up to whatever it was Atherton saw in him. I feel like I'm always a step behind."

Samuel let the silence float between them, not knowing much about how to console someone feeling sorry for themselves. He broke the silence with the only piece of relevant information he could remember. "I can't tell you what Atherton thinks, but I can tell you Kaleb thinks the world of you. He thinks you're going to be great someday."

Michael's face brightened and he came out of his slump. "Did he say that?"

"Yes, he did," Samuel replied.

Michael pulled his feet up onto the bench and rested his chin on his knees, his smile beaming from ear to ear. They heard the ring of the latch and the door to the workroom swung open. Atherton stepped out and closed the door behind him.

"Time to turn in, Michael," he said. "We have a lot of work in the morning."

Michael stood and nodded to Samuel. "Thanks, Samuel."

"You're welcome," Samuel said. Michael made his way around the corner and up the stairs.

"He's very taken with you, you know." Atherton said. "All the mystery and the secrecy. He wants to help you."

Samuel turned to the old artificer. "I know. He's a good kid."

"Yes, he is." Atherton replied, his demeanor hardening once again. "And it will stay that way. I don't know what you and Kaleb are into, nor do I care to know. But Michael has a bright future, and I won't have him running off like—running off and wasting it. I'll repair your arm, and I'll have you on your way. Don't drag him into this, do you understand me?"

Samuel sat, stunned and unsure what to say. "Of course, sir. I had no intention of—"

"Oh, I'm sure you didn't." Atherton cut him off. He took a breath before continuing. "I'll have most of the parts fashioned by mid-morning and be able to begin work tomorrow mid-day. As I'm sure you are aware, I do not fashion quarters for constructs, so you will have to stay down here tonight."

"That's not a problem," Samuel said. "I'll try not to make a nuisance of myself."

"See you don't." With that, Atherton turned and followed Michael upstairs.

The Chronicler Saga

Chapter Thirteen

Samuel spent most of the night in quiet contemplation, trying to reach into the recesses of his mind for any clues to his situation. He hadn't thought to ask Atherton about the marking on his shoulder, but made a mental note to ask him tomorrow during the repairs. Aside from that one thought, nothing he did penetrated the time before he was born to fire. Above all else he wanted to know how he came to be in that room in the first place, and whose blood had stained the floor where he awoke. He pulled his cloak down from where it hung near the bench, reaching into the inside pocket for the serpent ring.

He sat on his bench with the ring around the tip of his wide middle finger, examining every detail he could make out in the dim lamplight. On the face of the ring in gold were two winged serpents, facing each other, their talons digging into one another's hides, their tails wrapping around the outsides to form the edges of the relief. In each serpent's eye gleamed a tiny cut gem, one black and the other a translucent red split by a vein of milky green. Beneath the relief, the ring itself was cast of a single piece of silver with a hole wide enough for two fingers, attached to the gold face by a complex setting. Inside the ring, Samuel saw fine grooves that may have once been an inscription, but had long since worn off. As beautiful a piece of work as the ring was, it still triggered no clues or memories for Samuel.

81

A noise from the stairwell drew his attention. Flickering light painted the floor from behind the archway leading to the stairs. Samuel stuffed the ring back into the cloak pocket and leaned back as Michael entered the room carrying a small candle on a dish. His hair was tousled, and he was still in his nightclothes. He made his way to the back of the shop and sat in the same spot as earlier, setting his candle down on the bench next to him.

"Can't sleep?" Samuel asked.

"Nope," Michael replied. "I can't stop thinking about you, and Kaleb, and everything." The boy paused before continuing. "I mean, why would someone get rid of all your memories? What use would you be to anyone then? It would take months, or years, to rebuild knowledge like that, even with Atherton's skill." He shook his head, once again pulling his knees into his chest and resting his head on them. "Have you and Kaleb been traveling together long?"

"Not too long, by your standards," he said. "But nearly my entire life, as far as I know."

Michael laughed. "How is he doing? I mean..." Michael trailed off, looking thoughtful. Samuel waited for him to finish. "I mean, people say things. To some people around Morrelton, Kaleb doesn't have the greatest reputation."

The boy's question bothered Samuel, but he put it away for the time being. "He helped me when I needed it," Samuel said. "I wasn't sure I'd made the right choice by leaving Taeman's caravan, but after hearing Atherton's comments, I'm convinced Kaleb helped me out of a bad situation."

"Taeman's a sleaze," Michael said. "The way he treats his constructs is awful."

"Now I know why Kaleb has so much faith in you, Michael." Samuel said, bringing a smile to Michael's face. He stood to replace his cloak on its hook. "I'm glad to know you'd never treat me that way."

"Never!" Michael exclaimed, then settled back down with his chin on his knees. "It's hard for me to believe any...   ...such a terrible... ...considering...   ...amuel?!"

The room wavered in Samuel's vision and then was gone, leaving nothing but blackness.

Trapped. Nowhere left to run, nothing left to do but wait. The doorknob turns, but the deadbolt prevents the door from opening. An angered, guttural scream from the hallway precedes a hard thump on the door. The jamb cracks, but does not give way. A wordless growl, another scream, and the door bursts inward, splintering the latch and frame.

Before him stands a boy in his teens. His shaggy blond hair is wet and clings to the sides of his face, his countenance locked into pure rage. He labors for heavy breaths. A dislocated right shoulder lends an odd cant to his arm. Tears stream down his face from bloodshot eyes.

"Quite a chase you've led us on." another says as he enters the room. The man's jawline is strong and his face angular but common. Two extraordinary features distinguish him from plain: a long, angry scar across his cheek and piercing silver eyes. Behind him, another man enters, his face shrouded between a tall collar and the brim of his hat.

"I won't let you take me." His own voice sounds foreign, yet feels familiar.

"Oh, I should hope not," Silver Eyes says. "This chase has been far too fun to end in something as pedestrian as surrender."

The boy stands at the man's shoulder, seething in mindless fury, waiting to be unleashed.

"Is the boy to be my demise, then?" he asks. "Do you throw away the lives of children in your pursuits?"

"Him? He's just a tool. A means to an end. A distraction." The boy lunges forward around the scarred one's shoulder. He brings his metal hand across the boy's face, hoping to deter any further attacks rather than cause real injury. The boy screams in rage as he stumbles sideways, then turns and launches another blind attack. This time, he takes no chances, landing a thunderous punch. Bones collapse under the force of his knuckles. The boy slumps to the ground, no longer a danger.

He wants to turn back to the other danger, but he can't move. A hand slides around his side, and a voice slithers over his shoulder, whispering, "Gotcha, copper-pot." Another hand applies the lightest of pressure to his shoulder. He topples over, coming to rest on his back. Those piercing silver eyes come into view over top of him, and he senses hands on his torso.

"This has been a long time coming," The man with silver eyes says. He raises

his right hand and licks the ends of his fingers and thumb. "You've been one of our more...difficult charges." Wet fingertips press against the center of his chest, and he is taken with a sense of deep cold. Slowly, he loses all sensation in the extreme reaches of his limbs, the loss of feeling creeping toward his torso.

His vision fills with blue-white light, wavering like a waterborne reflection. In the dancing light, the second man's face looks down on him, slipping amongst the waves in his vision, indistinct. He feels, more than hears, the same creeping whisper say, "Bye-bye, you ragged old toy," as his vision fails. There is a sharp vibration in his chest and a feeling like all the air rushing from the room, and he is gone.

His movements are uncoordinated, almost drunk, making the journey take much longer than it normally would. As he walks, his movements become smoother, but not faster. Nothing he does restores his control, making him feel like a puppet at the hands of a torturous puppeteer.

And what is the reason for his return? He wants only to be away from this place, to be away from himself, but he is driven back here. The need to return overwhelms his desire to leave. In spite of his fight against it, he is powerless to stop himself. His vision stutters as his consciousness wavers, causing him to stumble in the alleyway before righting himself against the back wall of some featureless building. Not far now.

The back of the manor house comes into view, and he heads straight for the rear entrance. He ascends the stone steps to the kitchen entrance and stops, placing a hand on the doorframe to steady himself. The compulsion to enter wars against the logic telling him to run, to get away from here. His resolve weakens, and he opens the door.

His hand leaves a tacky crimson streak on the jamb as he enters. Two steps in and his balance gives way. He falls in a heap on the kitchen floor.

Chapter Fourteen

Samuel's senses swam and he couldn't see. "I need you to stay quiet," the voice whispered. "I'm going to take it off of you, but you have to stay quiet, okay?"

He couldn't move, so any form of acknowledgement was impossible. The speaker would have to trust he wouldn't make any noise. Something moved on his face, covering his mouth. A screeching noise was quickly squelched and a jolt ran through his body. Vision snapped back to him, along with the rest of his senses, as something was peeled away from his face and thrown aside. Samuel lay on his back, staring at the heavy beams and metal plates of Atherton's workroom ceiling through dimness broken only by the flicker of lamplight. He tried to turn his head, but couldn't. Feeling flooded back into his limbs, save for his left arm. He realized he was strapped down.

Michael's face came into view over him. "Does everything feel normal?"

"Yes, I think so." Samuel's voice came out loud, and Michael winced.

"SSSHH!" Michael's eyes snapped to the doorway, then back down to Samuel. "Quieter!"

Samuel hadn't needed to speak in a quiet tone yet, and hoped he would get it right with his next question. "Michael, what's going on?"

His voice didn't whisper like a person's would, but came out at a much lower volume.

"We have to get you out of here," Michael said.

"What happened?" Samuel asked. "I must have blacked out. I saw…"

"I don't know, Samuel," Michael interrupted, his voice raw with fear. "You and I were talking, and you just fell over. Your eyes went dark, but you were still moving…like…twitching and stuff. I…I called Atherton and we were able to get you rigged up in the hoist and onto the table. Once we got you strapped down, he…changed. He pushed me out of the room, and wouldn't answer any of my questions. I just wanted to know what was going on, but he wouldn't talk to me. He got angry and yelled at me to leave, then locked you in here and wouldn't let me come in." Tears rolled down Michael's face. "I don't know what's going on."

"Michael, it's okay," Samuel said, trying to be reassuring. "I want to help, but you've got to unstrap me from this table."

Michael took a deep breath, wiping the tears away from his eyes. "I can't yet. I'm going to get your arm back first, and I'll need to leave you strapped down for that."

"Michael, just let me up. We can worry about that later."

"No, Samuel, it'll be okay. Atherton's asleep. He thinks I'm locked out of here but I snuck out and got the door open. I'll be quick—I can do it quick." Michael stepped out of Samuel's view, and Samuel heard him moving around the room gathering tools. Being strapped to the table was making Samuel anxious; he wanted to be up and moving.

Michael sat down next to the table and began to work. The sensation was something between irritating and unnerving as Michael worked tools into the metal structure of Samuel's shoulder, bending damaged parts back into place, or at least out of the way so he could move in deeper. Now he knew why Michael wanted him strapped down; he wasn't sure he'd be able to bear this otherwise.

Samuel tried to distract himself with a question. "Michael, what were you pulling off of my face when I was waking up?"

Michael continued working while he spoke. "A siphil. It's an animal that feeds on *khet*. I had to get it out of the way so I can work on repairing

86

the flow to your arm." A pause. "They attack people in forests and jungles by dropping on them from above. Once they've latched on, they'll drain a person in minutes. All their *khet* gone, until they die." Samuel felt him shudder through the tools in his shoulder. "They don't have the same effect on constructs. They'll try to drain the *khet* out of the construct's core. A siphil can't destroy a construct, but they can disrupt the flow of *khet* enough to immobilize one."

"That's what it was doing to me," Samuel said.

"Yeah. Atherton must have put it on you after he kicked me out of the workroom." Michael took in a sharp breath, choking back his emotion. "I don't even know why Atherton would have one here. It's illegal to keep them in Morrelton. They're too dangerous... What was that?"

Samuel had heard it, too: a noise from the front area. Both of them fell silent. Michael held his breath. The noise was faint, but sounded like footsteps. Michael leaned in close to Samuel, his whisper almost too quiet to hear. "Someone's out there!"

Samuel felt Michael return to his shoulder, his search for the malfunction becoming frantic. "Michael, unstrap me." he said, as quietly as he was able.

"It's fine," Michael whispered, quickening his pace. "I've got the door bolted from the inside. Listen to me, Samuel. Once you're free, you need to head east, into the mountains."

"Why are you telling me this?" Samuel heard the door latch click several times, but the door did not open. After a moment of silence, there was a clanging rap that jarred Michael from his concentration, then another, followed by a third. The pauses between each were long enough to let the ringing of the iron die.

Michael shook his head and turned back to Samuel. "You need to go north out of town, then head east up the main mountain road at the fork. It'll take a few days on foot, but look for the Bleeding Pine and head north into the woods on the trail there. It'll be hard to see, but Kaleb can follow it. There's a cottage in the forest there where my friend Pare apprentices. His master can help you. I know he can. Can you remember that?"

Samuel nodded.

"Come out, Michael." Atherton called, his voice muffled through the heavy door. "Don't do anything…rash." His tone was calm. Unsettling.

Michael's constitution held and he did not respond.

"Michael?" Atherton said, trying to sound amiable. "What are you trying to accomplish? That construct is dangerous, Michael."

"Why?" Michael yelled back at his master, his voice cracking. "Why won't you tell me what's going on?"

"You're too young to understand!!" Atherton screamed, snapping in anger. "Damn your foolishness. Come out of there right now!!"

Samuel couldn't hold his voice any longer. "Why are you doing this, Atherton? Please, just tell me what's happening."

The pause was longer than Samuel liked. "You removed the siphil, Michael?" Atherton's voice was quiet now, burning low with rage. "What have you done?"

"Hurry, Michael," Samuel said. "Hurry and unstrap me."

"I'm almost there!" Michael said. "I can see it now! I can fix it! Here…" Michael reached up and released the strap holding Samuel's head. It wasn't much freedom, but it was something. He looked over at his shoulder, expecting to see a mass of bent metal and openings, and was surprised to see much of the work Michael had done was to repair the external structure. It looked less damaged, but one of the plates covering the front had been removed, and several tools were clamped into place deep within the opening.

Atherton's voice came louder, more forceful this time. "Malthoranic!" Samuel didn't understand the word, and Atherton paused before repeating it. "Malthoranic, awake!"

Then Samuel understood. An inactive construct in the corner of the room sprang to life, its eyes glowing a deep green. It stood, awaiting orders. Michael's hand stopped moving and he gaped at the construct.

"Michael, *hurry*!" Samuel barked. Michael shook his sight free of the construct and began working again.

"Malthoranic, unlatch this door for me," Atherton said.

Malthoranic moved stiffly, its joints creaking from disuse. It reached for the door. Grabbing the inner hardbolt, the construct pulled, tearing it free of the door in the process and dropping it on the floor.

Samuel didn't know what level of intellect this construct possessed, but he was quite sure it was not aware of its own strength.

A twinge of feeling shot down Samuel's left arm, all the way to his fingertips, then receded back to his shoulder. Samuel turned and saw Michael smiling. "I've almost got it." he said, unbuckling the straps that held Samuel's arm in place.

The latch on the door slid free. Atherton hauled it open and stepped through. "Thank you, Malthoranic," he said, closing the door behind him. "I knew you'd be useful at some point." Atherton placed his hands on the door and there was a *whoosh* of air, and a faint tinge of light glittered across the metal of the room's interior armor plating. He turned toward Michael but did not approach, and Michael did not stop working.

"Oh, Michael," he said, spying what the boy was up to. "Malthoranic, stop him, please." The construct took several jerky steps toward the table where Samuel lay.

"Hurry up, Michael!" Samuel said.

Michael wiped sweat from around his eyes and tried to steady his hands. Malthoranic rounded the end of the table. Michael glanced quickly over, pressing a long metal tool into the opening in Samuel's shoulder and letting it rest against the side of the opening. Malthoranic covered the gap in two long strides as Michael reached to retrieve his other tools. The construct grabbed his wrist and pulled him upward. Samuel heard two loud cracks as the boy's wrist snapped in Malthoranic's grip. Michael screamed as the construct held him up by his broken arm.

"Let him go!" Samuel yelled, struggling against the restraints.

Atherton approached the table on the other side, bending down to retrieve something from the floor. Before him, he held a small creature with two short, clawed appendages and a long tail, its back covered in blue feathers and its underside leaking a viscous fluid onto Atherton's hands. A long cut marred the creature's back, and blood ran down its sides. "You killed it, Michael? You killed my siphil?" Michael couldn't respond, only sobbing in pain as he hung from the construct's grip. Atherton's attention turned to Malthoranic. "Drop him," he said. "But don't let him near Samuel again." The construct released Michael who fell in a heap on the floor. Atherton set the dead siphil on the workbench and stepped up next to Samuel.

"Why?" Samuel asked.

Atherton leaned over and looked Samuel in the face, his lips curled in a sneer. "Because I know what you are. It was your kind that was responsible for the death of the Queen Consort," he said through gritted teeth. His voice was thick with contempt. "I'll not have you destroy everything I've built here, everything I've worked for!"

"My kind? I don't understand, Atherton! I hold no malice toward you. I don't want to harm you."

"Just your presence is a blight that could ruin me," Atherton sniped, his words tinged with fear. "Handing you over will guarantee my safety and protect my prosperity." His face softened, just a little, and he lowered his voice. "You're a fascinating creature, Samuel, but you're not worth my life and livelihood."

"Just tell me what you're talking about! Maybe I can help!"

"There's nothing you can do!" Atherton screamed, his anger boiling to the surface. "And nothing I'd let you do!"

Atherton's eyes darted to the door as the sound of the front entryway closing echoed through the front room. "Samuel?" It was Kaleb's voice. "Michael? Atherton?" Atherton's hand pulsed a deep blue as he placed it just below Samuel's chin. Samuel tried to speak, but was unable. "Samuel?" Kaleb repeated.

"KALEB!" Michael yelled. "Help us! Atherton's gone crazy!"

Atherton shot a look at the boy, but didn't remove his hand from Samuel's throat.

"What?" Kaleb yelled. The door latch clicked, but would not turn. "Atherton? What are you doing? Michael?"

"You can't come in here right now," Atherton yelled. "Something's gone wrong with Samuel, and it's dangerous." The artificer's eyes were frantic, searching the room.

Michael sprang to his feet, grabbing a mallet off of the rolling table next to Samuel, striking down onto the tool he had left in Samuel's shoulder. Samuel's arm flooded with life, feeling and strength returning all the way to his fingers. Malthoranic swung a backhanded blow that connected with Michael's cheek, sending him reeling into the workbench behind him.

Samuel pulled his newly restored arm free from the loosened straps, shoving Atherton, who lost his grip and stumbled to the ground, his head striking the side of one of his workbenches. "Kaleb, get in here now!" he shouted, trying to loosen the buckles on some of the straps holding him to the table.

Samuel had almost freed his other arm when Atherton, the side of his head covered in blood, barked at Malthoranic to stop him. The construct grabbed Samuel's left arm and pulled it back to the table, pinning it down. He wasn't sure if Malthoranic was stronger than him or not, but the mindless construct had leverage on its side, which made all the difference in the moment. Samuel hadn't been able to pull his right arm free, and now Malthoranic stood over him, pinning his head and his left arm and staring down at him with those glowing green eyes. "Kaleb! Get in here right now!"

There was a loud *whump!* outside the door, like the sound of someone striking a feather pillow with their open hand.

"You won't be able to get in that way." Atherton said, leaning against the leg of his workbench and holding a hand to the injured side of his head. "I've warded it." He let out a weak laugh.

"Samuel, can you move?" Kaleb asked.

"Not at the moment," Samuel replied, struggling to free himself from Malthoranic's grip.

"Michael! I need you to open the eyeslot on the door!" Kaleb said.

Michael moved around behind Malthoranic, keeping as far back against the opposing workbench as he could, then turned to sprint towards the door.

"Stop him, Malthoranic!" Atherton said.

The construct released Samuel's arm and gave chase after Michael. Samuel freed his right arm and began working on the other straps. The boy reached the door and grabbed the handle of the eyeslot, slamming the thin metal portal open. "Michael, look out!" Samuel yelled. Michael turned, a half-second too late.

"Wait!" Atherton screamed, understanding the order he had given, and what he'd given it to.

Malthoranic struck Michael with a sweeping backhand that caught him at the base of the jaw, shattering it. The blow flung him into a bookcase on the opposite wall. His head struck the frame at a terrible, impossible angle and he went limp, tumbling into a pile of loose parts.

"NOOO!" Atherton bolted across the room, racing to his fallen apprentice. Malthoranic turned his attention back to Samuel, who had managed to free his arm and torso. The construct clouted Samuel hard in the face, slamming his head back to the table. With one hand, the construct pinned Samuel down by the neck while using his other to ward off Samuel's attempts to free himself. There was another *whump!* in the air, this time louder and inside the room. Something struck the back of Malthoranic's head and a splintered plank of wood flew over Samuel, landing with a clatter in the corner.

"Um..." Kaleb said, stepping back, holding the broken end of the plank. "Sorry, Samuel, but I think I just pissed it off."

Samuel struck at the construct's arm, trying to free himself from its grip. With his legs still strapped down, he couldn't get much force behind the blows. "Just cut my legs free!" he yelled to Kaleb.

Kaleb drew a knife from his belt and moved around the table, cutting the strap at Samuel's ankle. Malthoranic swung his free hand to strike Kaleb and missed. Kaleb moved swiftly, freeing Samuel's leg. Samuel twisted and struck Malthoranic in the back with his knee. He followed with a blow to Malthoranic's head that knocked the construct just off balance enough for his grip to falter. Malthoranic stumbled backward and Kaleb lunged, cutting the last two straps around Samuel's other leg.

Samuel slipped away, Malthoranic's crushing, two-handed blow splintering the table where Samuel's head had been. Samuel rolled off onto his feet and ducked another swing. Rebounding, he grabbed Malthoranic by the neck. The construct took another swing, which Samuel caught with his free hand. Samuel's fingers dug into the construct's neck, crushing the plates where it attached to the jawline. There was no doubt in Samuel's mind he was stronger than this mindless hulk.

"I'm sorry," Samuel said. With one great pull he ripped Malthoranic's arm free and released his neck. As he staggered, Samuel grabbed the severed arm at the wrist and took a mighty swing into the side of the construct's head, tearing it away and flinging it into the workbench with a crash. The remains of Malthoranic tried to take a step, stumbled into the worktable, and fell to the floor motionless. Samuel dropped the severed arm and stared down at the construct he'd just destroyed. He didn't know if Malthoranic could even understand what was happening, but hoped with all his being he could not.

Samuel pulled Michael's tools from the opening in his shoulder and laid them on the workbench. Kaleb leaned against the foot of the table, his head bowed. Ragged sobs echoed from the corner of the room where Atherton, on his knees, clutched Michael's lifeless body to his chest. Samuel had liked Michael, and his inability to cry for the loss didn't make it any less painful.

He stepped forward and placed a hand on Kaleb's shoulder. Kaleb didn't turn, but Samuel felt he was coiled like a spring. His face was wet with tears. At his chest, he held his dagger in a white-knuckled grip. Samuel understood the sentiment. "This isn't the time, Kaleb," he said.

Kaleb's muscles unclenched, and he lowered his head, taking a deep breath. He sheathed the knife and turned to Samuel, his eyes still lowered. "Why would he do this?" Kaleb's expression had shifted from fury to anguish. He looked up at Samuel. "Why?"

"I couldn't even begin to know, Kaleb." Samuel said, remembering the look of hatred on Atherton's face only moments before. "I have no idea what's going on."

Kaleb nodded. "We, ah..." He cleared his throat. "We need to get out of here. The guard will be here any minute after this racket, and we need to be gone." Samuel nodded.

The two of them headed for the door, but Samuel stopped Kaleb, turning back toward Atherton. "Do you think we should—" He wasn't even sure how to finish the sentence.

Kaleb's face hardened again. "No. Leave him. Let him live with what he's done." He heaved open the iron door, and Samuel followed him into the front room. Two working arms made donning his cloak easier, and while they walked through the shop, he checked to make sure the serpent ring was still in the pocket. Samuel stepped out into the alleyway and Kaleb shut the door, holding onto the doorknob for an extra few seconds as his jaw worked and he took shallow breaths. Samuel dared not speak or interrupt. It was dark out and it had started to pour, rainwater draining off of the front of Kaleb's face as Samuel watched him try to reconcile all he had just seen.

Kaleb nodded to himself, then looked up at Samuel, his eyes red. "Let's go."

Chapter Fifteen

Kaleb led them through the winding back alleys of Morrelton. The wind whistled between the buildings, driving the rain into their faces as they tromped through thickening mud. Samuel wasn't sure where Kaleb led and just tried to keep pace, never questioning. They moved as quietly as they could, stopping at every intersection so Kaleb could be assured they wouldn't run into any guardsmen. Samuel heard the sound of the stream; they'd have to move to the main street to cross it. Before they reached the water, Kaleb led them into an even smaller alleyway, ducking into an alcove. Overhanging eaves on either side covered each of them from rain, but the runoff from both formed a waterfall between them.

"You need to tell me what happened, Samuel," he said, looking up at the construct. "Atherton's not exactly a saint, but a turn like this is... What happened?"

"I..." Samuel wasn't sure how to phrase it, "...blacked out. Michael"—Samuel had to pause, images he no longer wished to see burning themselves into his memory—"Michael said I fell over in the middle of our conversation. He called Atherton and they hauled me into the workroom, and then Atherton...he turned on Michael, yelling at him to leave. Michael didn't know what was going on."

Kaleb shook his head. "I don't understand."

"Neither do I," Samuel said. "They couldn't know what I saw..."

Kaleb's look was understandably questioning.

"I... I don't know what it was, Kaleb. It was like...I think maybe I was seeing...memories. But I'm not sure. It was a flash of random images—thousands of them, all at once. Some of them felt like memories, but some..."

"What, Samuel?" Kaleb pressed, somewhere between inquisitive and angry.

"Some felt...like *visions*. Like I was seeing the future."

"That's impossible, Samuel."

"I saw my own death, Kaleb." Samuel said. "I saw a blond man with silver eyes standing over me as he destroyed me."

Kaleb shook his head, leaning against the wall of the alcove and sliding to the ground. "I don't know what you saw, Samuel, but you're still standing here. Whatever it was, it wasn't your death. And it wasn't the future. Maybe your memories are starting to come back to you. But that doesn't explain anything that happened back there." He dropped his head to his hands.

"Atherton... He was *livid*. He kept saying he wouldn't let me ruin him. That he was going to turn me over to someone."

Kaleb's only response was to shake his head, looking at the ground as he rummaged through his thoughts. He splashed his face in the streaming water and stood up straight. "Come on, Samuel." He said, heading out into the alleyway. "We need to get out of here."

Samuel followed, more confused now than before, but he understood the need to leave this place. Their path wound through the unseen spaces of Morrelton, avoiding main streets and open spaces at all costs. After an interminable silence, Samuel had to speak. "Kaleb, do you know what Atherton was talking about?"

Kaleb shook his head, but kept moving. "No. It doesn't even make sense. I don't know why Atherton would act like this."

"Could he be in some sort of trouble?" Samuel asked.

"Atherton doesn't get into trouble anymore." Kaleb said. "And even if he were, he wouldn't be for long."

"Maybe he owed someone?" Samuel said. "Maybe he was trying to..."

He cut himself off as Kaleb came to a sudden stop and held up his hand, warning Samuel to back up. "Damnit," he whispered. "Backbackback!" Kaleb waved his hands, pushing Samuel back down the alleyway. Samuel turned, but stopped in his tracks as two men, dressed in black leather baldrics with smallswords in hand, stepped out from the intersecting alley and blocked their way. Kaleb and Samuel turned to go forward again, but three more men stood before them. The closest, a giant of a man, rested his hands atop a long, angry-looking mace whose head sat in the mud between his feet. Cort grinned down at them, the rainwater streaming down from his bald head to drip off of the end of his thick, oft-broken nose. "Well, well. Looky wha' we found, boys!" he said through a thick accent.

Kaleb stood straight, throwing a quick look over his shoulder. "Keep an eye on those two, would ya, Samuel?" Samuel turned to spy the two blocking their rear exit.

"Got yourself a new ladyfriend, I see!" Cort said, to the stolid chuckles of his crew.

"I see your sense of humor hasn't changed." Kaleb said.

Cort's demeanor hardened. "You got som'fin o' mine, my friend," he said. "An' I intend to get it back from ya. You c'n hand it over, or I c'n take it from ya." His smile darkened. "Please, cully, make me take it from ya…"

"Well now, Cort," Kaleb said between breaths. "You were pretty much gonna do that, no matter what, now weren't you."

Cort laughed. It almost sounded genuine. "Maybe you know me be'er than I thought." The smile disappeared from his face. "No one makes me look like a fool, Jacob, especially not you."

Jacob? Samuel looked at Kaleb, but Kaleb was too preoccupied with watching Cort to return the glance. He caught movement out of the corner of his vision and saw the two men behind them had begun a cautious advance.

"You do a fine job of making yourself look like a fool, Cort."

Cort lunged. Kaleb sidestepped as Cort's mace came crashing into the mud behind Samuel's feet, forcing Samuel to step toward the two advancing thugs. He had no intention of hurting these men. For all he knew, they might have a legitimate gripe against Kaleb—*Jacob?*

The first one took a wild swing with his smallsword, missing his target as Samuel stepped in and pushed him back into the other. His sword left his grip as the two men bounced off the alley wall and tumbled into the mud, rolling on top of one another.

Kaleb ducked under another swing. This time Cort's mace crashed into the alley wall. Kaleb kicked the haft of the mace, flinging it from Cort's hand and tossing him off balance. From behind Cort there was a deafening *crack* that echoed through the close quarters, and a piece of the wall near Samuel's head exploded outward, showering him in splinters. A sharp, smoky odor filled the alley. Cort turned and slapped something out of his lackey's hand that clattered off the wall and into the mud.

"No guns, you moron!" Cort growled. The goon retreated a step under Cort's menace. "Do you want to get us all executed?"

Samuel felt something pulling at him, a faint tugging at the corners of his consciousness. He saw Kaleb take in a deep breath and make a wide circular motion with his hands before drawing them in toward his chest. A disturbance wavered in the air around him, materializing in glittering blue light that flowed toward his hands. Cort's attention snapped back to them and strode toward Kaleb, meaning to put an immediate end to the fight.

Kaleb thrust his hands forward. The light was doused then, with a bright flash, a concentrated blast of air struck from his outstretched hands. Cort raised an arm and, though he staggered, the full force of the blast seemed to slide around him. His two companions were flung back into the alley, one landing with a *slap* in the mud more than thirty feet away, the other striking an eave and landing heavily on a barrel.

"Nice parlor trick," Cort said. "But ya need somethin' a lot heavier to knock me down!"

Samuel, at first startled by the report of the pistol and then transfixed by Kaleb's display, cost himself precious seconds versus his two opponents. The two recovered, splitting to either side of the alley and rushing him. One of them thrust his sword and forced Samuel to dodge, the other stepped in and struck Samuel in the side with something that sent a wave of shock through his entire body and caused his legs to wobble underneath him. He struck Samuel again on the shoulder with a sound like a pocket of sap exploding on a burning log. The blow was more intense this time, driving Samuel to his hands in the mud. The sensation frightened him and ignited his anger.

"No!" Kaleb yelled. Samuel was buffeted by another blast of air that took his attackers off their feet, but didn't stun them for long. "It's a mafi-stick, Samuel! Don't let him hit you with it again or they'll kill you!" He barely got the words out before Cort's fist slammed into his jaw, staggering him into the wall.

Samuel regained his feet just as the two men mounted another charge. The first came with his sword and Samuel put up his arm to block the blow straight on, the blade shattering on the metal of his forearm. In spite of the ineffectual attack, Samuel felt enraged. The ruffian with the mafi-stick charged, but the stick was short, giving Samuel an advantage in reach. He dodged the first swing but the thug's second connected with his thigh and he staggered. The shockwave was intense, but localized to his leg this time.

The goon went for the kill, taking another swing straight at Samuel's head. Samuel caught the blow in mid-flight and twisted his attacker's wrist, turning the man's elbow backward with a crunch. The mafi-stick dropped into the mud. He stood, still holding the screaming man's damaged arm, and turned on the second. With less effort than he thought it would take, he swung the first man around, flinging him into the second and sending them both crashing into the wall. This time, neither of them got up.

"Samuel!" The word was almost unintelligible, a croaking sound from somewhere beneath and behind him. Samuel turned and saw Cort straddling Kaleb, the bald giant's face twisted in rage and his huge hands wrapped around Kaleb's neck. Kaleb's head sunk into the mud and his eyes rolled back into his head. He pounded at Cort's thick forearms with no effect. The rain beat down on them as Kaleb's face turned bright red, then a nasty shade of purple.

Without thinking, Samuel took off at a run, covering the distance in four strides. He hauled back with his hips and kicked Cort square in the side. The crack echoed through the alleyway as the bald giant's ribcage buckled. The kick lifted Cort into the air and he slammed into the ground in a plume of muddy water, sliding a full ten feet before coming to rest. He let out a single loud, ragged cough, spewing blood over his face and neck before settling onto his back, unmoving.

Kaleb pulled himself up out of the mud, sliding back and leaning against the alley wall, coughing and sputtering for breath. Samuel looked down the alleyway at the man he'd just struck as the rain pelted his face, mixing with blood and saliva. He turned to the hacking Kaleb and found his anger had not subsided—only found a new target. He knelt down, waiting for Kaleb to catch his breath.

"Thank…" Kaleb coughed, not quite ready to speak. "Thank you," he said in a whisper like shifting gravel.

Samuel was still furious, unsure which question to ask first. "What's a mafi-stick?"

Kaleb was panting, speaking between breaths. "It's used for…taking down…unruly constructs." He paused and composed himself a little better. "A few hits and it just shocks you—immobilizes you. Enough in a row, in the right spots, and it'll drain your core, leave you mindless."

Samuel nodded and reconciled his actions in his mind as justifiable self-defense. "What did Cort want from you?"

"I…I don't know," Kaleb replied.

Samuel's tone turned to an angry growl. "Don't lie to me."

Kaleb looked like Samuel had slapped him across the face. "A trinket, nothing more," he said. "Something they were hired to guard."

"Something you stole."

"Retrieved." Kaleb's tone was defensive now.

"What did Cort call you just then?"

Kaleb's defensiveness melted away, the question catching him off guard. His jaw clenched and unclenched, but he didn't answer.

"Damnit, Kaleb," Samuel said, pushing himself to his feet. Kaleb stared up at him from the ground, one hand rubbing his throat. Even though Samuel wasn't sure he wanted to know the answer to his next question, he still asked it. "Is Kaleb even your real name?"

Kaleb's mouth opened, but no sound came out. He turned his eyes away, and Samuel got his first taste of true disappointment. The rain continued to beat down on the two of them in a back alley in Morrelton, one at a loss for words and the other suddenly unsure what to do next. Samuel shook his head, overcome by the realization he had no idea who the man in front of him really was. The thief's eyes dropped to his hands as he attempted to wipe some of the mud clean using the pouring rainwater.

"It's only been a few days, Samuel," he said without looking up. "There's a lot you don't know about me."

"That's your reasoning?" Samuel replied, astonished. "Your reasoning for lying to me this whole way? I just *killed someone* for you, and I don't even know your real name!"

"Don't put this all on me, Samuel."

"Where should I put it, then?" Samuel asked. "These men were after *you*. For something *you* stole. And you put me right in the middle of it!"

"You made that choice yourself!" the thief yelled, glaring at Samuel under an angry brow. "I didn't force you into anything! You came along of your own accord. You can try to lay as much of tonight off on me as you want, but you bear just as much responsibility for Cort and Michael's deaths as I do."

The mention of Michael's name staggered Samuel. He took a step back, hovering somewhere between shocked and infuriated. The comment dug deep, pointing out how little he even knew of himself, much less of the stranger sitting across from him. How much responsibility would he have to bear for Michael's loss? And how long would the weight of it bear down on him before he could even provide a framework to make sense of it? The confusion and anxiety of the last several days barely held a candle to the swirl of emotions and questions produced by the last several hours.

"Sometimes, Samuel, we just do what we need to do."

Samuel had no response, barely able to gather his own thoughts. Again they were still, each contemplating his own move. Both snapped out of their thoughts when the sounds of voices echoed through the alley, coming closer by the second. The man whose arm Samuel had broken began to stir, moaning and moving his head. The necessity to vacate the scene made all other decisions moot. Samuel pulled the hood of his cloak over his head and turned to leave.

"Samuel, wait." A momentary pause. Samuel didn't turn. "I...I can show you the back way, help you figure out where to go next."

"I know where I'm headed," Samuel said. "And I don't need your help to get there."

Samuel walked away, leaving the other standing in the muddy alleyway under a torrent of autumn rainfall. He stepped around Cort's body without looking, but made note the other two men were breathing. They were, at least, still alive. At the end of the alleyway Samuel pressed himself against a wall, leaning out to check the intersection. With no pursuers in sight, he moved across the street, following the sound of the stream and hoping he'd eventually run into the main road. He stopped, for just a moment, and allowed himself to look back over his shoulder into the alley where he'd fought for his—and one other's—life. No one was there but Cort and his men.

Traversing the town on his own proved more of a chore than Samuel had anticipated. Morrelton's streets and alleys were curvy and unpaved and had turned to a soft muck in the rainy evening. Each intersection was a new lesson in anxiety. As he moved closer to the street where he…they…had turned toward Atherton's shop, he saw more and more guardsmen, and even some townsfolk making their way out into the blustery evening to see what had happened. Avoiding detection would be easy amongst the windy passageways and odd-shaped buildings of the strange forest town. Finding alcoves in which to hide was simple, and in the driving rain, guardsmen were more preoccupied with staying dry than performing a diligent search.

But keeping his sense of direction wasn't easy here. As he moved, the sounds of people and guardsmen became less frequent. Several times he had to stop as his mind tried to reconcile the flood of random images that had come to him after he blacked out. He hadn't had another bout of visions yet—and hoped he wouldn't anytime soon—but trying to push the ones that were there to the background long enough to concentrate on the task at hand was difficult, especially without the stress of defending himself to keep his attention focused.

At one point, the alley spilled out onto the main road, with no easy intersection to go back to and find another way round. This far to the north end of town the road was almost empty. For the few people he did encounter, he buried himself deep within his cloak and hurried by, making out like he didn't want to be out in the rain any more than they did. He was glad no one took a lingering look at his feet. Even though the main road may have remained uncluttered until the edge of town, he decided to veer onto another series of side streets for the remainder of his trip out of Morrelton, just to be safe.

Eventually, the buildings thinned and gave way to more and more foliage. Larger gaps between the buildings were filled with trees and shrubbery rather than grass and mud, and the forest canopy grew thicker. Samuel wasn't too keen on travelling through the raw forest if he could avoid it and so took the chance to return to the main road.

When he saw he was out of town, he froze. With the rush of imagery still slamming his brain, the anxiety of his escape, the betrayal of the only person he'd been able to call a friend, and the raw emotion of what had happened in Atherton's shop, Samuel stood paralyzed by the roadside. There was no telling how long he'd stared off into the rain before he regained himself, but it was the memory of Michael's instructions—find the Bleeding Pine and the trail to his apprentice friend in the forest—that snapped him out of his stupor. He bid Morrelton farewell and set off into the night.

Chapter Sixteen

Colton was glad to put Cinth at his back, but his anger at backtracking across the plains toward Winston was inconsolable. Cinth wasn't the most pleasant of cities, but at least it was a *city*. A place where one could find anything, for the right price. A place where you could vanish and never be seen again, if you wanted. Winston and the rest of the towns in the eastern plains were nothing more than collections of ambitionless dirt farmers who didn't have the wherewithal to make something better of themselves.

If Colton was angry, Bales was outright livid. The idea he had missed something dug under his skin like a splinter, and he was more determined to prove it a lie than to make it right. He rode lengths out ahead of Colton, barreling down the plains road as the driving rain and whistling wind battered his face and hands. He was going to kill his horse, and perhaps himself, if he wasn't careful. Then again, when was Bales *ever* careful?

They'd been on the road all day and into the night, and it didn't seem Bales had any intention of slowing. Colton didn't object; they needed to be back on task as soon as possible. He kept mulling over the burned-out skeleton of Ferron's shop in Winston. The melted remains of the construct sat exactly where they had been, and Ferron's bones lay charred in the room close to where they'd left him. Anything else that might've been in the room would be nothing but charred dross. It pained him to admit it, even to himself, but he was beginning to agree with Bales—something here wasn't right.

At this rate, they'd reach Winston in two days, and who knows what might be left of the artificer's shop by then. All he could hope was there'd be some kind of clue pointing them in the right direction. Taeman's caravan was, no doubt, already well south of Winston by now, too far to detour if what his letter said was true. If they found nothing of importance in Winston, they would head north, possibly as far as Morrelton. Colton despised that forest town more than almost any place he'd ever seen. The duplicity of a nature commune with an affinity for constructs made his skin crawl, and he wished the forest would burn and take Morrelton with it.

The rain continued to fall in sheets, making their nighttime flight across the plains a blind one. Wet and cold seeped through to Colton's bones, but he pushed thoughts of his discomfort aside, driving his horse harder to keep up with Bales's relentless pace.

Walking along the main road at night, in the rain, was only marginally easier than slogging through the alleys of Morrelton. The road was solid somewhere underneath, but with each step, Samuel's feet sank into the soft surface and came free with a *plok*, leaving behind little pools of muddy water. The wind howled through the treetops and thrashed the branches of the tall evergreens together. Needles and leaves fluttered down around him as the relentless rain battered the forest. Samuel hoped he was alone on the road; the cacophony kicked up by the storm made it impossible to hear another's approach.

The rain continued throughout the night, but Samuel didn't stop for shelter. Without a companion who required sleep or sustenance, he resolved to continue moving until he'd found what he was looking for. It was late into the night when he came to the crossroads, the left fork leading off at an angle into the forest while the right fork headed due east, rising into the hills. Consideration of the left fork never even rose in Samuel's mind. There were questions to be answered, and he was going to find someone who could answer them. Besides, it wasn't like he had another lead to follow.

The rain abated near the end of the second day. The road was a steady eastward climb into the hills that would become the northern end of the mountain range to the east. The mixed forest of the lowlands gave way to tall pines and firs, hemmed by thick undergrowth. Several times during his walk, Samuel was forced to stop, his balance failing him as the images swirling through his mind reorganized and attempted to reconcile with one another. None of the scenes seemed to connect, each a separate and encapsulated string of imagery with no beginning or definitive closure. Although he never blacked out like he had at Atherton's, faces and names ran roughshod over his mind, blotting out his surroundings until he could calm the maelstrom and push it to the back of his thoughts. Some memories were weak, flashes of still imagery or half-recalled details, while others were clear and strong, like the face of the scarred man with silver eyes.

His memories bore with them a calm detachment, a lack of emotion Samuel found unsettling. The images played in front of him, accompanied by an analysis of facts and outcomes, but never lending insight on how he *felt*, as though he were looking at his own memories from the outside. Amongst the emotionless visions, pangs of sadness echoed through him at more recent memories of Michael. He was the only person who had been genuine with Samuel from the start. At best, he could almost convince himself Atherton's madness had been at fault in Michael's death; at worst, it was a question he didn't know the answer to.

He slowed his pace one morning, searching the roadside in earnest for anything falling under the description of Bleeding Pine. The forest closed in on either side, tall walls of green framing a thin strip of white sky high above. He was grateful the branches didn't cross the road as much as in the lower forest. It felt brighter here, less claustrophobic, which he hoped would make finding the Bleeding Pine easier. It wouldn't be long before sunset, and he knew he'd have to stop until morning whether he felt he could go on or not. With only partial knowledge of what he was looking for, Samuel worried he might already have missed it. Every tree within sight of the road had been scrutinized—

whether it was a pine or not—and he'd found nothing he could even associate with the name. Nothing red, nothing oozing, no distinguishing marks or interesting properties.

As Little Blue chased Big Sister past the gap in the trees overhead, a weak reflection glinted at the edge of Samuel's vision. He moved to the middle of the road and found the source about a hundred yards away. Samuel abandoned his careful search, pursuing the reflection in the fear, with the movement of the suns, he might lose it. He moved fast, his sight fixed on the one spot where a multitude of tiny reflected lights danced before his eyes, and instantly understood.

Before him stood an ancient pine tree, almost eight feet across at its base. It didn't seem any taller than its neighbors, but it was obviously older. Gnarled and twisted branches were covered with thick waves of long, heavy needles toward their ends that grew thin closer to the trunk. The roots of the old tree twisted up out of the ground and back in, claiming sole ownership of a wide area around its base where no other undergrowth could be seen. From the dark forest soil to as far upward as Samuel could see into its branches, the trunk was covered in layer upon layer of running sap. Sticky rivulets wound through a craggy landscape of long-hardened pitch. The fading sunlight sparkled in starlight reflections on its surface and penetrated the translucent amber so rich in color its reddish-brown hue almost glowed.

Samuel was relieved to have found the landmark, but his trek was not yet over. According to Michael, his destination lay some distance into these unknown woods, along a trail that might not be so easy to find or follow. Now that Samuel was on his own, what if he couldn't find the trail? Getting lost in the northern wilderness wasn't high on Samuel's list of things to do. Then again, standing out on the mountain road staring into the forest wasn't either.

The suns sank out of view over the treetops to the southeast, burning the sky a dusky orange as nighttime approached. Samuel stepped off the road and into the embrace of the Bleeding Pine, looking for any clues he could find in the failing light. A circle of hard-packed earth with little vegetation surrounded the tree, ringed at its edges by the low bushes and vines typical of the rest of the undergrowth here. The hedgewall at the outside of the circle was broken in several places, but none led very far back into the forest. Samuel moved around to the north side of the tree, opposite the road, a wide break in the foliage offering a sign of hope. The sun must have slipped over the mountains; the red had faded from the sky and the forest descended into darkness.

Samuel took the plunge into the gap in the brush, deciding he was better off moving than standing still. He felt invigorated after reaching the Bleeding Pine, and moving onto the trail brought with it both excitement and uncertainty. As twilight deepened he stopped, his vision momentarily hindered as his world transitioned from color and light to the blue-grey monotone of his night vision. There would be no starlight or moonlight here to provide the glittering highlights he'd seen on his first night out on the plains, but even in the darkness under the forest canopy he could make out every tree, leaf, root and rock in sharp detail.

After moving a few feet out of the Bleeding Pine's influence, the path could barely be called a trail. Samuel thought he might not have even been able to follow it in daylight, but his vision in the darkness gave him a unique view, the greys and whites of the surrounding leaves framing a thin black path where the undergrowth moved aside for regular travelers. The path was not cut away or cleared, so to untrained eyes it might not be visible, especially not at night. Although the trail was easy for Samuel to *see*, he knew it would not always be easy for him to negotiate as he traveled deeper into the woods. He had no idea what to expect of the terrain, and no concept of what he'd find at the trail's end.

Chapter Seventeen

Much of the ruin of the artificer's shop had been cleaned or removed. Ferron's bones no longer lay in the back room. The melted slag of former constructs would have been taken as scrap and sold, no doubt to Taeman as his troupe passed through Winston on their path southward. Driving rain ran in a constant stream off of the corners of Colton's hat. His boots were covered in grey-brown muck as the running mud mixed with ash.

Bales had been in a foul mood as they approached the plains town, muttering obscenities and slurs against the rural populace, exclaiming his distaste for being driven back here by what he called a "filthy load of lies from the hand of an untrustworthy slug." He'd insisted they ride straight through from Cinth, which extended even Colton's abilities to their limits. When they reached Winston, their horses were already dead, only waiting for Colton to release them. The effort of driving them forward had exhausted him, leaving little energy for the search by the time they unsaddled the horses and carried their tack to the edge of town.

"Damnit." Bales stared into a pile of bricks and burned supports, which now covered the floor of what was once the shop's back room. He let out an unintelligible scream, kicking a blackened ceiling support that cracked under the blow. The sound died quickly in the storm, but Colton was sure the entire town must have heard him.

111

"I haven't the strength to keep diverting their attention from your petulance, Bales." Colton said through gritted teeth. Beneath his rain-soaked leather coat he was sweating, which only enhanced the chill.

Bales stamped over to Colton, pulling off his hat and running a gloved hand over his greasy black hair. "Then what, your mightiness, would you suggest we do now?"

"I'd suggest, first, you calm down and quiet yourself." Colton stepped around Bales to the back of the ruin, took a deep breath, and rooted through the rubble. It looked as though much of the debris from the front part of the building had been removed, but some had been tossed into semi-organized piles. Nothing of value remained and the room was now buried in broken supports, skeletons of bookshelves, and pieces of unsalvageable workbenches.

"Nothing escaped this!" Bales yelled over the din of the driving rain. "There's no way any construct survived this fire!"

Colton couldn't deny what Bales was saying. The fire was intense enough to cut off any construct's connection to *khet* long enough for their core to drain. The more pertinent fact was that Colton had ensured their target was immobilized and near destruction before Bales had even set the fire, which was necessary to destroy the evidence of Ferron's murder. They'd seen the construct's remains in the front room of the shop the day after the fire. Even if *something* had escaped the fire, it wasn't their quarry, but even that seemed impossible. The destruction from the fire was complete, thanks to Ferron's alchemy, and there was no way out of the building.

"You might be right," Colton replied, hoping he hadn't said it loud enough for Bales to hear. He worked his way around the back of the room, kicked aside burnt remains of bookshelves, and found an almost intact volume underneath. He picked up the half-charred book and propped it open on his hand as he stepped outside where the shop's back wall had once stood. It was a thick, leatherbound volume on the alchemical properties of minerals and their applications that read as dry as he would have expected it to. He snapped the book closed, taking a wider look at the room from outside its periphery, seeing nothing else that offered any clues. Bales stared at him with his arms crossed, looking like a drowned rat without his hat on. Colton shook his head and tossed the book onto one of the debris piles in the corner as he made his way back to where his partner waited.

The book landed heavy. A loud *crack* escaped from beneath the debris. The entire pile fell into the earth, landing somewhere far below with a splash.

Colton turned, confused, and Bales raced forward to join him. At the rear corner of the room, a deep hole in the ground replaced the pile of burned boards. The two of them stood over the opening, watching rainfall race past them into the blackness below. Around the rim of the hole was a wood-and-stone framework, the far side of which supported two heavy iron hinges attached to the stubs of broken boards. On the side closest to them, ladder rungs were mounted into the stone side of the hole and descended into darkness.

"What the fuck is that?" Bales said.

Colton felt his anger rise, but with it the familiar exhilaration that accompanied the beginning of a hunt. A malevolent smile turned the corner of his mouth. "A hole big enough for a construct to fit through."

Bales looked at him wide eyed. "Oh, no. No no no." He turned and started walking away, exasperated. "This doesn't mean a damn thing."

Colton turned, but did not follow. "What?"

Bales swung around, glaring at Colton through the rain. "Why does it matter if there's an escape hatch? We know Ferron didn't get out"— he thrust his finger in the direction of a wall that no longer existed— "and Esiphilicus melted to slag right over there. You've got a bottle full of *khet* for our troubles with him."

Colton's unnerving smile faded.

"So," Bales continued, "let's say something or someone *did* escape the fire. At worst, it was another random construct and of no concern to us."

Colton took a deep breath and looked over his shoulder at Bales. "No concern?" Colton said. "At best, whatever escaped this fire is a witness. Taeman might not be the most honest of businessmen, but he doesn't lie to *me*. He's too familiar with the consequences. Whatever prize it was he lost said it came from this place, and now we know how."

Bales ground his teeth together and said nothing. Colton could see his mind working, trying to find any angle that didn't result in pursuit.

When it was clear he couldn't, he slammed his tricorne back on his head and stormed away from the burned-out shop without a word.

"If you're going to sulk, find us some horses while you're at it, would you?" Colton said behind him, returning his gaze to the mouth of the hole. His smile returned.

Samuel found no solace in being right. He trekked through most of the night, following a trail made visible only by his unique vision. As dawn broke, however, ease turned to frustration as the increasing light of day made the trail blend into the surrounding undergrowth. Whoever used the trail on a regular basis must have known the landmarks that would guide them, otherwise they'd end up wandering aimlessly through the forest.

Dawn's awakening brought with it a cacophony of sound, from the simple swish of the wind through the branches to the calls of any number of forest animals as they went about their daily business. Squirrels leapt around the high branches and small birds flitted about the undergrowth, hunting for bugs. The forest here teemed with wildlife, more so than the forests along the road to Morrelton. At one point, Samuel spotted an elk between the trees in the distance, but his crashing traversal of the disappearing trail scared it off.

Around midday his luck turned and the trail widened into a track Samuel could see without effort, giving him no choice but to follow. He made better time, and not having to push between close bushes and branches allowed him to take in the sounds of the forest as he walked late into the day.

It was beautiful here, in a different way than what he'd experienced so far. While Morrelton was a testament to the inhabitants' attempts to live in harmony with the nature around them, it was still a town, and the people there still outsiders to the forest. Here, this far away from the mountain road, the forest seemed unspoiled, a place so untouched by man where wildlife could rule freely.

As Samuel contemplated the nature around him, he noticed a change. The once prevalent sounds of animals died down to almost nothing. Birds no longer chirped; squirrels no longer filled the air with their raspy, clicking cries. He stopped, peering into the trees under the flat light of the grey sky. In all directions, the forest was devoid of movement other than blurry shadows as they played along the surface of the undergrowth, moving in time with the swaying of treetops in the breeze.

He'd only taken a single step before he stopped, almost stepping on a creature in his path. The large rodent stood with its forepaws off the ground, sniffing at the air in Samuel's direction. Its whiskers twitched back and forth as it balanced on stout hind legs and a short, flat tail. Samuel thought it was rather cute and wondered what kind of relationship it must have with the people who normally traveled this trail that it would be so bold in its approach.

Something struck Samuel on the shoulder, just hard enough to disrupt his balance, and weight bore down behind his neck. The little animal in the trail laid its ears back and chattered in anger before darting into the bushes. Samuel felt something slip under his arm and wrap around his chest—a long, furless tail. He swooned, dropping to his knees. His hand found something sitting on his shoulder beside his neck, clamped into his cloak. He grabbed hard and tried to pull it off, and came away with a fistful of blue feathers.

Panic engulfed him as he tried to pull the siphil free. He knew it couldn't kill him, but he wasn't about to let it knock him unconscious. The creature dug one talon into his shoulder and the other grasped for purchase on the other side of his neck. He swooned again, almost the exact weakening sensation he'd felt while trying to escape the fire in Winston. He couldn't get a solid grip, only managing to tear out feathers and unable to find any vulnerable spots that would make the siphil release its hold. With his strength waning, he failed to tear away the creature's tail.

His vision wavered just as he regained his feet. Before blindness could set in, he headed for the nearest tree at a dead run. Lowering his head and his shoulders, he moved as though to tackle the tree right out of the ground. His shoulder slammed into the trunk with a wet crunch, shaking loose a rain of needles as his strength and senses slammed back into his body. The tail around his midsection slackened, and the siphil fell away into the undergrowth.

The eyeless creature lay on its back at the edge of the trail, working a four-pointed beak-like mouth open and closed as it grasped at the last moments of life. Samuel stood forward and unclasped his cloak, swinging it off of his shoulders to survey the damage. There was a large hole at the base of the hood and the top was covered in translucent yellow goo. Samuel was contemplating how to clean away the slime when a flash of blue feathers tore the cloak from his hands.

A second siphil hit the ground, rolling into the path and turning over to balance on the two talon appendages, using its tail as the third leg of the tripod. The feathers on its back flared and it made a screeching hiss, striking several times at the fallen cloak before realizing it was empty and turning its attention toward Samuel. Samuel backed away on the trail and the siphil followed him, still hissing but cautious now of its prey. The thing reared onto its tail, exposing the four pointed beak beneath. The siphil belted out three screeching barks, then returned to the hissing sound. It filled the forest and sounded like it was coming from all around him.

And it was. At least six more siphils hung above him over the trail, dangling from branches by their tails and hissing in concert with the one on the ground. Samuel panicked, and didn't wait around to find out how many more were out of sight, taking off down the path at a sprint. The one on the ground leapt at him as he passed, sailing over his shoulder into the bushes. It recovered and slid out into the path in front of him. He stepped hard in the middle of it. Blood and yellow slime splattered the trail as Samuel crushed the creature under his weight, barely losing step. Behind him, he could hear the barking of the other siphils over the swishing of tree branches as they followed through the canopy. The screeching cries were being answered from further off in the forest; more would be on the way. He didn't dare look over his shoulder for fear of seeing what kind of trouble he was in. One of these things might not be able to destroy him on its own, but he had no idea what an entire pack could do.

He felt another jolt on his shoulder and he stumbled forward but kept his balance, a siphil bouncing in front of him as it failed to find a solid grip. As it skittered to a stop, Samuel kicked it aside and into a tree.

More and more dropped from the canopy, just missing him in his flight. The trail narrowed again, brush and ferns slapping against his arms and legs as he ran.

His balance almost failed him twice as his feet found roots and vines that crept across the narrow trail. His flight was not subtle or quiet, and after a while all he heard were the sounds of branches scraping and cracking against his metal plates. It dawned on him the sounds had changed again. He heard only his own clumsiness, so he dared a look over his shoulder.

Almost all the siphils were gone, and those he could still see had stopped their pursuit, dispersing into the trees. He pulled to a stop and looked back, glancing upward first and staying on his guard for a sneak attack. The siphils' retreat appeared genuine, but even that put Samuel on edge, wondering why they had lost interest. Or worse, what had driven them off? Samuel was relieved to find he hadn't lost the trail in his panic.

Soon, the sounds of the forest returned, dominated by the chittering din of nocturnal bugs as darkness descended. Night fell as the trail continued to narrow and Samuel hoped tracking it would be as easy as the previous night. Again, he stopped and waited while twilight passed, the failing light leaving him with an awkward mix of color and monotone.

The Chronicler Saga

Chapter Eighteen

As the greens and browns of the forest bleached to monochrome, Samuel noticed the same flickering glow he'd seen on the plains under the light of the moon and stars. A clear sky meant additional moonlight, even this deep in the forest. The glow, however, seemed to be localized to an area about a hundred yards off the trail, and the rest of the forest around him was still just varying shades of grey. *Maybe there's a break in the clouds and moonlight's only hitting that one spot.* For several minutes he watched. The glow never moved, faded, or changed location.

The undergrowth pressed in on him after he left the trail to investigate, vines tangling at his feet and branches blocking his path. He pressed forward with a clatter, sweeping the foliage out of his way as he approached. The light that had drawn him from the path took on a different cast. The forest wavered in his vision like a mirage, and minute points of bright light that shone blue even in his night vision rose from the ground and danced into the sky like sparks from a campfire. At the edge of the distortion, the undergrowth fell away to form a small clearing where nothing but grass and wildflowers grew.

The foliage inside the light popped with color in Samuel's vision. The wildflowers in the clearing were open and turned upward, as though drinking in light from the noonday sun. Samuel moved around the periphery of the clearing and a faint reflection moved with him, ghosting

119

in the surface of the light. Across the clearing, behind his reflection, a dark shape moved silently behind a tree, the grey leaves at waist level shivering back into place.

Samuel had flinched when he saw the movement, but hoped whoever spied on him had not seen it. He continued to move around the light, acting as though he studied it while he moved toward the tree where the shadow hid. The moment he approached, he lunged into the brush where he'd seen the movement...and found nothing. No one hid behind the tree, and no evidence of the spy could be found. No broken branches, bent leaves, or footprints. As out of sorts as Samuel had been, he chalked it up to a figment of his imagination.

Samuel turned his attention back to the clearing. A pine cone tossed into the center of the circle disturbed the swirling sparks and shone in color inside the light, but produced no other effect. Pushing his arm through the light produced similar results. Samuel grew frustrated with how much time he'd spent on his investigation. As beautiful as the lights were, and strange in how they affected his vision, they seemed harmless and he decided to move along. He found the path again and threw the dancing lights one last lingering glance before heading on his way.

The path skirted around a rise in the forest floor to his right, which made his direction easier to decide, even if the path wasn't clearly visible. The gentle rise gave way to jagged rocks as he walked, becoming a high stone wall jutting out of the forest floor. The path wound closer and closer to the outcropping until it met with the wall at a pile of fallen stones.

A draft blew his way from deeper in the forest, bringing with it a hint of the familiar smell of smoke. A wood fire meant one of only two things: either the forest was burning, or there were people nearby. He couldn't imagine bandits this deep in the wilderness, and his hopes soared that he'd found what Michael led him toward. Skirting the rock wall, he took the path of least resistance first, hoping whatever he was to find would be down here and not up on top.

More blue lights came into view as he rounded the corner, the same as in the clearing, but this time running in a straight line away from the rock wall into the trees. On the other side of the wall, the color returned. The path veered away from the outcrop and through the wall of light, widening into another clearing. A wispy trail of smoke curled into the sky from the stone chimney of a small cabin. Faint light flickered behind small, round windows beneath a rough shingled roof. The heavy front door was painted dark blue with a carved symbol Samuel didn't recognize.

After days of trudging through the forest, Samuel was elated to have found his destination, but was unsure of how to approach it. If it was the homestead of an adept, like Michael said, Samuel would tread dangerous ground by stumbling up onto it in the dead of night. There was no way around it, but he didn't want to just wait out in the forest until morning, so he started down the trail. His anxiety had him almost jogging when he reached the dancing lights, and he slammed headlong into them, bouncing off and landing unceremoniously on his back in the trail.

"You can't pass through it, construct." The voice came from somewhere to his right, above him. "You're not even supposed to be able to see it."

Samuel stirred and tried to stand.

"Stay down where you are, if you please," the voice said. It was male, and younger, probably about Michael's age.

"All right," Samuel said, remaining seated as he looked for the source of the voice. "To whom am I speaking?"

"You're not in any position to ask questions." Samuel began to zero in on the direction of the voice, and hoped he would keep talking. "Few know of this place, and all of them know me. You are not amongst them."

"This is true," Samuel said. "I was told of this place in Morrelton."

"Whatever you seek here, you won't find it." Samuel spotted the speaker, crouched on a ledge about thirty feet up the rock wall, next to where it intersected the lights. He wore tight clothing and a leather vest from under which a hood sprouted, keeping his face hidden. "Turn and leave. You will find no friends here."

Samuel looked directly at him. "I certainly hope that's not the case. I am in desperate need of some friends right now." Samuel moved to stand, but hard brown roots sprang up to entangle his hands and feet, working their way up over his upper legs to pin him down.

"Either you leave this place," the boy on the ledge said, "or be buried here forever." The roots tightened around Samuel. The soil beneath his feet loosened and his heels sank in deep.

"This is unnecessary," Samuel said, trying to remain calm. "I'm only looking for some answers, and I mean no one here harm." The roots stopped pulling at his feet. "I'll leave if you demand it, but I would instead ask for your help. Please."

The tension slackened and the roots retreated into the trail. "I cannot help you. If you are truthful that you mean no harm, then…"

He stopped talking as the front door of the cabin swung open. An old man, short and wiry, stood in the doorway in a nightrobe, holding up a bright candle. His face was gaunt, the thin remnants of his white hair standing from his head. Shadowed eyes searched the darkness from beneath bushy grey eyebrows.

"Come back inside, my boy." The man's voice was powerful and deep, in stark contrast with his appearance. "Come back in out of the cold, and bring the construct in with you."

The old man's command was met with a frustrated sigh. The boy stepped off the ledge, dropping thirty feet straight down and landing without a sound, bending his knees as if he'd only dropped a few inches. He walked toward the cabin, his eyes never diverting from Samuel. "Are you sure that's wise? We don't even know…"

"Of course it's wise!" the old man said. "I said it! Now do as you're told and bring him inside."

"Yes, sir," the boy said. He pulled back his hood to reveal close-cropped hair and a stern face. "Come on, get up," he said. Samuel stood. The boy raised his hand to the wavering light, and the rising sparkles split around a narrow opening. Without a word, the boy gestured for Samuel to step through. As he did, the color drained from the world once again, save for the auras of light from the old man's lamp and the windows. He turned back as the boy stepped through and closed the gap, noting the forest to the other side of the lights was now bathed in color.

"Are you going to stand there all night?" When Samuel looked back, the old man had retreated into the cabin and the boy was halfway down the trail. He stared back at Samuel with his arms crossed and an exasperated look on his face. If Samuel could have smiled, he would have delighted in frustrating the boy even more with his grin.

By the time they reached Morrelton, Colton and Bales were tired and saddle sore. They had stopped to camp one night along the way to save the horses, and Colton was thankful Bales hadn't insisted they keep moving through the night. Now that they were in town, Colton's only imperative was to find a comfortable bed and recuperate. Vials of Drift could only get a man so far, especially when he didn't have the time or means to properly distill it. A time came when real rest was required.

Colton glowered at the forest town, his face bent in a thin scowl. The people of Morrelton were nature-loving dirt-mongers, and their town little more than a commune for those unable to adjust to life in the real world. The buildings here were standing contradictions—twisted shapes built to coexist with the flora, but still constructed of materials harvested from the surrounding forest—that illustrated the townsfolk's unreasonable views on natural balance. The streets and alleys meandered like the minds of the town's builders, showing little thought to direction or efficiency. There was no symmetry to this place, and that disgusted Colton.

They entered Morrelton just after nightfall, so there were still a fair number of folks out along the main street. There were almost as many constructs as people, and Colton spied the naked contempt painted across Bales's face as they made their way deeper into town. If Bales had his way, he'd sweep through the town and eradicate every single one of them just to be sure they got the one they were looking for.

Bales rode with the heel of his right hand pressed to his temple. "This place hurts my head." He said, his voice weaker than Colton expected. "So much noise."

"Keep it together," Colton replied. "We've got work to do, but let's just find a place to sleep for now."

Bales steered his horse to the side of the main road, where a stocky man was loading crates into a small buckwagon. "You, there!" Bales barked, dispensing with any pleasantries. The man set a crate in the wagon and turned. "An inn!"

The man raised an eyebrow in a look of disdain, and pointed up the street. "The Woodland Rest, 'bout five buildings up on the right." Bales turned and rode away without so much as a thank you. Colton smirked at the gesture the man made to Bales's back.

The Woodland Rest was nicer than either of them were accustomed to. The three-story building, one of the larger buildings in town, seemed one of the few with straight walls. An elegantly carved sign hung over the oversized double doors that displayed the inn's name in flowing script. Large windows looked into the main hall, which was divided into a tavern and a dry goods shop. If the rooms were half as nice as the sign and the downstairs establishments, they might just find one redeeming quality to Morrelton.

The pair dismounted and tossed their reins around the inn's hitching post. Bales clomped to the entrance, the large front door groaning on its hinges as he yanked it open and stormed inside. Colton shook his head and followed, keeping his distance. The tavern was small but well-appointed with cushioned seats in the booths and candles on every table. It was about half-full and the patrons were oddly subdued, speaking in somber tones and not engaging in the type of tavern revelry Colton expected. A barmaid wound between tables, alternately taking orders and cleaning. Bales stood at the bar with his fingers mashed into his temple, the barkeep speaking to him with an eyebrow raised. Their conversation was short and Bales handed over some coin, then tromped over to Colton.

"I'm going to my room," he said, his eyes closed. "You're next door, room 14. If you disturb me, I'll slit your throat in your sleep." He headed outside, slamming the main door open on his way. Colton couldn't help but smirk at his companion's bearing. Bales always reacted this way around large numbers of constructs, and it always brought a smile to Colton's face. Bales's sensitivity to the flows of *khet*, especially around a construct's core, made him uniquely suited for their assignment, but too much of anything could drive a man mad. The door slammed open and Bales once again stomped in, dropping Colton's traveling pack at his feet. "They're taking the horses to the stables." He said over his shoulder as he headed off to his room.

Colton found an empty table near the center of the room and dropped his bag beside it. He got the barmaid's attention and waved her over, ordering a beer and whatever dinner the kitchen happened to be providing. After she departed, he pulled a glass vial from a side pocket on his pack and fiddled with it while he opened his ears and mind to surrounding conversations.

It didn't take long to get a bead on the room. More than half the patrons spoke in hushed tones about the death of several town guardsmen, and half again more were actively thinking about it. Colton couldn't get much in the way of specifics, but it was recent enough and significant enough the town was still shaken by it. He was pulled from his concentration as the barmaid returned with a clay mug filled with cold ale and a plate of some sort of roast and vegetables, all covered in brown gravy.

"What meat is this?" he asked the barmaid, trying to sound pleasant.

"Elk," she said with pride. "Big haul this season, and we've got some fine cuts. Let me know if you want any more."

As she departed for the bar, Colton remembered he wasn't fond of elk. He took a probing bite and noted at least the gravy was tasty and disguised the flavors of the meat and vegetables. He ate quickly, wishing to dig around some more and find a direction before heading to bed. He pushed his plate aside and took up his mug of ale, but didn't drink. With mug in hand, he turned to the two men at the table behind him.

"Good evening, gentlemen," he said.

The two eyed him, their appraisal lacking suspicion but loaded with annoyance. "Evenin'," said the closest one, a short man with a lined face and a bushy grey moustache.

Colton lowered his voice, taking on a respectful tone. "Why's everyone so quiet in here tonight? I just got into town and was expecting this place to be a bit more...lively."

"Ain't gonna find much liveliness around here for a while," said the other one, a stockier man with pale red hair and respectable sideburns.

"Why's that?" Colton asked.

The closer man shifted his chair so he wasn't peering over his shoulder at Colton. "Couple nights ago, the guard lost some men."

Colton widened his eyes. "Really? What happened?"

"Some sort of brawl," Sideburns said. "Rumor has it they was trying to arrest a murderer who turned sorcerer on 'em."

"A murderer?" Colton asked, feigning interest. To this point, the story had no bearing on Colton's plight, but he'd dug himself into the role of interested tourist and had to play it out properly. "Who did he murder?"

"A local apprentice boy," Moustache said. "Shame, too. Michael would've made a fine journeyman." The two men dropped their eyes and shook their heads, and Colton followed suit.

"How do they know he...turned sorcerer, as you put it?" Colton asked, hopefully working this out to be his last question.

"Well, it was only the one of 'im against five guards, includin' Cort 'imself," Sideburns said. "Stories say the boy caught 'im stealin' cores from his shop. After the thief killed the boy, Cort and his men trapped him in an alley, and he took out all five. Only sorcerers could pull that off, especially with Cort in there."

Colton wasn't sure who Cort was, but didn't want to ask that question. "Do they know who it is?"

"They say it's a drifter, name o' Kaleb Hargrove," Moustache said.

"And that's crap!" Sideburns retorted. "Kaleb Hargrove's been in my shop before, and he ain't the man to do somethin' like this. He especially ain't the man to use a gun."

"He had a gun?" Colton asked, his interest now genuine. So what if the story wasn't helping him find this rogue construct? Stories about murder and intrigue were more than Colton expected to encounter here.

"Yeah," Moustache continued. "Took a shot at the guards an' missed, then still took 'em all out. They said Cort's ribs were crushed, and ain't no normal man pullin' that off. Jeffers survived the attack but died a few hours later, and Strew's still unconscious. Everyone's hoping he wakes up soon."

"How do they know he had a gun?" Colton asked.

"Bullet in the wall," Sideburns said. "Plus, he left it behind." That part sounded a little fishy to Colton. Guns were so heavily outlawed, even the hint of ownership warranted execution, much less a potential eyewitness to a discharge inside a town.

"Wow," Colton said. He widened his eyes and blew a big breath, shaking his head. "I bet that's more excitement than this town's seen in a while." The two men nodded their heads. Exhaustion was catching up

126

to Colton, so he decided to wrap it up. "Thank you, gentlemen," he said, nodding to each. "I'd love to chat more, but it's time for me to turn in."

The two nodded back and Colton turned around, setting down his ale and pulling his pack up onto the table. He replaced the glass vial and started rooting around inside for some coin to pay for his meal.

"There is no way it was Kaleb Hargrove," he heard Sideburns say behind him, pausing between *no* and *way* for added effect.

"Why not?" Moustache shot back. "Not like Hargrove's got the greatest reputation in this town anyway!"

"Three reasons," Sideburns said, without so much as a pause, "One: Hargrove might be a lot of things, but he's not the type to kill anyone."

"You don't even know him that well," Moustache said.

"Maybe you're right. Anyway… Two: absolutely no way he uses a gun. I may not know the man well, but I know he wouldn't risk his freedom by using a gun. Besides, how many adepts you know would even touch one? No way." Colton heard a grunt of agreement from Moustache.

"And three: Kaleb doesn't travel with a construct." Colton's hands stopped and his ears perked up. Moustache said something in response Colton didn't even hear. He tried not to look overly interested as he turned back to the men.

"Wait," he said. "What did you just say?"

"I said I think I need another beer," Moustache said, his inflection on the last word rising like a question.

"No, you," Colton said, nodding toward Sideburns. "About this Hargrove fellow."

"Oh, I said he doesn't travel with a construct."

"There was a construct involved in the fight?" Colton asked, his heart rate rising.

Moustache turned, scowling. "There's ain't no evidence of that," he said.

Sideburns waived his hand at Moustache in a dismissive gesture. "Atherton said he left the shop with a construct. Nothin' to say that construct wasn't at the fight with Cort."

Moustache turned back to his tablemate. "There were no construct footprints anywhere!"

"Atherton don't have any reason to lie," Sideburns said. "I'm sure he prob—" Colton stopped listening and turned back to his table, neither of the men even noticing his departure.

A construct involved in a brawl that killed several guardsmen. A solid lead on his target was just about the last thing he expected to hear from these two. Taeman hadn't mentioned a companion of any sort in his letter, but it was plausible the construct could have picked one up along the way. The lead was about as concrete as he could think of, but even in his excitement he was exhausted, and decided to pursue it further in the morning. He gathered up his pack and stood, then saw Bales coming down the stairs. His eyes were wide and a hand held up to stay Colton from speaking.

"There's one here," Bales said through gritted teeth, his voice wavering with anger. He jabbed his finger down toward the floor. "Right here in Morrelton!"

"Wait," Colton said, unable to mask his confusion. "What are you talking about?"

Bales sat, taking a long draught off of Colton's untouched beer. "I'm telling you, there's one here." He took another drink. "Hard to pinpoint with all the background noise in this dungheap, but it's here."

Colton gestured for him to keep his voice down, then sat back in his seat. "How far?"

"Not sure yet," Bales replied. "But it's definitely in town. Maybe it's our guy."

"I doubt that," Colton said, looking distracted.

"What?" Bales was annoyed, as usual. "Wouldn't this confirm your little letter?" The last two words came out in a childish, derisive tone.

"Yeah," Colton said, maintaining his calm. "But if Taeman's lost treasure were one of them, don't you think you'd have caught wind of it in Winston?"

Bales sat back, his lips pulled into a thin, tight line. He shook his head and gulped down more beer. "This doesn't make any sense," he spat.

"Maybe not." Colton said. "Either way it doesn't matter. If there's one in town, then we've got some business to take care of."

Bales nodded, his expression unchanged. "Damned right we do."

"Besides, I've got a lead on Taeman's little goose chase," Colton said. "We have to talk to—"

"Yeah, yeah," Bales said before standing and finishing the last of the beer in a couple of large gulps. He dropped the mug back on the table with a *thud*. "We'll take care of that after."

"No, we'll go question…"

"After," Bales said, cutting Colton off again. He walked away, disappearing back up the stairs to the rooms. Colton ground his teeth, Bales's attitude setting his nerves on edge. Tomorrow was going to be a busy day.

Chapter Nineteen

The interior of the cabin was larger than Samuel expected, a marvel of organized clutter. Every bit of wall space was covered with bookshelves, and every bookshelf filled to overflowing with texts. The only unoccupied wall space was in places where they simply could not be mounted: the three small, round windows, which looked like portholes set deep into the bookshelves, the stonework fireplace on the far wall, and the entryway to a hall leading to the back half of the cabin. There were even shelves on the ceiling, hanging at a downward angle that should have resulted in a rain of books on Samuel's head, but the books stayed in place with no visible restraint.

The boy from the woods sat on a short bench just inside the door and removed his boots. A plush blue rug lay before the hearth, scattered with an array of pillows in lieu of furniture. Against the wall beneath one of the porthole windows stood a long worktable filled to the edges with stacks of books and a number of mechanical contraptions. Every space was filled with something, all of it meticulously organized. Samuel believed he could approach a bookshelf and understand straightaway where he might find any particular volume. The old man who ushered them in now sat atop a short stool near the end of the worktable, watching Samuel with a critical eye as he took it all in. Samuel was keenly aware the boy on the bench still eyed him.

"Off to bed with you, now," the old man said to the boy, waving him off to the other part of the cabin.

"But…"

"You're absolutely right. Get your butt to bed." There was humor in the old man's words, but his tone was stern and unforgiving. "We're apparently to have an interesting day tomorrow, and you need to sleep. Now go."

"Yes, sir," the boy said, proper, with little to hint at his disappointment. A deep sigh and his body language told Samuel a different story as he padded, slouching, across the cabin. He glanced over his shoulder as he passed into the hallway, and then vanished into the darkness beyond.

"Please, have a seat," the old man said, gesturing to the floor where the cushions lay. Samuel moved over to the middle of the room and sat, rather awkwardly, on the floor. "Are you comfortable?" the man asked.

Samuel wasn't sure how he defined comfort just yet. "I…um…"

"Of course you're comfortable," the old man said, standing up and placing his hands on his back above his hips. He arched his back and Samuel heard several pops and cracks. "Ah!" he said, returning with a smile. "Well then, I'm off to bed." He started toward the hallway.

Samuel was so astonished it took him a moment to speak. "But, sir! I need help with…"

"You came to me in the middle of the night," the old man interrupted. "You'll be fine until morning, but I need my rest, as do my young charges, who are no doubt lying awake talking about you right now."

"What am I to do, then, while you sleep?" Samuel asked. "What if I intend you harm?"

Samuel's questions were met by a dismissive wave. "If you were here to kill me you'd be scrap already. You can't leave this room—you can trust me on that—and if you try to damage any of the possessions in here, the house will take care of you." And with that, he, too, disappeared into the dark.

Samuel wasn't about to test the old man's words, but that also meant he was stuck in this room all night. Could he touch anything? What actions might the house take offense to? Samuel stood with caution and moved to the workbench. At the edge of the table, to the side of a large stack of parchment, stood a small candle holder and a candle, from the top of which light flickered. When Samuel noticed there was no actual flame, he also saw that the candle and holder were actually one piece, ingeniously carved out of delicate wood and painted to look like the real thing. Even the wick was part of the construction and beamed a flameless light that emulated real candlelight.

Upon the table, a small frame with numerous compartments contained an array of carving implements. Whittling knives, small chisels, round files, and other tools stood upright in neat rows, next to a stack of small squares of sandpaper. A book stood open on the table, attached to some sort of device, a delicate construction of wood and fine copper. The contraption clipped to the book's spine and arms extended to the outside corners of each open page. Samuel moved around the table, taking the false candle with him for light to get a better look at the book, which was written in a language he didn't recognize. When his finger touched the edge of the page, the attached contraption moved, causing him to recoil. He watched in amazement as the arm of the device picked up and turned the page for him. He touched the next page, and the device turned it for him again.

"Huh." Shaking his head, he spied the other items on the table and noted there were several unfinished gadgets, the uses for each Samuel couldn't even begin to imagine. The endless spines of books occupying the shelves behind the table contained precious few words amongst their titles he could read, and even those were intertwined with unfamiliar language. His eyes wound from shelf to shelf amongst the leatherbound volumes, coming to rest on a thick spine embossed in white with the title *Artifacts & Constructions*.

Samuel placed a finger atop the spine to tilt the book out of its place, but it wouldn't move. Applying more pressure yielded no results, not even creasing the leather or denting the spine of the book. It simply would not budge. He moved back down the shelf, testing random books along his route, and all of them stuck in place. No physical binding held them, but now he understood why the shelves could run at odd angles and even up onto the ceiling without worry. The old man must have some way to unlock the volumes, but Samuel wouldn't find out until morning.

The fire had died down to one small flame amongst a pile of glowing grey and orange embers. Samuel found the firelight comforting, and moved to add a log to the fire. Before he reached the circle of cushions, a long, bronze arm tipped in a two-pronged iron claw swung down from beneath the mantelpiece. The claw dipped into the woodpile, plucking a medium-sized log off the top and placing it in the fireplace, prodded around in the coals to stoke the fire to life, then folded itself back up under the mantle. Samuel sat down again on the plush blue rug, taking in every detail of the small room while he waited for its owners, the people who might just be able to help him discover who he was, to awaken. This was a wondrous little cabin in the woods.

Chapter Twenty

Cool blue light filtered in through the small round windows, offering Samuel a different view of the room than he'd had all night. As the morning grew brighter, the deep hue of the bookshelves lent a warmth to the cabin's colors as the flickering light of the fire was replaced by sunlight. In anticipation of the morning, the bronze arm loaded several extra pieces of firewood into the fireplace, stoking up a large, warm fire.

Not long after, a girl, a bit younger than the boy Samuel met the previous night, emerged from the back hallway in deerskin slippers. Her chestnut hair had been recently brushed and flowed down into the open hood of her long, forest green robe, which was cinched around the waist with a thin leather belt. Inquisitive blue eyes spied Samuel from above freckled red cheeks, betraying not even the slightest hint of fear. She smiled, bounded into the room, and plopped down on a small pile of cushions facing the construct, taking one into her arms.

"Hello! What's your name?" she said, a hint of wonder in her voice.

Samuel was struck by her friendly and genuine nature, an approach that put him at ease. "I'm Samuel," he replied. "What's yours?"

"I'm Eriane. I like your voice."

Samuel laughed, which seemed to catch her by surprise. "Thank you, Eriane. Yours is pretty, as well."

"Well, I wouldn't call *your* voice *pretty*, really," she said, blushing. "It's just..."

"Different from other constructs?"

She smiled again. "Yeah. I guess you've heard that a couple times?"

"A few. So, where are the other two?" Samuel asked.

"Oh, I'm always up and about before either of them," she said. "Master Mane will probably be up soon, and he'll have to kick Pare awake after how late he was up last night."

"Well, would you do me the honor of introducing me?"

"Of course," she beamed, tilting her head in mock propriety.

Samuel felt a wave of elation run through him at hearing her mention Pare, the name he had been given by Michael. There had been little question upon finding the cabin that it was the right place, but over the course of his night alone a sliver of doubt and fear wormed its way into his mind. Knowing he landed in the right spot gave him more hope than he'd had since the thief took him to Atherton's shop. All he could hope, now, was this encounter turned out better than the last.

A deluge of questions came to Samuel's mind, but he was enjoying his light conversation with Eriane. There would be plenty of time to pose the more difficult queries to Mane later on. "So, what's so special about my voice?"

"I dunno. It's just...smoother than other constructs I'm used to. Icariascus always sounds so tinny, and most of the ones I've met in Morrelton have this weird vibrating sound, like they're always gargling something. Your voice is...well, it kinda sounds more like a normal person's voice."

"Icariascus?" Samuel asked, focused on the name.

"Oh, that's our construct," Eriane answered. "He's in back, but I'm sure you'll meet him soon."

"Eriane!" The voice of the boy from the previous night startled them out of their conversation. Pare stood at the hallway entrance in a similar robe to Eriane's, but his was a deep brown and belted with a wide, leather band. Tall, meticulously maintained leather boots emerged from beneath the hem. "Back away from it right now," he barked.

"Well, well, well," Eriane said, peering at him over her shoulder, "look who's awake before the crack of midday!"

Pare took a step forward. "I'm not kidding around with you, Eri. This thing is dangerous."

"Oh, Pare, settle down," she said with a dismissive wave. "Samuel's not dangerous. Besides, you know the house would take care of me if he tried anything anyway." Samuel couldn't help but wonder just how deep the cabin's capabilities ran.

Pare moved to Eriane's side. He grabbed her by the arm and pulled her to her feet, causing her to drop her cushion. "Pare! Ow!" she said. There was a spark and a dull flash that caught Pare off guard, flinging away his grip on her arm and bouncing him backward.

"That was really good," he said, distractedly rubbing his hand with the opposite thumb. After a pause, he came back to himself. "You can't just rely on the house all the time. Use your head!"

Eriane glowered at him. "Would you calm down? Do you honestly think Master Mane would let him in here if he were dangerous?"

"Well," Pare stammered.

She didn't let him continue. "That's what I thought." He glared at her. She stuck her tongue out at him, then turned back to Samuel. "Pare, I'd like you to meet Samuel." Samuel made his way to his feet. "Samuel, this is Pariadnus Jameson. But you can call him Pare." Samuel held out his hand for Pare to shake.

The boy turned his gaze on Samuel and crossed his arms, ignoring the gesture. "Only my friends call me Pare." He crossed the room and sat on the stool by the worktable.

Eriane turned back to Samuel and sighed. "Oh, ignore him." She said in a conspiratorial tone. "He's all bluster, and sometimes he takes things too seriously." She raised her voice on the last half of her sentence, goading Pare.

"Yeah, well you could learn a lesson about taking *anything* seriously!" He picked up something small off the desk and threw it at her, but she waved her hand and deflected it with a flash about a foot in front of her. Pare's eyes narrowed and he crossed his arms.

Eriane smiled at Samuel, then retook her seat on the stack of cushions.

Master Mane's voice came from the hallway opening. "That'll be enough of that, you two." His hair was combed and he wore fresh robes rather than nightclothes, almost making him look civilized. Samuel now saw a thinning grey goatee adorned the tip of his chin, and his eyes were dark brown, almost black. "This fellow," he gestured to Samuel, "is our guest, and we will treat him as such. In fact, he specifically sought us out, am I right?"

Samuel nodded. "Yes, sir. I was hoping to find someone who can help me."

"Ah, yes," Mane replied, moving over next to Pare and leaning back against the worktable. "But you must not have come here on your own accord. Very few know of this place, and those who do will not tell of it lightly." Mane raised an inquisitive eyebrow, Pare shot Samuel a threatening look, and Eriane's bright eyes were questioning above her little smile.

Samuel nodded. "I was told to come here by an artificer's apprentice."

Pare's posture changed, his curiosity obviously piqued by Samuel's claim. For a moment, he looked as though he would speak, but then he sat back and deferred to Mane.

"What was the artificer's name?" Mane asked.

"Atherton," Samuel answered. Pare straightened, almost shooting out of his seat. For the first time since he'd arrived the hint of a smile touched Pare's lips, and in that expectant moment, Samuel was crushed. He knew the conversation that was to follow.

Mane moved to walk behind the work table, speaking as his back was turned. "How are Atherton and Michael doing these days?" He asked. Samuel felt Mane already knew his reply, and had elicited a direct answer on purpose.

Samuel hesitated. Pare's smile faded and the color drained from his face, his expression now angered concern. Samuel's posture deflated and he could not maintain Pare's gaze. With great effort, Samuel formed the words. "Michael's dead."

"What?" Eriane's scream careened into Samuel's head like the blow of an axe.

Pare shot to his feet. "I told you he was dangerous!" His hands came up beside his hips, palms toward Samuel. His fingers sparked with blue power and Samuel was forced to a standing position by some invisible force. Pare's hands pulled back, the power pulsating and drawing inward toward them.

Eriane's shocked expression tore at Samuel when tears welled up in her eyes. As he lifted upward, she broke her tortured stare and turned on Pare. "Pare! Put him down!"

Samuel couldn't move. His arms were pinned to his sides and his feet left the floor, if only by a few inches. Pare advanced on him. "What happened?" he yelled at Samuel.

Mane, the picture of calm, walked up and placed a hand on Pare's shoulder. "Put him down, Pare." His voice was gentle. "And please, do so lightly. I'd prefer to not have to repair the floor."

Pare's jaw worked back and forth, setting his teeth to grinding. There was a moment where no one in the room moved; Samuel floated, helpless as Pare held him in stasis with his muscles clenched and hands in claw shapes at his hips. Mane tightened his grip on Pare's shoulder, but maintained his calm expression. Tears broke free of Eriane's eyes and rolled down her cheeks.

All these people knew Michael, in a much deeper way than Samuel had been allowed in the short time they'd shared. As profound an effect as the boy's death had on Samuel, he couldn't even imagine how the people in this room must have felt upon hearing the news. Pare's fingers loosened and Samuel was lowered to the floor, regaining his feet. Eriane moved around between him and Pare, swiping her cheeks dry and looking at him with a pained question in her eyes.

Samuel sat and recounted his time in Morrelton to the detail, beginning with a short synopsis of his time with the thief, whom he refused to refer to by either name. He wasn't sure if these three knew of him, but they didn't press for more information on that front, focused as they were on hearing about Michael's fate. He told of his time at Atherton's shop and of his blackout, skirting the details of his visions. At last he spoke of Atherton's reaction and Michael's actions leading up to that one terrible moment.

"Michael is a hero," he said. Eriane held a hand over her mouth as she wept. Tears even streamed down Pare's stony visage. "To me, at least. He fixed my arm." Samuel moved his repaired shoulder to illustrate. "And I have no doubt what he did saved me. I don't know what

Atherton had planned. I'm afraid even to speculate." His story told, he sat silent, his head bowed.

Pare was the first to break the silence. "So my friend died so some random canner could keep walking." Samuel looked up, greeted with open contempt. Pare stormed out of the room.

Eriane watched him leave, then sniffled and turned her red eyes back on Samuel. Her hand came away from her face long enough for her to utter a quiet, "But…", and then she, too, ran from the room. A tall, thin construct had entered and raised his hand as though to gain the attention of the two as they pushed passed him, but did not speak in time.

"Master Mane?" the construct said, turning back to the old man.

"It's all right, Icariascus," Mane said. "Just leave them be for now." He approached Samuel and placed a hand on the side of his head. "It will take them some time, Samuel. They were all friends, and spent time together whenever Pare and Eri had occasion to go to Morrelton."

"I'm sorry," was all Samuel could manage.

"What you've gone through is unfortunate. Death is never an easy thing to deal with."

"Shouldn't make any difference to me," Samuel snapped. "I mean, I'm not supposed to have emotions, right?"

Mane took in a long breath, then moved back to sit on the stool where Pare had been seated. "Well, you're not exactly a normal construct, now, are you?"

Samuel looked up at him. "That's the question I'm trying to find the answer to."

"And why should we help you find that answer?" Mane asked.

Samuel took a moment to contemplate his reply. "A week ago, I would have said I don't have a good answer to that question. I'm just a lost construct with nothing to offer you for your help. I see, now, something more important is going on. Death has followed me from the moment I awoke, and if I can't find out who—or what—I am, I'm powerless to stop whatever it is that's coming for me. Before, it was all about figuring out who I was. Now? I…I don't want Michael's death to be meaningless."

A small smile crossed Mane's face. "Good answer," he said, standing. "I'm willing to help you, Samuel. But to do so, you need to tell me the parts of your story you left out."

Samuel knew better than to try and lie to this man, or omit anything further. "My blackout wasn't passive. It came with a rush of visions—memories, I think. The problem is they're...incomplete. There's no discernible order to them, and they all seem jumbled. Unconnected."

"Hm," Mane said, stroking his goatee with his thumb and forefinger. "I have to wonder if there's been damage to your core that segregated your memories. Strange things can happen to a construct when their core is tampered with."

"Could that sort of tampering have given me...emotions? Could someone have been trying for that result?" Samuel asked.

Mane scratched his head and leaned back in his chair. "Anything's possible, Samuel. I know one thing; someone's been tampering with you in ways I can't even begin to hypothesize yet, not without knowing more about where you came from. Instilling emotion into a construct has been a tempting and dangerous goal for artificers for centuries. It's not something one attempts lightly, or without thought of the consequences."

"What do you mean?"

"Oh, think about it for a minute," Mane said, exasperated. "Emotion is the heart of conflict. If feelings were never injected into disagreements, do you think we'd ever have arguments? Or fights? Or wars? The majority of artificers strongly disagree with the idea of even *trying* to infuse emotion into an artificial being, believing emotion is a gift of nature, not to be tampered with. The potential for disaster is too great."

Mane paused and took a deep breath. "What good would artificial beings be as servants and workers if what little independent thought they're imbued with was also colored by emotions? Without feelings, the concepts of freedom and individuality are rendered moot, which is exactly what people want out of a construct. Your apparent feelings are unique, Samuel, and of much more interest to me than your origins."

"Both weigh equally for me, Master Mane," Samuel said. "My emotions may be unique, but it's my history that puts me in danger."

"Very true," the old man responded. "And don't call me Master. You're not my apprentice. Mane will do fine."

"All right," Samuel said. "What comes next, then?"

"First and foremost," Mane replied, "We must allow Pare and Eri time to grieve, and I have work to do if I'm to convince them you're not to blame."

Samuel looked down at his hands. "Who's to say I'm not?"

"Oh, rubbish," Mane said. "The person responsible for Michael's death was Atherton, and no one else. That man's been an erratic mess for as long as I've known him. I can't even begin to wonder what would have driven him to do what he did, but one can never tell with someone as unpredictable as him. I'll have no more of your self-pity, whether it be real or affected."

Samuel nodded, but did not reply.

"Now, this thief you spoke of." Caught off guard, Samuel snapped his head upward. Mane smiled. "Ah, you thought I wasn't paying attention, eh? Or I'd just let it go? Things don't slip by me as easily as the other two, Samuel, and you'd be wise to remember that."

"You have to understand," Samuel said, "I'm not trying to deceive you. I'm just—wary."

"And rightly so," Mane replied. "But if you're going to ask for my help, then I will ask for yours in return. You cannot afford secrets right now, and the more I know, the more I'll be able to help you."

"You're right," Samuel said.

"Of course I am. Now, I have to assume this thief you spoke of was Jacob Tensley?" Mane asked.

A flash of anger ran through Samuel at once again hearing the thief's real name. "The name he gave me was Kaleb, but I only discovered this other name just before we parted ways. I don't know his last name."

"Yes, that's him. Kaleb is a name he goes by sometimes." Samuel looked away, stifling an angry retort. "You mustn't hold it against him, Samuel," Mane said. "Men like Jacob spend most of their lives protecting themselves, and almost always at the cost of genuine relationships. The name Kaleb is as real to him as his given name, and probably used more often. It's nothing more than a defense mechanism."

Samuel thought about Mane's words, but they didn't lessen his anger. "Perhaps. But that is a discussion for another day." The name wasn't the only issue he had with the thief, it just served as an easy focal point for the entirety of his deception.

"Very well." Mane let it drop. "Tell me about what you saw in the forest, after you evaded the siphils."

"How did you…?"

"Pare tracked you most of your way through the forest," Mane said with a sly grin. "He said he got lucky at the clearing; he'd thought you'd made him out. It's that clearing I wish to know more about. What did you see there?"

Samuel thought back. "It was a ring of light. This blue, wavering wall of light that shimmered with sparks. Aside from altering my vision somewhat, it seemed pretty but harmless."

Mane's eyebrow went up again. "Interesting. I'll need to work on that one, then."

"What do you mean?" Samuel asked.

"That clearing contains a powerful illusion," Mane said, leaning back in his chair. "Quite an ingenious one, if I do say so myself. I set it up as a deterrent for anyone looking for this place. Anyone looking into that clearing will see whatever will make them give up their search. I've found many people will see the image of a burned out husk of a cabin, complete with charred remains. It serves well to keep out unwanted trespassers."

"And what about the one just outside here?" Samuel asked.

"Ah!" The sorcerer flashed a proud smile. "That one's even more complex. Anyone looking this way will see, hear, and smell empty forest. If they wander too close, the illusion gently redirects them, causing them to walk completely around without ever thinking they've gone off course." He leaned forward, glaring at Samuel. "You, on the other hand, just trundled right into it. I'm glad I put up the bump field as a failsafe."

"It looked the same as the one in the clearing to me," Samuel said. "I thought I could just walk through it."

Mane snorted and shook his head. "It's baffling, is what it is! Those illusions are masterworks, and all you see is pretty lights. Well, you can rest assured if there were nothing else at all interesting about you, that alone would get my blood boiling enough to help you figure out what you are!"

Samuel's conversation with Mane became more sparse as day wore on into evening. Samuel learned how the books were removed from the shelves when Mane snapped his fingers and a small object floated down from somewhere near the ceiling. It was constructed of wood and bronze, with a round central core about the size of a clenched fist. Two flat, wooden panels, about a hand's breadth square and extremely thin, flared to its sides like wings, attached to the central core by metal connectors. It hovered before Mane and, upon receiving instruction floated off toward the wall near the hallway entrance. The flat panels rotated around in front of it as it moved. Approaching a bookshelf, the panels slipped neatly between books and enclosed one between them. It drew the book off the shelf, turning it flat and carrying it back to Mane. Mane took the book and waved his hand, and the little librarian floated back toward the ceiling, taking up a central position in a little rack where it rested until called for.

Mane spent much of the day poring over book after book, pulled for him by his tireless little flying construct, which he called Reet, a nickname for retriever given to it by Eriane. It seemed Reet was in constant motion that day, and Mane's search for information had been met with varying success.

Samuel described his visions, but Mane stopped him after he described at least four that involved his own death. Samuel told him these supposed premonitions were woven between other, more mundane scenes as well as potent images that did not involve his own death, but always some spectacular experience or extraordinary event. Mane listened carefully and uttered the occasional "Mmm…" or "Uh-huh…" or "Ah…mmm…" but offered no helpful advice, stating only that he didn't want to speculate until he could find something more substantial.

Icariascus wandered in and out of the room, speaking in low tones to Mane and shuffling back to the rear of the cabin, offering Samuel only perfunctory acknowledgment. Samuel did not see either Pare or Eriane for the remainder of the day, although he wished he could talk to them and offer some form of consolation. Mane suggested he give them time, let them approach at their own pace.

"You must understand, Samuel," he said, "both of these children have experienced profound loss in their lives. Why else would the two of them be living out here, learning from some grey-haired forest hermit? Neither of them expected to go through that kind of pain again so soon. They'll come around, in time."

When Samuel asked what had happened to the two of them, Mane would not answer. "That's not my place," he said. "That is a question for you to ask them, if circumstances allow, and for them to answer, if they feel it is right."

There was little other conversation to fill Samuel's time as the evening wore on. He spent much of the day observing Mane's reactions as he read and watching the fireplace contraption drop logs into the fire. Stacks of books covered every open space on Mane's worktable, all of which he seemed to be keeping for reference. After hours of poring over a particularly old and dusty volume, Mane pushed himself back from his table, leaning back in his chair and rubbing his eyes. With a grunt he hauled himself out of his chair, reaching his arms up into the air in a stretch that arched his back, causing it to pop several times.

"Well, Samuel," he said, "I'm going cross-eyed. I think these old peepers have had enough for the day, and my head's starting to hurt from translating some of these texts." Samuel must have been visibly disappointed, which caused Mane to step over to place a hand on his shoulder. "I'm making some progress, but this will take time. Making any coherent sense out of these spotty texts is about as easy as you making sense of all those jumbled memories banging around in your mind." He patted Samuel's shoulder and turned to leave. "But we have plenty of time, and you're safe here."

Samuel nodded. "Is there anything you can tell me tonight?"

"Nothing solid. If I thought I'd found anything worth pinning your hopes on, you can believe I would have told you by now." Mane turned to leave. "If you like, you can feel free to read the volume on the worktable. It is one of the rarest in my collection. It's a little archaic, but the tongue is common enough I'm sure you'll be able to muddle out an understanding." The old man disappeared into the back of the cabin, and Samuel was left alone for another night. At least this time he'd have something to read.

Chapter Twenty-One

The dim light of an overcast morning did little to brighten the cabin's main room. Icariascus emerged first, long before Samuel expected any of the other three to be out of bed. The old construct had a smaller build than Samuel, taller and more wiry. A short, thin slit indicated a mouth in an otherwise featureless plate, toward the bottom of a noseless face with large, round eyes. The construct shuffled over to where Samuel stood at the worktable.

"Good morning, sir." Icariascus's voice sounded thin and reedy, with a tinge of an unrecognizable accent.

Samuel was surprised by the greeting; Icariascus hadn't spoken to him since he arrived. "Good morning, Icariascus."

Icariascus nodded a friendly affirmation. "May I ask you a question?"

"Of course," Samuel replied.

"Are you"—the thin construct paused, almost as though he were afraid to continue—"independent?"

Samuel considered how to answer the question. "To the best of my knowledge I am. If I'm not, I have not yet found my master."

"Oh." Icariascus nodded and looked down at the table full of books. "You cannot feel a link?"

"I cannot," Samuel replied. "But I wouldn't know the feeling even if I could."

147

"You would know," Icariascus said. "The link to your master is a driving imperative that begins to override all other thought the further from them you are."

"Are you linked to someone, Icariascus?" Samuel asked.

"Not anymore," Icariascus said. "At one time I was, but it is my choice to stay with Mane and the children. They do not feel the need for that level of...control."

"Then you are also independent," Samuel said.

"Not as independent as one may think." Icariascus said. "In some ways independence is a blessing for a construct. But be warned, there are some who would just as soon have you imprisoned or destroyed as allow you to remain free. There are places in the world not as accepting as Morrelton, places where independent constructs are viewed as a threat to the peace. Be mindful with whom you share your independence."

Samuel understood much of the fear and paranoia toward constructs. The book which Mane had given him to read detailed a five-year war with constructs that ravaged the countryside generations prior. Constructs had become so common almost every family and business had them working as laborers. Advancements in the technology had begun to produce constructs of many different shapes and sizes, specialized for different tasks. In a single, coordinated stroke, indentured constructs across the continent turned against their masters, killing a great many wealthy and powerful people and igniting the conflict. By the end of the war, the cities of Cyril and Balefor were almost razed to the ground, but the constructs were overrun, their numbers having dwindled to less than a tenth of their former strength. Many people still harbored an inherent distrust of constructs, even generations after the war.

"I'll make sure to be careful about what I say in public, then," Samuel said.

Icariascus nodded and walked away, pausing before he left the room. "I know of none better than Mane to help you find the answers you seek. You were right to come here."

"Let's hope so, Icariascus," Samuel said. The other construct disappeared into the darkened hallway. Samuel looked down at the book he'd been reading all night and absently touched the edges of the pages, causing the page-turner to flip them back and forth. Would the knowledge he gained from coming here warrant endangering three peoples' lives?

"He's right, you know." Mane's voice snapped him out of his thoughts. The old man's smile presented a wild visage under the disheveled white mess atop his head. His simple brown robes looked as though he may have slept in them. "I might not be a storehouse of knowledge, but my collection"—he gestured to the books around the room—"isn't one to sneeze at."

Samuel nodded. "It's not the answers that worry me," he said.

"Our safety isn't in question, Samuel," Mane said. "We'll know if anyone's coming before they even reach the Bleeding Pine. Besides, I'm a crafty old codger." A new grin, wilder than the first. "Anyway... Find anything in that book that I missed?"

Samuel shook his head. "Nothing pertinent. Plenty of interesting history, but I can't connect any of it."

Mane raised an eyebrow. "Well, that didn't work."

"What?" Samuel asked.

"I was hoping you'd do the research for me!" He chuckled to himself. "I figured maybe you'd spend the night getting through this book and find something in short order."

"Nothing but more curiosity," Samuel said. "I'm interested in the linking process. How does it work? How was it developed?"

Mane plopped down, tipping his chair back onto its rear legs and propping himself back with a foot against his worktable. He reached up and began stroking his beard. "It's a process of linking a person's *khet* to that of the construct. With a little spice thrown in, of course. It's a bit like a process once used to link constructs to each other, so they all respond to the same commands or are able to work together on a task with a sort of hive mind. The process to link to a human is more delicate, because you only want the link to work one way."

Samuel was focused on the past-tense of the phrase. "Do they not link constructs anymore?"

"Oh, no," Mane said. "Many think a link like that was used to coordinate the assassinations that sparked the war. Since then, linking constructs has been illegal. That doesn't mean it doesn't happen, of course, but it's generally frowned upon."

Samuel nodded. "Icariascus says I'd feel any link that might be bound to me. Is that always true?"

"Always true," Mane replied, dropping the front legs of his chair back to the floor. "A true link has to be tethered directly into a construct's core. You'd know it, even if you were linked to another construct." He raised an eyebrow. "I trust you'd tell me if you felt something?"

"Of course," Samuel replied. "So, I'm not linked to anyone or any…thing. But I still can't make sense of the memories that have been coming back to me."

"I've been mulling that one over," Mane said, "and the only explanation I can think of is something happened to cause your core to fragment."

"I was told a cracked core would explode." Samuel said.

"No, no, no," Mane said. "Fragmentation isn't physical, and it usually only happens during the creation of a core. Something goes wrong and jumbles everything about; makes the core useless. If it happens to a core after it's been imbued, any number of things happen to the construct, but they're never as…lucid as you."

"How does it happen?" Samuel asked.

Mane leaned back, shaking his head. "There's no real rhyme or reason to it. In most cases, the core's damaged and should have exploded or dissipated, but instead it fragments. In the few cases I've heard of, the effects range from rendering the construct mindless to splitting their mind apart. It's about as close to insanity as you'd ever see in an artificial being. Your case? Well, I'm not even sure that's what we're dealing with here."

Samuel grew frustrated with Mane's hedging. Mane continued before he could speak, as though sensing his impatience. "Your mind is intact. You're capable of rational thought, you can make your own decisions. You've even retained all your basic skills and a good chunk of your ingrained knowledge. The only thing that's been tampered with are your memories, and I'd venture these visions you've been having are actually vestigial memories not caught by the wipe. If I didn't know better, I'd say someone was trying to tamper with your memories or erase them without doing a complete wipe, and something went wrong."

"So that could be why they're so incoherent?"

"It's the best theory I've got so far, but it's just a theory. Fragmentation is rare," Mane said. "And that's putting it lightly. Most constructs whose cores fragment just shut down, or fall apart. Not literally, mind you. Well, sometimes, but..." He shook his head and made one of his dismissive waves. "I don't have a complete answer to that question just yet." The words Mane said didn't match his mischievous expression. He reached into a pocket on his robe. "But I would reckon it has something to do with *this*." His hand emerged with the serpent ring resting on his palm.

Only then did Samuel remember the fight with the siphils, and how he had discarded his cloak in his flight. He was hit with a rush of frustration at how easily he had forgotten the ring and left it behind with the cloak. When his wave of anger at himself subsided, curiosity about how Mane had acquired the ring quickly followed. "How did you...?"

"Pare," Mane said. "After you fled, he searched the cloak and brought me the ring."

"How did he escape the siphils?" Samuel asked, shocked Pare would have braved such a situation.

"He's very adept," Mane said. "Siphils aren't much of a danger to him anymore, which is why we bait them into the area."

It shouldn't have surprised Samuel the siphils were laid as a trap, but it still did. He wondered how many people may have been caught on that trail by that pack. More and more, Samuel wondered what it was about this old man that warranted so many protections and failsafes.

Samuel gestured toward the ring. "What is it, then?"

Mane grinned. "That's the really exciting part!" he said. "But before I tell you what it is, you have to tell me where you got it."

Samuel was more than a little frustrated with the stalling, but knew there was no way around it. "I pulled it from..." He hesitated, but remembered his promise of honesty. "From the hand of a dead man in the room where I awoke. In Winston. What is it?"

Mane was nodding, looking down at the ring and mumbling, "Ferron, you sly little bastard," to himself. He looked up at Samuel and held up the ring. "This, my friend, is one of the four Rings of Lorrem."

A smug smile crossed his face and he leaned back, unaware what he'd said meant nothing to Samuel.

"Or a forgery." Both of them turned to see Pare entering the room. He wore tight-fitting forest clothes and a wide belt, pulling on a pair of long-gauntleted leather gloves. "Meant to distract us." Pare looked at Samuel, the anger in his eyes slipping just a little bit before he turned to Mane as he walked toward the front door. "I'm going out."

"Back before dark, Pare," Mane said, with a tone that meant they'd had this discussion many times before.

Pare didn't respond. Samuel looked after him and wanted to say something, but couldn't form the words before the young man slammed the front door behind him.

Mane looked back, tilting his head toward the exit. "Headstrong, that one. Hard to convince of anything once his mind's made up." His mischievous grin returned. "Which is why it's so much fun to prove him wrong."

Mane had begun fiddling with the ring, which was still the primary focus of Samuel's attention. "Rings of Lorrem?" he asked.

Mane snapped out of his bemusement. "Of course, of course. The Rings of Lorrem were a set of four, purportedly forged by a powerful artificer after whom they were named many generations ago."

"What do they do?"

Mane tipped his head back and forth in that *it's complicated* sort of way. "No one really knows, to be honest. There are hundreds of rumors and theories about their properties, but no one's ever been able to say definitively what their use is."

"How do you even know they actually exist?" Samuel asked.

"Well, because two of the four are on display in the Central Museum in Balefor," Mane replied. "No one was ever able to unlock their secrets, so they were put on display as simple artifacts. The placard on the display says the other two rings were lost. It looks, my friend, like one of them's been found."

Samuel shook his head in annoyance. "But what difference does that make if we don't even know what the ring does?" He immediately regretted his tone of voice.

Mane took a deep breath and shot Samuel an admonishing look.

"There are any number of crackpot theories about the purpose of these rings. Some say they create wealth, some say they bring amazing luck to the wearer. We know neither of those are true, because one of the museum pieces was acquired from a destitute trinket vendor for a pittance, who killed himself after seeing the ring on display. Some say they command the elements. One ridiculous musing would even have us believe the four rings together have the power to destroy reality itself. All that's a load of rubbish."

Samuel tilted his head in a way he hoped conveyed confusion, so Mane continued. "One would have to be able to conceive of a way to destroy reality before being able to create an artifact capable of the task. Besides, why would anyone want to? Anyway... One of the more popular theories is they involve thought transfer, allowing the wearer to pull another person's thoughts and memories into their own mind or giving them the power to occupy the consciousness of another person, effectively transferring one mind into another body."

Samuel perked up. "Maybe the person who I took it from was trying to transfer himself into my body? If he was interrupted..."

Mane stopped Samuel with a wave. "No, no," he said with a definitive tone. "A construct core doesn't work that way—it wouldn't have the capability to sustain the complexity of a human consciousness. And believe me, men have been trying to find a way to prolong life through constructs ever since the invention of the construct. I even tried to figure it out myself for a little while." He looked down at the ring and shook his head. "No, even if the theory about these rings is true, it just wouldn't be possible."

"Then why?" Samuel asked. "Why would I even find it there?"

Mane chuckled. "Because Ferron was just the type of man to try it anyway," he said. "Never in my life have I met a man more driven by the pursuit of artificial life. It got him into trouble more often than not, and is likely what got him killed. You probably just got caught in the crossfire."

Samuel shook his head in disappointment. This was the only reasonable theory about the presence of his emotions he'd heard, and Mane had just summarily shot it down. Even though he had grabbed the ring on something less than a hunch, the longer he held onto it, the more hope he invested in the idea of it being the key that would unlock his own mysteries. If not tell him who he was, at least provide some insight into a small aspect that would further his knowledge. He'd carried it around this whole time, and all for nothing. An interesting and powerful artifact, yes, but if it couldn't help Samuel figure out his life, it was worthless to him.

"Look," Mane continued, setting the ring on the table, "just because the ring isn't the answer doesn't mean we aren't making progress. It also doesn't mean the ring has nothing to do with all of this." Samuel looked up at the sorcerer. "If Ferron was trying to use this blasted ring to dump his own consciousness into your body, he could very well have mucked up the works in there, and that might be what caused the fragmentation." He rapped his knuckle on Samuel's chest.

Samuel looked down on Mane, who was shorter than Samuel originally thought. "What do you mean?"

"These rings are extremely potent," Mane said. "If Ferron managed to unlock even a fraction of this one's power, then tried to use it on your core, just the output of *khet* alone could have scrambled things around. Manipulating *khet* is more art than science, and when you get that much of it flying around, it's easy to mess things up. I'm actually surprised you're still here."

"So, if the ring isn't the answer," Samuel said, "then where do we go from here?"

"It might not be the answer, but I think it's a clue," Mane said, moving back around the table and plopping down in his chair. "With some time to research the nature of this ring, we have a good chance of figuring out how the fragmentation occurred and working out how to fix it."

Eriane came into the room, her hair pulled back into a tight braid and tied with two green bows. Her eyes were red. She crossed the room to where Mane sat, leaning over him in his chair and giving him a tight hug, which he returned in earnest. He patted her on the back and she knelt beside his chair. They exchanged a quiet word and she nodded, wiping away a tear as he kissed her on the forehead.

Eriane rose and walked to Samuel, knelt beside him, and wrapped her arms around his neck. He swelled with surprised gratitude and was overcome with heartbreaking remorse. When she didn't move, he returned the hug.

"Thank you, Samuel," Eriane said in a quiet voice.

"For what?" he replied.

"For telling us about Michael's final moments. For showing us…" she swallowed. "For not letting us think he died for nothing." She sniffed and let go, wiping a tear away with the cuff of her tunic.

"Thank you, Eriane," Samuel said.

"For what?"

"For not blaming me, like Pare does," Samuel said, looking down at his hands.

Eriane took in a deep breath and leaned back, looking Samuel in the eyes. "Pare's angry and stubborn," she said, "but he's not stupid. I don't think he blames you, really. But he's so hurt right now he'd never say it, you know?"

Samuel nodded. "I'm so sorry we had to meet this way."

Eriane tilted her head at him and smiled. "You really are, aren't you?" Again Samuel nodded, and she sat back on her feet. "Wow." She hopped up and moved back over to the worktable, sitting on the stool at the end and flipping through the piles of loose books. "So, what did you figure out about him?" she asked Mane.

Mane grinned. "Not much, just yet, but we did find something interesting. Do you want to know what it is?"

She smiled back and leaned forward expectantly. "Of course!"

Mane held up the serpent ring.

Eriane's eyes went wide and her mouth opened like she was going to speak, but instead she snatched the ring from Mane's hand and studied it with awe. "One of the Rings of Lorrem!"

"That's the one," Mane replied. "Right here in our house."

"But what does it mean?" Eriane asked, confused.

"Well," Mane replied, "I think an artificer tried to use it on Samuel, but I don't know why. I think it might be the key to why Samuel's memories are in so much disarray."

Eriane jumped up from her seat and moved over to where Samuel sat, plopping down on some nearby pillows. "What *do* you remember? Do you know where you came from? How old you are? Who made you?"

Samuel shook his head. "Nothing, really. The only memories I have are so broken I can't make sense of them."

Eriane's shoulders dropped. "What happened?" she asked.

"That's what I'm trying to figure out," Samuel replied.

"Hopefully Master Mane can help you." Eriane hopped to her feet and smiled down at him. "I have to go study, so I'll be in back. Call me if you need my help with anything." With that, she handed the ring back to Mane and headed off to the rear of the cabin.

"What do they study here?" Samuel asked.

Mane tipped his head back and forth. "A bit of this, and a bit of that," he said. "They both have an acute sensitivity to *khet*, but I've had more trouble than I thought helping them find their talents."

"What do you mean?"

"Each person is different," Mane said. "Some people can't even tell there's *khet* in the world, much less find ways to work with it. Others, like myself, are good at using it in a variety of ways with very little training. Some people, though, have specific, unique natural abilities. The types of things a talented adept can do are as varied as snowflakes, which is why it's so hard to pin it down with these two. I'm closer to working it out with Eriane—she's much more connected to the world around her than Pare, but her abilities are rather unique. Pare's got an instinctual aptitude to apply new uses once he learns them, but he's so closed off it's been a struggle figuring out what he's truly good at." He shook his head. "He'll figure it out someday. I can only hope I've helped him along the path."

"Well," Samuel said. "If you're half as diligent with him as you've been trying to help me, I'm sure he's on the right path."

"With Pare, it's not his knowledge that worries me. He has so much anger in him. Sometimes he... control...   ...wonder if he'll ever...   ...dangerous... "

He can't tell how long he's been out. It feels like he hasn't moved in literal ages. A bright blur is all he can see at first, then the world in front of him pulls into colorless focus.

A squat, balding man sits a short distance away, resting his hands palms-

up on a table. Tears stream down his cheeks and he inhales sharply, gritting his teeth in pain. Blood seeps from raw, open blisters at the tips and along the lengths of all his fingers. The man stifles a scream and stares at his hands, sobbing.

He tries to turn his head but can't move and, in fact, he can't even feel his limbs. Someone swings a chair into his view, and a stout man with cropped hair sits heavily into it. He tosses aside the small rag he'd been using to wipe his face, revealing the scar running from his nose to his jawline across his cheek. Even without the benefit of color, the man's eyes gleam in an unsettling way as he leans forward to speak.

"You weren't easy to find, my broken friend," the scarred man says, his tone almost amicable. "It took us a while to dig you out of this one's scrap heap"—he jabs a thumb over his shoulder at the sobbing man behind him—"and even longer to get you back up and running."

Another voice scrapes across the side of his head, but he can't see the speaker. "That was my idea."

"Yes, yes," Scarface says, nodding in annoyance. "I wanted to do this quickly, but my partner here insisted you be…aware, so we had Corman back there get you all fixed up." The balding man let out a strangled sob. "He's been working for two days straight with no rest, but here you are!"

Scarface licks the tips of his fingers and thumb and presses them into his chest, leaning in so close he can see over the man's shoulder. His vision falters and coldness overtakes him. His hearing is the only thing left to him as the cold gives way to numbness. Over the constant sobbing of the balding artificer, a whispered voice ushers in the darkness. "With as long as you've been out, I'm not even sure you can understand me. After all that time waiting, I wanted you to know who it was that finally brought you to your end. And will bring all of you to your ends."

The door of the shop stands a slightly ajar and the light of an oil lamp flickers within. He stops short of the entryway and approaches with caution.

"Master?" he calls, pushing the door open further. There is no answer.

Lamplight shines from the main shop at the far end of the hallway, but he sees no movement or sign of people. A few things are out of place, which feels strange for such a well-kept business. He calls out again, all but knowing he will get no response.

Across the rear of the shop stands the door to the owner's office. He hears no sound from within and hopes it might stand empty, its occupant away on other important business. He grasps the handle and the door swings open on creaky hinges.

The office beyond is smashed. Shelves have been emptied, and the desk in the corner overturned. A shadow sways on the opposite wall, cast by the limp body of the shop's owner suspended by a noose looped over one of the rafters. Something is pinned to the man's chest, but he can't bring himself to approach. He turns to leave, but feels a hand at his back and a chill rush through his body. He can't move.

"You shouldn't have run, canner." The voice is calm and measured, quiet like a crack forming in deep ice, felt more than heard. The hand on his back releases and he slumps to the floor, every faculty cut off. He can't move or speak and his hearing dulls, but his vision remains so he can witness every vivid detail of what is to follow.

Chapter Twenty-two

"Samuel?" The light, sweet voice drifted into his hearing. "Samuel, are you awake?"

Overloaded bookshelves filled his vision as it swirled back to him in a blurry haze. What Samuel thought, at first, to be the bookshelves along the wall were actually those that lined the cabin's ceiling, which told Samuel he was lying on his back in the main room of Mane's cabin. As his sight snapped back into focus, he sat upright.

"More memories?" Mane asked, kneeling beside him. Samuel nodded. "Tell me everything, starting with the first thing you saw."

Samuel's mind swam, submerged in a deluge of imagery as they collided with his previous memories and he attempted to make sense of the jumble. He began rambling off descriptions, starting with the scene in the artificer's shop. Mane took in every detail, the occasional earnest nod indicating he had taken note of something that caught his interest. When Samuel reached his fifth or sixth scene, Mane waved a hand to stop him.

"It's only the first few that are important, I think," he said, moving to his worktable.

The windows behind Mane were black and the room dark, lit only by the small, artificial candle and the fireplace. Pare reclined in a chair on the far side of the room, near the hallway, having a quiet conversation with Icariascus. Samuel turned to Eriane, who sat on a small stack of pillows at his side, leaning forward.

"How long have I been out?" he asked the girl.

"Most of the day," she said, her brow scrunched in concern. "It was early morning when you…when you passed out. Is that the right word? Can constructs pass out?"

Samuel shrugged. "Apparently *I* can," he said. "This isn't the first time." He pushed himself to his feet and moved over to where Mane was flipping through one of his books. "What did you mean about the first few?" he asked.

Mane leaned back in his chair and took a deep breath. "Well," he started, reaching up to stroke his beard, "What's the first and brightest memory that comes to you every time you have one of these bouts?"

Samuel thought back over the times he had passed out, recalling every piece of imagery that flashed into his mind. In every single instance, the first memory had been the strongest, most intense feeling he could imagine. "They've all been of my own death," he said.

"Right," Mane said. "But not your *death*. Not really, anyway. I think the memories you're seeing are of major memory wipes. Times when you've been put down and…reset, as it were."

That made some small bit of sense to Samuel, but there were still pieces that didn't add up. "Then why am I seeing the same man in so many of my memories… hearing the same malicious voice? And why do they always seem like they're chasing me… fighting me?"

Mane was nodding, with his hand over his mouth. He removed it to speak. "Because, I think, your pursuers keep trying to wipe your core, and keep failing. Keep trying to put you away, maybe because of something you've seen."

"Or something I've done," Samuel said.

"Perhaps," Mane replied.

"Then why wouldn't they just destroy me?" Samuel said. "And who keeps putting me back together?"

"Destroying a construct isn't as easy as it seems," Mane said. "At least, not destroying the core. Oh, sure, the *act* is simple enough, but doing it without causing collateral damage or bringing attention to yourself is almost impossible. A wipe, at least most of the time, is much easier and quieter."

"So," Samuel said. "They're trying to keep me quiet."

"Wow," Eriane said in a quiet voice. She leaned back and clutched a pillow to her chest, listening as Mane continued.

"That first image is important to us," Mane said. "First off, it's powerful enough to overcome whatever's mucking up your works, coming through vivid and clear even though the rest of the memories are incomplete. Second, it lets us know someone's been tampering with your core and your memories for a long time, maybe enough times to be the cause of the fragmentation." He slapped the book on his workbench shut and stood.

"Last, and probably most important," Mane continued, "it tells us you're being pursued by someone, and we might be able to use these visions to figure out *who*."

Samuel searched the imagery that tumbled through his mind for similarities, and one face was almost too easy to single out. "There's a man who shows up every time," Samuel said. "Short, blond hair. Angular features. Nondescript, except for the scar. And his eyes." Mane raised an eyebrow and Samuel continued. "He's got a long scar running across his cheek from the bridge of his nose to past his jawline. And his eyes...they're silver. Not grey, but a bright, almost polished silver. Piercing." Samuel paused. "Cold."

Mane leaned back on the table, burying his mouth in one hand and looking downward, lost in thought. None of them dared interrupt. After a moment he raised his hands in the air, shaking his head. "I don't know who that is," he said. "And I know just about everyone of note, sheriff to charlatan, from here to Cinth. I'd remember someone with silver eyes and a scar like that, but I don't know who this man is. You say he's shown up in every flash?"

Samuel nodded. "This is the man that's following me. And I can't be sure, but I think he's got a partner."

Pare stood from his chair, no longer talking to Icariascus, and crossed in front of Samuel to sit on the stool next to Mane's worktable. "Why do you say that?" he asked. A slight smirk crossed Mane's face as he watched his apprentice take on the demeanor of investigator.

"There's another voice," Samuel said. "I never see a face, but there's a voice. A sort of...creepy, slithering voice in every vision I have with the silver-eyed one."

"What does the voice have to say?" Pare asked.

Samuel searched his jumbled memories. "Nothing nice."

Colton stood in the mud of the alleyway, facing the door of the small shop at the edge of Morrelton, staring up at a carved wooden sign that read simply *Atherton, Artificer.* Bales had already knocked on the door twice, but no one answered and now he was trying the knob to no avail.

"He's not answering," Bales said, "but I'd bet real money he's here."

Colton didn't move, still captivated by the artificer's simple wooden sign. Bales looked at him, then back at the sign, then back at Colton, his features twisted in confusion.

"Look at it, Bales," Colton said, gesturing to the sign. Bales stepped around beside him and looked up with a huff. "Look at the craftsmanship. There's nothing imposing or ostentatious about it, but the attention to detail is startling. Two words, carved in relief into an ironwood plank, but done with such care you wouldn't be able to find a tool mark if you tried. The man who carved that sign is an artist."

Bales shook his head and turned to his partner. "The man who carved that sign has information we need." He pointed at the door. "I've done my part, so just unlock it, would you?"

Colton shot a disapproving look at his abrasive counterpart and moved up to the door, placing his right hand over the knob. After a moment of stillness, a series of muted clicks indicated the lock had been defeated. Colton turned the knob and the door swung inward.

The meticulous neatness of the shop was marred at the back of the room, where several shelves had been knocked out of their brackets, spilling construct parts and other random materials along the floor. There was no light in the room save that which filtered in from the front window and a thin sliver of flickering orange that escaped around the edges of a heavy metal door at the rear.

Colton surveyed the room for exits, spotting three: the front door, the metal door at the rear, and a darkened archway to the left, beyond which he saw a stairway leading up to what was likely the artificer's apartment. Bales moved in first, intent on investigating the light from the room at the rear, but with more caution than Colton would have given him credit for. When he was halfway through the room, Colton moved in to follow. He only made it a few steps when he felt something cold and hard press against the back of his head, stopping him dead in his tracks.

"Bales," he said, his shoulders locking up with tension. The dark haired man stopped near the back of the room and looked back over his shoulder.

"It's not nice to break into another person's place of business."

"Atherton, I presume?" Colton asked of the voice that had come from behind him. "You know you could be executed just for owning that iron you're holding."

"If I cared about legality, I wouldn't be holding you at gunpoint." Atherton asked. There was a flat quality to his voice, a deadness that worried Colton. "You'll turn around and leave, the both of you, and forget you were ever here."

"After all the trouble we've gone through to find you," Colton said, "why would we do a thing like that?"

"To avoid a bullet to the brain, would be my first suggestion." Atherton pressed the barrel of the gun harder into Colton's skull. "And stop trying to dig around in my head. Whatever you're trying to do, you'll never get past my defenses before I can pull this trigger."

Colton exhaled a disappointed sigh and let his shoulders drop. "You're paranoid."

"I like to think of myself as well-prepared," the artificer shot back. "Hey, you—Bales, is it? Step forward and join your friend here."

Atherton moved around to the side, one small pistol poised at Colton's head and another trained on Bales as he moved across the room. Colton noted his sunken eyes and cheeks, his disheveled appearance. If not for the strength in his voice, Colton would have been hard pressed to believe this was the owner of the shop, the man who meticulously carved the sign over the door and who undoubtedly handcrafted the two cap-lock pistols now trained on him and his partner. The man looked like he'd been through the wringer, which made the guns in his hands that much more dangerous.

Colton crossed his arms and turned toward Atherton. "Why would someone with talents like yours even need little burners like those?"

Atherton's hands drew closer together as Bales stepped behind Colton's shoulder, staring down the old man like a dog waiting to pounce. "For men just like you, whose talents run wilder than mine." He took a sliding step backward. "On any other day, in any other life, I might have asked you what you wanted here. But on this day, I'll be satisfied if you leave. You can do so walking, or being dragged. Makes no difference to me."

There was dead air between them now, neither one with anything to say and neither able or willing to back down. Bales cleared his throat, and Colton shifted his weight to his other foot. "I'll walk out of here, old man, but not before you help us find what we're looking for."

"I've no intention of helping you, son. Leave before I kill you."

"You'll help us, Atherton," Colton said, stepping forward. "Whether you want to or not." Atherton's muscles flinched. His guns did not change position even when Colton and Bales moved to the side. He now aimed at the opposing wall of his shop. Bales let out a grating little chuckle as he leaned against one of the racks in the center of the shop.

"Amongst his many talents, my partner here," Colton gestured to Bales, "possesses an unworldly aptitude as a breaker." He leaned in close to the frozen Atherton and whispered into his ear. "This little short time we've been talking, he's been worming in behind your defense, chewing at the supports like an overgrown termite." Bales's grin drained from his face.

"And, now, you'll do whatever I tell you to," Colton continued. "For instance, if I were to tell you to put the barrel of one of your guns in your mouth..." Atherton did just that. "Now, see how easy this is?"

Tears squeezed out of the corners of Atherton's eyes and he let out a ragged breath, the barrel of his pistol rattling against his teeth, sweat beading on his forehead. His limbs jerked in tiny vibrations as he struggled against Colton's hold. The barrel of his pistol pulled slowly free of his mouth, but was still pointed at his face. The struggle of it was starting to show, Atherton's face turning bright red with effort.

"Ho ho!" Colton watched with amusement. "You're stronger than most! It's been a while since someone's had the balls to put up much fight. But…" Atherton's breath released and the gun was back in his mouth. "Now, I'm going to ask you some questions, and you're going to answer them, but you can't very well do that with a gun in your mouth, can you? Go ahead and put them on the shelf over there."

Atherton lowered his guns. His movements stiff, as though he were walking through mud, he made his way to the wall and set the pistols on a shelf. When he turned back to Colton his struggle had ended. The old artificer's eyes were dry. He sagged in a look of both exhaustion and sadness.

"That's good," Colton said, no longer prodding or smug, just getting down to business. "We heard you had some trouble with a construct recently. Tell me about it."

"Jacob brought him in," Atherton said, his voice droning out the words and devoid of any human tone. "Said he needed a shoulder repaired. Seemed legitimate enough to me. Jacob took off on an errand, and he left the construct behind. During his first night here, something happened…"

"What?" Bales asked.

Atherton turned his dead eyes onto Bales for a moment, but then turned back to Colton. "The construct passed out. His eyes went dark and he toppled over. I thought he'd dissipated, but he'd flicker to life every so often and mutter something incoherent. We hauled him onto the work table, and that's when I saw it."

"Saw what?" Colton asked, even though he knew he didn't need to.

"The inscription on his shoulder." Atherton said. "Ancient. Almost unreadable. On a plate that's never been replaced. I couldn't make out the whole word, but I'd venture an educated guess it said *Aesamaelus.*"

Bales started. "Impossible," he spat at the old man. "Your eyes were playing tricks on you."

Atherton said nothing.

"Are you sure that's what you saw?" Colton asked.

"Of course I'm sure," Atherton said, his visage still exhausted, but otherwise blank.

Bales wagged a finger at Colton. "This is horseshit and you know it. There's no way I didn't know."

Colton raised a staying hand and Bales settled, grinding his teeth. "What did you do next, Atherton?"

"We strapped him to the table. There's an Assessor from Cinth who comes to Morrelton on the regular, and I was going to hand him over, until he tried to help the construct escape."

"Who?" Colton asked. "Who helped him to escape?"

Atherton's lips quivered and his shoulders shook, fresh tears streaming from his eyes. His jaw clenched and unclenched, but he did not speak.

Colton pressed, his frustration bubbling to the surface. "Who, Atherton? Tell. Me."

"Mmmm..." Atherton still resisted, turning red again. "Mmmm... Mmmichaelll." He released another explosive breath, tears flowing freely now. "M-M-Michael h-helped him. Repaired his shoulder and freed him. Jacob came b-back while I was trying to stop him, and the construct left with him."

"Did the construct tell you its name?" Colton asked.

"Samuel. Its name is Samuel." Colton shot Bales a questioning glance, which was met with a confused look and a shrug.

"Where did Jacob and Samuel go, Atherton?"

"I... I don't know," Atherton said, his voice quiet. "M-Michael would know, but... but he's not here."

"I want you to take us to Michael," Colton said. "Right now."

A pained look crossed Atherton's face. "I can't," he said, his voice still flat. "He's dead."

Bales exhaled a whispered chuckle and shot Colton a grin. Colton leaned in close to Atherton's ear. "That won't be a problem."

Chapter Twenty-Three

Colton took small pleasures in making Atherton recount the night of Samuel's escape, demanding every lingering detail the old artificer could dredge up about the fight with Malthoranic and Michael's death. Bales sat to the side, closing his eyes and taking in long, blissful breaths as he listened to Atherton's tale.

Although waiting until nightfall to leave the shop meant fewer people in the streets, bitter cold followed the darkness, so their pace across the small forest town was brisk. Colton had released Atherton from his mental grasp, having demonstrated what would happen to him if he made any move of betrayal. The old man acquiesced, offering to do whatever they wanted so long as they left him alone after this night. In spite of Colton's talent, Atherton's strength was a struggle to overcome and the artificer's broken will suited him just fine. The struggle between them had been taxing and had Atherton's life not taken the unexpected turn of a few nights prior, Colton knew it would've been even worse.

The three of them walked in silence, both Atherton and Bales carrying long shovels. Atherton leading two strangers across town in the middle of the night would have drawn the guard's attention even on a normal day, but since the deaths of Cort and his men, Morrelton was under a strict curfew. Without the strain of controlling Atherton on his shoulders, Colton was able to focus on any nearby guardsmen as they

167

passed, redirecting their attention and securing free passage across the city.

A small cemetery stood in a clearing near the edge of town, ringed by a low wooden fence and surrounded by trees. Burial grounds gave Colton the creeps, and every sound in the trees overhead pricked at his paranoia. Atherton paused at the gate, closed his eyes and took a deep breath, then stepped over the threshold and up the center aisle, turning near the middle of the yard and coming to a stop before Michael's grave. Atherton's jaw clenched as he looked at the simple headstone, frozen for a moment with emotion. He held his shovel out to Colton.

"There," he said, his teeth still gritted. "Do what you need to and I'll be on my way."

Colton flashed an unpleasant smile. "I don't dig. Not unless you want the guard all over us in a matter of minutes."

Atherton's face flashed with anger. "I will not do this. I've come as far as I will."

Colton stepped up close so their noses almost touched, then gripped Atherton's hand and squeezed it around the shovel. Colton felt the artificer's breath on his face, felt him begin to shake. The scraping sound behind him let him know Bales had already started digging. He was certain Bales was actually looking forward to this part.

Atherton let out a slow breath. "Will you leave me be, then?" he asked, his voice so weak Colton barely heard him. Colton stepped aside and Atherton moved across from Bales, plunging his shovel into the already broken surface of Michael's grave.

Bales worked like a dog unearthing his favorite hidden bone. Atherton's work was labored, but Colton didn't intervene, letting him dig at his own pace. Once the hole was deep enough they could no longer dig from above, Atherton and Bales took turns climbing down into the grave to continue digging. After three solid hours, Bales's shovel struck the hardwood of a casket with a loud *thunk* that caused Atherton to flinch. Another several minutes of clearing and Bales exposed most of the plain pine box's lid.

Colton stood at the edge of the grave, looking down on Bales with a mixture of annoyance and disgust. "Peel it," he said, his tone abrupt. He often wished Bales could develop a talent for what he was about to do. His greasy-haired companion was always enthralled by the process, but Colton found it distasteful, even when necessary.

Atherton moved to the end of the grave, his curiosity taking over before he realized what he was doing. Bales tossed his shovel up out of the hole and reached down to the edge of the box, prying his fingers under the side of the lid and spreading his feet into the dirt walls of the grave to brace himself. With a mighty yank the nails came loose and the cover hinged open, spewing forth a musty-sweet stench that caused both Atherton and Colton to recoil.

"Out," Colton ordered.

Bales leaned the coffin lid up against the dirt wall and climbed out, bowing to Colton with a hand upturned at the grave. "Table for one and a half, sir?" he joked, ever the morbid jester.

Colton shot him a disgusted look and climbed down, straddling Michael with a foot on either side of the coffin. The apprentice's body was bloated, his face still grotesquely swollen with the bruises and cuts from his encounter with Malthoranic. Colton grabbed the edges of the boy's vest at the armpits and hauled his body upward into a sitting position. Michael's head lolled to the side at an impossible angle. Colton heard Atherton retch twice, then vomit as Bales snickered. A broken neck would make Colton's task even more difficult—he might only get a few words out of the boy.

From a pouch at his belt Colton withdrew a small glass vial, inside which white light stirred in lazy tendrils like captured fog. He grasped Michael's head by the hair and drew it upright. The boy's face was a mess, all bruises, swelling, and unpleasant fluids. Placing the vial against the dead boy's forehead, Colton closed his eyes and took a deep breath, which he held for several seconds.

Colton let out the breath and opened his eyes. Michael's right eye was open wide, his left open and staring but partially buried under swollen flesh. Without blinking or breathing he offered Colton only an open gape, his pupils so dilated they met the whites of his eyes. Colton removed the empty vial from Michael's forehead, replacing it in his belt pouch before gripping Michael by the sides of his head and looking deep into his eyes.

"Michael," he said, rather loudly. "Take in a breath." Michael drew a long, labored breath through his nose, but did not exhale. Colton knew he would only have this one breath to retrieve his answer, so he hoped his question would elicit something understandable, or at least something Atherton could help interpret.

"Michael. Where did Jacob and Samuel go?"

Michael's eyes narrowed in a confused expression. His mouth opened and air began to slowly escape, but he did not form any words. Colton couldn't understand why it wasn't working and he was running out of time. He'd have to find a way to rephrase the question, or ask another one, before the breath was gone.

"Atherton!" Colton snapped, looking up out of the hole for the artificer, who wasn't in sight. "Why doesn't he understand?"

"Kaleb," Atherton's weak voice croaked over the edge of the hole. "He never knew Jacob's real name. Michael knew him as Kaleb."

Colton snapped his head back around, gripping Michael's head even tighter. Michael's mouth was still open and there was a light hiss as the air escaped his lungs. "Michael! Where did Kaleb and Samuel go?"

Michael's jaw worked up and down twice before his lips started to move. "Bbbear's hhhhooouuusssee," he hissed as the last of his breath fluttered into the night air. His eyes were still open, but no life was left in them, natural or artificial.

Bear's house. Senseless words. Colton shoved Michael's body back into the coffin and stood, gritting his teeth and shaking his head. Bales held a hand down into the hole and helped him climb out. Atherton sat on the ground, leaned against a nearby tree, his arms dangling in the dirt at his sides as tears washed trails down his dirty cheeks. He looked as though he'd aged ten years in the last twenty minutes. Colton stalked over to him and knelt, grabbing a fistful of his shirt.

"What does *bear's house* mean?"

Atherton turned his head, looking at Colton as though he'd spoken a foreign language. Colton pulled him forward by his shirt, then thumped him hard back against the tree. Atherton coughed. "What are you talking about?"

"It's what Michael said when I asked him where Kaleb and Samuel had gone. What does it mean?"

Atherton turned his head, silently mouthing the phrase *bear's house* over and over. The old man looked more confused by the second, and Colton's anger was coming to a boil. Colton let out a frustrated scream, using Atherton to lever himself to his feet. He paced back and forth at the foot of the grave with a hand on his forehead, trying to work it out.

"A cave, maybe?" Bales offered. "Bears live in caves."

Colton didn't stop pacing. "Maybe, I suppose. Doesn't help us, though. These hills are littered with caves. They could be holed up anywhere." His pacing slowed and finally stopped. He stood with his hands on his hips and his head tilted back, eyes closed as he searched to make any sense of what Michael had told him. If Atherton didn't even know, they were back at square one. "Fuck!"

Colton's scream died in the branches. Silence enveloped them; not even the wind rustled the trees. Finally, Atherton's weak voice floated over the night air. "Pare's house."

Colton and Bales both snapped their heads to look at the old man. "What did you say?" they said in unison.

Atherton coughed up a chuckle and looked at Colton, his contempt laid bare. "Pare's house. One of Michael's friends. Apprentices with this crazy old hermit who lives somewhere northeast of here." He let out a weak laugh and grinned knowingly. "You'll never find it. No one ever has. That old coot might be crazy, but he's powerful. More powerful than ten of you. You could spend the rest of your life searching and never find it, and you'd be ten feet away."

Colton looked down at him, his face so devoid of humor the grin drained from Atherton's face. "Where do I start?"

"Why should I tell you now?" Atherton spat back.

Colton placed his hands on his knees and leaned down, his lip twisted in an enraged sneer. "Climb into the grave." He said, through gritted teeth.

Atherton's jaw clenched hard and his eyes went wide. There was a half-second of pause before he struggled to his feet and walked over to the hole, climbing down to stand across Michael's still-open coffin. He looked up at Colton standing over him, and the last of his tears flooded out of his eyes before they went dry. He couldn't even blink.

"You know," Colton said. "I could make you tell me whatever it is you do know just by asking you the question again right now." He leaned over the edge of the grave. "But you've gone and pissed me off. Lay down." Atherton laid down on his back atop Michael, holding his head up to stare at Colton at the edge hole. Colton released his control just enough to allow Atherton to speak freely.

"The Bleeding Pine!" Atherton screamed. "Go to the Bleeding Pine, up the east road into the foothills! That's all I know, I swear... Please."

Colton stood up straight, shaking his head. "There was a time, Atherton—albeit brief—when I thought of you as strong."

"Please..." Atherton pleaded. "I've told you what I know. Please let me out of here."

Colton paid him no heed. "You're nothing but a betrayer, really. So easily you will turn on those who put their faith in you. Twice now you've betrayed your beloved apprentice's trust, even in death, and now you betray his friends. And for what? What's left for you?"

Atherton, his body rigid, cried in tearless sobs. "Please..."

"Stop blubbering," Colton said. Atherton's mouth snapped shut and his eyes grew large. His body went limp and his head came to rest in the coffin next to Michael's. Colton bent down and picked up the shovels, tossing one to Bales, who caught it with an unsettling smile. The two of them scooped up shovelfuls of fresh dirt. "I don't claim to be a good man, but at least I'm *loyal*."

Chapter Twenty-Four

It had taken an entire night for Samuel's thoughts to settle, slotting as many of his new memories into some rough timeline as was possible. So much of the imagery was just random, with no context or defining characteristics to identify a time and place. Unable to place them into any sort of timeline or associate them with his current knowledge, he was engaged in a constant—and exhausting—battle to compartmentalize them in such a way they wouldn't interfere with his ability to engage in normal, rational thought. If there were anything that could drive him to madness it might be this.

For several days he fought, alone at night in the front room of Mane's cabin, long after everyone had gone to bed. The manual process of organizing his memories frequently sent him into miniature blackouts, so he'd spend the nights attempting to work himself back to normality while Mane and his charges rested, leaving himself lucid for questions during the day.

It was upon waking from these blackouts he missed their company. Especially Eriane's, who seemed to be the only empathetic one of the group. Mane could not be blamed for his distance; it was his mind that Samuel was taxing for answers. Even Pare had softened some, using the questioning and research not only to occupy his mind, but also to force himself to interact with Samuel in some way other than anger. Samuel

173

suspected Mane had some hand in directing Pare's actions.

So many questions had been raised by his most recent flash of memories. There was no way of knowing how close his pursuers were, or even if they were still pursuing him. Besides, would they even be able to find him, buried out here in the wilderness behind protective barriers so complex?

The face of the silver-eyed man intruded on Samuel's every thought. He was an enigma on his own, surrounded by questions that had begun to supersede Samuel's own search for purpose. Why was he after Samuel? What did Samuel know—or worse, what had he done— to draw this kind of attention? Images of the murdered woman lurked behind every question, every thought. What was the link between the murder and his fugitive flight?

Pare and Eri were up early one morning, diving right into the investigation. Mane hadn't emerged yet so Pare sat behind the worktable, poring over books and asking Samuel the occasional question. Eri's approach was more compassionate, wondering how Samuel was feeling and if his mind had settled. As focused as Samuel was on figuring himself out, he was comforted there was someone who cared more about his well-being than the mystery at hand. It was a quiet moment, with Pare buried in a book and Eriane lounging on the cushions by the fire, when Mane entered the room.

"Look who's up!" he said to the kids with a smirk. "What terrible fate has befallen the world to get you two out of bed so early?" Eriane laughed and Pare just shook his head, returning to his book. "Have you been out to practice yet, Eriane?"

"No, sir," Eriane said. "But it's early, I still have plenty of time today."

"Let's get you dressed and out to practice," Mane replied. "Early to rise just means you've got more time for study."

"Yes, sir," Eriane said, rising from her pillows. "But if you find out anything at all about Samuel, you'll come get me right away, right?" Samuel wished he could smile.

Mane chuckled. "Of course. Now run along with you; go get dressed."

Eriane made her way back to her room. Pare took a deep breath and closed the book he was searching, rubbing his eyes. "I think I'll join her," he said, standing.

Mane waved his hand. "No, Pare. I need your help today."

Pare's surprise melted into confusion. "Um, okay."

"What's this?" Mane said in mock astonishment, moving over to his desk. "I thought you'd relish the opportunity to help me investigate."

Pare shrugged. "It's fine, but Eri and I haven't practiced together in quite a while."

"Well, Pare, that's partially by my design." Mane put a hand on the boy's shoulder. "I think Eri's close to a breakthrough, and she needs some time to work it out on her own."

"Really?" Pare asked. Samuel thought he heard a hint of genuine excitement seep through. "What's she onto?"

"Now, now, Pariadnus. You know better than to ask that question. That's for her to tell us, is it not?"

Pare was crestfallen, rubbing one thumb into the opposite palm. "I think I could help her," he said to his hands.

Mane plopped down into his chair. "You remember what it was like at that point, don't you, Pare? The last thing you wanted was my interference, and I think she's feeling the same way about both of us right now."

Pare nodded and took a seat next to the desk. He took a deep breath. "What are we looking for?"

"Boring things," Mane replied, handing Pare a thick, leatherbound volume with two stripes of horizontal piping wrapping around the cover. Pare split his book toward the beginning and set it on the desk, leaning forward onto his elbows.

Icariascus emerged from the back, wandering across the room and fiddling with something in the corner Samuel couldn't see. Eriane followed a moment later, dressed in tight-fitting leggings and tall boots. Samuel caught a glimpse of a leather vest over her usual tunic as she tied up the front of a long, hooded cloak.

"A little overdressed?" Pare shot over at her.

175

Eriane flushed. "It's cold outside, Pare," she said, annoyed. "In case you hadn't noticed, it's autumn, and we live close to the mountains." Mane chuckled.

Pare leaned back into his book, rebuffed. "I was only kidding."

"I know," she said. "I'm just being prepared, like you always tell me. I'm surprised there isn't already snow." She moved over to give Mane a brief embrace before heading for the door. "I'll be back before dark!" she said over her shoulder as she left.

Samuel turned back to Mane. "How can I help?"

"Actually," Mane replied, "You can't. You've been cooped up in here for days, and I think you need to get out of the cabin for a bit. I'm sending you to gather some firewood with Icariascus, today."

"Sir?" Icariascus replied, and stood unmoving for a moment before nodding his head. He and Samuel both spied the stack of firewood already gathered by the fireplace. "Yes, sir," Icariascus said, leaving his task in the corner behind to cross the room. "Please come with me, Samuel," he said as he passed. Samuel stood, noting both Pare and Mane watched him from the desk. Nodding toward them, he turned to follow Icariascus.

The morning sky flared bright white. Dense fog loitered amongst the forest trees, cutting visibility to only a few feet. The sunlight was diffused through the cloud layer and fog into a pervasive glow that made the day feel even brighter than it actually was, an effect helped by the light blue shimmer of the illusory wall.

Icariascus moved around the side of the cabin without waiting for Samuel. The thin construct's movements were stiffer than Samuel's, but he suspected Icariascus might be more limber if the need arose. His design was simpler and his joints uncluttered, which would allow a wider range of motion, at least it seemed to Samuel, than the clunky plates around his own joints. He rotated his once-broken shoulder, looking at the final repairs Mane had done a few days before. Perhaps not Atherton's quality of workmanship, but he'd done a fine job and Samuel was grateful not to see a gaping hole there.

The two constructs walked quite a distance into the woods, along a well-worn trail that cut a straight path through the undergrowth and between the tall fir trees. "If we were to walk quite some distance, this trail would take us east and to the river," Icariascus said, acting the tour guide as they moved through the forest. "We won't be going that far today."

They continued to walk, and Samuel realized Icariascus knew they'd been sent on a wild goose chase as well, expelled from the cabin so Samuel could get outdoors and Mane could concentrate uninterrupted. There was plenty of firewood to gather, yet they gathered none. Samuel was the first to speak.

"Icariascus?" he said. The smaller construct paused and turned to face him. "How old are you?"

Icariascus started to turn away and looked back in a stuttering motion, then continued to walk. "I...I don't actually know," he replied. "We believe I've undergone at least one complete wipe, so I do not remember my origins, and we cannot determine my construction date. From my design, the best we can surmise is that I'm between one hundred and one hundred-fifty years old."

Samuel was staggered, as that put Icariascus at almost fifty years older than him. "Michael thought I might be about one hundred, but didn't know for sure."

Icariascus gave Samuel an appraising look. "Your design is much older than that," he said. "Older than me." There was no hesitation or question in his voice.

Samuel stopped in his tracks. "How do you know?" he asked.

Icariascus stopped and turned. "The wear to your frame. Your joint design and plate design are somewhat...archaic." He stepped forward, rapping a finger on one of Samuel's shoulder plates. It made a solid sound, almost no ringing echo. "It's been a long while since an artificer designed an armored construct." He rapped his own chest and it produced a hollow ring. "Most constructs are built lighter, more agile. We become easier to transport...easier to manage. I won't break Mane's floor if I fall."

Was that a joke? Samuel couldn't tell if Icariascus was being earnest or sarcastic.

"So, I'm older than you," Samuel said, mulling over how this revelation expanded what little frame of reference he had for his returning memories. The images and feelings he was recovering could be just from his last wipe, or from hundreds of years of experience. The breadth of his experiences could be even wider than he thought, which might explain why he was having so much trouble organizing them. And how long had he been followed by the man with silver eyes? What had triggered— A sharp, loud *crack* snapped him back to reality, but there was something odd about it. He listened for a moment and heard no echo, and wondered if what he'd heard was real.

"It's not that surprising, you know," Icariascus said. "Constructs have been around for..."

Samuel held up a hand to stop him as he listened. "Did you hear that?"

"Hear what?" Icariascus asked.

"A sound...loud." Samuel said, listening.

Icariascus looked around, then shook his head. "I've heard nothing, Samuel..." Another *crack* hurtled into Samuel's hearing, again with no echo. "There!" Samuel said, almost yelling. The forest seemed undisturbed by the sound, but Samuel recognized it, even without the echo.

He jerked his attention back to Icariascus, grabbing him by the shoulders. "Where does Eriane practice?" he said, his tone sharp.

"Her favorite spot is in a depression at the base of one of the knolls near the river," Icariascus said.

"Where? What direction?"

Icariascus looked at his surroundings, then raised a hand. "That way..." he said, pointing.

Right in the direction of another *crack*. Samuel was already running.

"I don't hear anything, Samuel. Where are you going?" Samuel was already at the edge of the clearing.

"Something's wrong! I think Eriane's in danger!" he yelled over his shoulder, just before crashing through the brush at the treeline and bolting into the forest.

"In danger? But Samuel—" Icariascus said, but Samuel didn't hear the rest. He ran as fast as his legs and eyes would allow, taking no heed of the underbrush that tried to tangle his feet or the branches that whipped his head and shoulders. He had little care for stealth, and was stirring up quite a commotion with the local wildlife on an otherwise quiet autumn morning. He stumbled, pushing off of a large pine to keep himself upright as the ground began a gentle downward slope he hoped would lead to the depression Icariascus mentioned.

Another *crack*, louder and closer. He'd heard this sound before, but only once—in the alleyway in Morrelton where he had defended himself against Cort and his men. Gunfire.

Samuel feared what he'd encounter when he reached Eriane, and only hoped he could get there in time. The treeline vanished and he exploded into a clearing across from the cliff face. In front of him was a dome of energy, perhaps fifty feet in diameter and perfectly round, a cascade of sparks and blue light slicing through the forest and surrounding trees, intersecting a small stony rise on one edge.

Eriane, at its center, turned quickly with an astonished look. In that same moment another loud *bang* took Samuel by surprise, a bright orange flash lighting the side of Eriane's face, stopping him dead in his tracks. Something struck the rock face just above the dome with a loud zipping sound and the branch of a tree just over his shoulder exploded in splinters. A flock of birds crashed through the higher branches and into the air.

A moment later Icariascus burst from the treeline to Samuel's right and stopped as well. Samuel watched as the look of surprise drained from Eriane's face and was replaced by fear, tears welling up in her eyes. She moved to her cloak, which was piled on the ground a short distance from her feet, and stowed something under it. Samuel could still see the curved side of a wooden handle with an ornate brass cap. She then snatched up something from the ground, and the dome of light disappeared. The young girl, now full of rage, stormed toward Samuel.

"What are you doing!" she yelled. "You scared me half to death! Someone could have been hurt!"

"I..." Samuel stammered, "I...heard something. I thought you were in danger."

"Well, as you can see, I'm fine." She stopped about ten feet from Samuel, crossing her arms and shifting her weight to one hip, her jaw clenched.

It was Icariascus who broke the silence. "What were you doing, Eri?"

Her eyes shot over to the other construct, who was now approaching them both. "Practicing, Icariascus, what do you think I was doing?"

"Practicing what?" Samuel asked.

Eri's head snapped back toward Samuel, and a tear ran down her cheek. She didn't say anything, instead letting out a huff and turning toward her belongings. "It's none of your business!" she said over her shoulder. She knelt over her cloak, being sure to keep herself between it and the two constructs. Samuel recognized the same sharp, smoky smell he'd first encountered in the alley in Morrelton. He turned to Icariascus, who was already looking at him, and could sense Icariascus knew the smell, too.

"Eri," Icariascus said in a soft voice, stepping forward.

All the girl's movements stopped for a moment and she was still, the clearing quiet. She shook her head before pulling her cloak around her shoulders and turning to leave. Icariascus stepped into her path and held up a hand. Tears ran down her face as she tried to sidestep him, but he moved to bar her path again.

"Get out of my way, Rascal." Her demeanor shifted from angry to pleading. "Please... Please don't..."

Icariascus stood silent, but did not move. Samuel stepped over to them. "Eri?"

She pulled her cloak tightly closed in front of her, biting her lip and looking away as she tapped one of her feet. As her adrenaline began to wear off the tension in her muscles drained. Her shoulders and eyes both dropped.

"Can you get in trouble?" Samuel asked. Eriane didn't respond.

"Yes, she can," Icariascus said, still watching the girl. "Why would you risk this, Eri?"

"Because it's what I'm good at," she said, probably louder than she intended, finally looking back up at the two of them. Her eyes fell on Samuel. "Besides, I need to learn to protect myself anyway." She turned back to Icariascus. "You're not always going to be around, and neither are Pare and Mane."

"That's true," Icariascus said, "but why this? You're so talented...why would you waste it on this? If you were ever caught with a gun..."

"Don't you understand, Rascal?" she said, staring into his eyes. "This *is* my talent." A fresh round of tears burst down her cheeks. "I'm *good* at this. Somehow, I'm better than I should be. It's like I can just…I can just feel my way through it." Icariascus just stood silent, staring at her.

"Maybe you should just talk to Mane about it," Samuel said. "Maybe it means something."

New fear sprang into her eyes, and she darted over to stand in front of Samuel. "You can't say *anything*! Either of you!" she said, looking over her shoulder at Icariascus. "Rascal, you know Pare can't find out. He'd never look at me the same way again!" She was openly sobbing as she turned back to Samuel. "You have to promise me! You won't say *anything*. Not *ever*."

"Eri, I—"

"Promise me, Samuel. You too, Icariascus."

The pleading in her eyes dug at Samuel. He wanted more than anything for this young girl and her strange little family to trust him. How could he let her put herself in danger like this, though? On the other hand, what place was it of his to say anything?

Icariascus was looking away, off into the forest, and Eriane was watching him. Finally he nodded, and said nothing more. Eriane turned her reddened face back to Samuel.

"I promise, Eri," he said.

She let out a breath and closed her eyes. "Thank you. Both of you."

"Just be careful," Icariascus said.

Eri turned and put her arms around the thin construct's shoulders. "I always am," she said, before planting a light kiss on the side of his head.

Eriane started back toward the cabin, with Samuel and Icariascus following at a respectful distance. The three of them walked for a few minutes before Samuel could no longer hold in his thoughts. He stepped up to Icariascus and tapped him on the shoulder.

"Rascal?" he asked.

Icariascus turned back to the trail. "A nickname," he responded. "When we first met, she had trouble pronouncing my name, and wasn't fond of it even after she could. So, she shortened it to Rascal. I see it as a term of endearment."

"I'm sure it is," Samuel replied. He quickened his pace to catch up with Eriane, who turned her head as she heard him approach.

"Look, Samuel," she said, pausing. "I don't want to talk about it, okay?"

Samuel nodded. "Oh, that's not what I wanted to talk to you about, actually." Eriane shot him a questioning glance. "I'm curious about the dome?"

She nodded her understanding and reached into her cloak, drawing out a small stone about two inches across. "It's called a guilestone," she said, handing the rock to Samuel. "They can be used for all kinds of things, and each one is different based on whoever's using it."

Samuel examined the stone as she spoke. The surface was polished smooth with a precise spiral shape etched into its surface. Beneath the surface sheen, small flecks of crystal sparkled amidst the rust color of the rest of the rock.

"A guilestone like this can be used as a general focus, or it can amplify a talent," she continued. "I was messing around with it one day, trying to find out if I could use it to create a larger, more powerful bump field, like the ones I practice with Pare." She sighed. "I still can't get the full power of a bump field through it, but the shield I can make will block all sound, and I use it so my practices don't disturb the forest." Her brow crumpled up in confusion. "But...you said you *heard* something. That's impossible."

Samuel handed her back the stone, which she dropped back into a pocket inside her cloak. "You say that dome was blocking sound?" he said. Eriane nodded. "That would explain why there was no echo." Her look of confusion intensified. "Mane has already discovered I don't sense constructions of *khet* the same way as others. I am able to see through his illusions, and I was able to see your little dome. I must have been able to hear the sounds coming from within it, but because the dome was blocking the travel of the actual sound, there was no way for it to echo off of the trees."

Eriane shook her head. "That's just weird, Samuel."

"Yeah," he replied. "What about me isn't, so far?"

She laughed, a sight and sound that relaxed Samuel. It was nice to see her smile. They continued walking in silence for quite some time with Icariascus trailing behind before Samuel spoke up again.

"So..." he said, hesitant to continue, "What...how did you figure it out?"

There was a long pause before Eriane spoke. "Look, I...I can't talk about it, okay, Samuel?"

He nodded and let it drop. The remainder of the trip back to the cabin was silent, and seemed to take twice as long as it had taken in the opposite direction. They had been gone for a few hours by the time they came back into the front room, where Mane was still hunched over his table and Pare had taken up a spot near the fireplace. Both were surrounded by an assortment of books, and neither looked up as they entered.

"You three are back early," Mane said, squinting at some text he seemed to be having trouble deciphering.

Eriane hesitated, casting an anxious look at the two constructs before replying. "I got hungry," she said. "Ran into these two on the way back."

"Is that right?" Mane said, raising an eyebrow from his book toward Eriane.

"Yeah, that's right," she said, smiling back at him. "Is there anything to eat?"

"There's some bread and some leftovers from last night, but it's all cold," Mane said, almost mumbling in his concentration.

"That's fine," Eriane said as she disappeared into the back of the cabin.

"I'll get some food ready," Icariascus said, following her.

Samuel took a seat on the floor near Pare, being careful not stray too near the stacks of books surrounding the boy. "Any luck?" he asked.

"Not much," Pare replied without looking up. "At least not useful. Plenty about the *effects* of fragmentation but not much about how to fix it." He jiggled the book in his lap. "I have a feeling about this one, though. It's a historical text about capital artificers in the early days. Pretty fascinating, actually, some of the designs they pioneered."

Samuel turned toward Mane, who heard what Pare said and raised his head. "We'll see if it leads anywhere, though. Every account of a fragmented construct I've found has resulted in either insanity, catatonia, or explosion. I can't find any accounts of one remaining cognizant."

Samuel's hopes sank. It seemed as though the deeper they researched, the further away from an explanation they traveled. He kept that opinion to himself. No use in further interrupting them, and he was in no great hurry to find an answer to his own riddle at the moment, anyway. Samuel occupied himself with sorting through his memories again, trying to link as many as possible and find any needle-like clues he could dig out of the haystack of his mind. He was jarred from his concentration by the snap of a closing book, and he looked up to see Mane rubbing his eyes and shaking his head.

"Something wrong?" Pare asked.

Mane took a deep breath. "I don't think we're going to find anything here," he said. "My collection is extensive, but it's not focused in the right place. I only dabble in artifacts, I don't specialize in them."

The weight of Mane's admission bore down on Samuel. Frustration and fear began playing at the edges of his mind. His first real lead was beginning to fall apart, and who knew what would come next.

Pare took in a breath that broke the silence. "What about..." He shook his head and cut himself off. Mane was staring at him, but he took another deep breath and didn't continue.

"Well," Mane said. "Spit it out."

"It's a stupid idea," Pare said.

Mane leaned toward him. "Stupid ideas might be all we've got left."

Pare took another breath. "What about Acthemenius?"

Samuel surmised, from the length of the word, it was a construct's name.

Mane leaned back in his chair. "You're right," he said. "That's a stupid idea."

Pare looked incredulous. "He might be a little...off...but if there's anyone that might know more about Samuel and his problems, it would be Acthemenius," he said, his tone defensive.

"Who's Acthemenius?" Samuel asked.

"He's sort of a...construct...I don't know, cult leader?" Pare said. The look on his face told Samuel he knew how ridiculous he sounded. "That's the best way I can describe him. But that's not the important part. Acthemenius is probably the most knowledgeable construct historian for a thousand miles."

"Unfortunately," Mane said, chin in hand, "He's about as crazy as a construct can get. He believes himself to be the oldest construct in the world, and claims not only to know the history of his kind, but also their future."

"The historical knowledge alone would be enough," Pare said.

Mane took his hand away from the bottom of his face. "Maybe so. Even if he wasn't a fraud, though, it's a worrisome trip this time of year."

"Yeah, but not an impossible one," Pare continued, "Besides, if Acthemenius is no help, there's always the library at Kelef. I mean, I've never been there, but the artificers in Morrelton talk about it like it's their holy ground. There's bound to be someone there who can help."

Mane looked thoughtful, running his fingers and thumb over his beard. "We might get up there and find ourselves snowed in for the winter."

Pare began to show signs of excitement. "Would that be such a bad thing?" he asked. "A little time away from the cabin might do us all some good."

Mane took another breath but didn't respond, leaning his head back and staring at the ceiling above his chair. Eriane and Icariascus—Samuel couldn't help but hear him called Rascal every time his name came to mind—returned, the construct taking up his customary station near the rear hallway while Eriane sat down on the step near Samuel. She tore off a sizeable chunk of bread and took a bite, smiling up at him as she chewed. It was a moment before she noticed the silence.

She swallowed. "What's going on?"

"The snows haven't started in earnest yet," Pare said directly to Mane, ignoring Eriane's inquiry. "We could make the journey before winter starts."

"Journey?" Eriane asked. "Where?"

Mane continued to examine the books on his ceiling. "If the autumn weather holds like last year, we may not get any serious snow for another month," Pare continued. "We could…"

Mane held up a hand to stop Pare from continuing. "There's a lot of ifs in this plan, you know."

"True, but you're always the one saying the most important knowledge is gained from taking risks."

Eriane forgot her bread and watched the exchange, rubbing her arms to ward off the cold. "Careful now, Pare," Mane said, "or you might let your cabin fever cloud your judgment."

Pare flushed. "I…" he began, but shook his head and thought better

185

of whatever he was going to say. He took a deep breath. "You're right. I won't deny I'm feeling a little...cramped. The prospect of some time away from Morrelton and the cabin is enticing. You can't deny it's a good idea, though. It's our best next step."

Eriane's eyes were wide as she listened, and Samuel saw her shiver. At first, he thought it was a sign of excitement, but the way she had her arms crossed told him she was just cold. He looked over to see that the fire had died down to only one small flicker of flame. The fire had never been this low since he arrived, and the fireplace mechanism made no move to stoke or fuel it. He was about to comment on the oddity when Mane continued.

"Well, I think you're right on that count," he said. Pare set his book aside and stood, his face split by an almost childlike grin. The look caught Samuel funny, being such a departure from his standard stern demeanor. Mane raised a hand again. "But we don't need to leave right this second. If we're going to be trudging into the mountains, let's take a day or two and make sure we're—"

A sudden rush of air staggered Pare backward a step and fluttered papers all over the room. There was a loud *whump* and a crash of energy splashed outward in ribbons at shoulder height. The dissipating energy revealed a cloaked figure in a half-crouch, who took an awkward tumble amongst the pillows with a grunt. Mane sprang to his feet and was in front of his workbench while everyone else in the room sat stunned. A look of genuine alarm crossed Mane's face. It was the first time Samuel saw him shaken.

The figure twisted beneath its long cloak, turning to face them. Gloved hands emerged from the folds of charcoal grey fabric, moving to pull back the hood. From behind an unkempt tangle of dark, shoulder-length hair, Jacob's eyes darted around the room, resting on Mane, whose alarm shifted to a mix of confusion and anger. Jacob spoke, his voice thick.

"They're coming."

Chapter Twenty-Five

"Who?" much to Samuel's surprise, was Mane's first question. Jacob still remained half-crouched, his position so awkward Samuel wondered how he held it until he saw Pare's hands. He'd felt Pare's grip and knew Jacob couldn't move.

"Two of them," Jacob responded. "Looking for Samuel. They...they killed Atherton after...after he told them about your cabin."

"Atherton didn't know about my cabin," Mane replied.

"Please, let me loose," Jacob pleaded. "We don't have much time."

Mane nodded. Pare gave a reluctant grunt and released Jacob, who stumbled sideways before getting to his feet.

"How did they find us, Jacob?" Mane insisted, his voice deadly quiet.

"One of them...his name's Colton...he gets in people's heads. Made Atherton take them to Michael's grave." Jacob hesitated. "He gave Michael the Breath."

Mane's face flashed with anger, and he flicked a glance at Pare, who stood with his jaw locked at Jacob's description.

"They've got a breaker with them," Jacob continued. "A damned good one."

"That must be how Jacob was able to get in," Pare said, deflecting

Mane's attention. As if on cue, a book loosened from its moorings in the ceiling and dropped to the floor, pulling everyone's attention.

"He's corroded every protection between the Bleeding Pine and here," Jacob said. "He must be talented if you didn't know."

"Which means we have even less time," Mane said, turning to Icariascus. A few more books began to fall, and more were slipping. "Take them in back and get them ready." He turned back to Pare. "Pare, pack up. Take Samuel and Eri to the waterfall."

"That's a mile into the woods," Pare said, calm and matter-of-fact.

"They'll never make it, Mane," Jacob said, shaking his head. "They've rounded up a mob. Eight or ten who believe they're tracking a murderer."

"They're not far off the mark," Pare spat, getting in Jacob's face.

"We don't have time for this," Mane said. "Pare, Eri, go in back with Icariascus this instant." Mane's tone was unmistakable; Pare and Eriane did as they were told.

"How far can you translocate?" Mane asked Jacob.

"Distance isn't the issue," Jacob replied. "It's knowledge. I have to have a pretty solid working image of where I'm going, or I could end up way off course…or worse."

"Knowledge won't be a problem," Mane said. "Is a mile?"

"I don't know. I've never had to try."

"Well, you will now," he said, the command in his voice amplified by his anger.

"How many?"

"Pare, Eri, Samuel," Mane said.

"What about…" Mane's look stopped him from finishing his question. Pare and Eriane returned carrying heavy rucksacks, their winter clothes hastily thrown on. Something heavy clattered to the floor at Pare's feet and Samuel saw Reet rolling off the step.

"What's going on?" Eriane asked, tears brimming at the edges of her eyes as more books shook loose.

Mane waved Pare over. "I need you to think of the waterfall cave."

"What?" Pare asked.

"You've been there hundreds of times," Mane said. "Quickly! Every step on the way, everything between us and that cave. Think hard and bring it to your mind."

Pare closed his eyes. "Okay, now wha—"

Mane placed the heels of his hands on Pare's and Jacob's foreheads. There was a sound like a cracking branch, and Jacob staggered backward, blinking his eyes and shaking his head.

"Can you get there now?" Mane asked.

"How did you—" Jacob began.

Mane cut him off. "Can you?"

"I think so, but I can't be sure."

"Be sure," Mane snapped. "You didn't risk yourself to come all the way out here only to give up."

Jacob set his jaw and gave a single nod.

Mane turned to Eriane. "You and Pare are going to take Samuel to Kelef." He looked up at Pare as he said the words, then back to Eriane. "You need to help him find out who he is, and why he's being followed."

"Wait..." Eriane said, refusing to cry even though a tear had broken free. "What about you?"

Mane stood. "I'll be along," he said, stepping back and waving Samuel over. Samuel moved to Jacob's side and Pare stepped forward to Eriane.

"No!" Eriane screamed. "What are you doing?" Pare put his hands on her shoulders and she shook him off, flinging her arms around Mane. Mane ran his hand down her hair, then nodded to Pare, who had to pull Eriane free and hold her back. "NO!"

"When you get there, look for a woman named Jo Tellis," Mane said, his face grave. "I...knew her once, a long time ago."

Jacob placed his hands on Pare's and Samuel's shoulders. Mane nodded. Jacob took a deep breath, and a dark burst of energy ripped everything away from Samuel's vision.

Samuel felt as though he was being dropped from a great height, tumbling through nothingness as his sight and hearing were obscured. There was no sense he was traveling with others, at which point he became frightened he'd been separated from the group. His fear seemed to stop time, and in a panic he wondered if he'd ever come out the other side.

Reality rushed back in a cacophony of light and sound. The world around him blared and he hit something solid at an odd angle, rolling out onto the hard ground facedown. As his sense adjusted to their new surroundings, he pushed himself up onto his hands and knees, his fingers digging into moss-covered stone. A rough circle of light, softened at the edges by mist, undulated before him. A roar filled his hearing, and the waterfall outside the cave mouth finally crystallized in his sight.

The others were all around him in varying states of composure. Eriane sat with her back against the wall near the spot where she had recently vomited, crying. Pare sat on his knees, clutching at his side, taking labored breaths. Jacob was on his hands and knees, shaking his head and muttering something to himself Samuel could not understand.

"Is everyone okay?" Pare said, his voice strained. No one responded, and Pare did not ask the question again. The boy worked his way to his feet, grimacing in pain in the process. Samuel and Jacob followed suit but Jacob swooned, collapsing to the stone floor. Pare seemed not to take notice, moving toward the cave mouth. Samuel knelt and saw a trickle of blood from Jacob's nose, but his breathing was steady.

"Pare?" He asked behind the boy, who didn't listen, exiting the cave and stepping out of sight. Samuel followed.

The narrow path wound up the cliff and out from behind the sheet of water tumbling from the river above. The footing was slippery, but Pare navigated it without any trouble, following a switchback that led to the top of the waterfall. Samuel followed, wanting to know where Pare was going in such a hurry. Jacob was unconscious, Eriane was in shock, and Samuel was no caretaker.

Samuel could no longer see Pare on the trail, so he moved along as fast as the footing allowed, emerging in a clear spot at the top of a tall cliff, along the bank of the river. Pare stood at the edge, looking out over the forest below. Samuel approached him with caution.

"Pare?"

"Do you see it, construct?" Pare asked.

"See what?" Samuel asked.

"The cabin." Pare still looked out toward the forest, which sprawled before them. "You probably can't." Their vantage point stood at twice the height of the trees below, and the landscape sloped downward away from them. Pare raised a finger. "Just there, below that rise." Samuel followed Pare's instruction, looking to the forest at the base of a tree-covered hill. "If there were a fire burning, you'd see the smoke," Pare said. "I've always been able to see the smoke."

"Pare, I…" Samuel stopped, unsure of what to say, instead taking a place a few steps back from the boy and looking out onto the forest. They stood, listening to the waterfall and watching the trees, as the first snowflakes began to fall around them.

"Can you imagine, construct," Pare continued, "what must be happening down there right now?" Samuel could, but he didn't want to. Pare's refusal to address him by name had become unnerving.

The explosion almost blinded them both. A brilliant multicolored flash tore through the forest at the base of the rise where they looked, where they both knew the cabin to stand. A gout of blue energy expanded from the center of the flash. Even from a mile away the devastation was plain. Pare sank to his knees as the flash and cloud expanded, and the rumbling report of the blast reached their ears. Samuel felt himself falling, blackness enveloping his world.

The first one who entered the cabin didn't live long enough to regret the decision. As his body struck the ground, another entered, and another, stepping around their comrade's lifeless form and piles of fallen books, splitting into two groups. Only two approach him, while Mane must now deal with three. The two rush him and he blocks their blows with little effort, striking them both with force enough to ensure they will no longer be a threat. By the time he finishes, Mane's opponents have been dispatched. The old man's nose is bleeding, either from injury or exertion.

The second wave comes on fast and with more precision. Objects strike from all sides, energy crackles in bolts and waves, and defensive shields absorb blows. A deafening report rocks the cabin. He looks to Mane. Blood spills from between the fingers of a hand clutched to his breast. The old man loses balance and sinks to the floor. A tall, bald-headed mercenary strides in from the doorway, smoke drifting from barrel of his pistol.

The remaining attackers approach with caution, leaving their former target to bleed on the floor, two of them drawing mafi-sticks. The first of them makes the mistake of coming close enough to reach, and he caves in the side of the thug's skull with an easy blow. A mafi-stick strikes his opposing side with enough force to stagger him. As he drops low, he strikes downward into one of the thug's legs, the back of its knee slamming into the floor.

Another mafi-stick blow drives him fully to the floor, and the thugs subdue him with several more blows before a voice calls them off. They back away toward the door of the cabin, toward the new voice. "I'd rather he be aware for this part."

The blows of the mafi-stick have sapped him of most of his fight. Even through his hazy vision, he can see their leader's piercing silver eyes scan the cabin.

A white flash draws his attention to the side of the room, where the bald-headed man is kneeling over Mane's lifeless form. "The old man is dead." The mercenary says as he stands, wiping blood from a short-bladed knife. The murderer walks calmly over to where he kneels, bending over to talk to him. "I'm going to enjoy watching this," the man says, tapping his chest. He knows what he must do.

He has just enough strength left to deliver a rocking blow to the thug's sternum, launching him across the room and into another mercenary, who slams into the doorjamb and crumples, unconscious. The bald man rocks to his knees and struggles for breath. He raises his head and growls through gritted teeth, then turns and draws a pistol from his fallen friend's belt. Silver Eyes has just enough time to scream an obscenity before everything goes black. He never hears the shot.

"Master?" he calls as he rounds the corner, moving into the long hallway leading toward the kitchen from the front of the house. There is no response, save for a wet noise that repeats with a light slap, like someone coring a pumpkin and throwing the seeds aside. He's halfway down the hallway when the noise ceases, replaced by a quiet scraping and grunts of effort, someone lifting something heavy. He pushes the kitchen door open and freezes, unable at first to process the scene before him.

Blood splatters the walls and cabinets, dripping off the edges of countertops and doorhandles. The tile floor is obscured by an expanding pool of viscous red liquid that fills each grouted seam as it creeps toward him. Streaks break the surface of the red, intersecting small piles of pink matter steeping in the crimson morass. His gaze follows the trail and stops at two bare feet as they slide through *the pool toward the back of the room.*

Delicate legs lead his gaze to a woman's body, still gushing blood from a belly-level opening too large to be called a wound. Entrails snake out of the evisceration and drag on the floor beside her. A spasm draws him upward to her face, her eyes open and somehow still alert, pleading with him for help behind tears that streak down her face. Her shoulders are held in her murderer's grasp. His face is hidden behind long, dark hair that hangs heavy, soaked in blood. One of his hands moves from under the dying woman and draws a small knife across her throat, opening veins that spew upward and add to the carnage.

The killer's head rises. White eyes shine bright against the dark gore surrounding them. He knows he should run, leave this place as fast as he can. The killer drops his victim as she bleeds to death on the kitchen floor. He turns to run, bolting down the hallway toward the front door.

Chapter Twenty-Six

Something sharp dug into Colton's cheek. Forest air tinged with an acrid odor drifted into his nose. Opening his eyes was a chore. Dirt and ash filled his view. His right side throbbed with a dull ache, and the metallic tang of blood filled his mouth. His right hip screamed and his joints moved as though filled with sand. The brightness surprised him until he was able to fully open his eyes, and see that where he sat was no longer deep forest but open to a wide, white sky.

"Hm. You finally woke up," Bales said. He sat against the shattered remains of a large pine, putting the finishing touches on a ragged bandage around his right thigh. "Wasn't sure you would."

"How are we not dead?" Colton asked around the dry cotton wad of his tongue.

"Bump field," Bales replied. "Managed to get it up, but not as fast as I would have liked. Did the job, though."

Colton maneuvered to his feet, brushing the dirt and ash off his clothing as well as possible. The blast crater was a hundred feet across and intersected the hillside they saw on their way in. Falling snow mixed with blowing ash from trees incinerated by the fireless heat of the explosion.

"How many do we have left?" Colton asked.

"Five," Bales replied. "Surprisingly intact, save for one broken arm."

Colton nodded. Nothing remained of the cabin or its inhabitants.

He moved into the space where the structure once stood, but not even a splinter of wood or a shard of glass betrayed there was once a dwelling there. He found his target, a man lying face down under a growing blanket of ash, and worked his boot under the man's side to flip him onto his back. The bald-headed mercenary lay motionless, the flesh on the side of his head blistered and one arm twisted in an unnatural way. Colton spat on his face.

"Dumb son of a bitch." He turned back to Bales. "I told you guns were a bad idea."

Bales's head was leaned back against the tree, his eyes closed. The other mercenaries sat in a cluster some distance behind him, amongst the still-standing trees. "Seemed to do a number on the old man. Not a total loss."

Colton couldn't argue that point. "Then perhaps we should have brought men with enough brains to know not to shoot at a construct."

"You're just pissed because you didn't get to do your thing with this one," Bales said.

"No, I'm angry I was almost killed by stupidity, and in this destruction we won't even be able to find out how they got out before we showed up." Colton winced as he took a breath, then tried stretching out some of the pain with limited success. "I don't suppose *you* know how they got out?"

"How am I supposed to know?" Bales said. "I didn't even go in." He leaned his head back against the broken stump and waved a hand lazily about. "Is there some sort of escape tunnel like back in Winston?"

There was nothing, but he looked around anyway. The crater floor was smooth all around, unbroken by any structures or tunnels. "Nothing." Colton buried his frustration. "Is there anything left?"

Bales shot him an incredulous look, but said nothing. Instead, he took a deep breath and closed his eyes. After a few moments of deep breathing and tilting his head, he opened them. "Nothing. I broke it all. I didn't leave—" Bales turned his head and went rigid, like a bird dog in a point. "Wait..." Bales snapped to his feet, limping past Colton and into the crater. He raised his hand over his head, feeling.

"What is it?" Colton asked.

"I...I don't..." Bales opened his eyes, reaching a hand into the air above him as though he stroked something very delicate. "Yes…right here. Colton, give me one of your vials."

Colton knew better than to hesitate when Bales got like this, and immediately handed him a small vial filled with the iridescent fog of gathered *khet*. Bales felt for the spot in the air again and, once satisfied, held the vial up and uncorked it. The contents rose, swirling into the snowy air. Both men watched, transfixed, as the vapor curled upward. Like smoke drawn through a keyhole, the vapor pulled into an empty spot in the air between them and vanished. A darkness descended into Bales's visage. "They have a slip."

"Which means they can't be very far." Colton said.

"But they could be anywhere," Bales replied. "We don't even know where they're headed. *They* probably don't know where they're headed."

"They can't go back to Morrelton," Colton said. "And, if this canner is what we think it is, then there's only one place left for them to go."

"Kelef." Bales turned on his heels, waving at his thugs to follow.

"Not right this second," Colton said. "We'll camp for the night and leave in the morning."

Bales scoffed. "You can stay here as long as you want. I'm going after them."

"No, you're not. You'll wait, because you know better," Colton said. "None of us are in any condition for another fight without some rest. We'll catch up to them tomorrow, and put an end to this cat and mouse. We'll head back to the clearing. I don't want to stay here." Colton gestured to the mercenaries, who began pulling themselves to their feet.

Bales ground his teeth and stepped up close to Colton. "If they get away from me? I'll put you down and go after them myself. Accidents happen all the time on the road."

"Duly noted," Colton replied.

"You're a slip," Pare said, hovering between a question and a statement.

"I can translocate, yes," Jacob replied. "But if you call me a slip again, I'll let you choose which arm to keep."

The two of them had been hovering at the edge of a full-blown argument since Pare returned to the cave. Eriane half-listened to their bantering, the numbness from Pare's news still filtering through her limbs, her chest aching from crying.

"How have you evaded the Interdictors?" Pare asked.

"Simple, I'm not stupid," Jacob said, looking around the cave. "Where did you say Samuel was again?"

Pare looked away. "Still above."

"He's been up there a while," Jacob said. "We should go get him so we can be on our way."

Pare smirked. "On our way to where, exactly?"

Eriane pulled her feet under her and wiped her face, fed up with listening to the two of them go at each other. "Kelef, like Master Mane said."

"I'm not going anywhere near Kelef," Pare said.

"What are you talking about?" Jacob asked.

"I'm going back to Morrelton. That construct can rust for all I care."

Eriane looked at Jacob, who was staring at Pare and looking just as dumbfounded as she felt.

"Master Mane and Icariascus are dead because of him," Pare said, like he was quoting a math problem. "Not to mention Michael and Atherton, and who knows how many others."

It was difficult for Eriane to process what Pare was implying. "But Master Mane told us to take him there," she said.

"And he told you to help get him there," Jacob added.

"Did you not hear what I just said?" Pare raised his voice, and addressed Eriane directly. "You don't seem to get it. Mane. Is. Dead. And it's the canner's fault."

"Don't call him that." Eriane's blood boiled and she closed in on Pare. "*You* don't get it, Pariadnus. Mane died *for* Samuel, not because of him."

"What difference does it make, Eri?" Pare's voice was quieter, but no softer. "We're on our own, now, and I'm not risking my neck for a canner," he said, turning his back.

198

"Does the canner get a say?" Samuel stood silhouetted in the cave entrance, the waterfall roaring behind him.

Eriane ran to embrace him, relieved to see him standing. "I'm so glad you're okay."

Samuel hugged her back and continued. "I can't really say what it is I'm looking for. I don't know why I'm important, but I know now there's something in these memories I need to make sense of, and whatever it is, it's a lot bigger than just me."

Eriane turned to Pare, whose back was to the group. "You should at least hear him out, Pare." Pare turned around, his arms crossed like a shield against discussion.

"What do you mean, Samuel?" Jacob asked.

"I now know for certain these memories," Samuel said, "the fragments of visions that come to me whenever I black out—they aren't actually mine."

Eriane was confused. "If they're not yours, then where did they come from?"

"All I've got is bits and pieces," Samuel said. "Some are stronger than others, and I know for sure they aren't all mine, because"—he paused, as though building up the resolve to explain—"because I saw Icariascus's last moments, through his own eyes."

"What?" Eriane said. A shock welled up from her gut and pushed behind her eyes, threatening a fresh round of tears. Pare finally turned around.

"I think that's what this is," Samuel said. "I'm seeing the memories of other constructs, after they are destroyed. I don't know why, or even how I'm linked to them, but after the explosion, I had another rush of images, and the strongest was from inside the cabin, from just a little while ago. I saw the fighting, I saw Mane…and then…black. One of the intruders pulled a pistol and shot Icariascus."

Samuel's words were a punch to Eriane's gut. She put a hand over her mouth as her stomach lurched. Jacob let out a breath, running a hand through his hair and turning away.

"And it wasn't just the last moments," Samuel said. "It was just like the others. I've got images from all throughout Icariascus's life. A lot. A lot of you two, where he was before Mane. But it's all a mess. Disjointed.

Incomplete. If this Acthemenius can help me fix it...put it all together...then maybe we can figure out why I'm being followed, and put an end to the ones following me."

Pare scoffed and turned away again, and Eriane followed him. She couldn't let his pig-headedness win out this time. "He's right Pare, and you know it. This is why Mane wanted us to help him." Pare stopped a few paces away, putting a hand on the cave wall. She waited as he contemplated, but he never turned, never spoke.

"The people following me, Pare," Samuel said, "they've destroyed a lot of constructs, and hurt a lot of people in the process. The others they've destroyed, they never—they never felt fear, or anger. I want to turn the tables on them. I want them to pay for what they've done." Samuel stepped forward. "And I need help."

Eriane waited to hear Pare's response, but he didn't turn or speak. She approached him, fighting back the urge to scream. "You don't get to do this, Pare. You don't get to turn your back on this. This time it isn't just you."

"Everything's different now, Eri." His voice was almost inaudible. "I...we have to start all over again. We're on our own."

"Yeah, but we don't have to be. This is our decision to make, now. Ours." She took a breath. "Right now, we're the only people in the world Samuel can trust, and he needs us."

Pare's eyes flashed as he turned to her. "He doesn't deserve our help."

"How can you say that?" Eriane said, putting a hand on Pare's arm. "Please, Pare... We need your help. I need your help. Don't leave me now. Not now."

Pare set his jaw. "Who's leaving who, Eri?"

Eriane raised her voice, no longer able to contain her anger. "Don't you dare, Pariadnus," she said, wiping her eyes.

"What, Eri? Tell you the truth?"

"You're so full of it!" Eriane said. "All you care about is yourself and your stupid grudges!"

"It's self-preservation, Eri," Pare snarked. "It's kept me going so far. You're going to walk into a fight you have no part in—the fight that took our home away from us."

Someone behind Eriane said something she didn't hear. "Samuel came to us for help, and I'm not going to let you make me feel guilty for doing what's right."

"What's right?" Pare asked. "How do you know Samuel there isn't the bad guy, huh? How do you know the people following him aren't right?"

"How can you even say that, especially after what they've done?"

"HEY!"

Eriane finally registered Jacob yelling at her and turned on him. "What!" she yelled, but what she saw pulled her up short. Between them, a steady stream of iridescent mist poured from a point in the air just above head-level, then dissipated into the moist air of the cave. As it began to die down, she looked at Jacob.

"We have to go. Now," he said, without waiting for the question.

"What is that?" Eriane asked.

Jacob was already gathering what few things he had with him. "It means someone's still alive down there, and they know there's a translocator with you. They know I helped you escape."

"What?" Pare asked. "How is that possible?"

"I'll explain later," Jacob said. "Right now, we have to leave."

Eriane scooped up her rucksack and moved toward the entrance just behind Jacob. Samuel still stood near the entrance but didn't move as Eriane approached. She looked over her shoulder and saw Pare hadn't moved.

"What are you doing?" she asked him. He set his jaw and did not respond.

"Pare, you have to come with us," Jacob said. "If they can follow that trail, they could be here soon."

The whole group paused, waiting for a response. When it didn't come, Eriane was the first to speak. "I'm done arguing with you about it, Pare. I'm going."

She turned around, the rock in her chest descending into her gut. Pare had been in her life ever since Mane had taken her in, and she struggled with every step away from him. Knowing what needed to be done didn't make the doing any easier.

She paused a step past Jacob and Samuel, both of whom were still waiting on Pare, who maintained the same silent posture. "Are you sure, Pare?" Jacob said. After no response, he turned to Eriane. "Are *you* sure?" he said.

Eriane blinked, then nodded. Samuel looked at Pare. After a long pause, he found no words, and followed Eriane out of the cave.

Chapter Twenty-Seven

Samuel followed Eriane's lead, heading beneath the waterfall in the opposite direction than he'd gone earlier. The wider path rose at a gentler slope, rounding a corner into a cut in the cliff instead of following a switchback to the top. Eriane trudged ahead of Jacob without a word, and Samuel brought up the rear. The shock of seeing the thief again was settling in, and he wasn't sure how to reconcile his feelings of betrayal from Morrelton with his gratitude at being saved from his would-be captors.

At this point, Samuel decided, he had no choice but to trust Jacob. The discussion of what happened in Morrelton would have to come later, when Samuel found both the courage and the humility to ask without allowing his anger to dictate the conversation. For now, they were travel companions again, and something about that felt good.

Steep rock walls gave way to a clearing at the top of the cliff along the riverside. To their right the flat ground disappeared into the trees and jagged, white mountain peaks towered over the forest. The sky was stark white, and the snow didn't seem to be taking hold yet.

"That way," Eriane said, pointing out a narrow path that led into the treeline. "That will take us back to the road in about half a day, if I remember right."

"Are you sure we shouldn't go back?" Samuel asked.

Eriane's lips were a thin line and she shook her head. "Pariadnus has always been a stubborn goat," she said. "Once he's made up his mind..." She headed up the trail without another word. Jacob shrugged and they followed.

Before long they passed under the forest canopy and the trail wound between the narrow trunks of high alpine trees. It was a silent walk and the mood was dark. Samuel was torn about leaving Pare behind, regardless of his attitude. Despite his reluctance, the boy had been helpful and had just started warming to Samuel before they were forced to leave the cabin. Samuel knew Pare was self-sufficient, but still had no desire to see him fall to harm.

Pine boughs overhead obscured the winter sky as the trio walked, the distance traveled in almost complete silence. Their path was clear and all Samuel wanted was to put the horror of the day behind them to focus on the task ahead. He held onto the hope their pursuers—*his* pursuers—would not find a way to follow them through Jacob's translocation and that they'd make it to Kelef unmolested. Ever since Winston, Samuel stumbled from one disaster to the next, narrowly avoiding a terrible fate. Kelef, and whatever awaited him there, was an opportunity to put everything together and work on finding a way out of his situation.

Lost in thought, Samuel almost ran into Jacob as they came to a stop on the trail. Ahead of them, Eriane stood at a place where the trail split and meandered off in opposite directions. Samuel and Jacob waited for Eriane to decide which path to take, but when she said nothing, Jacob spoke first.

"Eriane?" he asked.

She turned to face him, unable to disguise her worry. For a moment she looked as though she were about to speak, but instead turned back to the fork, her head nodding and shaking as she weighed each option in her mind. In a small voice she said only, "I don't know which way."

Jacob was silent, looking up each trail in much the same way Eriane had, so Samuel stepped forward. He hadn't yet known certainty in his short waking life, so this was just another obstacle to overcome. It was clear Eriane's uncertainty terrified her. "That's okay, Eriane. Let's just try to work through it."

"Okay, okay," she said, taking a breath. She turned back toward the intersection. "These are tracker's trails, so one will take us back to the main Morrelton road. The other would wind deeper into the forest along the foothills, or possibly back to the river at some point. So..."

Jacob and Samuel held their anxiety while waiting for her to finish.

She took a step to the left trail, stopped, and shook her head. Her shoulders twitched in the same direction one more time, and she stopped herself again. "There." She pointed to the right trail. "That should lead us back to the pass." She hesitated, then nodded toward the two of them and headed down the trail.

"Well, you almost had it right."

The voice startled all three of them and they turned in a flash, Jacob drawing a knife from beneath his cloak. There, leaning against a tree next to the trail, stood Pare, his rucksack slung over one shoulder. Eriane bolted past Jacob, leaping up and wrapping her arms around Pare's shoulders. "I knew it!" she said, her voice muffled as she buried her face in his shoulder.

"I couldn't let you try and lead them to Kelef on your own," he said, mustering an almost convincing nonchalance. "You couldn't even find your way out of bed in the morning without help."

Eriane let go of Pare's neck and didn't even flinch before slapping him across the face. Pare dropped his eyes with a sheepish nod. "The right path leads along the river for a while, but curves back away from the mountains a few miles down. The left path heads toward the mountains and will take us back to the road just before the pass."

Jacob nodded. "Then we'd better get moving. Maybe we can make it to the base of the pass before nightfall, and still have trees to camp under for one more night. Oh, and Pare? I'm glad you decided to come with us."

Pare nodded his thanks and pointed himself up the trail, moving to the front of the group. "Pare, I..." Samuel said, but the boy indicated no acknowledgement, instead starting off at a brisk pace with Eriane beside him. Jacob shot Samuel a look, then motioned for the two of them to be on their way as well.

The trail wasn't wide but it was uncluttered, save for the occasional root. Samuel and Jacob hung back from the other two, allowing them their time together. Every so often, Eriane would speak to them about where they were headed, obstacles they might encounter, or other tidbits about their upcoming trek. Pare rarely addressed either of them, and only ever Jacob.

Samuel couldn't really blame him. All Pare's fears had been proven accurate and now he didn't even have Mane to tell "I told you so." Regardless, Samuel was grateful to have him along. With his knowledge and skills, he would prove to be a useful companion. As the day crept to a close, they neared the intersection with the main road to the pass.

"Do you think they can trace you back to the cave?" Pare asked Jacob.

"Not unless they have a translocator of their own," Jacob replied. "At best they'll know you were pulled out, but they shouldn't be able to track where."

"Good," Pare said. "We'll stay here for the night. We don't want to head into the pass in the dark. All we can hope is that they don't know what direction we went, at least not right away."

"What if they catch up to us on the main road?" Eriane asked.

"I'll be here, on watch," Samuel said. "You're all exhausted. Get some sleep."

Pare paused, as if to size up Samuel's trustworthiness. Weariness won out and he nodded. After looking around, he pointed out a small depression a ways back from the trail. "There."

"Seems like a good spot," Jacob said. "I'll go gather some firewood."

Pare stopped him. "Before you go." Pare reached up to touch Jacob's head and Jacob flinched away, to which Pare gave him a scowl. Jacob nodded and stepped back up. Pare placed his hand on the side of Jacob's head at the base of his neck, and there was a sound like blowing leaves. Jacob blinked and shook his head.

"What did you do?" Jacob asked.

"Back at the cabin. You said one of them could get in our heads," Pare said. "It's a mind-wall trick Mane taught me. It should protect us, at least for a little while."

"What about the breaker?"

"I can't do much to stop him, if he's good," Pare said. "But even if he's good it'll take some time, and you'll get a warning. I'm not sure how it'll manifest; it's different for everyone. Just pay attention to anything out of the ordinary. You'll know."

Pare turned to Eriane, placing a hand at the same spot on her neck. The same quiet sound blew by, instigating the same gentle shake of the head from Eriane, as if to clear it. Pare leaned down, speaking to her in his best big-brother voice. "You need to pay attention, okay? Anything could be a sign of tampering, and there's no way for me to tell."

Eriane nodded. "What about Samuel?"

Pare just shook his head. "There's nothing I can do. These things really only work on people. Besides, even a breaker can't do much against a can—construct."

"Oh," was all Eriane could say. Her look to Samuel was tainted with pity before she turned to follow Pare to their camping spot. Samuel didn't know how accurate Pare's assessment of his safety was. He had little choice but to sit watch and hope he could do his part to protect the people who were trying to help him—some against their better judgment.

The suns had retreated for the day and the forest darkened. Eriane busied herself making camp and building the small fire, waiting for Pare to return. He had headed off into the woods without a word. Eriane knew all of them wondered what he was up to. She assured them he'd be fine—he knew these woods better than anyone—even though her own worry was clear.

Pare's life had been upended once already, not as long ago as it seemed sometimes. Mane had taken him in and had been everything to him for longer than Eriane had known either of them. And now Mane was gone; they were on their own again. The thoughts of Mane caught in Eriane's throat but she fought back tears; there wasn't time for weakness right now.

She shook herself out of her thoughts when she heard Jacob say her name. "Hmm?"

Jacob took a spot next to her on the log next to the fire, leaning in close. "So, are you any good with those irons you're packing?" he said, keeping his voice quiet.

Her eyes snapped to Samuel, who sat across the fire and back a ways into the woods. She felt Jacob's hand on hers.

"No one told me, if that's what you're wondering," Jacob said.

She was confused. "But, how?"

"You don't translocate two people and a construct over a mile without learning a little bit of what they've got on them," he said.

Eriane flushed, her chest tightening again. "Jacob, you can't say anything. You just can't!" she said.

Jacob nodded and raised a hand. "You don't need to worry about that," he said. "So, are you?"

"Am I what?" Eriane asked.

Jacob smiled. "Any good with them?"

Eriane smiled, but she didn't feel very convincing. She dropped her eyes. "Yeah," she said. "Really good."

"That's good to know," Jacob replied. "But you need to be careful."

"I'm always careful," Eriane said. "I know how to handle these things."

"That's not what I'm talking about," Jacob said. "Those pistols need to be an absolute last resort." He sounded like he wanted to say more, but trailed off instead.

"What do you mean?" Eriane asked.

"I mean," Jacob said, looking around. "I mean I don't know how Pare would react."

Again, Jacob caught her by surprise. "I know that," she said. "But how do you?"

"That little mind trick Mane pulled back in the cabin," he said. "It wasn't exactly, well, *clean*."

There were things about Pare's history even Eriane didn't know. She wanted so much to ask Jacob for details, but it felt wrong to invade Pare's privacy, so she rephrased the question. "How much did you learn?" she asked.

"Enough," Jacob said. "Look...Pare's got some demons buried way deep, and I think it's in our best interests to keep them buried, if you know what I mean."

She did. "I'll be careful," she said. "I just hope we can handle all of this."

Jacob put a hand on her shoulder. "You're strong, and so is Pare."

He gestured over to where Samuel was sitting. "And I'm willing to bet that big lunk over there is more worried about you than he is himself."

Eriane smiled, this time for real. "I hope Acthemenius can help him. I hate not knowing what we're running from."

"You and me both, kid. You and me both."

They sat for a while in silence, warming their hands by the fire, before Eriane spoke up again. "Jacob?"

"Mmm?"

"What's..." Eriane hesitated, unsure whether she wanted her question answered. "What's the Breath?"

Jacob leaned back and took a deep breath, then blew out in a long exhale before speaking. "It's a way to make the dead speak," he said. He paused, looking as though he didn't want to continue, but Eriane kept her eyes on him to prod him along.

"Are you familiar with Drift?" he asked.

She was intimately familiar. Drift was the street name for a form of concentrated *khet*, gathered from a living being and distilled by an adept into a dangerous drug. Eriane's jaw locked at its mention. Drift addiction was a blight on anyone who succumbed to it, and making the drug was one of the most despicable things an adept could engage in. Eriane ground her teeth and returned a curt nod.

"The Breath," Jacob continued, "requires a vial of Drift...at full potency." He paused again, clearly uncomfortable.

Eriane felt her face curl into a scowl. Jacob's hesitancy was well-founded. To make the drug at, as he put it, full potency required the *khet* to be drawn from a victim until the drain killed them. Drift distilled from latent *khet* or drawn from a person or creature without killing them was perilous enough. At full strength, the drug was an unforgivable corruption of the use of *khet*.

Jacob placed a hand over Eriane's. "I had a feeling it was something you wouldn't want to know," he said.

It took a moment for Eriane's jaw to unclench enough for her to speak. "But I needed to know," she said. "Whether I want to or not. Now I have a better idea of what we're up against."

Jacob's brow furrowed, and he nodded. "Hopefully we won't be put up against them anytime soon."

Pare returned with a small clutch of long-tailed ermine hanging from his hand. Samuel saw Jacob and Eriane pull away from their close conversation and inhale as they visibly attempted to relax. They greeted Pare and his catch, Eriane commenting on how well they'd eat tonight. Samuel was fascinated by watching the three of them skin and clean the animals, as though it were second nature to them. Wilderness survival was not something foreign to any of them, and that put Samuel's mind at ease for the trek to Kelef.

Jacob turned in early and wasted no time falling fast asleep, buried under his winter cloak. Eriane and Pare stayed up for some time after, speaking of practicing while Pare tested Eriane's defenses with pine cones and small stones, all of which deflected away from the bump field held a foot in front of her upraised hands.

"Eventually you need to learn how to do this without your hands, Eri." Pare said.

"I've never been able to figure it out." She replied. "I need my hands to hold up the field."

"You know you don't." Pare said. "It's just a matter of confidence." Eriane nodded, deflecting another pine cone with a wave of her hand.

In spite of everything that had happened in the cave, it seemed they were trying for some semblance of normalcy. Eriane was the first to succumb to her fatigue, but her sleep was troubled, and Pare watched her as long as he could before he lay down himself without so much as a word or glance at Samuel.

That night, as Samuel watched over them, he struggled with the idea of leaving them behind. How could he endanger the lives of others any longer, when he knew his path and could travel it alone? His practical side told him the trip would be easier and shorter were he to strike out on his own, and perhaps he could draw the danger away without any further harm to these three strangers, who had laid down so much for him already.

That was the key, though, wasn't it? They had already given so much for him, and had dared to stay with him in the face of the dangers he had wrought. Leaving them now would spit in the face of all they had sacrificed. Maybe, in taking on his pursuers, Pare and Eriane would have the chance to get some closure for all Samuel had already cost them.

Chapter Twenty-Eight

Sleep had come and gone without notice. Exhaustion could sometimes be a blessing, the body's needs overriding the mind and heart's unease. Eriane was the last to wake, gently prodded by Pare, wakefulness bringing the sting of remembrance. Eriane choked back the tightness in her throat and buried the previous day with a deep breath.

After only a short walk, their trail opened up on the main road, where they paused under a blanket of light gray clouds. A right turn would take them back down through the foothills and into Morrelton. To the left was the road to the pass, taking them into the mountains and on to Kelef.

Pare had closed his eyes and paused, but Eriane made the decision for them by stepping out onto the left-hand path. Jacob started off in her wake, with Samuel close to follow. Pare scrambled to catch up, sliding past Samuel to take up a spot behind Eriane and Jacob as they talked.

"So, what was that we saw back in the cave?" Eriane asked Jacob. Her breath was visible in the morning air and her nose ached from the cold.

"It was gathered *khet*," Jacob said, "probably Drift. When someone translocates, they're using *khet* to bridge two places and jump between them. It leaves a trail, a sort of…hole. It's not visible, and normal things like air or fog won't be affected by it. But someone on the other end released Drift, which was drawn into the trail."

"For someone to have enough to just release some in that way," Pare said, "they must have a stockpile. And you don't pull together that much through well-meaning methods."

"I watched this guy give Michael the breath back in Morrelton. And what he did to Atherton..." Jacob trailed off and shook his head to clear away the image. "There's nothing well-meaning about him or his methods."

Eriane let the silence hang, gathering the courage to ask the next question. "Was there nothing you could do for Atherton?" she asked.

Jacob's teeth ground and his posture alone gave Eriane her answer before he even spoke. "I was...already a wanted man in Morrelton. To expose myself, especially to these two, would've landed me in jail, or worse. Besides, Atherton—" He shook his head, and Eriane sensed he'd cut himself off. He looked over his shoulder at Pare. "So how far is it to the pass?" he said, deflecting any further discussion of the topic.

"It'll take us the better part of daylight," Pare said. "We could probably make it to the mouth of the pass a little faster if we push it."

"We shouldn't need to, today," Jacob said. "We shouldn't dawdle, though. How far to Kelef?"

Pare shrugged. "Kind of depends on the condition of the road. Once we're in the pass, the road narrows and there are a lot of places where it's cut right into a cliff face. We're not on horseback and have no carts, though, so it shouldn't be too hard to navigate, unless there's a rockslide." He shivered a little, then looked up at the steel grey sky. "Or it starts snowing in earnest."

The day passed Samuel by, the road growing a little steeper with every passing hour. The group soldiered on, no one willing to express any desire to stop or rest. Eriane handed out small pieces of bread and cheese, and they ate and took drinks from their canteens as they walked.

The forest began to thin, the soft loam of the forest floor giving way to gravel and rock outcroppings, and the trees themselves taking on a craggy, rugged look. The road grew narrower and harder, curving through the lowest points between the foothills that were now growing into genuine mountains. Around a corner the road straightened, pointing at a narrow switchback that worked its way up a steep face before cutting into a cleft at the top.

They all stopped to take in the sight. Although none complained about the walk, it was evident how tired they all were, and how daunting the switchback seemed. Jacob stepped off to the side of the road, plopping down to sit on a medium-sized boulder and stretching out his back.

"Well," Eriane said, "let's get on with it."

"Are you sure you don't want to rest for a bit?" Samuel asked. Eriane stopped and looked back.

"That sounds like a brilliant idea to me," Jacob said. One of his boots sat next to the boulder on the ground, and he was rubbing his foot.

Eriane glanced over at him, then back to Pare. "What do you think, Pare?"

Pare considered the cleft in the rocks, weighing his options while Jacob looked on with an expectant expression. "I'd rather get to the top and worry about rest after we get there. The going's easier once we're through that gap."

Eriane nodded and turned to continue. Jacob rolled his head back and sighed before pulling his boot back on and stepping up next to Samuel, leaning in close. "What do you think?" he asked.

Samuel wasn't sure what the actual question was. "About what?" he said.

"Master Pariadnus up there," Jacob said.

Samuel knew what Jacob was getting at, but he bit anyway. "I think I'm glad he decided to come along. This trip would have been a lot harder without him. And I see how his presence lifts up Eriane. I don't know how we would have handled all this had he not joined us."

"Oh, I don't know," Jacob said. "I don't think you give that girl enough credit. She's strong...and smart. What she did back at the waterfall was hard for her, but it was exactly what needed to happen for Pare to come along."

"Maybe you're right," Samuel said, watching the two of them up ahead as they bantered. "But having him along is still a good influence on her."

"Are you sure we can trust him?" Jacob asked.

Samuel hesitated. "You're an odd one to ask that question," he said.

Jacob eyed the road at his feet and nodded. "I suppose I deserved that," he said.

"Why *did* you come back?" Samuel asked, surprising himself at how soon the question surfaced. "What part do you want in all of this?"

"I told you before, Samuel. I abhor boredom. And you're anything but boring." Jacob grinned. "Besides, after what those two did in Morrelton, I couldn't exactly just leave you to them, now could I?"

"Took you long enough to get there," Samuel said. He hoped it sounded at least a little snarky.

"Hey!" Jacob put on a face of mock offense. "I didn't even know where you were! It's not like there's signs guiding people out to that cabin, you know. Besides, I spent some time after we parted making sure neither of us could be followed." He shook his head. "At least not by anyone less crafty than these guys."

The thought of the cabin pulled at Samuel and he slowed his pace. As angry as he had been at Jacob since the alley in Morrelton, his experiences since and the scope of the danger they were in made his actions toward the thief feel petty. "Jacob...I'm sorry," he said. It was the first time he'd spoken Jacob's real name, and with that one word, he felt a world of tension lift from between them.

"For what?" Jacob replied, astonished.

"For Morrelton," Samuel said.

Jacob put up his hand and shook his head. "I know I'm not always the easiest person to trust, Samuel, so don't sweat it."

Samuel nodded. "I have to ask you, though... What was it you took from Cort?"

"Retrieved," Jacob reminded him.

"Retrieved," Samuel repeated.

"Someday, my friend," Jacob said. "I'll tell you that story. But today is not that day." He smiled, then bounded up the trail to where Pare and Eriane were talking.

Samuel's eyes followed him as he went, then slid past the group and on to the cliff-face before them, up and up. They had covered almost the entire distance to the mouth of the pass, and the switchbacks leading up loomed above. This would be the most physically taxing part of their journey and, even though Samuel knew he would barely notice it, it looked daunting even to him.

As they all stood staring at the path in front of them, Pare was the first to break the silence. He looked at Jacob, motioning toward the top of the cliff face. "Why don't you just...you know?"

Jacob shook his head. "I'm still burned from yesterday," he said. "On any other day it might be possible, but I just translocated farther than I ever have, carrying the largest load I've ever carried." Jacob looked up, seeming almost to consider it before dismissing the idea. "I can't. Even if I could get us up there, I'd be too prone to mistakes. If it were just me, maybe, but the lot of us... The last thing any of us need is to come out the other end halfway through a tree. Besides, I wouldn't want to make it too easy for you now, would I?" Jacob's grin seemed designed just to put Pare's teeth on edge.

Pare's eyes narrowed and by the time Jacob had finished, Eriane was already halfway up the first switchback. "Hey! Wait for us!"

The Chronicler Saga

Chapter Twenty-Nine

The road leading up the face wasn't treacherous — it was wide enough for a cart or wagon to navigate, with large turnabouts at the ends — but it was steep. Before long Pare, Eriane, and Jacob were sweating, their backs bowed with the effort of the climb. None of them spoke as they trudged along, everyone concentrating on just putting one foot in front of the other.

Samuel watched each of them deal with their own exhaustion in different ways. Pare hunched over, soldiering forward without lifting his head or changing his pace. Eriane fell in behind him and used him as a guide, losing pace every so often to scratch an itch or mop her brow, then pushing harder to catch back up. Jacob took intentional breaks, stopping to stretch his back and shoulders before pushing back up to the group. None of them spoke of stopping to rest, though, all intent on reaching the top.

When they reached the last bend where the road entered the gap at the top of the cliff-face, the pace quickened. Samuel wasn't sure how long it had taken them to reach the top, but once they broke through onto the plateau above there was a sigh of relief and the three of them collapsed onto the ground beside the road.

A snowflake fluttered down and landed on Jacob's upturned cheek. "Well, I'm not sure I'm so happy about that," he said. The others looked up as a few more flakes followed the first out of the bright white sky.

"We shouldn't rest long," Pare said. "We should cover as much ground as possible before much of this comes down, and if enough of it falls it might just slow up anyone coming in behind."

"Damn bugs!" Eriane said, scratching behind her ear before pulling out her canteen and taking a long draught. She passed it to Jacob, who took a drink and passed it along to Pare.

"I haven't gotten bit," Jacob said, smiling at her. "Bugs must just like you, for some reason."

Pare was in the middle of taking a drink when he stopped himself, inspecting something on the side of the canteen. Without a word he stood up and bolted over to Eriane. "Eri, show me your hands."

"What?" She said.

"Your hands. Now!" Pare said.

Eriane held her hands out for Pare, who grabbed her right wrist. There was blood on the tips of her fingers. Her eyes went wide, and she reached back behind her right ear, coming away with even more blood. The color drained from her face.

"How long have you been scratching?" Pare asked her.

Eriane's eyes flitted about, searching. "I... don't..."

"How long, Eri!"

"M-maybe halfway up? I think?" she said.

Pare backed off and began mumbling and pacing.

"Pare I..." Eri stammered. "I didn't know... I thought..."

Jacob was on his feet, running to the edge of the cliff beside the road, with Samuel close behind. The entire valley opened up before them, almost all the way back to Morrelton, and Samuel's eyes followed the road as it wound back into the woods. Nothing stirred save the wind in the trees and the birds.

"There," Samuel said, pointing. Movement on the road, a long way away, but not far enough. The rest could barely see, but a group of people rounded a corner and appeared in an opening for only a moment, and then moved back under the cover of branches.

"Damnit. How could they be so close?" Jacob spat. "How could they know?"

Samuel moved back to Eriane's side. "What does this mean?" she said, holding out her bloodied fingers.

"It means their breaker is close enough to start working on us," Pare said.

Eriane took in a sharp breath.

"Then we have to get moving," Jacob said as he and Samuel returned from the edge. "As fast and as hard as our legs will take us, we have to go." Eriane kept nodding. The two of them headed back to the road and Samuel followed.

Pare was pacing, his hand on his forehead. "Think, think, think," he kept saying to himself.

Jacob had picked up the packs, and was holding Pare's out for him. "We can think later, Pare. Right now, we have to run."

"No, no," Pare said. "You don't understand. If he can reach our protections from this distance, then we have to stall him. Running won't do any good—he'll just keep working until he breaks through."

"Then what do we do?" Samuel asked.

Eriane made a noise, like a scream cut short, and slapped her hand over her right ear.

Pare was at her side, looking over her with a mixture of fear and confusion. "No no no no no..." he was saying, to no one in particular. "Not so soon!" he muttered, standing again and staring down at Eri.

Eriane dropped to her knee with a gasp. "Pare, hurry!" she said.

Pare had both hands in his hair, stalking like a caged animal. Eriane was breathing hard, her eyes closed and her hands trembling.

"Come on, Pare," Jacob said, kneeling and putting an arm around Eriane. Pare didn't even register, instead continuing to mutter to himself.

Eriane let out another strangled cry and pitched forward onto her hand. Pare bolted back, skidding to a halt on his knees in front of her. He reached forward and gently lifted her chin in his hands. She looked at him through wet, unfocused eyes.

"Eri?" Pare said, as though she couldn't hear him. "I'm going to try something that'll stop this, and stall the breaker. Eri?" She gave a weak nod. "Look, Eri... This is going to hurt, okay? There's no way I can stop him without it hurting you, too."

She nodded again, and forced out some words which came out in more of a croak than in her voice. "Couldn't be much worse," she quipped. She slammed her eyes shut and groaned through clenched teeth.

Jacob moved away, dashing back to the edge to look down on their pursuers. Samuel watched as Pare put his hands around the base of Eriane's head again, much the same way he had in order to set the protection in the first place. He closed his eyes and pressed his forehead against hers. She grabbed his wrist with her free hand. He took a deep breath and let it out, very slowly, then took another and held it. Eriane's eyes and mouth snapped open and she froze, as though she were suffocating and trying to pull in air. And then Samuel felt it.

BOOM.

But it wasn't a sound, and there was no concussion. It resonated through all of them. Like a thunderclap that surrounded them and pressed in on them, the *boom* hit hard and then rebounded outward. Eriane screamed and Pare almost couldn't catch her as she fainted, because he wasn't in much better shape. The echoes of a terrible scream, cut off as quickly as it had started, reached them on their perch from the valley below.

Jacob was back by Samuel's side, and the two of them looked down on Pare as he held the unconscious Eriane in his arms. Her head lolled to the side and there was blood running over her mouth from her nose. Pare's eyes were half-closed and he was panting from effort, but he looked up at the two of them and nodded.

"I think that worked," Pare said.

Colton had kept them at a relentless pace after their initial night's rest, jogging up the Morrelton road in pursuit of their fleeing prey. There was, of course, no argument from Bales, and he kept up without complaint. Without a word, in fact, which Colton thought was a nice change of pace. To their credit, the mercenaries at their back also kept up well, the promise of payday spurring them forward.

They knew they were getting close when Bales had sensed the protective constructions ahead of them, shielding their quarry from

Colton's senses. Bales characterized the protections as crude, but powerful, and noted he'd have to work on them carefully to avoid detection. Once one of the protections was down, Colton was in, and this whole ordeal would come to a messy close.

They jogged along while Bales worked, half of the time with his eyes closed, navigating the road better blind than some of the mercenaries were with their eyes open. He'd found the one chink in the armor and had begun working on it several hours prior, but had stumbled over his attempt multiple times.

"Well?" Colton said, for what must have been the tenth time. When Colton had tried to question him before, Bales just shooed him away. This time, though, the breaker's eyes opened and his face split into a greasy smile.

"I think I've got—"

BOOM.

It came from somewhere ahead, high above, and traveled with frightening speed. All of them felt it, like a gathering wave, rolling through the forest, intensifying as it came. Bales doubled forward with his hands over his ears, splitting the mountain air with a feral scream.

His wailing cut off when a fountain of blood sprayed out from his nose, all across the front of Colton's coat as Bales was lifted off of his feet. It was as though a giant hammer had struck him from where he stood, launching him into the air and over the heads of the others behind him, to land in a hard heap in the center of the road about thirty feet away. Even Colton stood stunned at the ferocity of it.

As Colton moved to check on him, Bales groaned and rolled, trying to get a hand down to push himself up off the ground. Colton was simultaneously relieved and disappointed at Bales's movement, but couldn't deny how much he would need the breaker if his target could fight back on this level. Bales turned himself around and sat up, his entire front covered in blood. He ran an arm across his face under his nose to clear some of it away and winced. His cheeks showed signs of swelling.

Colton crouched down and looked at him, but couldn't hide his own satisfied smirk. "I see they've chosen to fight back," he said.

Bales leaned forward and placed a thumb on the side of his nose, closed off a nostril and blew hard out of the open one, splattering

Colton's boots with more blood. "I'm going to kill them. With my own bare hands." With a deliberate movement, he closed off his other nostril and repeated his action. It was Bales's turn at the satisfied smirk. Colton turned his back and stalked away.

Chapter Thirty

Sounds came back first, before Eriane could open her eyes. An eerie quiet, cut only by fast footfalls and rustling clothing. She felt herself swaying rhythmically back and forth, listening to the sound of the footsteps. She took a deep breath and opened her eyes. It was bright, the sky above her stark white and shining right on her face. Snowflakes were falling all around her. It was almost peaceful.

Until the pounding in her head came crashing back, and her stomach lurched. She clenched her jaw and fought back the bile in her throat. Her nose hurt, like she'd been punched in the face. When she tried to reach up and touch it, she found her arms swaddled close to her body in her cloak. She turned her eyes on the brown blur above her, and Samuel's face came into focus.

He's carrying me. She kept looking at him, like somehow that would answer all her questions. Instead, she grew more confused, and wanted to know where they were going. Her dry throat prevented her from speaking, so she turned her head to see where they were. Something pounded in her head like she had sloshed her brain against the side of her skull. Her stomach turned harder, and this time she vomited into the snow.

She wanted to apologize to Samuel, but couldn't form the words. The world went black again.

They were still running, but the sky had turned from bright white to a charcoal grey, snow still coming down around them. The sound of the footfalls had changed from a scuffling to a crunching, and she could see a long cliff face stretching up away from them on one side.

She turned her head much slower this time, and saw a dark figure further up the trail, keeping pace at a solid jog, trudging through the deepening snow. She followed the line of the cliff face up to the left, then saw no such barrier on the right, and turned her head further, only to see the road to their right fall sharply away, a valley stretching far below.

Her heart caught in her throat and her muscles locked with a wave of vertigo. She whipped her head back around and closed her eyes tight, which only made her swoon and her insides turn to liquid. She tried to calm herself but couldn't catch her breath, so she pulled herself in as close as she could to Samuel's chest and tried to take slower breaths. He pulled his metal arms in closer, tightening his hold on her as they trudged through the falling snow.

Her breathing slowed and her mind wobbled, and after a moment she again descended into darkness.

When Eriane awoke again, they were no longer moving. She was warmer than the last time, and smelled woodsmoke. When she opened her eyes this time, she wasn't in Samuel's arms, but bundled up in her cloak on the ground, with something soft supporting her head. A low campfire of small sticks threw weak orange light onto the walls of what looked like a tall cave.

She coughed once, trying to clear her throat, and Jacob came into view. "Look who's awake," he said, his voice soft and concerned.

She cleared her throat again and attempted to speak. "Won't they smell it?" The effort of a yell produced only a whisper.

Jacob smiled. "Ever the pragmatist," he said. He gestured to the walls of the cave. "It's more of a crack than a cave, and luckily the air flow carries our smoke back and up rather than out toward the pass."

"Why are we stopped?" she whispered.

"We needed rest," Jacob said. "Pare's asleep. Samuel's on watch at the mouth of the crevice."

"What about you?"

"Just can't sleep," he said. He put a hand on the side of her head, so soft it didn't even hurt her like she thought it might. "Close your eyes, Eri."

She did just that.

Eriane heard someone crying from where she stood. She turned around and saw a boy kneeling on the ground before her, facing away. Heaving sobs echoed off of unseen walls, somewhere off in the black. As she moved closer she saw he was leaning over a body—no, *clutching* a body to his chest—and crying.

The young girl he held wasn't moving. The front of her sun dress was covered in red splatter. One step closer and she saw two more bodies lying just beyond. A stout older man lay face up on the ground, and a reedy thin middle-aged woman lay across his chest, her face touching the ground. The boy stopped sobbing, taking in a slow breath. His head turned, his puffy eyes boring into hers.

"You did this to them," Pare said, his voice so loud it hurt her ears. "You did this to *me*."

She had no words to respond to him, she only stared as he lay the young girl down in a pool of her own blood and then stood to face her. He held his hands open, palms toward her, out low to his sides and covered in the young girl's blood.

"You did this to me," he repeated.

"No, Pare!" she cried. "I didn't... I didn't..."

He nodded his head toward her. "You did. You did this to me!"

Eriane looked down and saw her pistols in her hands, smoke trailing from the tips of both. Horrified, she threw them to the ground and stepped toward Pare. "NO! I didn't do this!"

He nodded once and the pistols were again in her hands. This time, when she tried to throw them away, she found she couldn't move. Her eyes tracked back up to Pare, whose hands clenched in claw shapes at his sides.

"You did this to me!" he screamed as he advanced on her. She tried to say something but her voice failed. Pare closed down his fingers, and she felt his power constrict around her, crushing away her breath.

His eyes flashed blue and his skin turned black. His jaw elongated, revealing rows of sharp white teeth. His arms thinned and his shirt burst from the back where two curved horns grew from his shoulder blades, coming to points beside his head. His hideous form terrified her, but all she wanted was to tell him it wasn't her, that she didn't do it. His grip on her tightened and she knew she would die, with him breathing his carrion breath into her face.

"YOU DID THIS TO ME!!"

He closed his fists.

"Eri! ERI!" A raspy voice drew her awake.

There was a hand over her mouth. Something held her down, her arms pinned to her sides and a weight on her chest. She struggled, trying to break free. Her eyes focused on Pare's face, close to hers, shushing her. She took a deep breath and relaxed.

Pare took his hand away from her mouth and released the restraint on her body, and Jacob knelt beside her. Samuel stood behind both of them, looking down and then back over his shoulder.

"I'm sorry," she said.

"That must've been a pretty intense nightmare," Jacob said.

Eriane eyed Pare, his look of concern marred by the images from her dream. She exhaled a stuttering breath through her nostrils and nodded.

"How do you feel?" Pare asked.

Her head wasn't spinning anymore, and her belly seemed to have settled. The headache was still there, but it was just a dull throb now. She pushed herself into a sitting position. It didn't make her sick. "Better, I think." It was her full voice this time, and not a whisper.

Jacob handed her a tin cup with cold, clean water. She took a tentative sip, then gulped the rest down and held the cup out to Jacob, gesturing for more. "I'm starving," she said.

Pare stepped away, and when he returned he handed her a bread roll and some dried venison from the provisions they'd cobbled together in the cabin. She tried not to scarf it down in one bite.

"Do you think you can walk?" Pare asked.

She did a quick mental check and didn't find any immediate problems, and swallowed a mouthful of bread. "Guess I'll find out," she said. She finished the last of the bread and venison and pulled her legs under herself.

Once she was standing, Jacob was at her side, steadying her. Pare had a hand on her shoulder and looked right into her eyes.

"I'm fine, Pare," she said, feeling weak but able to walk.

"Are you sure?" he said.

That question always annoyed her and made her feel good, all at once. "Yes, Pariadnus," she said. "I'm fine. At least as fine as I'm going to be, for now. And if I'm not, you'll be the first to know."

Pare hesitated, then nodded and took his hand away. With a hand on Jacob's arm she gave him a gentle nudge, and he stepped away, so she could try a few steps on her own. Her legs weren't as wobbly as she expected, so she walked up to Samuel and put a hand on his chest.

"Now that we're rested, we have to get going," Pare said.

"Okay," Eriane agreed. Her knees softened for a moment and Samuel caught her, a querying tilt to his head. She patted his hand and moved past, sidling up behind Pare at the entrance to the crack where they camped.

"We've got a ways to go until the road to Kelef," Pare said. "And hopefully the snow has slowed them down enough we can build a lead."

"Then let's get going," Eriane said, now sick of the delays. She wished they'd all stop looking at her like she was about to break in half, and just get on with it. Pare was still looking when she pushed him out onto the road.

The Chronicler Saga

Chapter Thirty-One

The wind picked up, swirling powdery snow around Eriane's feet and buffeting the lot of them against the cliff face as they trudged along. Conditions had worsened overnight; snow was piling up in their path, covering obstacles and making footing treacherous. Samuel took the lead now, barreling through the calf-deep snow and acting both as a wind-break and a plow. The drop to their right had her heart in her stomach, and even with Samuel cutting a trail, Eriane's feet seemed to find every crack and rock in the road. She stumbled once or twice, which wasn't helping the looks she was getting from Pare and Jacob.

The curving road followed the line of the incline into which it had been carved. It felt like they'd been pushing forward all day, but in truth Eriane had no idea how much time had passed. As the day wore on and her feet and fingers and the parts of her face not covered by her scarf got colder and colder, each moment extended into an eternity. Every bend looked the same, bringing a frustrating sense of déjà vu.

And yet they kept going, bundled in all the winter clothes they had been able to gather. Reaching the road to Kelef was all she allowed herself to think about. When her mind wandered to what might come after, or what would happen if *they* caught up, she started to shut down, just wanting to curl up in a heap and sink into everything that had happened to them. But that was unacceptable.

After another one of the endless bends in the road, Eriane felt a tap on her shoulder and stopped. She turned and saw Pare's eyes peeking out from behind the cloth mask he wore wrapped around his face under his hood. He didn't speak, but instead pointed out into the expanse of snow and void that had hovered to their right all day long. They had turned a bend that showed her their path, and she could see a great distance of the road extending out behind them until it finally disappeared around another curve.

She looked back at Pare, his eyes betraying the smile hidden by his mask. Being able to see their progress made her feel at least a little better about the cold clawing at her bones. Jacob almost ran into the two of them where they had stopped, his head bowed and his gloved hand holding his hood shut around his face to ward off the cold. Samuel stopped several paces ahead, and the four of them looked out across the chasm at where they had been.

The cold faded to the background as Eriane took in the sight of it, the massive mountain stretching up and away, the empty expanse below them filling with white. It was a humbling scene, awesome and beautiful in the swirling snow, and all she could do was marvel at those who had come before, those who had forged the path across this pass and carved a trail for others to follow, until Samuel came clomping back to them in his own footsteps.

The construct leaned around Eriane and tapped Jacob on the shoulder, then pointed out into the storm. Eriane and Pare both followed the direction of his outstretched arm along the road all the way to where they could barely see it disappear. Pare moved behind Eri, a hand on her shoulder and closer to Samuel's arm.

Eriane couldn't see anything save snow and rocks, until a gust of wind blew through the chasm and cleared the way for just a moment. Pare's grip tightened on her shoulder, and there they were: several figures—little more than black dots against the white snow—moving around the bend along the same road, pushing forward in their trail. With as long as Eriane had been unconscious, she wasn't sure if they'd gained ground or not, but they were closer than she expected—or wanted—them to be.

Pare pulled down his mask and leaned close to her. "They're

gaining," he said, yelling over the howling wind.

"How is that possible?" Jacob asked.

Pare's look was exasperated. "How am I supposed to know?" he said. Jacob just looked back across the expanse.

"They're going to catch up," Eriane said.

"We need to find a way to slow them down," Jacob said. "How close are we to the Kelef road?"

Pare leaned around Samuel and looked ahead. "I'm not entirely sure," he said. "Especially in this…" He gestured up at the sky and let the statement hang.

"Then the best we can do right now is pick up the pace," Samuel said. "We can't defend ourselves here. Maybe there's something up ahead that can help us against them."

Eriane wasn't even sure what to make of the conversation. Their discussions had shifted from pushing through to Kelef to finding a defensive position in the pass. All the thoughts she didn't want to have came tumbling through. *Where did you think all of this was leading?*

"Come on," Samuel said. "Stay close behind me and keep up."

Samuel set off at a trot, blasting the snow away as though he didn't even notice it. Eriane focused on his feet and powered on, thinking of nothing but keeping close to him. She could hear the metallic clank of his feet and knees as they came down hard in the snow, even over the sound of the wind. She couldn't hear the others behind her, but at this pace she dared not look back, for fear of losing her footing or one of them running into her.

Their path had been a steady uphill climb all day, but the new tempo brought that climb into sharp focus. It wasn't long before the muscles in her thighs burned, and when she shifted her gait to compensate, her calves followed suit. Even breathing through her scarf had begun drawing frozen air, chafing her throat and nostrils. No matter how much she wanted to, she couldn't stop, couldn't let up. She couldn't let Samuel down, especially not now. She blinked some of the cold out of her eyes and gathered her second wind.

They passed under a large outcrop and, for the first time all day, she saw a few scraggly trees above them, growing out of a crack in the rocks on the incline. The ridgeline was much closer now, only about fifty feet above them. A sharp whistle over the gale pulled her and Samuel up short. Pare and Jacob had stopped just past the outcropping, and were standing against the cliff wall talking. She couldn't hear what they said, but Pare gestured toward the trees and the ridgeline. She looked back at Samuel and waved for him to follow her back to Pare.

"What's going on?" she asked as she approached.

"I'm not so sure about this, Pare," Jacob said.

"We don't have a lot of choice," Pare said. "If they're gaining at that rate, they'll be on us soon. Can you do it?"

Jacob stepped out away from the rock wall, looking up at the top of the ridge. He moved up the road a ways, still examining the same spot. Eriane just watched him, confused, until he returned to the group. "I think I can, yeah," he said to Pare.

Pare looked back up the road, into the snow that had become a whiteout in the pass. He took a deep breath and looked right at Jacob. "Then do it."

Eriane looked back at Jacob, who nodded without responding. "What are you doing?" she said, looking back at Pare.

"We have a plan," Pare said, the wind over Eriane's shoulder blowing back his hood.

"What plan?" Eriane said, turning back to Jacob.

But he was already gone.

Chapter Thirty-Two

Colton spurred the mercenaries before him, giving them a subtle boost that kept them at a steady, high pace. They were close enough the tracks left by their prey hadn't snowed in. The groove cut by the group ahead made going easier, but not by much. The sellswords were heartier than Colton expected, and driven by their goal and the payday that would follow. Luckily for Colton, none of them would realize how far past their limits he had pushed them until it was too late.

As usual, Bales was on edge, insistent they move faster, pacing at the back of the group like a wildcat held back from a kill. His cheeks had swollen and turned a nasty shade of mottled purple and yellow, but his bloodshot eyes were still wide open, unblinking.

"Can you feel them yet?" Colton yelled over the gale.

Bales glared over his shoulder. "No," he snapped. "And if you ask me again, I'll teach you how to fly." His face was still covered in blood, and any exposed skin that wasn't purple was turning red and chafing in the chill. The effect would have been comical had he not looked so feral, but Colton was still taking joy in Bales's earlier defeat.

"Look at the tracks, Bales," Colton said. "Less and less snow as we go, and now we're close. We need to know *how* close." The mercenaries slowed their pace.

Bales looked back again, then turned forward and bowed his head.

A muffled grunt escaped his lungs and he drove the heel of his hand into his temple. A new trickle of blood escaped his nose, and his eyes snapped open. "I can't. It's too much."

"I don't like going into this blind," Colton said. "You can't break one of them?"

Bales rolled his eyes. "You're asking a man with two broken arms to swim," he said. "I can't even find them, much less"—his eyes closed in pain and he turned, staining the pristine snow with a dark red clot from one nostril—"much less try and break anything." He pinched his nose with his forefinger and thumb. "I think that little sot physically broke my nose."

"I guess we do this the old fashioned way, then," Colton said. Again, the mercenaries slowed their pace. When Bales noticed, he spun on Colton, grabbing his cloak and forcing a forearm into his chest.

"Don't you dare slow them down," Bales said. "You keep them moving until they drop."

"They're no good to us if they don't make it, Bales," Colton said.

"Then you keep them standing as long as you can. I want this over with."

Colton gave Bales a little shove and nodded forward, indicating how far ahead the mercenaries now were. Bales sped to catch up, with Colton taking the rear. They rounded the next corner and the whole party came to a halt. It looked like Bales would get his wish.

Ahead of them in the road, a cloaked figure knelt in the snow, tending to another, smaller one who sat against the rock face, holding a knee in both hands and rocking in evident pain. Bales reached back and grabbed Colton's shoulder. Colton could feel him shaking. Right behind the two in the trail stood an ancient-looking construct, clad in armored plates that made it look like some sort of archaic war machine.

"That has to be it," Bales said, almost a whisper.

Colton nodded. "Then let's end this and get back to someplace warm, shall we?"

Colton's thugs advanced and the kneeling cloak stood up, wheeling about in the road. The other also stood and moved back behind the construct, who stepped up, taking a protective stance. The one in front made a circular motion with both hands, the snow in front of him swirling as though caught in a vortex that grew and grew until it cleared most of the powder from the path.

The mercenary in front broke rank, drawing a smallsword and rushing forward with an idiotic scream. There was only so much control Colton could exert before being found out, and the exertion of controlling this many in any meaningful way wasn't worth the effort, so he let the man go. The whirlwind swept forward, slinging the man outward over the chasm before pulling him back around and slamming him hard into the rock wall, where he slumped unconscious into the snow. The display surprised both Colton and Bales.

"Hold, men," Colton said to his posse. He stepped forward to address his opponent. "Well done!" he said, sounding something close to genuine. "There is no need for this to escalate, though. Give us the construct and we'll be on our way, and you can be on yours."

A pause. "Yeah? Is that all it would take?" Colton heard from the cloak, and was again surprised; it was just a boy.

"Let us have him," Colton said, "and we'll help you and your injured friend back to town."

"Well," the boy said. "That *is* a very interesting offer. How do I know you'll keep your word?"

Colton nodded. "A fair question, simply answered: I have no quarrel with you, or your friend. This construct has committed a grievous offense, for which it must atone."

There was a gap of silence, filled by whistling wind. The boy looked over his shoulder at the construct, contemplating, and his companion stepped out.

"No, you can't!" The voice was delicate—a young girl. The surprises just kept piling on.

"The two of you don't have any idea what you're wrapped up in," Colton said. "You can still step away from this, unharmed. This construct has to pay for what he has done."

Another silent breath, the boy mulling over his answer. His head waved back and forth, contemplating his construct companion and Colton's crew, appearing to weigh his options. The young girl just shook her head. The construct didn't move.

The boy turned back to Colton. "For what he has done," he said, "or what he has *seen?*"

Colton shook his head, lowering his eyes to the snow. "That, my young friend, was a mistake." Every man in front of Colton was stretched taut, about to snap. Bales seethed at the back of the pack, his chest heaving under heavy breaths with his quarry in sight. Colton raised his head and the mercenaries began to advance when a movement caught his eye. A small rock bounced down the cliff face from an outcropping above.

"Back!" Colton yelled. Throwing his power outward he clenched his hands and pulled, the entire group sliding toward him in the snow. A rock the size of a man's torso slammed into the road and broke in two, the pieces bouncing off into the abyss. The whole group looked up to see where it had come from, taking their eyes off the boy and his companions.

In that moment of distraction, the man in front screamed, impaled in the thigh and hip by thick icicles. The boy across the way loosed another volley and Colton stepped up, sweeping the projectiles aside with an impertinent gesture. "You're out of your depth, boy," he said, twisting the last word. "Even with your friend up top, we'll get what we want."

As if on cue, a hail of fist-sized rocks came down on top of the hunters, but stopped short by an unseen barrier a few feet above their heads. Bales grunted with effort, his barrier having done its job but having also taken a toll.

One of the mercenaries drew a mafi-stick and lifted it before his face, light twisting from beneath the cuff of his coat and into the thin black rod. He hauled back over his shoulder and heaved it forward. Instead of tumbling end over end like Colton expected, the baton shot straight and true, like a fired arrow only twice as fast, and struck the construct square in the chest, knocking him onto his back with a great plume of snow. The mafi stick returned to the man's hand with a slap.

"Samuel!" the girl screamed, rushing to the construct, who was trying to pull itself up to a sitting position.

Colton turned to the mercenary. "Nice throw," he said. The gruff man grinned. "I knew I was paying you imbeciles for something." The smile drained away at Colton's backhanded compliment.

Bales turned. "Samuel."

Colton nodded. "Move forward!" he yelled. "And don't worry about falling rocks." He looked at Bales, who gave a curt nod and, with straining effort, raised another bump field.

The group started moving again, eyeing their downed companion against the rock wall. Even the man who'd been hit by the icicles made his way forward, prodded by Colton a little harder than the rest. A few more rocks came down from above, creating sparkling blue flashes as they struck Bales's overhead shield. The boy made another attempt at drawing the wind, but with a simple gesture, his effort was broken apart by Colton's counter. A rain of dirt and needles deflected harmlessly away above them, and Colton began to wonder if it could really be this easy.

The thought had only just formed when Bales let out a grunting cry, and the forward end of his field was torn apart by the weight of an entire fir tree falling upside-down from on high. The top of the tree struck close to the wall and it toppled over the two men at the front of the party. Soil-laden roots carried the tree over the cliffside with the two men still tangled in the branches, screaming as they fell away into the chasm.

As their howling faded, the boy, fingers curled at his sides, made a pulling motion and the next two men lurched forward, falling on their faces in the snow. Bales was on his knees panting. Colton tried to raise his hands to offer up another counter, but found them pinned. Then, the whole world came crashing down the hillside.

Their plan had gone almost exactly as Pare had told her it would.

Even as the ruse played out, Eriane had been unprepared to confront the scarred face of the silver-eyed from Samuel's visions. His stature exuded menace, even at this distance, and Eriane had no interest in finding out what else he was capable of. The others all looked like hired hands, the kind of men who would drink and do business in the parts of Morrelton Pare and Eriane were told to avoid. Pare smirked when he saw the man in the back, his face swollen and covered in dried and frozen blood. "That must be their breaker," Eriane said. Pare nodded.

When the first rock came down, their enemy was caught off-guard but it missed its target, and their breaker raised a bump field to cover their advance. The hurled mafi-stick took them all by surprise, especially Samuel, who lay on his back in the snow trying to recover. Even after the unexpected attack, Pare still held back, drawing only on the nature around him for simple constructions of wind and ice—things Eriane knew he could do in his sleep, especially in a place with those two elements in such abundance. It was his way of feigning weakness, and it worked to draw the group in, further under the outcrop.

It seemed almost too simple to Eriane, the idea of just dropping rocks and debris down onto the advancing party as they stepped into the danger zone. Pare had kept something from her, though, and she had no idea what to expect when the tree came down, shattering the bump field and taking two men with it over the side. Pare and Jacob's combined efforts had managed to take out three of the men, but four more still stood, the falling tree causing them a moment's hesitation.

Pare's muscles tensed and Eriane saw the men at the front of the pack fall forward into the path. The others stood frozen in Pare's clutches but didn't fall, and she saw Pare struggle to keep his hold. His feet slid forward in the snow just as the loudest *CRACK* she'd ever heard split the air apart.

Rocks and debris rained down from the cliffside, and to Eriane it seemed like time slowed to a crawl. A huge boulder came down on top of one of the downed men, rolling away covered in red and leaving little recognizable beneath. More and more kept coming, striking closer and closer to Pare. He kept his hold; wouldn't give in. The others tried to break away as more debris came down between them. Eriane looked up to see the outcropping—the *whole thing*—tipping away from the cliff-face, an entire mountainside about to come down on top of them. Pare wouldn't release his hold. Eriane's feet slid as she rushed to his side, pulling around in front of him.

"Pare!" she screamed. "Let go now!"

Blood trickled out of his nose and one ear from the strain. He shook his head. With no time to think, Eriane rushed him, burying her shoulder into his stomach. Fueled by panic, she threw up a bump field just as the impact of a huge pile of rocks and soil and brush blew her forward in a blinding blue flash. The two of them crashed to the ground, detritus sliding away from them to fall into the chasm. Eriane flipped off of Pare and felt herself grabbed by the collar, both her and Pare sliding backward on the road as Samuel pulled them further out of harm's way.

The second crash was more deafening than the first, as the entire bulk of the outcropping struck the road. Rather than disintegrating into a heap, the outcropping kept its shape, the force of its strike crumbling the road beneath it. The noise of it was extraordinary as rocks and trees continued to slide down the hillside, not piling up in the road but instead falling away into the space where the road used to be.

The noise echoed through the chasm for some time as the rockslide continued on below them. When it all finally subsided, the entire space of road between where Pare had stood and where the breaker had held up the back of his group was a yawning void, framed on either side by piles of dirt and rocks. The echoes died down in the swirling snow, punctuated by the occasional clatter of a tumbling rock.

The Chronicler Saga

Chapter Thirty-Three

Snow settled back into the space where there had been only chaos moments before, and the world calmed back down to a cold winter day in the mountains. Pare and Eriane lay on the ground in front of where Samuel sat, both of them panting with their eyes closed, the snow alighting on their faces.

"Are you okay?" he said to them.

Eriane answered first. "I think so."

"Yeah," Pare said. There was a pause, and then he continued. "Thanks."

Samuel looked out at where the road used to be. "Was that the plan?"

"Not exactly," Pare said, pushing himself up to his elbows.

"Seems to have done the job," Samuel said.

Pare pushed himself up further and Samuel got to his feet, offering help which, to his surprise, Pare accepted. Eriane knelt beside the cliff wall trying to catch her breath. Pare and Samuel stepped as close to the edge as they dared, loose dirt sliding away in front of them. What once had been a path carved into the mountain was now just a continuous hillside through a huge gap, with piles of flotsam on either side. Samuel could only see one body across the expanse, but the rubble blocked most of his view of that part of the road. Nothing was moving.

"Jacob!" Pare yelled. "You still up there?"

241

The call was met by a long silence, and Samuel's anxiety spiked. "Jacob?" Samuel followed. "Are you okay?" Still no response.

Pare let out a long breath and shook his head, looking down into the space the slide had created. Samuel looked, too, but wasn't sure what he was looking for—or if he'd want to see whatever he might find. Another friend lost, and more death on Samuel's shoulders. Both of them were shaken out of the onrushing grief by a groan from across the gap, and movement as someone stirred.

"No way," Pare said.

His close-cropped hair was caked with blood, but Samuel could see it was the silver-eyed man who had recovered to his knees, his back to them, next to the other body Samuel had spotted earlier. He absently reached over and shook the other man, who also groaned and, after a moment, sat up with a hand over his eye. With a loud grunt, Silver Eyes forced himself to his feet and stumbled, disoriented. Both Samuel and Pare were transfixed, watching this man will himself upright. The other, a gruff looking man with salt-and-pepper beard, was looking around with his uncovered eye when his gaze stopped on them and lingered.

"Sir," the man said, his voice barely audible.

Silver Eyes froze, then turned around to face them. He took in a sharp breath and walked forward to the edge, threatening to pull them into the break with the sheer force of his hatred. Pare stepped back as though struck. All Samuel wanted was to be on the other side of the gap, to put his hands on this man, fling him over the side, and implore the universe to trade him for all the loss he had wrought.

The other man was on his feet now, and the four of them stood still and silent in the falling snow, staring at one another. The leader's silver eyes were wide and crazy, his nostrils flaring as he fumed. Samuel knew they should turn and run, but neither he nor Pare moved. The bearded mercenary broke the silence.

"What now?" The question was simple, but the scarred one reacted as though he had been stabbed, turning his malevolence on the mercenary. The man stepped back, but not before Silver Eyes had a hand on his chest.

"Now, Samuel," he heard Pare say, his voice low. "We have to go now."

In the space of a breath Pare was already behind Samuel, helping Eriane to her feet. Samuel wanted to leave, but was paralyzed by what he saw. The bearded man had gone rigid, his eyes wide and his mouth open in a soundless scream. Silver Eyes drew his hand away from the man's chest, streams of *khet* following it from all along the mercenary's front, as though he had grabbed the man's skin and was pulling it straight off of his body.

Silver Eyes flicked his hand and the streams of blue power shot across the empty space and struck Samuel in the chest, then wrapped around him and took hold of his torso. The bearded man staggered forward, his breath ragged as he looked up to the scarred one.

"No, no... please, no... don't..."

Samuel took a step back and the bearded man stumbled sideways, the stream having formed a tether between them. He couldn't move without moving the other man, and walking away would drag him off of the edge.

"Come on, Samuel!" Pare said from behind him.

"I can't move, Pare..." Samuel said.

He heard Eriane say "Oh, no..."

"Please, sir...no...please no..." the mercenary begged.

Silver Eyes stared straight at Samuel, ignoring the pleas of his man. He put a hand on the bearded man's shoulder, took a breath, and pushed. The tether slackened as the man floated above the abyss, then snapped taut as he fell to its end, swinging downward and pulling Samuel off balance. His screaming followed his path from below as he passed by, and, at the apex of the swing, the momentum of his fall dragged Samuel over the edge.

The Chronicler Saga

Chapter Thirty-Four

Eriane sat down hard when Pare pushed her aside. He faced the edge, his muscles rigid, white knuckles adorning clenched fists at his sides. A groan escaped his throat between neck muscles drawn into taut cables from his jaw to shoulders. His entire posture took on a backward lean. Sweat beaded on his forehead as his whole body shuddered with the strain.

She scrambled to her feet and ran, kneeling at the edge. Samuel hovered before her in mid-fall above the chasm just below the edge of the road. A tether of blue energy clawed at his torso, extending to suspend the bearded mercenary far below. There was a moment of stillness before Samuel's whole body jerked, shifting a few inches downward before his limbs slammed back into his sides and he stopped again. Pare grunted in pain.

Eriane was on her feet without knowing it. She flung her arms around Pare's waist and pushed. Even with the extra effort she felt him sliding, the weight of Samuel and the tethered mercenary pulling them both toward the edge. Pare took in a coarse breath and tensed against the pull, trying to power through his lack of leverage. Panic set in and she pushed again, hoping to add to his strength. It felt as though she pushed against solid stone.

A new sound scraped across the rocks and echoed around them.

The silver-eyed man watched their struggle from across the gap, laughing. Her face went hot with anger.

Pare's feet slipped again, dragging her backward. They were only a few feet from the edge now. She could hear the mercenary far below pleading with them for help through sobs of fear. She buried her weight into Pare's midsection.

"Don't..." she heard Samuel say. "Don't let me take you over this edge. Pare, just let go."

Eriane's chest tightened. Tears flowed down her face as she pushed against Pare. He grunted again, louder.

"I can't hold it, Eri," Pare said, his voice almost inaudible through gritted teeth.

"Don't you dare let go, Pare!" she screamed. "Don't you dare!" She poured all her strength into holding him up, pushing him away from the edge.

Samuel spoke again. "Eri, don't. If this is where it ends, then it ends with me. Please don't let me take you down with me."

"Shut up, Samuel!" How could he say these things, after what they'd been through? She wrapped her arms around Pare's waist as tight as she could. His breathing was shallow and his body felt like it was forged of steel. His feet slid again and she felt his body jerk back against the pull. Against her ear, she heard one of his ribs crack.

"Eri, I can't," he said.

His jaw trembled and the lower half of his face was covered in blood. She felt his body shudder, his muscles vibrating under the strain. Even with her help, the full weight of the construct and the mercenary bore against them. She stepped back, found a rock to plant her foot against. She put her hands on Pare's chest, shifting to gain more leverage. He grunted in pain.

"You hold him, Pariadnus Jameson," she cried. "You hold him and I'll figure this out." Even as she said it, she knew there was nothing to figure out. None of her knowledge or talents could help here. Her mind raced, but she had nothing to offer. Pare might have something up his sleeve, but in the split second it would take him to release his grip on Samuel and try something different, Samuel would already be lost.

"Eri," Samuel said. "You have to let me go."

She heard herself scream. Her nose ran. Tears froze to her cheeks. Every muscle in her body burned and quavered, and her breathing was ragged. Pare groaned.

"Promise me," Samuel said, "you'll go live your life."

Eriane felt Pare shudder again, and the shaking in his muscles became constant.

"Get away from here—away from them." All she wanted was for Samuel to shut up. "I've already done enough to you. Let me go, leave this all behind, and don't look back."

She began to hyperventilate. She couldn't let go.

"Promise me."

Pare's shaking was getting worse. Their footing was slipping.

"Eri…" Pare whispered.

She closed her eyes and forced in a deep breath. There was only one thing to do now. As the choice settled into her mind, she felt like it would eviscerate her right there in the snow. She looked up at Pare and her throat caught.

"I'm s—" A thump of air struck her in the back. There was a tearing sound and something snapped. Pare's muscles slackened and they were both flung away from the edge, Pare slamming into the cliff wall and cushioning her impact. She heard a scream die away over the edge, and then silence. Pare's strength must have given out, and he must have let go, throwing them backward as the tension of holding on to Samuel's weight was released.

She slumped to the ground over Pare's lap as he sat against the rocks and she began to weep. All she could feel was devastation, and her exhaustion was complete. With no energy for anything else, she just lay in the snow and bawled. To her surprise, she felt Pare's abdomen shake with sobs, as well. She was almost lost in her own sadness when she realized Pare wasn't crying. He was laughing.

It was too much. Pare had never been very fond of Samuel, but how could he be this callous? She flushed with anger again and sat up, about to launch into a tirade at his laughter. He just smiled at her and her anger melted into confusion as he nodded his head and looked over her shoulder. There, slumped against the rock wall in the snow was Samuel, his elbows on his knees and his head in his hands. Next to him, Jacob was on all fours, vomiting into the snow. Ribbons of black energy dissipated around them like steam.

Before any of them had time to register what had happened, a savage scream cut the mountain air. The man with silver eyes, his head thrown back and arms out to his sides, vented his pent up aggravation to the sky. As his head came back level, his eyes fixed on them and he stared, his face inhuman with fury. Movement stirred behind him, and she saw the breaker emerge from under a pile of debris, willing himself upright.

Her vision went red. She was on her feet, her thighs screaming in protest. She stalked toward the edge and fumbled with her winter cloak, clawing to get beneath and draw the pistol that dug into her back. This would end, right here and right now, and damn the cost. The heat of her anger blotted out all sense and her vision tunneled down, so intent on the silver-eyed man that all but his face blurred into nothingness. Her hands worked and worked but she still had not drawn the pistol as she neared the edge of the break left by the falling outcropping. She screamed in frustration and broke her gaze, looking down to see the tangle her probing hands had made of her winter clothes, just as she was enveloped by metal arms.

She was lifted from her feet and carried away from the edge, away from her target, away from the moment that could have put a stop to the entire chase. A wail of anger escaped her throat as she was borne away through the snow, around a bend that took the mercenaries out of her sight just as the breaker stood to watch their retreat next to his companion.

Chapter Thirty-Five

"I thought you let go!"

Jacob sat with his head bowed. Eriane had been alternating between yelling at each of them ever since they'd found a place to rest for the night. Her eyes were bloodshot and baggy, and when she wasn't turning purple in anger, her skin had taken on a pale tinge. Jacob knew she needed to vent, and it seemed like the others did too because they kept quiet and let her go. At the moment, she focused on Pare, but Jacob knew it would be his turn soon enough.

"Eri, come on..." Pare tried to interrupt. He winced and sighed, pulling an arm into his side over his broken rib.

"Don't you start with me, Pariadnus!" she said. "I feel like I'm the only one here who didn't know what was going on!"

"Eri, that's not fair," Samuel said.

"And YOU!" she turned on him. "'*Just walk away.*' What the *was* that?" She was almost hysterical now, but Jacob couldn't help but smirk. "'*Just go live your life.*' Are you joking? What were you even saying?" At that, Jacob let out an audible snort and realized his error too late.

"And YOU..." Now it was his turn. "Where were you? Why this last-second crap!"

"I was unconscious," Jacob replied.

"THAT'S NO EXCUSE!"

With that, Eriane pulled up short. Her eyes closed and she shook her head, sinking to a seated position with her face in her hands. All of them were beyond exhaustion, and for Jacob, the humor in Eriane's rant was gone.

"I'm sorry, Eri," he said. "I got there as fast as I could." When she didn't respond, Jacob nodded to himself and leaned his head back against the cave wall. He couldn't find a comfortable position. Every rock and bump brought to light another spot on his body that flared in pain.

"What *did* happen up there, Jacob?" Pare said, just as the silence had begun to settle in around them.

Jacob ran a hand over his face, trying to organize his thoughts. "It was the bump field that did it," he started. "I'd gotten to the top of the outcropping okay, and started dropping what I could down onto the trail. Pare's idea was solid, really. Any normal person, even if they could get to that position, wouldn't have been able to drop anything useful. But I was able to translocate some pretty heavy artillery down onto that path."

Jacob massaged one temple with his thumb. "When the bump field came up, I knew I had to go all out. That's when I saw the tree. It was growing out of a crack in the rock, close to the edge. When I slipped it out of its place, something shifted. The crack ran deeper than I expected, and pulling the tree out caused the whole thing to break loose. I was on the wrong side of the gap when the whole outcrop came away from the mountainside."

Jacob shook his head and closed his eyes. Talking about the incident just reminded him how tired he was, and of everything they'd been through. "It all happened too fast. I tried jumping as the gap widened, and misjudged. I missed the safe side with my feet, and hit the edge at my armpits, but my hands never found any grip. Everything was sliding, falling away, and I was going with it. I had no choice but to translocate blind. I came out too high, up in the trees, and the last thing I remember was a branch coming at my face. I guess that's how I got this." He pulled his hair back and winced as he came in contact with the nasty cut on his forehead, ringed by a fist-sized lump.

Eriane looked up from her seat and crinkled her brow, a look of concern washing away the tiredness in her eyes. "Let me take a look at that," she said, rummaging around in her pack and producing a small, leather-wrapped bundle. She sat on a rock next to him and leaned in, brushing his hair back and probing the cut.

"AAGH!" he blurted, recoiling from her touch.

"Oh, stop it, you big baby," she said, leaning back in.

"Do you even know what you're doing?" he asked.

"No, not really," Eriane replied. "But I'm the best you've got right now. You don't want Pare anywhere near this, but I'm sure Samuel could get in here with those fenceposts he calls fingers, if you want." Samuel clanked the fingers and thumb of one hand together to emphasize her point. Jacob's shoulders drooped. "Stop whinging and let me take a look. Finish your story."

With a deep breath, he leaned back toward her and continued. "When I came to, everything was quiet. I had no idea how long I'd been out, but there was no noise, so I figured everything was over. Until I heard the laugh."

Pare made a noise, something between a snort and a growl, and lowered his head. Eriane's hands stopped moving, only for a moment, and continued cleaning Jacob's wound.

"When I tried to stand, the world shifted around me—OW!" A look of disdain from Eriane, a deep breath from Jacob. "Like it was trying to buck me off. I fell down a few times before I got to my feet at the edge. Samuel had gone over, and I thought I was too late... but he wasn't moving. When I caught sight of the two of you, I knew you weren't going to be able to hold him, and I saw why."

"The tether," Pare said.

"Yeah..." Jacob took a deep breath, pushing back the sudden rush of adrenaline that comes with remembering a moment of fear. "I wasn't even sure what I did would work, but when both you and Eri got quiet, I knew I didn't have any time to think about it. I translocated right down on top of Samuel and the moment I made contact, I slipped us both back up onto the path." Jacob closed his eyes and pushed the heel of his hand into his temple, trying to ward away the deep throbbing within. "I guess it broke him out of the tether. I didn't even know if I could do it."

"Well, I'm glad you found a way," Samuel said. Jacob managed a slight nod.

"I'm going to need to stitch this," Eriane said.

Jacob's face flashed from fear to pleading, then resignation as Eriane threaded her needle.

It was early morning when Jacob woke with a start, the barest flicker of pre-dawn light finding its way through the cave entrance. Every inch of him hurt. Bile rose in his throat and his stomach churned, emptier than he thought possible. Joints popped and creaked as he pushed himself upright. Samuel and Pare were nowhere to be seen, but Eriane asleep on her bedroll meant neither of them would be far.

Jacob struggled to his feet, stretching the ache out of his back and shoulders. Throbbing pain shot through his face from the cut on his forehead. Eriane's stitching job was admirable, and Jacob hoped it would hold and not leave too nasty a scar. Running his hands over his face, Jacob breathed deep and felt his ribs creak. The acrid smell on his hands and clothes crinkled his nose, one of the aftereffects of his rapid translocations. The musty cave wasn't much better, and some fresh air was in order.

The black sky was fading to dark blue over the craggy mountaintops outside the cave. They'd camped not too far after the turn onto the Kelef road. This canyon was narrower and more rugged, but the road itself was wider and more level than the pass from which they'd come, and took on a welcome downward slope.

Neither Samuel nor Pare was in sight, but bends in the road meant Jacob couldn't see very far in either direction. Fishing around inside his cloak, Jacob produced a small glass vial from a pouch at his waist. A faint glow emanated from the bottle, generated by the swirling fog within. With another glance in either direction, Jacob uncorked the bottle. He lifted the vial to his mouth and pressed the opening to his lips. Closing his eyes he inhaled, his muscles flooding with relaxation, his mind swooning with unnatural calmness.

The relief was instant. Tension slid away from his frame, carrying the aches and pains of batter and strain with it. Jacob felt as though he were floating, lifting away from the world and the troubles inhabiting the ledge on which he stood. The weightless euphoria lasted only a second, but in that moment he reveled in the forgetfulness it brought with it. Gravity returned and he found his hands empty at his sides. His eyes fluttered open and he breathed deep the cold morning air, feeling it fill his lungs with a familiar but rare intensity. At his foot lay the little vial, having cut a bottle-shaped hole into the shallow snow as it fell. He bent to pick it up, and felt a blissful lack of soreness in his back at the motion.

"How long have you been on the whiff?"

The start wasn't as intense as it would have been in another moment, but it caused Jacob to jerk nonetheless. He turned to the source of the voice, and there Pare stood, bundled in his cloak and leaned against the rocks to the side of the cave entrance. Had he been there all along? Jacob couldn't remember.

"So that's how you've kept so warm," Pare said.

Jacob just nodded, not sure where the conversation was headed.

"Where do you get it?" Pare asked.

"What do you mean?" Jacob said.

"You know exactly what I mean," Pare said, his voice low.

Jacob hesitated, looking at the bottle still in his hand. He wiped the wetness of melted snow away from the glass and replaced it in the pouch beneath his cloak. "Around," he replied.

"Not good enough," Pare replied. "Where? From me? From Eriane?"

Jacob was offended by the implication. "Never. Never from another," he said in his defense. "Plants, animals, usually."

Pare's lip curled into a sneer. "Manipulating latent *khet* is one thing. Stealing it from the living and distilling it into a drug…that's…"

"It's not full potency." Jacob replied. "I'm a lot of things, Pare, but I'm not a killer."

"How do I know you're telling the truth?" Pare asked.

"I have no reason to lie," Jacob replied.

Pare was off the rocks and in front of Jacob faster than he could react. The boy leaned in closer than he liked, and he became keenly aware of the edge of the road and the drop at his back. "I thought you were someone who knew better," Pare said.

"You don't get to judge me, kid."

"No, but I do get to distrust you," Pare spat.

"Look," Jacob said. "You want to lump me in with Drift-addict waste or some undercity Breather to make yourself feel superior, you go right ahead. But I'm not hurting anyone."

"If Eriane finds out, she'll never forgive you."

A flash of anger heated Jacob's collar. "Don't use her to project, Pare. Hiding behind her doesn't become you."

"You don't even know what you're talking about," Pare replied. "And you have no idea how much it would hurt her—or the wrath you'd bring upon yourself—if she found out."

He looked down for a breath and then back at Pare, leaning in even closer. "Then she needn't know."

The wind picked up and whistled through the canyon, and carried with it the sound of metal footsteps. Pare blinked, inhaled, then turned away, stalking into the cave just as Samuel rounded the corner, coming down the road from the direction they had come the night before. Jacob shook his head and exhaled, allowing himself to breathe again.

"What was that all about?" Samuel asked as he approached.

"Nothing. It's...nothing," Jacob said.

Samuel paused and stayed quiet. Jacob shifted as Samuel looked on, so much like a person waiting for the inevitable continuation after an obvious put-off. It really was a marvel how alive the construct seemed sometimes, the feelings he could invoke with mannerisms that just never felt affected. Maybe that's why they all stuck with him, taking risks in his name and trying to protect him from those that would cause him harm. It was that connection that made Jacob uncomfortable now.

"Where have you been?" Jacob asked.

Big Sister broke over the peaks at the end of the canyon as Samuel turned to look across the gap. "Just...I couldn't sit in there all night without knowing we weren't being followed. I backtracked and made sure our...friends hadn't crossed the gap."

Jacob shook his head. "Well, thank you," he said, "but that was really stupid. What if they'd still been there?"

Samuel didn't turn, but just kept staring into the drop as sunlight painted the rockfaces orange. "They weren't." A pause. "Is there another way around?"

Jacob had been absentmindedly probing the newly stitched cut at his hairline. He stopped and ran his fingers through his hair, pausing to scratch the back of his head. "I honestly don't know. I've never been to Kelef," he said, wiping his hand on his trouser leg. "But I can't imagine this is the only road."

"That's not very reassuring," Samuel said.

"I don't know what you want me to say," Jacob said. "We're trudging through a narrow mountain pass in the winter snow, running from a pair of psychopaths who have now tried to kill us twice for unknown reasons, to see some mysterious prophet in a secluded city on the thin hope they'll be able to help us understand why you, my friend, are so important." He took a deep breath of cool morning air. "And right now, my only hope is that I can have a bath when we get there."

Chapter Thirty-Six

Samuel followed Jacob back into the cave where they had camped. Pare and Eriane huddled close, talking in low tones near where she had slept. There was a hitch in Jacob's step when Pare looked up from the conversation. Pare had been distrustful of Jacob from the start, but this tension was new, and something about it unsettled Samuel.

Jacob moved off to the other side of the small cave to look after his things. "How much farther do we have?" Samuel asked.

"If the mild weather holds," Pare replied. "Only a few days. From what I know, there are even some rest points along the way that the people of Kelef built into the trail for travelers."

"Barring any more entanglements," Jacob said, "it should be easier going, then?"

Pare didn't reply, instead turning back to cinch up the straps on his pack. "Yeah, hopefully," Eriane interjected, directing a furrowed brow toward Pare.

"What's this Kelef place like?" Samuel said, hoping to distract everyone from this newfound animosity. The last thing they needed was for any acrimony to crop up when they were so close to their goal.

Eriane shook her head. "We don't really know," she said. "Mane showed us...Pare and I have seen pictures in some old texts, and we've heard stories from people in Morrelton." Her face brightened. "A whole city carved into the mountain, surrounding the end of a steep valley, with a waterfall in the middle. It's supposed to be very beautiful." Her description had become wistful. "I've wanted to see it ever since I was little."

"Well, then," Pare said, wincing as he pulled on his pack. "Let's get a move on so you can."

Eriane jumped to her feet but grimaced through her smile. She took a deep breath and held her grin as she pulled together her own things and approached Samuel. "Only a few more days," she said. "A few more days and we'll know everything. You'll finally know who you are."

Her optimism was infectious. The last several days had been trying, even without a real frame of reference for the experiences. He could only imagine what these kinds of upheavals meant to the other three, whose entire lives had been upended. For Samuel, the chase was all he knew, but for them... And even through all those thoughts, Eriane's smile still made him believe his quest to find out who and what he was could almost be at its end. *Then what?* The question still nagged at him, but he pushed it aside and chose instead to revel in Eriane's enthusiasm.

Eriane crossed over to Jacob, who was just situating the last of his things underneath his cloak. "Jacob?" she said. He looked up and visibly stiffened, as if preparing for another of the previous night's tirades.

"Yeah?" he said.

For a moment Eriane looked as though she were formulating a response, but instead she stepped close and hugged him. Caught off guard, Jacob's hands hovered for a moment before coming to rest around her shoulders.

"Thank you," Eriane said.

A look of genuine confusion crossed Jacob's face. "For what?" he asked.

"For everything," Eriane said.

Samuel thought, for an instant, he saw a flash of emotion sweep across Jacob's face, but it was gone just as fast, steeled away behind a mask built of indifference. "Eri, I didn't...you don't need to thank me."

Eriane pulled her face away to look up at him. "Of course I do. If you hadn't come to the cabin, we'd have been ambushed. If you hadn't been up on that ledge, we'd have been overrun by those men. And if you hadn't been there afterward, Samuel wouldn't be with us right now. We all owe you, Jacob. Thank you."

Samuel heard a sharp intake of breath, and saw Pare headed outside. "Come on. Let's get going," he said, stalking out into the bright morning.

Jacob tapped Eriane's shoulder and gestured toward the entrance. "He's right. Let's get on the road." Eriane nodded and moved toward the door, smiling at Samuel as she passed by.

Samuel tilted his head toward Jacob, hoping for some sort of acknowledgement, but received nothing in return as he passed.

Compared to the last several days, travel along the new road was easy. Their view of the rugged cut in the mountains through which they traveled was frequently breathtaking. Samuel had taken the lead like before, in case the snow picked up, but at some point Jacob had separated himself from the others and moved ahead of Samuel, pulling into his cloak and trudging forward without a word. Behind him, Pare and Eriane's conversation began in serious tones but lightened as the day went on. They quipped and joked, much like siblings would, and Eriane's laughter echoed off of the cliffs around them. As they talked, they dropped back, and Samuel took the opportunity to approach Jacob.

"What was that back there, in the cave?" he asked.

"What are you talking about?" Jacob said.

"With Eriane. She was thanking you for saving my life. For saving hers—all of us. And you brushed her off."

"Samuel, I..."—A pause—"I don't know what I'm supposed to say to that. I'm no hero."

Samuel put a hand on Jacob's shoulder. "If you hadn't risked your life, I'd be a pile of scrap at the bottom of a canyon right now."

Jacob whipped his head around, a flash of anger on his face. "And where would we all be if I simply hadn't followed you in the first place?" Jacob pushed Samuel's hand away. "You'd all be better off if you'd never met me."

"What are you talking about?" Samuel asked.

"Think about it for about half a second, Samuel," Jacob spat through gritted teeth, keeping his voice down so Pare and Eri couldn't hear. "*I* took you to Atherton's shop. The only reason why any of this happened to any of these people is because of my interference. Michael…Atherton…Mane… I mean, even Cort and his men. All on me." He turned his angry gaze back on Samuel again. "All that? It's *all on me.*"

"You were pretty quick to dump a lot of that on my shoulders back in Morrelton." Samuel said.

Jacob's eyes narrowed and he shook his head. "Yeah… Well, it's hard to maintain denial when that girl," he nodded toward Eriane, "looks you in the face with reverence in her eyes. Reverence I don't deserve."

Samuel felt his own anger rising. "You're forgetting one crucial point, Jacob."

"And what's that?"

"Those two…psychopaths? They're following *me.*" Samuel tapped his own chest a little harder than he'd intended, resulting in a loud *clang*. "Not you. Not them. *Me.* So any claim you think you have to this guilt is tenuous, at best."

"Exactly, Samuel. They're following you. And I'm the one who brought you into all of these people's lives."

"So, what are you saying then?" Samuel shot back. "You'd rather have left me with Taeman? To be collected and scrapped by the same people who are following me now?"

Jacob's eyes narrowed and he stopped, Samuel stopping behind him. "Maybe that is what I'm saying." He turned and stalked up the trail, leaving Samuel standing in the light snow, reeling as though he'd been struck.

"Oh, thanks," he shot after Jacob as he walked away.

"What was that all about?" It was Eriane, who'd caught up and now stood beside Samuel in the trail.

"It's nothing," Samuel said, shaking his head.

"Well then, what are you standing here for?" Pare said as he brushed past.

Jacob's words ricocheted around in Samuel's mind like a fired bullet. It was bad enough to have to have his own reservations about his presence in these people's lives. To have that thought voiced by another drove the pain home in a way Samuel didn't know was possible. He hadn't even noticed Eriane take his arm in hers.

"Are you all right?" she asked.

"No, not really," Samuel said, unable even to sugar coat how he felt in the moment.

"Me either," Eriane said. The statement shook Samuel out of his stupor. He looked down at her, and realized how tired she looked, and how that look of wear seemed so foreign on a face so young.

"What do you expect, Samuel?" Eriane continued. "After the last few days? None of us are okay." She let go of his arm and took a few steps forward, then turned around in the trail to face him. Her mouth was curled into a small smile that belied the exhaustion in her eyes. "But that doesn't mean we won't be."

And through all that, she'd done it again. She'd driven that little stake of optimism through the heart of all the anger, guilt, and doubt, and broken through his fear just enough for him to pick up his feet once more and be on his way.

Early that night they happened upon one of the prepared campsites. The space was level and open, the end of a small dry gully that intersected the trail and contained enough soil for a few alpine firs to grow. The high sides of the enclosure protected them from the mountain winds, and the trees would be enough cover to keep them out of the snow. The fresh smell alone was enough for Jacob to consider it an improvement over a damp, musty cave.

At the center of the space slabs of flat rock ringed a firepit. Several large tree rounds, cut and sanded into makeshift stools and coated in some sort of protective resin to prevent rot, surrounded the pit. They had been here for quite some time, and appeared well-used. Soil and a blanket of fir needles covered the ground outside the ring, a heavenly mattress compared to a hard stone floor. A small stack of firewood sat near the base of a fir tree not too far away.

"I'll build a fire," Pare said, dropping his pack and a few other belongings off to the side. Jacob and Eriane had done the same, and Jacob was already situating his things for sleep.

"I'm gonna take a look around," Eriane said. Her tone caught them all off guard. She pulled her cloak close and walked out of the campsite to the rear, into the gully. Both Samuel and Pare stopped what they were doing. Pare started to get up, but Jacob stood and motioned for them to continue setting up camp and, with a nod, walked after her.

It took a few minutes to catch up to her; it seemed as though she'd picked up her pace after the edge of the campsite. She stopped ahead as Jacob approached and turned. "Look, Jacob," she said, "I just want to be alone for a few, okay?"

Jacob furrowed his brow. "What's going on?"

"I don't really want to talk about it."

After Eriane's outburst the night before, Jacob was glad she didn't immediately start tearing into him. He hoped that also meant Pare had kept his secret safe, at least so far. Still, he felt like he was treading unsteady ground. "It's…" he paused, not sure how to proceed. "Are you upset with the situation, or with one of us? Me?"

"No, it's not any of you," Eriane said. "It's just… I don't know."

"Hey, I know you might not want to talk, and that's fine," Jacob said. "But maybe you need to, whether you want to or not."

She closed her eyes for a moment and took a frustrated breath, then found a place to sit. She leaned forward with her hands steepled in front of her face, but didn't speak. Jacob took a seat beside her and leaned forward with his elbows on his knees.

"We've all been through the grinder." Jacob said. "And no one's going to blame you if you need a shoulder."

"That's not it, Jacob," she said, not looking at him. "I haven't had…don't have…time to worry about feeling sorry for myself. I'm just…"

This time, Jacob waited, fully expecting her to launch into him about what Pare had told her. He wasn't sure where the conversation was going yet, and he braced himself for the worst. It took a moment for her to continue, but she did so without prompting.

"Does it make me a terrible person to be angry at Samuel?"

Jacob could not have been more relieved. Was that all that was bothering her? He smiled. "Eri, there isn't a person in your situation who wouldn't harbor at least a little bit of anger or resentment. Of course it doesn't make you a terrible person."

She exhaled and turned back to her steepled hands, her expression unchanged.

"Samuel and I had a discus—an *argument*—about that very subject. Look, we're all in this because of Samuel, but we all made these choices on our own, right? The consequences are more than any of us expected, but that doesn't mean we don't have the right to that bit of anger. All that matters is how we act on it...you just can't let it fester. You have to—"

"You don't understand what I'm saying." She cut him off.

"Then what do you mean?"

"I'm not angry at him for the situation in general, Jacob," she said. "My anger toward him is very specific." She turned to face him. Her eyes were wet, but hard. "I'm pissed he stopped me. That I didn't get to shoot that silver-eyed son of a bitch."

That admission was not among the many things Jacob expected to hear from Eriane. Her rage in the moment was understandable, after the silver-eyed man had attempted to kill them. The rage still lingered, marring her young features and stripping Jacob of any child-like or innocent image he still held of her.

"Oh, Eri..." he said, not sure how to continue.

She jumped to her feet and turned on him. Her face flushed with anger, but there was something altogether different than what he'd seen in her the night before.

"Don't 'oh, Eri' me, Jacob," she said. "I had him. Right then, right there. This could all be over."

"Do you honestly think he's the only one interested in Samuel?" Jacob ran a hand over his mouth and dropped his eyes. "Kill him, and there'll be another one right behind him, right up until we can figure out exactly why Samuel's being followed in the first place. Besides, you don't need to be in such a hurry to kill someone, Eri. Trust me."

"Even if it means stopping them from trying to kill us?"

"Yeah, actually," Jacob said. "Even then."

"I don't understand you, Jacob," Eri snapped. "You were the one up on that cliff, trying to drop a mountainside on their heads, and now you're telling me I shouldn't have shot him?"

Jacob stood up and looked Eri directly in the eyes. "That's exactly what I'm telling you, kid. I'm not saying we weren't looking for the same result, but I am saying you don't need to be so eager to get it done. It doesn't matter what it benefits you in the end, killing someone is something you never get rid of. It'll hang with you for the rest of your life. It may get you out of one hole, but it damned sure puts you right in another."

Eri stood silent and still, a small shake revealing how hard she was holding onto the furrow of her brow and the set of her jaw. Jacob looked back at her with equal intensity, but broke first and sat down.

"Besides, you don't need Pare seeing that if he doesn't absolutely have to," Jacob said. "We got out of there in one piece, and that's good enough for one day."

Eriane's shoulders sank a little more with each breath, until she sat next to him. "I don't need you guys to protect me from adulthood," she said in a small voice.

The comment took Jacob aback. "It's already too late for that, Eri," he said. "This has nothing to do with being an adult. If or when you need to take that shot, you'll know it. But don't seek it out. And don't be angry at Samuel for delaying it—you should revel in that, because who knows how much time he bought you."

An early evening meant an early start, and they were up and on their way just as the western sky began to lighten. Not long after they set out, the road began climbing, a shallow grade, but uphill nonetheless. Campsites became more common, in gullies and caves, and even one built as a viewpoint over a wide part of the canyon, surrounded by a low stone wall.

Samuel spent both day and night in quiet contemplation, piecing together as many memories as he could access. The murdered woman was a recent vision, and he made the short leap of logic it was the reason he was being followed. There were any number of his newfound memories that could warrant his fugitive status, but none were so vivid. It was one of the most recent memories he could conjure—at least that's how it felt—so it would stand to reason everything he'd been through was triggered by this one event.

What worried him was the disconnectedness of all the memories. He'd started comparing all the visions he'd received to his own memories—the recent ones he knew for fact were his own—and none of them felt...whole. Seeing the memories of so many other constructs had Samuel wondering if he'd ever get back any of his own. Were his memories—the ones experienced and gathered by this body, this core, from before the fire—still in there somewhere, or were they gone forever? Sifting through the ages of emotionless images that twittered around his mind made him feel like he was standing in some foreign land, learning a whole new language and culture from scratch. In a way, that's exactly what he was doing.

No matter how hard he concentrated on the woman and her killer, he couldn't connect the timeline of his visions, and there were still gaps he wasn't able to fill. Her face was the one unifying image. So clear and complete, so easy to study, to memorize. Every line in her pleading eyes, the shape of her whispering mouth, the smears of blood on her cheeks, were all burned into his waking vision. At no point, however, was he able to get a clear view of her murderer, his face so masked in shadow and gore. All he knew were the clear whites of dark eyes that bore into him from under a curtain of matted hair. He had no doubt if ever he were to look upon those eyes, he'd know exactly who he'd found.

It was the identity of the woman that haunted him, though. Could this be the Queen Consort herself, and could these be the memories of the construct believed to be her murderer? If that were true, the very knowledge within him could exonerate the framed construct, and bring to light a new killer. That knowledge alone warranted the pursuit, and putting it all together was beginning to give Samuel the smallest inkling of the scope of his danger.

If this was the Queen Consort, then why was she murdered? Who was the mysterious killer, and why was a construct framed for the crime? At camp the next night Samuel presented his theory to the group, who listened and shared his concern. According to Jacob, Samuel's description of the murder matched the whispered rumors of the circumstances of the Queen Consort's death, the details that were much too graphic to make public but had found their way into circles of people in the know. Samuel's theory, and the very real likelihood he was right, meant their pursuers would be desperate to keep him quiet, to erase the knowledge he'd been gifted.

The other implication, the one Samuel didn't voice, was that his pursuers somehow knew the knowledge had been transferred to him, which meant the process by which it occurred must be more than simple coincidence. If they were following him, they must know how he was connected to the other constructs whose memories he'd acquired. Worse yet, the fact that they were tracking down and destroying other constructs meant the others had been granted similar knowledge, and must have a much deeper connection to Samuel than happenstance.

In a way, knowing there were other constructs like him, and connected to him, was comforting. Although the three people with whom he camped had become genuine companions, if not outright friends, his disconnection from other constructs had seeded him with a deep sense of loneliness. If there were other constructs in the world that could receive memories like he could, maybe there were others with the type of emotions that made him unique. That connection also meant he wasn't just being followed. He—and every other construct of his kind—were being hunted and systematically eradicated, all to protect the identity of a murderer and maintain the façade that the Queen Consort's death came at the hands of a construct.

The more Samuel mulled over the idea, the angrier he became. He wondered why Icariascus had kept silent instead revealing his nature and helping him to find his place. Was the threat so dangerous Samuel couldn't even trust his own kind?

Through their travels the next day he fumed in silence, sifting through every fractured memory he'd acquired to try and fill the gaps in the story, to bring his recollection to a coherent whole. Sorting the memories felt more and more like someone had tumbled hundreds of puzzles together, handed Samuel a fraction of the pieces, and asked him to sort out which ones went together. Without the rest of the information, even out of order, trying to make sense of the fragments was nearly impossible.

Samuel trudged forward at the head of the group, oblivious to all but maintaining his walking pace. The mountains, the snow, his companions, and even his destination faded away, leaving only his singular drive to make sense of the images. To find a killer.

Samuel wasn't aware of how much time had passed when Eriane stepped into his path, breaking his fugue by forcing him to stop and acknowledge her. When he inquired why she'd stopped him, she only turned to look, drawing his eyes to one of the most amazing sights in his all-too-limited experience.

The gates of Kelef.

Chapter Thirty-Seven

Kelef stood much like Eriane's description, but with a grandeur her words could never have conveyed. The canyon cut deep through the center of the city, narrowing toward the far end and terminating into a steep cliff face. Jagged, snow-covered peaks surrounded them on all sides like giant, natural crenellations. The first visible structure on the approach to the city was an immense archway that extended across the chasm, housing a wide city gate before them on the road and disappearing into the rockface on the opposing side of the canyon.

The archway formed by the gate bridge framed a stunning picture of the city, built of granite structures that seemed hewn directly from the mountainside. The setting sun glittered in the surface of stone buildings arranged in layers of angled terraces, reminiscent of striations in broken rock, all of which climbed upward from the archway toward the opposing end. At the end of it all, past the last of many bridges connecting the two sides of the canyon, a tall, thin waterfall emerged from the base of a massive fortress that burrowed into the crease between two mountains and stood vigil over the city below.

Samuel was rooted to the bend in the road, looking up at Kelef with a mixture of anticipation, awe, and relief. In the previous days, their journey had become excruciating, a long trudge toward an unknown goal. Their destination being made real before him was overwhelming.

The city was astonishing, not just in its presence but its beauty, accentuated by a fresh round of falling snow.

"Wow," Eriane said, the first to speak.

"You can say that again" Jacob said, his eyes never leaving the sight ahead of them.

"Wow."

That drew a smirk and a sidelong glance from Jacob, which was met by a mischievous grin and a glint in Eriane's eye Samuel was glad to see. A genuine smile had been rare since their encounter with their pursuers, so a moment of true relaxation was as welcome a sight as the city spread out before them.

One by one they broke their stances, advancing on the road toward their first sign of civilization since leaving Mane's cabin. Samuel was the last, taking in the sight of the city that likely contained not only the answers to all his questions, but the key to his identity—maybe even his salvation.

"So, how do we find this Acthemenius?" Samuel asked.

"Whoa, hold up there," Jacob said. "I know you're eager, Samuel, but I need a bath. And a hot meal, and a bed, and perhaps some nice company for the evening. I don't even want to think of this Acthemenius until I've"—a pause, as his eyes flicked toward Eriane—"*slept.*"

The group of them stopped not too far from the gate, which stood open with a minimal guard. "As much as it pains me to say this," Pare said, "I have to agree with Jacob. Aside from the simple desire to be clean and rested, none of us are in any condition for research right now."

Samuel said nothing. As foolish as he knew it was, he felt resentful of their needs. He could set off into the city himself, if he so chose, not needing the rest his companions required, and find the answers he had traveled so far to seek. Maybe it was best to let them head off to some inn to bathe and sleep in a feather bed while he investigated on his own. *They've been with you this far, Samuel. Don't deny them the whole purpose of their journey over simple impatience.* Acthemenius could wait.

Samuel nodded. "You're right," he said. "Let's find some place for you all to sleep. In the morning we can try to find the woman Mane sent us after, and maybe she can help us find Acthemenius." The group nodded their assent, and as they turned to enter the city, a voice rang out from the street on just the other side of the gate. "Kaleb?"

A thin older man wearing a fur-lined winter jacket approached them through the gate. Jacob turned at the mention of his alter-ego.

"Sorrell?" Jacob said.

"Kaleb!" the man repeated. He approached the group, extended a friendly hand toward Jacob. The two grasped forearms like old friends, pulling each other into a brief but familiar embrace. Eriane turned a confused expression to Pare to which he responded with a shrug.

Jacob backed away from Sorrell, looking him up and down. "What in the name of all the Vells are you doing in Kelef?" Jacob said.

"Would you believe I live here now?" Sorrell replied, holding his hands out to his sides.

"No, honestly," Jacob replied. "I would not believe that."

"Well, that's what's happened," Sorrell replied, stepping back to take full measure of Jacob. He shook his head. "You look like a Padorean vagrant!" he said with a jovial smirk.

"You would not believe what I've been through in the last few weeks," Jacob said. Pare coughed, and Jacob swung around as though he'd forgotten he wasn't alone. "Oh! Everyone, this is an old...business partner of mine, Sorrell Antenum. Sorrell, this is Pariadnus..."

Pare nodded, and Sorrell returned the gesture.

"...Eriane..."

Eriane eked out a weary smile. "M'lady," Sorrell said, with a shallow bow. As he righted himself, he shot a questioning glance at Jacob.

"...and our servant construct Jethaltanon. You can call him Jeth, for short." Samuel wondered where Jacob had pulled the name from this time. At least 'Jeth' would be easy to remember, and he hoped Pare and Eriane caught on.

Sorrell's appraisal of Samuel was quick and harsh. "Where did you pick this one up?" he said with a snort. "This might be the oldest construct I've ever seen! How much did his previous owner pay you to take him?" As a sarcastic afterthought, Sorrell turned to Samuel and added, "No offense, of course."

"None taken," Samuel replied, which drew a double-take from Sorrell.

"Don't let his looks fool you," Jacob said. "He's been a workhorse ever since we met." Jacob gave Samuel a sidelong smile. "He's practically indestructible."

"Hey, whatever you say," Sorrell replied. "I know it's been a long time since we saw each other, but I always thought you ran alone?"

"Yeah, well, I always thought you'd be in Balefor until your dying day," Jacob said. "I guess things change some times, huh?"

"That they do," Sorrell said. He paused, and shook his head, looking back at Jacob again. "Look at you. You almost look like a grown up now!"

Jacob laughed. "Well, if it makes you feel any better, you still look like the same haggard old fool as always."

"Ha! Well, you know what they say about age and treachery, my boy," Sorrell said. "Why don't you and your crew here come stay with me tonight? It's a bit of a walk, but I'm sure it can't be any worse than getting here."

Jacob raised his hands. "Oh, we shouldn't impose. We can find an inn for the night."

"I insist!" Sorrell said. "I've got comfortable guest quarters and floors that can withstand your canner's weight."

"I don't know," Jacob said, looking back to the group. Eriane's face was painted with an expectant grin, and even Pare's eyes were a little wider than normal.

"I have a full bath and the means to run it hot."

Before Jacob could reply, Eriane skirted around him and took Sorrell's arm. "Well, if you *insist*," she said, "then how could we *possibly* refuse?"

The two of them turned and began walking up the street. Eriane looked over her shoulder with a satisfied grin and nodded for them to catch up. Jacob scoffed just as Pare approached him.

"Can we trust him?" Pare asked. The tone of skepticism was unmistakable.

"About as much as I can trust anyone," Jacob said. "So watch yourselves."

"So," Sorrell said between laughs, "he comes stumbling out the back door, half-naked, drenched from head to toe, runs right into a lamp post—"

"The soap was getting in my eyes," Jacob interjected.

"—and, not five seconds later, a lovely young lady by the name of…oh, what was her name?"

"Muriel."

"Right! Muriel slams the door open and is also soaked, and—in an impressively athletic moment, I might add—nails Kaleb right in the back of the head with one of his own shoes!"

Everyone—even Pare, wincing in pain as he did—was laughing. Jacob had given Samuel some coaching on acting like a normal construct, which included keeping his laughter in check. Forcing himself to stay quiet was a price he was willing to pay in exchange for seeing the rest of them have a genuine moment of joviality.

"I guess I'd forgotten one in her room," Jacob laughed. "I was just happy she gave it back!"

Sorrell, in spite of Jacob's warning, had offered overwhelming hospitality. His house, a two-story marble building in one of the higher terraces of Kelef, was an impressive home befitting Sorrell's high station. They were bathed and fed, and now gathered in a comfortable sitting room drinking wine and coffee and listening to Jacob and Sorrell reminisce.

The smile on Pare's face was as close to unguarded cheer as Samuel had seen from the boy, and Eriane was laughing so hard she teared up. "Oh, I'm not even sure these are things I wanted to know about J-Kaleb."

The slip was minor, and it didn't appear Sorrell had noticed. Jacob covered well with more laughter, and Eriane buried herself in a huge gulp of her coffee. For Samuel, it illustrated how tenuous their situation here in Kelef still was, and brought into sharp relief his own need to travel under an alias. Remaining on guard was imperative, because none of them knew just how far knowledge of Samuel's pursuit had traveled. After Atherton's turn in Morrelton, how could they be sure anyone was trustworthy?

As the laughter died down, Eriane finished her coffee and stood, exhaustion taking hold of her features. "I think it's time for me to sleep." She smiled at Sorrell. "In a warm bed, again."

"I agree," Pare said, also standing. "I'm already nodding off in my chair." His expression was a bit more serious than his words suggested, and it was clear he was looking for an excuse to get out of the room.

Eriane covered her discomfort more eloquently. She crossed to Sorrell and kissed him on the cheek, which reddened at the gesture. "Thank you so much."

Samuel was impressed at the grace with which she moved through the situation. Her entire bearing had Sorrell believing she was just a grateful young girl, but Samuel knew better than to underestimate her. Even with her minor slip-up, it was little moments like that one which kept Sorrell off balance and reinforced their façade. As she left the room with Pare, he counted himself lucky the two of them were on his side. Jacob nodded to them as they left, then turned to Samuel.

"Jeth, can you give us a moment, please," Sorrell said.

Samuel was caught off guard at being addressed by Sorrell, but couldn't break character and so stood to leave the room. As he passed, Jacob's eyes narrowed and he gave an almost imperceptible, but reassuring, nod. Eriane and Pare needed their sleep, so he headed toward the quarters he'd been shown earlier in the evening. Two other constructs, looking much like Taeman's automatons, sat stone still at the back of the room and did not acknowledge his entrance.

Samuel's mood had unexpectedly soured. He wasn't sure whether to trust his instincts, but something about Sorrell gnawed at him. Their acceptance into his household seemed too easy, too convenient. Jacob had made it clear he was not to be trusted, and the more Samuel mulled it over, the more unsettled he became.

"What is it, Sorrell?" Jacob asked. Sorrell sending away Samuel had his hackles up, but he lounged in his chair to avoid revealing his uneasiness.

Sorrell took a draught of his wine, and set his glass down with practiced ease. "Why are you here?"

Jacob smiled. "Because you invited me in," he dodged.

"You know what I mean, Kaleb." Sorrell said, an edge to his voice. "Why are you *really* here?"

Sorrell was drawing Jacob onto dangerous ground. He recalled an old axiom: Never ask a question you don't already know the answer to.

A cautious dance had just begun.

"You're not usually one to ask such direct questions, Sorrell." Jacob said.

"Different times, different circumstance." Sorrell replied, falling back to an easy smile. He plucked at the front of his smock. "I'm a respectable businessman now." He made a sweeping gesture. "I can't risk all this."

Jacob took a slow drink. "You say that as though someone has asked you to."

Sorrell's smile faded. "You've shown up in Kelef, looking ragged and beaten, at a time of year when most don't journey here. The man whom I used to know traveled alone—always alone—and yet you appear in the company of a pair of children and an ancient construct. I need to ensure you've not brought chaos into my house."

Jacob let the implication hang, taking a drink of his wine and a long breath. "I met the kids in Cinth. They wanted to come to Kelef, something about the library. I might have dropped the hint I'd been here before." Another drink of wine. "I let them hire me as a guide. Protection."

Sorrell raised an eyebrow. "Have you ever been here before?"

"What do you think?" Jacob said with a disarming chuckle. "But you know me. Not much stands between me and a fool's money."

"So they're just clients?"

Jacob didn't like the question, but smiled just the same. He held out his wine glass, which Sorrell refilled from the decanter. "Just clients. They are to meet their aunt here in Kelef, who will pay me the remainder of my fee. We'd intended to stay at an inn tonight, but your hospitality helped us avoid it."

Sorrell nodded, topping off his own wine glass. "What about the construct?" Now he was fishing.

Jacob offered a disarming chuckle "Just a canner heap I picked up along the way."

"How old is it?" Sorrell asked.

"I don't rightly know," Jacob said. "I've only been in his company a few days." This was Jacob's opportunity to misdirect Sorrell's interest. "But I figure a construct that age, fully intact, could be worth a tidy sum."

"To the right buyer." Sorrell said, leaning back in his chair.

"Are you saying you're interested?"

Sorrell smiled. "Not my type of business, I'm afraid. I could put you in contact with a few people, if you like."

Jacob shrugged. "Perhaps," he said.

"What are your plans, then?" Sorrell's tone had lightened, which took a bit of the edge off for Jacob.

"Not really sure," Jacob said with a shrug. "I'll make that decision once I've dropped the kids and turned a bit of profit on the canner. I will, after all, be in a brand new city with some money to spend."

Sorrell took a drink. "Will you need a place to stay?"

Jacob took a deep breath, confident the danger of their conversation had been averted. "I might just take you up on that."

The longer he sat, the more uneasy Samuel became. He wanted desperately to know what Sorrell and Jacob were speaking of, and resolved to find out. Moving out of the construct enclosure, he made his way back down the hall as stealthily as he could and approached the entrance to the sitting room in the shadows of the darkened hallway. He inched his way as close as he dared, enough he could just hear the conversation within.

"...old is it?" he heard Sorrell ask.

"I don't rightly know," was Jacob's response. "I've only been in his company a few days. But I figure a construct that age, fully intact, could be worth a tidy sum." Samuel started, mortified by Jacob's words.

"To the right buyer."

"Are you saying you're interested?"

Was he hearing this right? Jacob, making a deal for Samuel as though he were nothing more than property? *Theft of independence*, indeed.

"What are your plans, then?"

"Not really sure. I'll make that decision once I've dropped the kids and turned a bit of profit on the canner. I will, after all, be in a brand new city with some money to spend."

A rising tide of anger and disappointment washed away anything else that had been said. All along it had been nothing more than another score driving Jacob's interest in Samuel's plight and now, after all this time, the other shoe had dropped. How valuable the information in his head must have been, for Jacob to have gone through all this just for a chance at a payoff. Jacob had admitted to him he was more interested in the adventure, so maybe part of this was about the adrenaline rush.

Every ounce of Samuel's being wanted to storm into that room. But what would he do? What would he say? Tipping his hand would put him at odds not only with Jacob but with Sorrell and likely make the whole of Kelef an even more dangerous place than it already was. And what about Pare and Eriane? They were blind to the trap, and he needed to tell them, needed to help them get away.

Samuel made his way down the dark hallway, sure to keep his footsteps on the wide running rug laid in the middle so his metal feet wouldn't sound on the hard marble floors. More laughter drifted out from the sitting room; Sorrell and Jacob had returned to commiserating. He reached Eriane's room and gave a light rap on the door. When there was no answer he opened it and found the room empty. The bed was untouched, and Eriane's things were nowhere to be seen.

A moment of panic set in, and he crossed the hall to Pare's room and entered without knocking, startling Pare and Eriane with his sudden entrance. Pare's pack was at his feet and he was clothed for travel. He raised his hands, ready to work some sort of defense, but he dropped them and looked at Eriane, shaking his head.

"Samuel!" Pare said in a loud whisper. "Get in here and shut the door!"

Samuel did as he was told. "What's going on?"

"Pare says we have to leave," Eriane said, exasperated. "He won't listen to me! He thinks Jacob is up to something with Sorrell. I'm trying to tell him Jacob would never do that to us. Not after everything he's done to help us. Tell him!"

When Samuel said nothing, Pare stopped moving and the two of them looked at him for a response. Pare tilted his head, awaiting some sort of rebuttal, but when none came, Eriane stepped forward. "Samuel?" She asked, the question laden with expectation.

"I'm sorry, Eriane," he said. "But Pare's right this time."

"What do you mean?"

All Samuel wanted was to tell her that everything was fine. The thought of detailing what Jacob said was almost too much for him. "I... I heard them talking, in the sitting room." He couldn't continue. "What tipped you off?" he asked Pare.

Pare shrugged. "I heard them talking earlier, after I'd bathed. All night I've been watching, and something's off. I don't want to take the chance."

Eriane's shoulders sank. She breathed in and her eyes narrowed. The disappointment was palpable, and the sadness on her face would have broken Samuel in two—if it had lasted. Just before he thought she'd break down, her jaw set and her face hardened, and she began to pack her things. Pare still had his head down and was strapping on his pack as Eriane finished bundling up.

"You ready?" Pare asked her in a low voice, his eyes still downturned.

"Yep." She said, shoving the last few things into her pack. The disappointment was gone from her face, replaced by...nothing. No anger, no sadness, not even resignation. No emotion at all. "Come on, Samuel. Let's get out of here." she said.

The three of them looked at each other, and both Pare and Samuel nodded their assent. After an all-too-brief respite, they were on the run again.

Chapter Thirty-Eight

Snow swirled and danced in the night air. Eriane's and Pare's breath hovered in white clouds before their faces. As they walked, Samuel realized none of them had even the slightest idea of how to find Acthemenius.

Walking through the city was like navigating an empty maze, but at intervals they could see the chasm and gain some sort of bearing. The quarters through which they walked had no taverns or inns and were thus empty of the usual nighttime revelry of a city. Samuel didn't know how long they'd been walking in the silent winter night when he noticed Eriane was no longer with them and he tapped Pare on the arm. She had stopped some distance behind and was staring up at the next terrace.

"It's the library" she said, her voice small but her eyes wide. They looked up at the building towering above them. "I've only seen it in drawings. It's so much more massive than I expected."

The building was an impressive structure amongst an impressive city. The granite-columned monolith of a building started on the second tier and extended all the way past the tier above, five or six stories tall and four times the length of the largest neighboring building.

"I bet they'd have a city map," Eriane said.

"There's no way we'd get in at this time of night," Pare said.

"Maybe we just need to ask someone," Samuel offered.

"Right, and draw attention to ourselves?" Pare said, incredulous. "*Um, excuse me, sir...can you tell me how to find your local crazy construct cultist in the middle of the night?*" he said in a dullard's tone. "Besides, the only people we've seen out is the night watch."

"That's perfect, then," Samuel said, looking up and down the street. A watchman rounded the corner a few blocks away. "Ah, here's one now. You two should step into the alley here for a moment."

The guard was clad in a fur lined cloak bearing the Kelef coat of arms, strolling up the street from below them. Before either of them could object, Samuel was on his way. He looked back to see Eriane take Pare's arm and duck into one of the stairwells leading to the terrace above. Samuel approached the guardsman.

"Excuse me, sir." Samuel affected the tinny monotone of a normal construct. "I was wondering if you might be able to help?"

The guardsman's voice was gruff, and he coughed once in the cold night air before speaking. "Oy. What do ye need, then?" he asked.

"One of our other servant constructs has gone missing, sir." Samuel said in his flat tone. "Our master believes it's gone looking for...well...you-know-who. Searching it out is not the type of task my master normally engages in, so he sent me to see what I could find out."

"Who's yer master, then?" the guardsman asked.

"Master Sorrell Antenum, sir," Samuel said, fully expecting the gamble to fail.

"Ah, Antenum," The guardsman said with a knowing shake of his head. "That man goes through constructs faster than Count Felinus goes through wives."

Samuel didn't understand the reference, but took on an affected construct-laugh and hoped he'd gotten the tone right. The guardsman flashed him a concerned look, and hurried to end the conversation. "Acthemenius's goons are usually down in the Grotto."

Samuel pressed on. "The Grotto, sir?"

"You don't know the Grotto?" the guardsman said, shifting his weight.

"I'm new to the household, sir." Samuel said. "And I'm afraid Master Antenum didn't give me much to go on."

The guard shook his head. "On the east bank at the downward end.

280

Cross over and head down until you can smell sewage, and you've found your way."

"Thank you, sir," Samuel said with a shallow bow.

"Don't thank me," the guardsman said, stepping around Samuel. "Good night to ye," he said, heading on his way.

After the guardsman passed the stairwell and rounded a corner up the street, Pare and Eriane re-joined Samuel.

"That was almost too simple," Pare said.

"And brilliant," Eriane added.

"I haven't been around long," Samuel said, returning to his normal voice. "But I've already learned people don't see constructs as anything but property. If I present myself like property, they won't suspect anything's amiss." He shrugged.

"Well, I'm glad it worked out," Pare said. "I didn't really want to have to take out a city guardsman tonight."

"Let's try not to think like that, okay?" Samuel said. "We've got enough trouble as it is, and our night's getting shorter.

"So, what exactly did you hear?" Eriane asked Samuel as they walked.

"Are you sure you want to know?" Samuel said.

"Of course I want to know," Eriane said. "I can't just walk into all this blind because you all think I can't handle the truth."

Samuel shook his head. "You're right, of course." Samuel recounted everything he'd heard between Jacob and Sorrell.

The look on Eriane's face hovered between confusion and disappointment. "Are you sure of what you heard?" she asked.

"I don't know whether my hearing can play tricks on me," Samuel said, "but I'd venture not. Their conversation was pretty straightforward."

Eriane sighed, then ground her teeth. "That son of a bitch."

"Eri!"

"Well! It's true," she said. After a pause, she continued. "We haven't been here even a full day, and he's already making deals to ditch us. After everything we've been through, I can't believe it was all about the money. I trusted him."

"We all did," Samuel said. This drew a skeptical look from Pare, but Samuel was thankful he didn't voice his *I-told-you-so*.

The sound of the waterfall was only just audible as they approached the downward end of Kelef, barely a trickle through a twisting braid of crystal and white. All three of them were awestruck by the fortress wall, soaring into the mountain cleft above the waterfall column, an impenetrable, unbroken curve of smooth granite. Away from the fortress, the terraced city spread out, its many bridges forming a seemingly unbroken canopy over the chasm through its center, capped at the opposite end by the dominant Gate Bridge. In the daylight the city was magnificent; all color and light shimmering in the surface of sparkling granite. At night, as the snow fell, it took on a powerful ethereal quality that was at once breathtaking and menacing.

When they reached the end of the bridge, the guardsman's advice became apparent. The musty smell of damp earth wafted up into the street, mingled with stale beer and rotten food. Stout marble gave way to flat stone façades that appeared to front spaces excavated straight into the rock. They'd entered an enormous natural cavern, the roof of which towered above the tops of the tallest buildings. Although the area was bright with lamp and torch light, the claustrophobic architecture made the cavern feel even darker than the night outside. There was no doubt they'd entered the Grotto.

Malicious figures stirred in every dark corner of the place. They picked up the pace through the narrow streets. As they descended, the façades became more utilitarian, sometimes no more than a doorframe blocking the entrance to a small cave mouth. Samuel saw Eriane raise a hand to her nose to ward off the rank, moist air.

The street opened up into a small square, surrounded by tall, dirty buildings, some high enough to be anchored to the cave roof. In the center of the square stood a bronze statue of a group of stout men hefting heavy pick-axes, standing astride a pile of broken rocks. Around the edges, narrow alleys spilled into the open space. The entire rim of the square seemed occupied, and rather than drunken revelry and brawls, everyone here seemed engaged in a low conversation, like all the underworld deals in the city were being brokered right here. They stopped near the statue, and Pare tapped Samuel on the arm.

"Take a look," he said, gesturing across the way.

Samuel peered into the torchlit darkness of an alleyway whose mouth was occupied by a single, still, cloaked figure. The man was tall and stocky, but nothing about him stood out against the rest of the denizens of the square. Samuel turned to Pare and shrugged.

"Just wait for it," Pare replied.

Samuel kept watching. The cloaked figure swung his head around, peering out from the alleyway and taking note of the space. From beneath the edge of the cloak hood emanated the soft green glow of a construct's eyes.

As they continued to watch, the cloaked construct held position, keeping a close eye on all within the square. If he noticed the group at the statue he gave no indication, but Samuel had no doubt they'd been spotted. A drunken vagrant stumbled toward the alleyway and was turned away by the construct as he tried to push past. Moments later, another cloaked figure, moving with a stiff gait that could only be replicated by a metal frame, was allowed past.

"Let's go," Samuel said.

Eriane grabbed his arm. "Wait, we can't just stroll up there!"

"Why not?" Samuel said. "We don't have the time for subtlety. In the morning, Jacob and Sorrell will come looking for us knowing exactly where we've gone. And I have the feeling neither of them will be as amicable as before."

"I think Samuel's right, Eri," Pare said. "We just have to go for it. There are other routes into Kelef than the one we chose, and after the fight in the pass, who knows how many people are after us now. We need to figure this out."

Eriane said nothing for a few seconds, and then just nodded. Samuel stepped around the statue, and made straight for the cloaked construct with Pare and Eriane in tow. The guardian's eyes locked on the group as they approached, watching them all the way across the square. As they drew closer, the other cloaked construct stepped out of the alley and to one side, also watching their advance. Samuel hoped this wouldn't turn into a fight, but he was more than ready to step into the fray if the need arose. After spending so much time running, removed from conflicts while others fought in his stead, he was feeling the urge to get in a fight himself, and wound himself up for one as he crossed the square.

"Ho, there." Although the voice had remained quiet, the words seemed to resonate in a deep, metallic rumble from the alley mouth as Samuel approached. The construct held up a hand.

Samuel made note of the other guard's movement to flank, and motioned Pare to stay alert. Eriane stood between them, her hands buried beneath the folds of her cloak. For her own sake, Samuel hoped she would not have to draw the weapons concealed beneath. Samuel pressed, allowing the guard's hand to come in contact with his chest. A surprising level of resistance drew him to a halt.

"I have business within," he said.

"None that I am aware of, construct," the guard replied, with a light push. "Be on your way."

The flanking guard pressed inward. Pare stepped forward to meet him, his hands raised, the air between his fingers shimmering with wavering light. Turning to follow the construct's movement, Pare pulled around to stand back-to-back with Samuel. Eriane's shoulders twitched as she sidestepped to clear her line of sight. Samuel pushed forward and was again rebuffed.

"I will ask once more politely," the guard said. "Be on your way, or we will send you on your way."

The guard behind took a step toward Pare, who widened his stance. "I don't want to hurt you, boy." Its voice was crisp and sharp, a higher tone than its companion's. "But I will if I have to."

"Pare," Samuel said.

Pare inhaled deeply and let out a blast of raw *khet* that struck the front of the approaching construct, tearing at its cloak and swirling back around to constrict on Pare's target. At the same time, Samuel sidestepped and swept away the arm of the guard, turning the guard's shoulder away with his left and landing a fearsome blow to the side of its head. The blow barely registered with the guard. He used his turning momentum to sweep around low, taking one of Samuel's legs out from under him and dropping him to his knees.

Pare's fingers tightened and the constricting energy coiled about the construct guard, stopping his momentum and pinning his arms to his sides. With a shrug, the construct released his own power, shredding

Pare's bonds into dissipating wisps of gray smoke. The construct advanced.

"That's not possible," Pare said.

The construct's hand closed around a clump of his shirt and pulled him close. "You have quite the sum to learn then, boy," he said, flinging Pare to the side with enough force to send him tumbling across the cave floor.

The distraction caused Samuel to turn his head just as a heavy blow connected with his jawline. His right arm raised to block the follow-up blow, and he saw the second construct advancing from behind. As the guard readied another volley, Samuel uncoiled his legs and backed into a smashing uppercut that sent the guard reeling, but his companion was already there, his arms closing around Samuel's torso like a vice clamp. From his awkward position, Samuel couldn't find the leverage to free himself.

"Stay your hand!" the construct said, pulling Samuel backward and off balance. Samuel allowed his feet to slide backward, dropping his weight down to his knees and bringing his captor forward. With a roll, Samuel toppled the construct over his shoulder and slipped from its grip, backing off and earning himself some space.

The guard stalked forward with clear intent, but his companion recovered and barred Samuel's way with a raised arm. "Stay your hand, Chronicler!"

Time seemed to stop. Samuel, taken aback by his new title, remained on one knee and did not advance. The guard's head jerked toward his companion, who nodded in response and rose to his feet.

"Are you sure?" the guard said.

"Without question," his companion replied. "He is a Chronicler, and thus must be afforded at least our patience, if not our deference."

Pare got to his feet, clutching his shoulder while Eriane helped him walk. "That's not possible," he said.

"That's the second time you've said that today," said the construct who had tossed him aside. "It seems there is much in this world you've left to learn." He turned back toward Samuel and held up a hand. "Please, a moment. I am Talecronelum, and this," he gestured toward the alley-guard, "is Cormanthul. If you will give me a moment, I will see to your audience with Acthemenius."

Cormanthul turned. "Just because he's a Chronicler doesn't mean he gets an audience unannounced. *Ekfaliuk la thental Acthemenius tol. Sol pelacruk en fatha su laman.*"

Talecronelum placed a hand on Cormanthul's shoulder. "*Se la fatha su temak estalen. Shema sem fa semta nes fasuk.*"

"They're speaking ancient Kelthan," Pare whispered to Samuel.

"Can you understand what they're saying?" Samuel asked.

Pare shook his head. "That language hasn't been in general use for hundreds of years. Given days of study and access to Mane's library I might be able to decipher written text, but I've never actually heard it spoken in conversation."

"It's kind of pretty," Eriane said. Samuel and Pare both eyeballed her. "What?" she said, with a shrug.

"What did you mean, it's not possible?" Samuel asked, turning to Pare.

Pare shook his head. "They called you a Chronicler."

"What does that mean?"

"The Chroniclers are practically a myth," Eriane said, and Pare nodded his assent. "If you even believe they ever existed, there certainly wouldn't be any of them left."

Pare nodded his assent. "The Chroniclers are an ancient legend. You'd have to be...five...six centuries old."

Samuel nodded over to the guards, who were still discussing him. "Well, they seem to think I'm one of these Chroniclers, and if that's enough to get me inside, then I'll run with it."

"Construct," Cormanthul said, addressing Samuel, who turned toward them. "Please approach."

Pare and Eriane looked up and he nodded, stepping forward with caution. Cormanthul reached up toward him and he flinched away.

"It's all right," Talecronelum said, raising a calming hand. "Please show us your right shoulder."

Samuel turned, exposing the back of his right shoulder to the two constructs, who began conversing once again in their ancient language. He righted himself and faced them, just as Cormanthul addressed him.

"You will have your audience with Acthemenius."

"Just like that?" Samuel asked, suspicious.

"He will want to see you," Cormanthul said.

Samuel kept his confusion to himself, and took what good fortune had come his way at face value. "Please follow Talecronelum," the construct guard said. "He will take you inside."

Samuel nodded and waved Pare and Eriane to join. Cormanthul held up a hand as they approached. "You may have your audience, Chronicler, but they are not permitted to enter."

"They're coming with me," Samuel said. "I'm not leaving them out here."

Cormanthul stood fast. "It is not permitted. They will not enter with you."

Samuel paused, turning back to Pare and Eriane. "Go, Samuel," Eriane said. "We'll be fine."

After a moment of hesitation, Samuel spoke. "Try to get into the library. Find out whatever you can about the Chroniclers. Who knows...maybe I'm in the history books."

Eriane nodded. "We'll see what we can find. Hopefully Acthemenius can help you, and this will all be over soon."

Pare nodded and Samuel turned to follow Talecronelum, who led him into the narrow alley. He turned in time to see Eriane wave one last time before Cormanthul blocked off the alley's entrance.

Stucco walls loomed to either side, only just wide enough for the constructs to pass through. The entire route was devoid of entryways, simply a small open space between the backs and sides of buildings that opened onto the Grotto square. The few high windows on the walls above them were shut; after all, what purpose would opening them really serve?

They rounded a slight corner in the alley and Samuel spied a wall of sparkling blue light, filling a dark opening in a wall of solid rock. Talecronelum paused, placing his hand at the top of the opening. The light curtain shimmered and faded somewhat, and Talecronelum gestured for him to step through. If the construct guard knew Samuel could see through the illusion, he made no note of it, and Samuel didn't feel the need to inform him.

They passed into a long corridor of cool gray stone cut into the mountain, lit at long intervals by oil-lamps set into sconces Samuel had to shift to avoid knocking into. The deeper they descended, the more uneasy Samuel felt. What did he really know about this Acthemenius? Was he someone to be trusted, or feared? Or perhaps ridiculed? Samuel began to question what kind of help he was in for here.

Lost in thought, Samuel almost ran into Talecronelum when he stopped at a small doorway. "When we enter," he said, "give me a moment to introduce you. Acthemenius will see you, but must be approached with a certain…caution." Samuel nodded his assent.

Talecronelum opened the small wooden door and the two of them entered a large, low-ceilinged room that smelled heavily of candle smoke. The stone walls were concealed by ancient, moth-eaten tapestries whose fraying edges were stained a sickly yellow-brown by the flames that kept the room alight. Along the edges of the room, stout tables stood buried under piles of artifacts, books, and even parts of constructs. At the back, a lone figure sat on a slab of granite, hunched over a cluttered workbench, lit by an artificial light held by an arm attached to the table.

Deep shadows played between dull reflections across the figure's shoulders and back, a patchwork of interlocking plates of tarnished copper and bronze. Stains of time gathered in each crevice, and light scraping sounds could be heard whenever the construct moved. Segmented back plates moved in subtle interactions as the figure twisted to access something on the workbench, and Samuel traced the line down to heavy plates on one visible leg. Several segments looked to be constructed of stone or wood, and the visible foot was split at the end into two articulated toes.

"Wait here a moment." Talecronelum moved forward to address the construct. The hunched figure raised its head but did not look at Talecronelum, only listened to what was being said without reply. It then turned as if to look, but stopped short of just that, instead replying to Talecronelum, who leaned in close and said something so quiet Samuel could not even register the sound. At this, the construct jerked toward Talecronelum, exposing a profile to Samuel.

The construct's face was ancient, the metal worn as though eroded by centuries of natural forces. Ghosts of lost details were barely visible beneath the few dents and dings that added any true landscape to the old construct's countenance. Small eyes looked out from beneath a once heavy brow, and a large line was cut across the lower half to form some semblance of a mouth.

With a slow, deliberate movement, the construct turned to settle his eyes upon Samuel for the first time. There was a hesitation, a slight hitch in the movement only Samuel could identify because the motion was otherwise so smooth. This construct, this ancient construct, moved with a fluidity that should not have been possible with the sheer mass of his build, and was nothing like what he'd seen in Morrelton and Kelef. The old one didn't move like a construct—he moved like Samuel.

Acthemenius rose, appraising Samuel, and crossed the room to where he stood. The whole time his gaze moved up and down, taking in every detail and nuance, as if calculating and comparing what he saw with something he already knew.

Samuel held his ground as Acthemenius approached. He found the other to stand at almost an identical height. Although there were differences in design, it seemed their base structure was very similar, and Samuel couldn't help but be awed by that fact. Maybe there was more to this old construct after all, more knowledge than he could have hoped.

Acthemenius placed his hands on Samuel's shoulders and looked him over once again, turning him to see the engraving on his shoulder. At the sight, he released Samuel and staggered a half step back, and put a hand up to his head in a gesture of disbelief.

"*Ek... ek faliq tu lemath Aesamaelus!*" he said, his voice quiet. "*Se felatuth en ma fatha te lakemaleuk! Aesamaelus en felatat shea mathathul!*" His tone was one of surprise bordering on shock. Samuel had the overwhelming feeling he *should* understand, but stood silent, unsure of what to say.

"*Osikatul en shatham?*" Acthemenius inquired.

"He... he doesn't understand Kelthan, Acthemenius," Talecronelum said.

Acthemenius gave a dismissive wave. "*Fa! Aesamaelus en fathiuk du samak!*"

Talecronelum approached and placed a hand on Acthemenius's shoulder, who looked back. "I don't know why. When we spoke Kelthan before him outside, neither he nor his companions understood. There is more to this than we know."

Acthemenius gave Samuel another appraising look, and clapped a hand on his shoulder. "It has been a long time, Aesamaelus! I...we all...thought you had perished!"

Unsure how to respond, Samuel remained silent. After Talecronelum's warning, he felt he was treading unsteady ground, and telling Acthemenius he didn't understand might endanger his chances of learning anything from the old construct. All the thoughts running through his head had locked him in indecision. He felt sure he was beginning to look like a fool.

Acthemenius proved him right by addressing Talecronelum. "Does he speak?"

Talecronelum looked at Samuel and nodded. "Yes, he does."

This broke Samuel out of his spell. "I'm sorry, Acthemenius. I...I'm not sure what to say."

Acthemenius tilted his head, an almost comical look of confusion. "Your...your voice is different. What has happened to you?"

"I...I'm not sure," Samuel replied. "It is a long story, if you have time for me to tell it."

Acthemenius took on an almost defensive posture. "You. You are not Aesamaelus." He turned on Talecronelum, who flinched. "Who have you brought to me? *Falan tham tor Aesamaelus! Es tolo fan thamutas!*"

Talecronelum raised his hands and gestured for Acthemenius to remain calm. "*Secorum an faeseuk fan thamutas. Plyar maes tor Aesamaelus.*"

Acthemenius's eyes darted toward Samuel and lingered there, and Samuel felt his entire trip to Kelef hinged on this very moment. "Whoever you are," he said, "you are not welcome here. Talecronelum was mistaken in his judgment of you, and I have entreated him to correct his mistake."

Samuel turned toward Talecronelum, whose posture had changed, taking on an imperious standing. Talecronelum was on guard now, and Samuel was on thin ice. At first he was unsure whether to stay silent or plead his case, but when Acthemenius started to turn away from him, his decision was made.

"I have seen the minds of other constructs." Samuel said. "But I am...incomplete. I believe my core has fragmented." Acthemenius

290

stopped, turning his head partway back toward Samuel. Samuel looked toward Talecronelum, who backed down and offered an encouraging nod. "I awoke in a fire only a few weeks ago. I barely escaped."

Acthemenius turned back, an inquisitive tilt to his head. Talecronelum began to speak, but Acthemenius silenced him with a raised hand.

"You were…lost to us." Acthemenius said. "I know now you are still lost to us."

"You are my last hope." Samuel said, his desperation unmasked. "I have nowhere left to turn."

"My work here," Acthemenius said, gesturing to his dim workshop, "has moved beyond you, whoever you are. I look now only to the future. I no longer have time for the past." He began fiddling with something Samuel could not see.

Samuel stood, defeated, at a loss for what he had left to say. Acthemenius walked back to his bench and sat, readjusting the lamp to provide more light for his work. Talecronelum's shoulders dropped and he shook his head.

"Someone's trying to destroy me." Samuel said. "I'm being followed. *My* future depends on finding out why." Nothing. Not so much as a twitch or turn from Acthemenius. "If you know half of what you're rumored to know, you're the only one who might be able to help me."

Nothing. Acthemenius remained steadfastly attentive to his work. Samuel had been shut out, his last chance at finding out who he was dying out in a dingy cave in Kelef. Defeated, he turned toward the door, and Talecronelum followed. As he reached the exit he paused, finding one last thought he hoped might turn the tide of the discussion. He turned back toward Acthemenius.

"Someone tried to use one of the Rings of Lorrem on me."

The sounds of Acthemenius's tinkering halted. A hand reached up to push aside the work lamp, and the ancient construct turned once again to face Samuel. They stared at one another long enough to make Samuel uncomfortable, but he remained silent.

Acthemenius gestured to a stone slab at his side. "Sit," he said. "Tell me everything."

The Chronicler Saga

Chapter Thirty-Nine

As they exited the Grotto, Eriane wondered how they'd ever get back to the square without Samuel's bulk to deter brigands. Malevolent eyes followed their every movement from the dark alleys of the cavern. Pare increased the pace of their flight when more than one seedy-looking denizen made a point to exit the shadows as they passed and fall in step behind them. Their pursuers did not give chase, exactly, but were a constant presence just over their shoulder. She dared not look back until they were at the mouth of the bridge. Some few dark figures lingered at the edge of the moonlight as many others faded back into the darkness of the Grotto.

Breathing the fresh, frozen air of the open city calmed Eriane's nerves. Morning was not far off. It hadn't felt like they'd been gone so long, but it made sense when Eriane put her mind to it. Impending sunrise brought with it a double-edged sword: Sorrell and Jacob would discover their absence and soon be in pursuit, but morning's light would also bring access to the city library—the one place they might be able to find some answers about Samuel's origins.

The city streets were still deserted, the only footprints across the snowy bridge their own. It wasn't long before they reached the stairwell leading to the terrace upon which the library stood and they ascended without another person in sight. At the base of the wide marble stairs that formed the front of the building, Eriane halted, stupefied by its massive façade. She had spent her entire life in small towns or Mane's cabin, and the sight of such a building awed her more than anything she'd ever seen.

"Come on," Pare said, breaking the trance. "We'd better find a way inside."

"What do you mean?" Eriane asked. "You don't mean to break in, do you?"

"Have you got a better idea?" Pare asked.

"It'll open soon enough."

"We don't have that kind of time, Eri."

"Do you really think you'll be able to get in there?" Eriane asked, incredulous. "Do you honestly think just because there are no people around, a place like this is unprotected?"

"Yeah, I guess you've got a point," Pare said. He took a deep breath, then turned toward the building anyway. "Let's at least go see if anyone's inside."

Eriane nodded. The two of them made their way up the steps to the large double doors in the center of the building. Pare reached out and tried the handle, but the door wouldn't budge. Eriane crinkled her brow at him.

"Hey, it was worth a try!" he said. Pare looked both ways along the building gesturing to the windows along the front. "Okay, you go that way, and I'll look over here."

The two of them split up, peering into the library's frost-covered windows. There was very little light inside, and Eriane couldn't see much beyond the tall stacks lining the front of the building nearest to where she stood. Even those few shelves contained more books than Eriane had ever seen, making Mane's collection seem puny by comparison. At the third window there was an opening with no shelves, and she glimpsed into the wide interior of the building.

At some point, Eriane's amazement took a subtle shift into dread. How could they possibly hope to find anything in this gargantuan horde of volumes? She saw at least four levels of balconied walkways overlooking the open main floor. Rows and rows of books vanished into the darkness to the rear of the enormous room. Even Mane's collection would have been daunting without the extensive constructions to help them search and Reet to pull and replace books. What could they ever expect to find in the amount of time they had left?

Pare made a noise, waving Eriane over to his window. With one last look inside her heart sank, and she broke away to join him. "Pare, how are we ever going to find anything in here?"

A twinkle of a grin broke across Pare's face, and he pointed at the window for Eriane to look. Inside was another break in the bookshelves, looking out onto rows of study desks in an open lobby. Toward the middle of the pack, the halo of a low light cut through the darkness, illuminating the head and shoulders of someone hunched over a desk. "There's someone here!" Eriane exclaimed, quite before she'd realized she'd done it.

"Just wait," Pare said. "Watch for a minute."

Eriane returned her attention to the studying figure, who seemed to be flipping through several volumes simultaneously. Another movement high in the room startled her, and then delighted her when she identified it. A tiny round shape, clutching a book from one of the higher terraces, zipped down through the air toward the seated figure, depositing the book at the adjacent desk, then picked up another, discarded book and zipped back away into the darkness. It seemed the library of Kelef had its very own Reet. Eriane felt a wide grin work its way onto her cold-numbed face.

"Let's get his attention!" she said.

Pare held up a hand. "And say what, exactly?"

"Don't worry, Pare," Eriane said with a wry smile. "I can take care of this one." Before he could respond, she turned and rapped lightly on the window. When the hunched figure inside failed to respond, she rapped a little harder.

It was apparent she had startled him, as he jerked upward in his seat so fast he knocked over a pile of books sitting near his elbow. The bearded figure fumbled about on the desk for a moment and found a pair of round-rimmed glasses, which he used to peer out the window. After a moment of confusion he stood and headed in the direction of the front door.

"Just play along, okay?" Eriane said as she and Pare scuttled over to the door.

"What are you going to say?" Pare asked in a forced whisper.

"Just follow my lead. I'm going to tell him we're—" Just then, the door creaked open and a grey-haired, bespectacled head poked out at them.

"What in blazes are you two doing out here at this time of the morning?" he said.

"I'm SO sorry to bother you, sir," Eriane said, employing an affectation that made her sound far more girlish than she actually was. "I know it's early, but is there any way you can let us in?"

The old man huffed, making his displeasure known. "I can not," he said, putting extra emphasis on the final word.

"But sir, please," Eriane pleaded. "We've both got papers due tomorrow and we haven't studied..."

"Well perhaps two young..."—the old man stuttered and huffed again—"...lovebirds like yourselves should figure out your... priorities!"

"Ew!" Eriane said. "He's my brother!"

"Yes sir," Pare chimed in. "Our father will be very cross with us if he finds us being lax on our homework again."

"And we don't want to make him cross." Eriane flashed a convincing look of fear, one that spoke of a deeper dread than a simple chastising.

The old man huffed again and sniffled in the cold night air, staring them down as if attempting to read straight into their souls. "Oh..."—another huff—"...all right then. But you will be quiet and respectful, and you will not disturb me while I work! And when the doors open this morning, you will act as though you only just arrived. And stop calling me sir! My name is Harven. Am I clear?"

"Absolutely, s- Harven," Pare said, nodding and giving the librarian an apologetic look as he moved into the library. Eriane emitted a lilting giggle and jumped up to kiss Harven on the cheek before bolting past him through the door. The old man huffed once again at no one, closing and locking the door behind them.

Frescoed ceilings soared sixty feet above the library's polished marble floor, supported by columns of the same gleaming stone. An inlay of granite, in an array of types and colors, covered the entire expanse of the central lobby floor, depicting an open book whose pages showed a crimson heart on the left and a silver star on the right. The book stacks on the main floor stood some thirty feet high. Moveable ladders at the ends of each row looked like they had fallen into disuse, and Eriane was sure the little Reet helping the old man had something to do with that.

Inside, there were six stories of balconies and further stacks, each level built of a different color of granite or marble. To their left and right were extensive rows of study desks, each with its own lamp and chair. A short pedestal at the back of each desk supported a small metal sphere. The fact that they were hundreds of retrievers took a moment to sink in, and when it did she felt a lump in her throat at the sudden memory of her master and surrogate father, hunched over his little reading desk by the deep round window, his absentminded commands sending Reet whooshing through the cabin for this book or that to help in his studies.

"Well, go on now!" Harven said, his voice a stern whisper. Only then did the two of them realize they'd been immobile, mouths agape at the sight of the Kelef Library. "I haven't seen you two in here before. Do you know how to use—"

"Yes!" Eriane interrupted, hoping the catch in her voice wasn't all too clear. "We've used them before."

Harven nodded and started back toward his desk. "Well, on you go then. And try not to get me into trouble."

"Um…Harven?" Pare asked.

Harven stopped. "Mmm?"

"Where should we start if we're doing research on Chroniclers?"

The old man's bushy eyebrows raised, but he answered the question without another word. "Construct History is on the second terrace north. Be on your way, now."

"Thank you," Pare said. "Come on, Eri, let's go."

Eriane was already halfway to the stairs before he'd even finished the sentence.

The Chronicler Saga

Chapter Forty

"You were,,,Aesamaelus was my friend." Acthemenius said. "I've known you for over five hundred years."

The implications of Acthemenius's revelation swirled in Samuel's thoughts. "How is that even possible?"

Acthemenius belted out a mirthless laugh. "Because that's what we were designed for!" he said. He stepped around Samuel to a workbench that looked long disused. Reaching into a wall cubby above the table he withdrew a small bundle, an item slightly larger than a foot square wrapped in oilcloth, and returned to hand it to Samuel. "We Chroniclers were meant for more than simple servitude." Samuel detected more than a hint of bitterness in the statement.

Samuel carefully withdrew the folds of oilcloth to reveal a thick bronze plate, designed to fit just below a construct's shoulder. Light tarnish discolored the surface of the metal that was otherwise in fine shape. What Samuel saw in the surface of the plate stunned him into a long silence: an ornate engraving that read, simply, *ACTHEMENIUS*.

Finding his voice seemed to take Samuel an eternity. "What were we meant for, then?" Samuel asked.

Acthemenius stood above him and shook his head. "Damn that Ferron. Once a fool, always a fool." He raised a hand to his head. "Does the name not reveal our purpose to you, Samuel?" Another resentful laugh. "Of course not, of course not. You're only a child."

Samuel wasn't sure whether interrupting Acthemenius's rant would gain him any benefit, so he remained silent.

"It's bad enough to core wipe a useful, normal construct. I can't even begin to divine his purpose for wiping a Chronicler." Acthemenius mumbled, his voice rising as he spoke. "He's one of the few who should have known better." He turned, tapping the side of his head with two fingers. "Think for a moment, Aesama... Samuel. Think about our name, and what it may imply."

Ever since Samuel had heard the term Chronicler, he wondered at its meaning. Having the time now to mull it over, he had come to the conclusion they were some sort of record-keeping constructs, little more than a way to store information. He still failed to understand the importance of that fact.

"Do you still not see?" Acthemenius said. "Other constructs...normal constructs...have almost the exact same capacity for memory as a person. Their recall is more accurate, but there is only a finite amount of things a normal construct can retain. A Chronicler, however..."

"Can retain an infinite amount of information?"

Acthemenius laughed. "*Infinite* may be a bit overzealous, but..." He leaned over Samuel, pushing his face in close. "I remember...*everything*. Every nuance, every detail. And I will remember for all eternity. Every. Moment." He punctuated each word with a ringing tap to the side of his head. "Every war. Every cataclysm. Every act of pettiness, of jealousy, of hatred. Every drop of blood on every blade of grass on every field of battle."

Samuel thought back. Everything was there. The fire, the tunnel beneath Winston, Taeman's caravan, the journey to Morrelton, Atherton and Michael and Mane. All of it in vivid, flawless detail. Samuel hadn't even realized how fresh it all still seemed in his mind, and how much of it he could extract with very little effort.

"We see all and remember without error," Acthemenius continued, returning to his seat. "We were, as our *benevolent* makers ordained, '*Designed to be the perfect historians. Possessed of an individual perspective, a single point of view, but untainted by the bias of emotion*'. We were to be the world's storytellers; the embodiment of a flawless, undying record of all we had witnessed." Acthemenius paused, looking to Samuel as if waiting.

Samuel nodded, unsure of how to respond and wary of Acthemenius's agitation. He needed answers, though, so he pressed on. "Untainted by the bias of emotion..."

Acthemenius scoffed, and leaned his elbows on his knees. "There were only a few. A few of us *gifted* with the ability to feel. We thought it a gift." He lowered his eyes and shook his head. "A gift."

Samuel stared down at the engraved plate in his hands. "Why can I see the memories of other constructs?"

Acthemenius's head remained bowed. "It was a failsafe, meant to ensure the integrity of our..."—a chuckle—"chronicle. We are connected, one and all. If one is destroyed, its experience is passed to the rest."

It all came crashing together. Every single construct who had been destroyed in the pursuit of Samuel's knowledge had passed their memories along that link to Samuel. The images he'd been seeing were real memories, and now he knew that somewhere, buried amongst all of them, was the key to finding out why they had all become targets. Samuel tried to take it all in, to figure out his place in all of it, tearing his eyes away from the plate and returning them to Acthemenius. "I believe whoever is following me has some way to track Chroniclers. To find us. If you say a destroyed Chronicler's knowledge is passed to all others, that means you have the memories of the recently destroyed just like me, right?"

Acthemenius raised his gaze to Samuel, and nodded.

"How... Then why haven't you...any of you...done something about this? These men have left a trail of destroyed Chroniclers and dead people in their wake, and no one has done a damned thing about it!"

"You...you still don't understand..."

Samuel stood. "What would you have me understand? That you are clearly, in spite of rumor, measured and intelligent, and would rather play at insanity than act? That you are too frightened or too lazy to use the knowledge you have gained? People have died and you sit on your hands doing—"

With surprising speed Acthemenius was on his feet and clouted

Samuel across the face with enough force to knock him to the floor. "How *dare* you speak to me in that tone!" he yelled. "You have perhaps *weeks* of memories, and you have the gall to impugn centuries of knowledge? Every sight, sound, and detail from five hundred years and countless lost Chroniclers. Perhaps you will not again question the structure of my sanity, or why I don't act on every single, solitary image that enters my consciousness."

Samuel stammered. "I didn't..."

"No, you did not," Acthemenius snapped. "Our...flawed design was devised by *men*. Men with limited foresight, and power they did not understand." Acthemenius waved his hand about, his voice laden with disgust. "Centuries of collected knowledge with little thought on how to organize or retrieve it. *That* is the end to which I work here."

He made a gesture to the surrounding workshop. "At first, I was trying to find a way to allow a Chronicler to organize their memories in some way to relieve the...pressure...of it. Fruitless." He made a dismissive wave. "The design was a fluke in the first place, so attempting to temper a harnessed accident with logic was an infuriating failure. Now? All I can hope is to find a way to expel it without destroying the essence of the individual."

"The essence of an individual resides in one's experiences." Samuel said, rising to his elbows. "Ridding a construct of their memories makes them...something else. I'm walking proof of that." He shook his head in frustration. "I don't want to be *rid* of this, Acthemenius. I want to *understand* what I've seen. If I am to be the only one who can act on what I know, then by my will I shall act on it." Each word was punctuated by the dull ring of Samuel's fingers beating into his chest. "I have left a trail of death and destruction in my wake, and the ones who follow me will not stop until *I stop them*. And if your only solution is to rid me of what I know, then everything I've gone through to get here has been for naught."

Acthemenius stalked over to Samuel in three long strides and knelt. With one hand Acthemenius shoved Samuel to the floor and held him there with overpowering strength. Samuel pulled at his forearm but it wouldn't budge. "You want to know?" the ancient Chronicler growled. "Then *know*."

Chapter Forty-One

Something pulled at the edges of Jacob's slumber. This was the first good night's sleep in a real bed he'd had in weeks, and waking up went against every signal his body was giving him. His subconscious was insistent, and once he was awake enough he could hear the knocking and the voice outside his door.

"Jacob, please wake up," Sorrell said. The sentence was friendly, but did not come out as a request.

Jacob took a deep breath and rolled his neck to stretch. "Just a moment, Sorrell. Give me a moment to get dressed."

"Very well," Sorrell replied through the door. "Please meet me in the sitting room."

Jacob hoped his sigh wasn't loud enough for Sorrell to hear. He forced one eye open and saw through the break in the curtains it wasn't even light out yet. What could Sorrell possibly need? Jacob flipped the covers and swung his legs off of the bed. Creaking joints and heavy protests from overworked muscles forced him to sit unmoving, willing his body back into working order. Every movement brought another crash of pain and a wave of nausea. *The exertion of the past week is catching up with me.*

Sliding his hand under the lush down pillow Sorrell had supplied, Jacob produced a small, stoppered glass vial. A decision that would have been instantaneous only a few weeks ago dragged on as Jacob made little movements, feeling out his broken body and finding every point of soreness and weakness. With such simplicity he could feel right again, at least for a little while, could walk out of the room without a constant physical reminder of everything he'd been through. For the first time, Jacob thought of what it had cost him over the years, and the look on Eriane's face at the mere mention of Drift hovered in his vision.

Those thoughts were tempered by the ease with which he could erase his pain. Eventually, ease won out and he uncorked the bottle, lifted it to his lips, and inhaled the contents in one swift motion. Within seconds his muscles relaxed and the soreness drained away. He closed his eyes and leaned forward, his hands on the edge of the bed, and held his breath while the Drift worked its way through his injuries and strain, and melted the pain from his aching bones.

There was another knock at the door. "Jacob, are you coming?" Sorrell's muffled voice said. "There's someone I'd like you to meet."

Jacob's eyes snapped open. *Someone to meet?* "Almost ready. I'll be right out." The last thing Jacob needed was for Sorrell to have pulled in one of his less-than-reputable associates or, even worse, called in a favor with the city guard. Some sleazeball merchant or local thug Jacob could handle, but involving the law would make an already bad situation untenable. He threw on some clothes and opened the door, startled to find Sorrell still standing in the hallway.

"Ah, there you are," Sorrell said.

"What's this about meeting someone?" Jacob asked, making a point of his displeasure as he led the way down the hall.

"Ease up now, old friend," Sorrell said, catching up. Only when he had his diplomat voice in full swing would he ever call Jacob *friend*. "I was contacted by an associate of mine whose…interests align with our own. His talents may be of some use to us once we find your friends."

Jacob pulled up short and grabbed Sorrell's arm. "Wait, what are you talking about?"

Sorrell took a breath that signaled equal parts displeasure and relief. "Your friends. They departed last night. Off to see…Acthemenius, I assume?"

Son of a bitch. Jacob held his tongue but did not hide his surprise, instead masking it into a look of false irritation. *No good night's sleep goes unpunished.* Samuel and the kids had taken off on their own, without giving Jacob the opportunity to plan, and now he would have to try and explain himself out of a sticky situation while standing in the middle of the muck. No doubt they believed he'd betrayed them. *Who could blame them after my stupid outburst on the Kelef road?*

Sorrell leaned toward him. "I'm not stupid, Kaleb," he said. "Perhaps, in the future, you might consider telling me the truth?"

"We have to go after them," Jacob blurted, hoping his desperation took the right tone to Sorrell's ears.

"Of course we do," Sorrell replied, continuing their walk to the sitting room. "They can't get much of anywhere, if they're headed to the Grotto. We'll have them cornered. Besides, let's have a chat before heading on our way, and see what my associate is able to offer us."

Jacob had forgotten they were meeting one of Sorrell's footmen. He was paying for his attempt at deception, and should have known better. Sorrell never was one to get his hands dirty, if he could help it.

They crossed the foyer, lit by flickering lamplight from the archway to the sitting room, where Jacob heard a new fire burning in the fireplace. Sorrell rounded the corner first and Jacob followed, lifting his head as he entered in search of the wine from the night before, and stopped dead in his tracks. The man standing by the fireplace could have been any ordinary thug, but the scar across his face and his piercing silver eyes were unmistakable.

Every nicety was stripped from Sorrell's once diplomatic tone as he spoke. "Jacob, I believe you may have already met my associate, Colton Harms?"

Jacob could've taught a master class in self-control when he saw those cold eyes turn to face him. Without hesitation he slipped past Colton to the hutch where he retrieved a brandy snifter and filled it from a decanter in the same cabinet. "I...wasn't aware you two were associates," he said.

Colton wore an easy smile as he followed Jacob's every movement. An angry bruise marred his jaw and an unstitched cut had formed a craggy scab at his hairline. Otherwise, the man seemed unmolested.

"It is a...recent acquaintance," Sorrell said. Colton still stood silent

305

as Jacob backed away, draining a healthy dose of his brandy.

"You must be the slip." Colton said, his derisive language flowered like friendly banter.

Jacob inclined his head.

"Where have your friends gone?" Colton asked.

Jacob smiled. "It's clear you already know the answer to that question."

Colton gave a single nod. "You are an intelligent man, Kaleb." The silver-eyed man sat down across from him. Jacob felt an unpleasant tingling at the back of his mind. "Which means you know what I'm trying to do right now. Your friend has a talent for protections, I'll give him that." Jacob attempted to mask his panic with another drink of brandy. His hand shook. As subtly as he could manage, he began pulling energy to translocate away. If he could get to Samuel in time...

"But just because I don't have your mind," Colton continued, "doesn't mean I can't close down your translocation when you're halfway finished." Jacob's stomach sank at Colton's anticipation of his intention.

Impossible. Only the—

"Five of my best years were spent as a Royal Interdictor." Colton said, as though reading Jacob's thoughts. "It would not do to have half a slip suddenly drop into the Kelef streets, now, would it?"

Jacob finished his brandy and set the glass down, clasping hands to stop the tremors. "I am curious about one thing, Mr. Harms," Jacob said. Colton nodded but did not reply, prompting Jacob to continue. "How, exactly, did you get here so fast?"

Colton's head tilted, a slight twitch turning the corners of his smile. He stood, took three smooth steps, and leaned into Jacob's space, closer than was strictly comfortable. Every instinct told Jacob to lash out or to break and run, but he held back in spite of his screaming nerves. The silver-eyed man came almost nose-to-nose with Jacob, his hard eyes betraying the smile on his lips.

"Tenacity."

Chapter Forty-Two

Memories crashed like a hurricane, sweeping Samuel's mind into a maelstrom. As images poured into him from Acthemenius, it was all he could do to stay conscious, although he wasn't even sure he was. His surroundings vanished beneath waves of other constructs' experiences, drowning him in a sea of history.

Do you see? Acthemenius was here with him, in the storm, omniscience rather than voice. *Does it all make sense to you now, child Chronicler? Is your goal somehow clearer?* Acthemenius's vitriol overwhelmed Samuel's thoughts. He latched onto it, anchoring himself to the foreign presence, trying only to not be swept away. Centuries of memories flowed into him like a flash flood. He clung to the ones he knew and held fast against the deluge.

It will be too much for you, Samuel. And only then will you have an inkling of my mind. Acthemenius pushed wide the floodgates. Samuel screamed, somewhere in his psyche, trying to hold onto anything familiar. As his own memories were subsumed into the swell, a single thought rose to the surface. A powerful image had driven Samuel from the moment he awoke: The pleading eyes of a dying woman.

"Is he home, Bezeltania?" the woman at the door asks. She'd been by the house many times over the last several months, more visits to her old master than she'd graced them with in the five years prior.

"I'm sorry, but he is not," he responds. "He's been out most of today, and he's late in returning home."

"Damnit," she says. "Something's happened. Something is different, and I think both Ezekeal and I are in danger." The woman paces the kitchen, her hand to her lips, muttering to herself. "I thought I'd been so careful."

"Would you like to wait here for him?" he asks.

"No...no," she answers. "I have something I need to take care of, so I'll come back in a bit. If he returns while I'm gone, please ask him to wait for me."

"Absolutely, your Highness," Bezeltania says.

"Thank you, Bez. And please," the woman replies, turning back toward the rear door of the house, "Just call me Heliah. Using my formal title could be dangerous. And besides... it may not apply for much longer." With that, she slips out the door. Bezeltania wonders where master Ezekeal has been, but this wouldn't be the first night he came home late. There is nothing to do but wait.

For the next several hours, he busies himself with house chores, sweeping and dusting, cleaning and straightening. It isn't until after dark he hears voices downstairs. A man and a woman talking, and then arguing. He can't hear what they are saying. These kinds of discussions are no business of Bezeltania, so he continues to finish his chores in one of the upstairs bedrooms until he hears the argument rise in pitch, ending in an abrupt silence.

There is no sound of a door, no sign either or both people have left, but the voices have ceased. Bezeltania makes his way out of the upstairs bedroom and down the stairs of the large house.

"Master Ezekeal?" he says. There is no response. He reaches the bottom of the stairs and stops, craning to look into the study and the large family room, empty on either side of the main entryway.

"Master?" he calls as he rounds the corner, moving into the long hallway leading to the kitchen from the front of the house. There is no response, save for a wet noise that repeats with a light slap, like someone coring a pumpkin and throwing the seeds aside. He's halfway down the hallway when the noise ceases, replaced by a quiet scraping and grunts of effort, someone lifting something heavy. He pushes the kitchen door open and freezes, unable at first to process the scene before him.

Blood splatters the floor and cabinets, dripping off the edges of countertops and doorhandles. The tile floor is obscured by an expanding pool of viscous red liquid that fills each grouted seam as it creeps toward him. Streaks break the surface of the red, intersecting small piles of pink matter steeping in the crimson morass. His gaze follows the trail and stops at two feet as they slide through the pool toward the back of the room.

Delicate legs lead his gaze to the woman's body, still bleeding from a belly-level opening too large to be called a wound. Entrails snake out of the evisceration and drag on the floor beside her. A spasm draws him upward to her face, Heliah's eyes open and somehow still alert, pleading with him for help behind tears that streak down her face. Her shoulders are held in her murderer's grasp, whose face is hidden behind long, dark hair that hangs heavy, soaked in blood. One of his hands moves from under her and draws a small knife across her throat, opening veins that spew upward and add to the carnage.

The killer's head rises. White eyes shine bright against the dark gore surrounding them. He drops the Queen Consort as she bleeds to death on the kitchen floor, standing straight and staring at him, blood dripping from the end of his knife. Bezeltania knows he must leave and turns to run, bolting down the hallway toward the front door.

"Don't run, Chronicler." The killer's voice slinks down the hallway, a creeping trail that follows Bezeltania out the front door. "You'll only make it worse for yourself."

Curious onlookers follow his flight down the nearly empty street. The only place he knows to go is master Ezekeal's shop, ten full blocks away. He ducks down a side street and into the alleyway that runs along the back of the row of shops where Ezekeal's stands.

The door of Ezekeal's shop stands ajar and the light of an oil lamp flickers within. Bezeltania stops short of the entryway and approaches with caution.

"Master Ezekeal?" he calls, pushing the door open further. There is no answer.

Lamplight shines from the main shop at the far end of the hallway, but Bezeltania can see no movement or sign of life. A few things are out of place in the shop, a place he knows to be meticulously kept by Ezekeal, who is organized to a fault. He calls out again, all but knowing he will get no response.

Across the rear of the shop stands Ezekeal's office. He hears no sound from within and hopes it might stand empty, Ezekeal simply away for the evening. He grasps the handle and the door swings open on creaky hinges.

The office beyond is smashed. Shelves have been emptied, and his master's desk is overturned in the corner. A shadow sways on the opposite wall, cast by Ezekeal's limp body suspended by a noose looped over one of the rafters. There is a note pinned to his chest, but Bezeltania can't bring himself to read it.

Ezekeal hadn't shared the reason for the Queen Consort's increase in visits, nor had he hinted at their nature. Something terrible has befallen both of them and he is at a loss to understand why. Now masterless and homeless, he has no idea what his place in all of this might be. A hand touches his back and a cold feeling rushes through his body. He can't move.

"You shouldn't have run, canner." It was the killer's voice. Calm and measured, quiet like a crack forming in deep ice, felt more than heard. "Now, I'll just go ahead and make an example of you."

The hand on his back releases and Bezeltania slumps to the floor, every faculty cut off. He can't move or speak and his hearing dulls, but he can still see everything in vivid detail. Unable even to turn his head, he is forced to watch as the blood-soaked man releases Ezekeal from his noose, lays him on the floor, removes the note from his chest and crumples it into a pocket, then methodically eviscerates him the same way he had the Queen Consort.

When the killer finishes his gruesome task, he calmly steps around the pool of blood that now stains the floor of Ezekeal's office and kneels down into Bezeltania's line of sight.

"See what you've made me do, canner?" he says, his voice barely audible. "You just needed to stay upstairs, and you'd never have been a part of this." The snake of a man plants a hand on Bezeltania's shoulder and his limbs came to life, but not under his own control. With some concentration the man is able to get the construct back on his feet, and even makes him walk with jerky, hesitant motions, forcing him to stand in the pooling blood. Every instinct inside Bezeltania fights the motion, but he has been separated from all control of his own body. He watches from inside his own shell as he bends over and covers both hands in Ezekeal's blood, and then turns as the killer puppets him out of the office and into the darkened alley.

His movements are uncoordinated, almost drunk. Although his movements become smoother as they walk, they do not become faster, and the return trip feels like an eternity. Although he tries to fight, to leave, he is powerless in the madman's grip.

At the rear of the manor house they ascend the stone steps to the kitchen door and stop, the killer making a point of planting one of Bezeltania's bloody hands on the doorframe as they enter. His hand leaves a tacky crimson streak on the jamb as he enters. Two steps in, past the slumped body of the Queen Consort, the puppeteer releases his hold. Bezeltania falls in a heap on the kitchen floor.

The dark haired man once again leans into his line of sight. "One last thing before I leave you," the killer says, a sly grin splitting his face. He tips a small dagger back and forth in the construct's line of sight and wraps Bezeltania's fingers around the blood-soaked handle. Bezeltania hears light footsteps down the hallway before the front door opens and shuts, leaving him alone.

Bezeltania tries to rise, but cannot move. He lay paralyzed in the coagulating gore, unable to tear his eyes away from the grisly scene laid out before him. The Queen Consort murdered, a woman he'd seen alive and scared mere hours before. And now he's set up to take the fall.

He's not sure how long he lay paralyzed before a noise draws his attention, someone at the door. Thoughts of the consequences of being found here, framed for murder, begin to erode his paralysis. The men give up the front and arrive at the kitchen door, so close to where he lay.

His fingers twitch. Knocks at the door become more insistent, the urgent calls of the men outside unintelligible. Willing himself mobile he manages to roll, still burdened with agonizing weakness. As he gains his feet, the knocks at the door transform into crashes, and the door bursts inward.

The men rush in. Their eyes fall to the Queen Consort's body and return to him, filled with fire. Raising his hands to protest his innocence, his voice fails him. Something strikes his shoulder, a ripple of weakness crashing through to his feet, driving him to his knees. Fires of hatred burn bright in their eyes as they continue hitting him, each strike of their mafi-sticks carrying more than just impact; sapping his energy—his life—away.

His face comes to rest in a cool, sticky pool of drying blood. Once again he sees Heliah's face, her eyes still open as though pleading with him for help, just as she had in the last moments of her life. The voice of the killer, louder now and strained, drifts into his hearing as his senses fail him, screaming "No, you idiots, don't—"

Another strike; everything is gone.

The Chronicler Saga

Chapter Forty-Three

Eriane slapped another book shut and pushed it away, flopping back in her chair with a hand up to rub her eyes. They'd found a row of study desks on the second level and began employing the retrievers, who were off on another mission through the gargantuan library. History texts of all shapes and sizes were piled on the desks around them. "This is pointless," Eriane said.

"They all say the same thing!" Pare said, exasperated. "I mean, they couch it in different languages or give a different angle on the history, but they all just regurgitate the same crap."

"How can something like this exist," Eriane said. "And have no history? I mean, they were built to be historians, right? Then why isn't there any writing about them?"

Pare shut his book, as well. One of the retrievers returned and set a book down next to him, and he waved it into a sconce where it would await instruction. "I don't know. I mean, the Great War was ages ago... How reliable were the historians then? Besides, the constructs were on the losing side of that war." He gestured to the books around them. "Who knows how reliable any of this information really is."

Eriane flipped a page back and forth in one of the open books on her desk and rubbed her temple. She couldn't remember the last time she'd slept. Sifting through history books wasn't conducive to maintaining an adrenaline rush, and she was starting to crash. Any assurance their library trip was of any help to Samuel was slipping away.

"Wait," she said, snapping her fingers. Pare looked up at her from another book. "What if… What if we're looking in the wrong place?"

"What do you mean?" Pare said.

"You've made the point that these history texts might be sort of… well… biased, right?" Pare nodded. "But what about the myths?" Pare's look was equal parts inquisitive and dubious.

"I'm not sure how that's going to help," he replied.

"Think about it, Pare," Eriane said. "Mane had tons of mythology books in his collection. He always used to say myths are, at some level, always based in truth, right? They may seem fantastic now, but at some point something really happened that triggered the story."

"Yeah, but it's still just stories. People make things up to explain the stuff they can't understand. It's a waste of time."

Eriane couldn't hide her annoyance. "And what we're doing right now isn't? Come on, Pare, do you have a better idea?"

Pare took a breath as though he was about to reply, but blew it out instead and shook his head. "No, not really," he said. "I guess we've got nothing to lose at this point."

Eriane ran to the edge, almost knocking over her chair as she stood. Leaning over the railing, she yelled down into the main chamber. "Harven!"

Harven started, and Eriane wasn't sure if she'd just caught him by surprise or woken him up. "Quiet DOWN!" Harven shushed.

"Harven, where is the mythology section?" Eriane asked.

The old man gave one of his now-familiar huffs. "Fourth floor north! The next time you need to ask me a question you come down here and do it like a civilized person!" He shook his head and went back to his study-sleeping.

"Thank you!" Eriane blurted, before bolting back to Pare. Running down the line of desks, she activated every retriever on the row, mumbling commands to each one. Some of them swooped up the books already in their possession, others zipped out into the open air and upward toward the fourth floor balcony. Within minutes, all but a few of their history texts had been returned and the retrievers had brought a stack of books on mythology surrounding constructs and the Great War.

The little constructs brought them volume upon volume of fairy tales and poems and epics about early constructs. Eriane dove in, her energy for research renewed. The myth of artificial people, she found, wound back much further into history than the reality of it. But even with her second wind, Eriane couldn't focus. Although she loved reading stories of artificial beings as children's toys, or housing the souls of the departed, or terrorizing villages, the information just wasn't very useful. She couldn't tell if her exhaustion was affecting her search or if the information she wanted just wasn't there. Worry and anger crept in, and she began to wonder why they'd been sent here at all.

Did Samuel actually believe the library might hold some long-lost key to his existence, or was he trying to get rid of them? Samuel had been trying to separate himself from them ever since the fight at Mane's cabin, and now maybe he'd found a way to do it. *Damn him!* Exhaustion took over, and she laid her head down on her arm.

"Um, Eri?" Pare's voice was quiet, but something about it caught her attention and she raised her head. "Take a look." he said, sliding a book over to her.

An ancient illustration showed four constructs, laid down on tables in a cross pattern with their heads toward one another. Standing over them were four serious-looking men in arcane robes, each with distinct features but all of them very old. Each man had his hand on the chest of one of the dormant constructs.

"Read here," Pare said, tapping his finger on a passage opposite the drawing. As she read, her heart crept into her throat. Her energy returned and she was overcome with excitement and fear.

"This can't be real," she said.

"Maybe not," Pare replied. "But you said it yourself: myths are based in truth. Maybe..." He hesitated, as though what he was about to say were difficult, "Maybe this is one of them."

"Let's go," Eriane said. Both of them bolted upright and Pare grabbed the book they'd been looking at and began to stuff it into his pack. "Wait...you can't take it with you."

"Why not?" Pare asked.

"Remember?" Eriane replied. "Big library? Protections? Do you think they'd let just anyone walk out of here with one of their books? We can't afford to draw any more attention to ourselves."

Pare nodded, taking the book out and setting it on the table. He flipped it open and leafed to the page where they'd found the drawing. He flipped forward and back a couple of pages in either direction, then coughed loudly, shielding the sound of tearing the entire block of pages out of the book. Eriane put her hand over her mouth in shock, but when he shrugged at her and stuffed the pages into his pack, she let out a quiet laugh into her palm.

"We have to get back to the Grotto." Pare said.

The two of them jogged as quickly as their weary bodies would carry them, down the stairs and into the main hall. A few patrons now sat at desks on the main floor; the library must have opened while they worked. "Thank you, Harven!" They yelled in unison as they trundled by, and he let out a hefty scoff as they bolted out the front door.

"So where's your puffy-faced breaker friend?" Jacob asked. The question had been bouncing around in his brain ever since they'd left the mansion, and now that they were strolling down the empty streets of Kelef in the burgeoning morning light, he wasn't sure he wanted the answer.

"Around, somewhere," came Colton's noncommittal reply. "When we come to a place like this, I can't always keep him under my thumb."

"Are you sure I shouldn't bring a few more hands on for this?" Sorrell asked. Colton had insisted Sorrell accompany them to the Grotto, and Jacob took what little pleasure he could from Sorrell's discomfort. Every one of Sorrell's attempts to bow out of the trek was met with further coldness from Colton, so he took the tack of trying to recruit more help he could hide behind if things went sour. Jacob was beginning to remember why he broke ties with Sorrell in the first place.

"I have no need of your sellswords, Sorrell," Colton replied. "We'll have all the help we need by the time we get where we're going."

Jacob wasn't sure what that meant, but he didn't like the sound of it. The further they walked, the more trapped he felt. His options were thinning, and he didn't see a reasonable way out. At least not for all of them. *Maybe it's time to just cut and run?* The moment the thought crossed his mind, Jacob felt the pangs of something he hadn't dealt with in a great many years: responsibility.

All of his life, Jacob planned three steps ahead. He lived with a contingency for every situation, as long as he was the only one involved. For the first time in a long time, he'd put himself into a situation where he felt responsible for someone else's welfare. From the moment he saw Samuel, Jacob knew there was something special about him, and that's what had drawn him in. That force had been so powerful his planning gave way to spontaneity. Then, the moment things went bad at Atherton's, any chance of forming a plan fell to pieces.

He'd done the one thing he told himself never to do: put himself right into the middle of another person's drama. The real problem, though, wasn't that he was involved, it was that he was *invested*. Whatever was going on was bigger than just Samuel, or Mane, or Atherton, or any of them, and now Jacob was driven not just by feeling responsible for what was happening to Samuel and the kids, but by one driving question that hammered at his mind: *Why?*

"Not thinking of stepping out on us, are you?"

Jacob was shaken from his thoughts by the shiver Colton's voice sent through his body. He had drifted behind Sorrell and Colton in his daze, and they had stopped to ensure his continued participation. Something else was sawing at Jacob's thoughts, but it felt like someone pounding at a locked door, unable to get through. He locked eyes with Colton.

"I'd appreciate it if you'd stay out of my head." Jacob could only hope it sounded as intimidating as he'd meant it.

"Just checking," Colton said before turning back to their path. Jacob silently thanked Pare for the mental shield. "I'm sure Bales will want to have...words with your friend—Pare, is it?—after their encounter at the switchbacks."

"No doubt," Jacob responded.

"How much further?" Colton asked Sorrell, his impatience showing through his calm exterior.

"It's a bit of a walk," Sorrell said. The merchant had begun to sweat, even in the cold morning air. "All the way to the end of the canyon and across the last bridge. Are you sure you—hk—" Sorrell's words were cut off in a strangled gasp. Colton turned and beckoned them to follow. Jacob still had no idea what his next move was, but now he at least knew his time limit.

Eriane crashed right into Pare's back as they descended the stairs to the lower terrace. She was about to yell at him for the sudden stop when he shoved her back into the stairwell and thrust his hand over her mouth. He pushed them into the shadows of a small alcove, his face so close to hers all she could see was the widening fear in his eyes. He released his hold on her mouth and put a finger to his lips. It was only seconds before she heard footsteps crunching in the still-falling snow and the voices that followed them.

It didn't take long for Eriane to pick out Sorrell's voice. She faintly recognized a second voice, and it made her skin crawl. She could feel Pare's heartbeat, fast and shallow, through his chest. With the way they were crammed into their hiding spot, she couldn't lean out far enough to see, so she mouthed *Who?* Pare, pointed at his eyes and drew a line across his cheek: the silver-eyed man. Her heart sped up in time with Pare's.

Anger burned away her fear the moment she heard Jacob's voice. Pare must have heard it too, because when she pushed against him to get free, he shoved her back into the alcove and covered her mouth again. Her pistols dug into her back, amping up her frustration. Pare shook his head, an emphatic *NO*.

Jacob's presence with Sorrell and the silver-eyed man cemented his betrayal. She wanted nothing more than to step out into the street and see to it he never betrayed anyone again. Even through her anger, she could see how shaken Pare was and understood that, once again, this would not be the time. It wasn't long before the party had passed by and Pare let up on his hold. The two of them crept out of the alcove.

"Why?" Eriane asked in an angry whisper. "We could have ended this! You and me!"

"No, we couldn't Eri," Pare said. "You saw the things he did in the pass, how powerful he is. He's too dangerous for us."

"We had them by surprise!" Eriane argued. "And I have m…"

Pare gave her a suspicious look. "You have what?"

"A couple of tricks up my sleeve," Eriane recovered. "We could have helped."

"And likely died in the process," Pare said. "And I don't intend to die tonight, Eriane, especially not for this."

"What's that supposed to mean?" Eriane asked.

Pare shook his head. "Nothing. I just don't want us to go and get ourselves killed, okay?"

Eriane let it go, but something about what he'd said didn't sit right. "Okay, fine. What are we supposed to do now, genius?"

Pare grabbed her hand and pulled her out across the street and down into the next stairwell, leading to the lower terrace. "We need to get to the Grotto before them. We need to warn Samuel and hopefully we can all get out of here in one piece."

"What, so we can just keep running?" Eriane asked as they hurried up the street to the mouth of the nearest bridge.

Pare stopped them and grabbed her hard by the arm. "Yes, Eri!" He managed to keep his voice down, but she could tell he wanted to yell. "This is beyond us! That man up there could – and would – kill us without a second thought. We don't even know where his breaker friend is, and *he* was good enough to get all the way through my defenses from half a mile away. I don't even want to think what he's capable of up close. So look – I'm not going to just leave Samuel to the wolves, because I know you care for him, but once we get to him we need to *run*."

Eriane ground her teeth, more out of frustration than anger. She was sick and tired of running, but Pare's words—his logic—were starting to sink in. "What if…"

"What, Eri? What if what?"

"What if Jacob was right?" Eriane said. "What if we had a gun? Even the playing field. And we could catch them by surpr—"

"Stop," Pare said. She regretted her words the moment she saw his face. The range of pain, anger, and betrayal that passed behind his eyes tore at her, wrenching in her gut. "Jacob at least had the excuse of not knowing me, but you don't have that leeway." He shook his head and stalked away.

It took her some effort to catch up. "Look, Pare, I—"

"Don't, Eriane," Pare said without looking at her. "I thought you understood."

"I do!"

"Do you? Then maybe it's not you. You're just a kid. Maybe it's Jacob's influence, I don't know." Pare stopped one more time. "You don't know the depth of what you're suggesting. It's something you don't walk away from. Something that haunts you every waking moment of your life, that bores into your soul and eats you away from the inside out. You can't know."

This was an argument Eriane knew she couldn't win. "Look, I'm sorry I even said anything, okay?" Pare didn't respond. Eriane realized she was panting with effort, and even Pare was moving slower than she knew they needed to. They were halfway across the low bridge at a brisk jog, but there was still a long way to go. The thought of the silver-eyed man getting to Samuel first, though, was enough to drive her through the pain. She picked up her pace and tapped Pare on the arm as she passed him by.

"Come on, Pare," Eriane said. "We're going to have to get a move on if we want to beat them to the Grotto." Pare nodded a weary assent and picked up speed to match her.

The lower path was straight and mostly downhill, but as they approached Kelef's downward end, Pare slowed their pace. The final bridge arched overhead, intersecting the terrace above them, and Eriane could see the gaping entrance to the Grotto looming behind it. They crept under the archway, stopping near the top of the stairwell that led up to the next level. Pare peeked over the wall and, satisfied their way was clear, ushered the two of them forward, keeping a watchful eye on their tail.

Eriane took a deep breath and looked back out of the Grotto's entrance. The morning suns were glinting off of the few mountaintops she could see, but even at their height the sunlight wouldn't penetrate very deep into the cavern. She noted there weren't any footprints in the newly-fallen snow other than their own, and gestured to Pare. "Look, Pare. We must have beaten them here."

Pare nodded. "Then let's get to Samuel before we run out of time."

Chapter Forty-Four

Returning to the Grotto was more intimidating than their exit. When they were leaving, at least there was an open place to run. Delving into it now, every alleyway reeked of danger.

Eriane's eyes darted around the street as they passed by locked doorways and guarded alleys. Something was different this time...something about the demeanor of the men and women they passed. What was once just appraising interest had taken a more sinister tone, as though value was no longer a concern. The deeper they traveled, the more cut off Eriane felt.

As Eriane watched, two men at the mouth of an alley blinked several times and shook their heads as though to clear them. When their attention returned to their quarry, both men's faces had taken on the look of blank and barely concealed anger.

Eriane moved closer to Pare. "Pare... something's wrong here."

"Yeah, I noticed," Pare replied, quickening his pace. "I'm not sure what's going on."

Eriane heard a shuffling noise behind them. Everything in her screamed not to look, but she did anyway. The inhabitants of the Grotto—everyone who was in the street as they passed—was moving out of their alleyways and shadows and following Pare and Eriane. A throng of people formed in their wake, their attention riveted to Pare and Eriane. The further they walked, the more insistent their pursuers became. The Grotto became a claustrophobic nightmare with nowhere for either of them to turn.

"Pare," Eriane said, taking a shallow breath. "What do we do?"

Pare reached down and took Eriane's hand. "Eri...we have to run," he said. "Now!"

Pare bolted. Eriane stumbled, but caught herself and fell in stride, sprinting down the main street, looking for the turn into the square where they had met Acthemenius's guards. The shuffling pack turned into a raging mob the moment they ran.

Instead of just being followed, now they were being chased. As they fled, Pare threw his free hand out in front of them and a dull flash of blue light knocked would-be assailants to the side, sometimes back into the sides of buildings. Their path stayed clear, but the mob was still nipping at their heels every step of the way.

"Pare!" Eriane said. "What is this?"

Pare blasted another small group of people out of the way. "I have no idea, but someone doesn't want us to make it to Samuel."

A hand grabbed at Eriane's arm and wrenched her out of Pare's grasp. She spun and found herself looking into the angry eyes of an old vagrant woman in ragged clothing. Despite Eriane's attempts to free herself, the woman would not release her grip.

"What do you want?" Eriane screamed. "Why are you doing this?"

Her question was met with incoherent raving. Without a thought, Eriane generated a concentrated bump field in front of herself, thrusting it outward and knocking the woman away into the crowd. Even as she fell, the woman's eyes never left Eriane's face, and never shook the frenzied wrath that had overtaken her expression. Eriane knocked another man down and kept the bump field in place as Pare beckoned her to him.

"There," he said, pointing to the street that would lead them to the square. The entry to the street was choked with more angry Grotto denizens.

"How are we going to get through that?" Eriane said.

"Stay with me," Pare replied.

Pare and Eriane moved in unison. The mob advanced but, for some reason wary now, did not move in close. The new group made no indication they would part or let them through. The hairs on Eriane's neck stood on end as small, bright ball of light formed between Pare's hands, gathering *khet* as it increased in intensity. With a sharp movement, Pare released the ball, which exploded amidst the mob with a blinding, soundless flash. Bodies flew in all directions as they were struck by an expanding shockwave that washed around Eriane's bump field.

A clear path formed ahead of them, framed on both sides by unconscious and dazed people. Eriane glanced at Pare, and they bolted for the opening.

You KNEW! Samuel had pulled his consciousness above the chaos, enough to confront Acthemenius's presence in his mind. *This whole time, you knew. Ever since her murder, you knew it wasn't a construct that killed the Queen Consort, and you did nothing.* Samuel fumed, unable to comprehend the level of apathy required for Acthemenius's inaction. *And my pursuers? You've just let them be? Let them go on destroying Chroniclers?*

Samuel felt a push, Acthemenius's renewed attempt to snow him under the waves of memories. This time, Samuel pushed back. *They know us. What we are, what we're capable of, what we were built for. And they can find us. How many Chroniclers have they tracked and destroyed? How many more would it take before they drive you to do something?*

Acthemenius's reply came softer this time. *More than I can count. What would I have done, Aesamaelus? Lead some sort of rebellion into another war? Expose the existence of Chroniclers so that rather than two hunters, there would be hundreds? I'm not an idealistic revolutionary. I'm nothing more than an exhausted old man.*

Samuel failed to find any empathy, instead finding only disgust. *Well I'm not. Whatever I was before that fire in Winston is gone, and the burden of apathy gone with it.*

You're going to get yourself destroy—

For a moment the stream of memories froze, overlapping images of unnamed people and places forming an indistinct collage. A flash of brilliant white-blue washed the chaos away and left only a murky darkness. Once again, a smell—the smell of stale ale and tree nuts—brought him back to his senses.

Acthemenius's head was thrown backward, matching the unnatural arch of his back. His arms hovered out to his sides, frozen in a gesture of surprise and shock. Over his shoulder, a face glared at Samuel with unhinged enmity. From behind a stringy curtain of dark hair, a damaged face housed familiar eyes. The eyes of a killer.

"How do you do it, canner?" The voice was unmistakable. From the moment Samuel awoke, the venomous tone of this man's voice had haunted his thoughts and marred his dreams. The memories of other Chroniclers had borne the voice to him on wings of death, and now that voice assaulted his senses in the real world. The voice, matched with those malevolent eyes, stirred a rising fear in Samuel as the connection between his acquired knowledge and the face of his predator made itself blatant.

Samuel skidded backward on the floor as the man screamed at him. "How do you do it?" Acthemenius twitched in the madman's grip, still locked in the gruesome pose that marked his paralysis. "How do you hide from me?" The man said. "I can sense your kind from a hundred miles away. I can track you across any barrier, and break anything and anyone designed to protect you. But I can't see either of you. WHY?"

There was madness now, a desperate fury played across a face already twisted in anger. Samuel rose on unsteady legs, shifting toward the door of the shop, which now stood open and unguarded. "I don't know what you're talking about."

"I don't believe you," the murderer said. "You don't hide from me without knowing how. You'll tell me, or the destruction of this rust pile will be on your hands."

Samuel steeled himself into defiance, remembering every moment of destruction he'd seen at the hands of this snake and his partner. He made the only desperate play he had. "Nothing I tell you is going to prevent that, but something tells me you'll need your silver-eyed friend's help to pull it off, and I don't see him here," he said, inching his way closer to the door.

The killer gave a derisive snort. "Clever, clever, little canner."

There was a jolt that caused Acthemenius to convulse before he went limp, falling with a hard crash onto his side. "There's no place for you to go now, Samuel. Nowhere for you to run anymore."

Samuel stumbled for the door. Sickly laughter followed him into the alley. He tripped over something, catching himself on the alley wall. It was Talecronelum, laid flat, his eyes dim but still alight. He tried to shake free of the fugue Acthemenius had left him in. Would there be help to meet him in the Grotto? More worrisome was the fact the killer did not give chase.

Cormanthul lay collapsed at the end of the alley. The square was clogged by a throng of enraged people, some of whom trampled over his prone form. When the mob took notice of Samuel they turned on him, rushing into the narrow space with little concern for their own well-being.

Samuel had nowhere to retreat. The first of them rushed up the alley, leaping onto Samuel and pounding at his head and shoulders. The sound of cracking bones punctuated each punch. One of them was little danger, but if the mob were to get to him en masse they could keep him pinned. Behind him lay destruction, ahead a mass of people who would throw themselves against his might until he was forced to harm them to make his way through.

"I'm sorry," Samuel whispered, grabbing his attacker at the crotch and shoulder and flinging him backward onto the cobblestones. The man landed hard and stayed down. Before Samuel could even process remorse another was on him. One half-step at a time he made his way forward. With each movement he downed another attacker with a shove or swing, piling incapacitated bodies to either side as he moved.

A new wave of fear pierced Samuel's thoughts, driving him forward into the mass harder and faster. His escape was only feet away, the statue in the square framed by the alley's opening. The crush seemed endless, the fight growing harder with each step. Amidst the battle a thumping noise caught his attention. A body lifted above the rear of the crowd, landing atop the group then vanishing between. There was a moment of silence and stillness as a bright blue light zipped into the alley mouth from the square. Samuel was knocked clear off his feet by a soundless explosion that flung the crowd in all directions, flying overhead and smashing into walls to fall in unconscious heaps.

"Samuel, get up!" Eriane's voice pierced the brief quiet. She and Pare stood ready at the opening, beckoning him to join them. Samuel scrambled to his feet and rushed to meet them.

"We have to go. Now," Pare said.

The noise in the Grotto picked up, and the mob that had been at Pare and Eriane's backs had caught up and was spilling into the square. Flashes of blue and white sparked through the air, Pare pulling constructions of *khet* from the ether to help clear their path. Eriane wielded a bump field like a battering ram. Samuel used the attackers' own momentum against them, flinging running men into others and knocking them aside. Their progress stalled near the statue as more and more people flooded into the square, spilling out of every alley and doorway in sight.

"We need to do something!" Eriane said. "We can't keep this up forever."

Pare's hands blurred and flashed as another small group was punted away from them. "I need time!" he yelled. "I can't think... I can't make anything as long as they keep coming like this!"

"What can we do?" Eriane asked.

Eriane saw fear and sorrow cross Pare's face. "I...I don't know."

She had to think. Pare's abilities were keeping them alive for the moment, but he wouldn't be able to keep up the pace forever. Her guns weren't an option; two shots would be meaningless against the horde, and none of them wanted to kill people who weren't acting of their own volition. Her pack was filled with provisions and gear for the trek, but nothing that could help them escape. She only had one other possession: the guilestone.

In all her time with the guilestone she'd never been able to use it for anything other than dampening sound. She'd pulled together minor constructions of light and air through it before, but nothing she'd tried in the past had held. Eriane pulled the polished stone from her belt pouch and held it out to Pare.

"What about this?" she said.

"A guilestone?" Pare was taken aback, but was forced to turn and defend himself. "That might work, but if it's attuned to you I won't be able to use it. You'll have to do it, Eri. But whatever you're going to do, do it fast!"

"I...I can't!" Eriane said, her confidence waning. "It's never worked like that for me."

"You have to!" Pare yelled. He was beginning to sweat, his voice giving out.

"Come on, Eri," Samuel said.

Eriane took a deep breath and pressed her thumb into the spiral engraved on the face of the guilestone. The only construction she was consistently good at was a bump field. It might not provide them a good offense, but if she could amplify one through the stone long enough to push back their attackers, it might give them a moment to think, give Pare time to formulate an escape.

She closed her eyes and tried to shut out the sounds of the combat around her. *Khet* flowed into her and coursed down the length of her arms, tingling in her fingers around the guilestone. The power crackled through the stone itself and she felt it grow. When she'd drawn enough *khet* for the field, she released it.

The shimmering blue-white glow sprung up around them, knocking some of the crowd down or pinning them under its edge. Mindless attackers threw themselves against its perimeter as it came to life, sparking and flashing like lightning. The onslaught was too much for Eriane to withstand, and the construction crashed down around them. Eriane sank to her knees, dazed by the breaking of the field.

"Eriane!" Pare yelled. "Get back on your feet!"

Eriane shook the fugue away and climbed back to her feet between Samuel and Pare. "I...I'm sorry. I'm not strong enough."

"Sure you are," Samuel said. "You just need some space."

Pare turned to Samuel and nodded. "We need to time this just right. Samuel, can you hold them off for a few seconds?"

Samuel nodded. "Only a few," he said.

"Eriane," Pare said. "Do you understand?"

She nodded. Eriane began gathering *khet* for another try, the tendrils of light materializing through the air all around her and

327

converging on her hands, wrapped tightly once again around the guilestone. The power built inside her, focused on the stone, and she felt it coursing through her like the blood in her veins, even stronger than before.

"Are you ready?" Pare said. She could barely hear him through the pounding in her ears.

She shook her head. "Almost. Not yet." Her own voice sounded muffled.

"Samuel?" Pare said. Samuel nodded. Pare broke off his defense and turned to stand close to Eriane, drawing his own *khet* into his waiting hands. The sphere of light gained brilliance as the construction formed, becoming almost solid as it floated in his grasp. Samuel fended off the enraged around him, his movements just registering at the edges of Eriane's vision. She could feel him getting closer, the perimeter he was able to maintain shrinking by the second.

The power built to a crescendo. Eriane nodded to Pare.

"Samuel, *down!*" Pare yelled. Samuel dropped to his knees facing the two of them, spreading his arms around their shoulders. Pare's ball of light shot upward, only a couple of feet, and erupted. The shockwave almost knocked the three of them flat, but Samuel held strong above them, protecting Pare and Eriane from the brunt of the force.

Eriane released her hold, firing a torrent of gathered *khet* outward from the guilestone. A dome of blue-white light erected itself from the ground up around the three of them out to the edge of Pare's blast zone. As the dome rose it intersected one of the extended arms on the bronze statue, which fell to the cobblestones with a clatter. In only a few seconds the dome was complete, a shimmering circle of protection that bent light like imperfect glass.

The space outside the dome erupted into a riot. Citizens of the Grotto flung themselves against the field, desperate in their frenzy to get to those protected inside. The field held strong as the waves of the enraged smashed and broke against it with no regard for their own well-being.

"I did it!" Eriane exclaimed, momentarily pulled from her terror at the sight of her success.

Samuel put a hand on her shoulder and nodded. "You did it."

Pare slumped back on the cobblestones, drawing ragged breaths, his face glistening with sweat.

"Now what?" Samuel asked him.

"I just…I just need a minute," Pare said. "Let me think of a way out of here."

Samuel turned back to Eriane. "Can this field move with us?"

She shook her head. "I don't think so." She thumbed at the guilestone on the ground and it didn't move, locked between two cobblestones. "Even the stone is rooted in place as long as the field is up. The amount of power it would take to make this thing move is…beyond me."

"We need to get out of here," Samuel said. "We may have bought ourselves a few seconds, but it does us no good to be stuck here."

Pare sat up, flinging an arm over one of his knees. "I might be able to use the field to… create some sort of ampli—" He paused, tilting and turning his head, scrunching his brow. "Do you hear that?"

The three of them stopped moving and listened. The noise outside the dome died down. People were no longer throwing themselves into the barrier. Instead, they stood motionless, staring into the center of the circle with unbridled hatred in their eyes. That's when she heard it: someone was clapping.

It was a slow, methodical clap, echoing from the walls in the chambered town square. Behind Pare, people stepped aside to create a lane up to the edge of the bump field. Jacob sprinted up the lane to the edge of the circle, a look of relief on his face that almost seemed genuine.

Chapter Forty-Five

"You son of a bitch," Samuel said.

"You don't know the half of it," Jacob replied.

"Bravo!" The silver-eyed man stepped into view. "I would have thought this obstacle enough to end this, but you are a resilient little band, aren't you?"

"Jacob, how could you?" Eriane said from behind Samuel's shoulder.

Jacob's look of heartbreak only angered Samuel more. "Now wait, just hear me out."

"We don't have to listen to a damned thing you have to say," Samuel interjected. His was not a tone of disappointment; he let his anger shine through. "You brought them right to us."

"It wasn't—"

"Oh, don't be so modest," The silver-eyed man cut in. "We would never have found them if it hadn't been for you two." It was only then Samuel noticed Sorrell cowering behind the two of them.

"Fuck you, Colton," Jacob said, never taking his eyes off of Samuel. "Remember what I said before, Samuel, about why I stuck with you? Well, it hasn't gotten boring yet."

Jacob turned suddenly toward Colton, his hand extended and dark threads of *khet* trailing from his fingers. Colton stopped him in mid-motion with an open palm. Jacob stood frozen in place, his hand only inches from its target. His face and muscles strained against the hold, but his eyes told Samuel he couldn't move.

Colton tutted. "Now, now, you filthy little slip," he said. "Did you really think I wouldn't see this coming?" Colton closed his outstretched hand and Jacob let out a groan as something in his chest made an audible crack. His eyes slid off of Colton and looked past Samuel toward Eriane before his face went blank and his eyes rolled back.

Colton opened his hand. There was a sound like a stomping foot and Jacob's body was flung violently into the air. He smashed hard into the high stone ceiling of the cave and disappeared over the roof of one of the taller buildings. Confusion delayed the dawning of Samuel's realization as he watched the spot where Jacob's limp form had vanished, hoping for any sign of life. Nothing moved.

Sorrell let out a strangled cry and made a break back through the open lane. Colton took a deep breath and the crowd closed down on the merchant, pulling and tearing as they bore him to the ground. There was one last blood curdling wail, and then silence.

"Good" Colton said. "Now we can talk in peace." A drip of crimson fell from his nostril.

"You really are a bastard," Eriane said.

"Is speaking the truth meant to hurt me?" Colton replied, pulling a handkerchief to wipe his bloodied nose. "Hm," he said, examining the result. "You know, you had your chance in the pass. If you'd just let the canner go, none of you would be here right now."

"Yeah, well, we don't leave our friends behind," Eriane said.

"You've only known your 'friend' for a few weeks," Colton replied. "Your 'friend' knows something he's not supposed to know, and it's my job to tie up that loose end."

Samuel stepped forward. "All of this, just so you could cover up that your partner killed the Queen Consort."

Colton looked at him, and then nodded. "Oh, that's only the tip of the iceberg," he said, a smug grin turning the corners of his mouth. "We have a vested interest in the continued and widespread mistrust of constructs. Bales's mistake wasn't in the killing, it was that he let the city guardsman destroy the Chronicler before I got there. I could've prevented those memories from ever being transferred, but the guardsmen used those mafi-sticks one too many times."

Beside and behind him, Samuel could feel Pare and Eriane tensing for a conflict. The very air around him tingled with energy.

"If you're so good at preventing the transfer," Samuel continued, hoping to buy them a little more time, "then why have I seen the destruction of so many at your hands?"

Colton's grin vanished. "Because I *wanted* you to see. I wanted *all of you* to know I was coming for you," he said through gritted teeth. "That message performed its task to perfection. Chroniclers have receded even further into hiding, and as long as they remain hidden, their knowledge remains hidden with them. The cowardice of Chroniclers allows for a, shall we say, *leisurely* pace to my assignment."

"Then why continue at all?" Samuel stalled. "If the knowledge stays hidden, then why the hunt?"

The smug smile was back. "Oh, I'd think the answer to that question would be obvious." Colton hesitated, placing his hand onto the dome, taking a deep breath and pressing inward. The edge of the field rippled and skewed, and Colton's hand—followed closely by the rest of him—passed through the barrier to stand inside. "Because I *enjoy it*."

A deafening crack of power struck the air, driving Samuel to one knee. Something wasn't quite right about the sound, though, and when he turned Pare and Eriane were no longer over his shoulder. Instead, both of them lay in a heap at the edge of the circle to his right. Eriane lay unconscious, or worse, and he could see blood pooling around Pare's face.

"No!" Samuel said, and tried to bolt, but a flash of white in his vision held him firm, and his body failed to react. Something seized his core, his limbs no longer his to control. Paralyzed, he could only look upon the downed children in terror as the realization of what had happened dawned and a familiar voice slinked over his shoulder.

"Big mistake, canner," the voice said. "After everything you've been through, and such a simple distraction is what proves to be your end."

Colton's partner released his grip and Samuel slumped to the ground on his side, his field of view filled by Colton's well-kept boots approaching where he had fallen. Colton knelt before him, pushing his shoulder so that his view turned upward. He tilted his head to look into Samuel's helpless face.

"I have to give you credit, Samuel," he said. "You provided me more entertainment on this hunt than I've seen in...I don't know how long." After what he'd seen, he wasn't sure if Colton's little speech was for his own benefit, or for all the Chroniclers that would soon be seeing what Samuel saw. "Hiding yourself so Bales here couldn't track you. However you pulled that off was a stroke of genius."

Colton pressed his fingers into Samuel's chest, and a numbing cold crept into his torso. "My friend over there," he nodded toward Bales, "wants to know how you did it. But you know what?" Colton leaned in close, his cold, silver eyes boring into Samuel's, so close he could see nothing else. "I just don't care."

The numbness started at the tips of his extremities and coursed inward. Colton had full control, and was drawing out every last second of Samuel's destruction, flooding him with the terror Samuel knew every Chronicler would feel. Confronting Chroniclers with that emotion—perhaps the first they would ever feel—would only serve to drive them deeper into hiding from this pair of madmen, and Samuel couldn't drive it back. As he lay helpless under Colton's draining grip, wondering if Pare or Eriane or even Jacob were still alive, the only thought on his mind was that he didn't want to die.

The dull cold stripped him of his senses as it crept into his core. His feeling was the first to go, filling him with the sensation he was floating. Hearing went next, then smell, smothering his perception of the world around him, as though he were sinking into an abyss. His sight began to fade, sparkling at its edges with an almost incandescent fog, but just before he was completely blind, Colton was gone.

Chapter Forty-Six

Eriane stood behind Samuel's shoulder, listening to Colton ramble. She concealed her hands under her cloak, reaching to the holsters at the small of her back, and wrapped the fingers of both hands around the grips of her pistols.

"Are you ready, Eri," Pare whispered, trying not to move his mouth, and never taking his eyes off of the silver-eyed man. Samuel had Colton engaged, his attention focused away from the two of them and solely on the construct.

She felt her heartbeat pounding against her throat. Her vision tunneled. A thousand scenarios had run through her mind since their encounter in the pass, and all of them ended the same way. Colton and Bales were too strong for them, too focused on their goal. No matter what Pare said or thought, this was the only way they were going to escape from them. It was the only way they would be free; the only way to save Samuel from these killers. She only hoped she could make Pare understand.

Samuel dragged out the conversation, giving Pare and Eriane the time they needed to ready whatever offense they could muster. The hair on Eriane's neck stood on end, feeling the power Pare gathered. She pulled in as much *khet* as she could, focusing all her thoughts. She would only have one shot at this, and it had to find its mark.

"Then why the hunt?" Samuel said. The stalling tactic was working, then Colton did something unexpected. Between Pare and Samuel's shoulders, she saw him warp her bump field and step through like it was no more than a bead curtain. The most powerful construction she'd ever conceived, and he waved it off like it was nothing. Any doubt in her mind faded away and her resolve crystallized the moment she heard Colton say:

"Because I *enjoy* it."

Pare's muscles tensed and hers followed suit, but before she could move, the air beside them ruptured with a deafening thunderclap and she was blown off her feet. She rose to meet the edge of her own bump field, slamming hard into it and falling to the ground. With no time to free her arms or protect her head, the impact left her dazed. She hit the cobblestones at an awkward angle and her left leg snapped beneath her. Sudden, searing pain flooded through her, stealing her breath. She couldn't even scream before she passed out.

Eriane wasn't sure how long she'd been unconscious. Light filtered into her vision as her eyes fluttered open, a shimmering wall of blue that wavered before her. As her disorientation lifted, throbbing pain in her twisted leg made itself known. Tears flooded her eyes as she gritted her teeth, determined not to cry out.

Pare was regaining consciousness too, if he had ever lost it in the first place. The lower half of his face was crimson, blanketed by the steady stream from his broken nose. He shook his head as if to clear it, scratching behind his ear and wiping away some phantom annoyance, then pushed himself up to his hands and knees. Flecks of blood and spit splattered the cobblestones before him as he exhaled sharply, his face a mask of rage as all-consuming as the mindless mob outside the dome. Was he a victim now, too? Had the silver-eyed man—Colton—finally gotten to him? No, there was something else there, a sense of purpose the others lacked.

Pare was coiled like a spring, readying himself to move. "Pare?" Eriane said, her voice weak as a wave of nausea struck her, spurred on by the ache in her leg and her head. Pare didn't respond; didn't even acknowledge her presence. Eriane shifted her head to see the target of his focus, and saw Colton and Bales kneeling down, leaned over Samuel, who lay unmoving on his side. She brought her attention back to Pare, who had arched his back forward and planted his feet into a runner's stance.

When she tried to speak she coughed, the words caught in the dryness of her throat. "Pare…don't," was all she could get out, but before he could even register her words, he had sprung from his stance and bolted for Colton.

Samuel lay on his side before Colton, the long chase ended. Others in Colton's position would've been angry at the chase this canner had led them on, but Colton reveled in the hunt, and most of their quarries had, of late, been a bit too easy. There was a satisfaction to this victory Colton hadn't felt in quite some time, and he intended to savor it.

He spoke to the canner as he pressed his fingers into the metal of his chest. "My partner over there," he nodded toward Bales, "wants to know how you did it. But you know what?" He said, leaning in close, "I just don't care." Colton could feel the flow of *khet* around the construct's core, a flow very different from the other Chroniclers he'd encountered. There was power there, beyond any normal construct, tinged with a flavor he'd never tasted. As he siphoned the construct's energy away, he basked in the anticipation of watching this one dissipate. A glass vial from his belt was already in his hand, the blue nectar of distilled *khet* flowing through the glass to fill the stoppered vessel.

A crushing blow struck Colton low in the side, lifting him up before slamming him onto the floor of the Grotto some ten feet from the construct. The vial of collected energy skittered away over the stones as his attacker forced him onto his back, landing a *khet*-augmented punch to the side of his face that cracked his cheekbone and bounced his skull off of the stones. "Stretched yourself a little thin, huh?" the boy screamed. The power of it was raw and unfocused, driven by hatred, but stronger than almost any Colton had ever seen. This boy had talent.

As Pare hauled back for another blow, Colton unleashed his own brand of raw power, a quick blast of gathered *khet* from the palms of his hands that rocketed the boy upward, slamming his prostrate form into the dome overhead. The dazed boy came down in a heap next to him but was already recovering. Colton unleashed another blast, sliding the boy across the ground to come to rest at the edge of the circle, giving him enough time to recover himself. Bales stepped over the construct and drew a knife from a sheath at his thigh, stalking past Colton and toward the boy.

"No," Colton said, righting himself. Bales stopped and shot him a frustrated look. "Go take care of the girl." The look of frustration faded into an ugly grin as Bales changed direction.

Colton was unsteady, the vision in his left eye still blurry from the punch, but he regained his feet as Pare struggled to crawl. Shaking away as much of the stupor as he could, Colton strolled over to the edge of the circle and bent to pick up his lost treasure. A crack ran down the side of the container, the last threads of his precious Drift dissipating through it. With a frustrated grunt, he threw the vial to the ground where it shattered on the cobblestones. Colton pulled another vial from his pouch, yanking the stopper out with his teeth and spitting it to the ground. He placed the vial to his lips and inhaled.

The fugue from being struck cleared, burned away by the Drift like morning fog on a sunny day. It swept away the pain in his side and crystallized his vision. Muscles shuddered as they were given new life, and Colton stared at the still paralyzed construct that lay in the middle of the circle.

With Samuel down and Bales on a mission, Colton was free to narrow his focus. The boy was still on his hands and knees, scratching at something on the back of his head and trying to focus through blurry eyes. Colton wouldn't even need to use his power this time, and took a moment of pleasure to land a healthy kick to the boy's midsection.

"Do you feel that? Got an itch?" Colton said, leaning down. "Bales is the best breaker I know. I'm surprised you didn't notice he'd already broken your little slip friend's barrier the moment we arrived." Colton moved to a crouch, glaring at Pare as he struggled to breathe. "You've got some power in you, boy; I'll give you that. Your adeptitude may even rival mine. It's a shame," he said, standing once again, "you could've been something great." Colton's lips bent into a snarl. "Get up."

There was hesitation, a vibrating shudder that ran the length of Pare's body before he rolled back up on to his hands and knees. His teeth ground together as he held that position, his arms shaking and the muscles of his neck drawn tight into his shoulders.

"Even now you manage some resistance, huh?" Colton said, pushing just a little harder. The effort to hold this one was taxing, but the second wind from the Drift gave Colton the extra push he needed to maintain his grip. "Get. Up."

The boy let out a grunting cry as he struggled against his own body, lifting himself into a kneeling position. His jaw strained against the control and his cheeks were wet with tears. Sweat poured down his flushed face. His body struggled with the effort of breathing. Without placing a hand on the boy, Colton forced him to turn his head.

"Look over there," Colton said. Bales was on his knees with his back to them, straddling Eriane on the cobblestones. "Everything you know is lost to you. Everything you've done was for naught. She'll die, as will you, but not before I make you see the consequences of involving yourself in matters that don't concern you. Matters that are *above* you."

Eriane shifted to see, but every movement screamed in pain. When she tried to sit up she fell onto her back, overcome by dizziness and nausea. She rolled to lay on her side and tried to will herself back to lucidity. Colton had thrown Pare into the barrier after he'd been tackled, and was recovering while Pare still lay prone. Even though the blow had taken Colton away from Samuel, Samuel was still on his side unmoving, and now the other killer was coming her way, the blade of a short knife flashing in his hand.

She rolled for a better position, reaching for the pistols in her belt. She fumbled for them as he approached, but they weren't where she expected them to be. He was on her faster than she could draw, shoving her down onto her back and straddling her.

Her hips and one of her arms were pinned under his weight. As he leaned over, strands of his hair felt coarse and unwashed against her face. His hot breath bore a combination of unfamiliar and nauseating smells. "Is it cliché to tell you I'm going to enjoy this?" Bales said.

Tears rolled away from her eyes as she struggled under him, rolling her shoulders to unpin her arm. Her broken leg allowed her no leverage with her hips, and her struggling had little effect. She struck at his face with her free hand but he almost seemed not to notice, grabbing her wrist and holding it against her chest. His knife dipped down to point at her abdomen, and he leaned his weight into it.

"No!" she screamed, wrenching her pinned hand around just in time to stop the knife's blade an inch from her skin, her bump field crackling with light. All her thought and effort was bent into the field, held up by her upturned palm like a shield as the killer's weight bore down on top of her.

"Clever," Bales hissed. "But I'll break it, you know I will. Just like I broke your friend's little protections. I'll break this and have you anyway."

Around Bales's side, Colton was on his feet; Pare on his knees before him, facing her. The silver-eyed man's smug grin had returned, and she knew Pare was no longer under his own control.

Her concentration slipped, only for a moment, and the blade of Bales's knife dropped downward under his weight, the tip resting against the skin of her belly before she reinforced her defense. Bales said nothing, only staring into her eyes with a hate-filled gaze that filled her with terror. Their weight shifted, and she felt something dig into the muscles at the back of her right thigh.

Her pistols.

The belt on which they were holstered must have shifted when she fell, and now their only hope lay pinned under her leg. Bales bore down into her. Eriane felt his power clawing away at her construction. Any loss of concentration or movement of her hands would weaken the bump field that was keeping her alive. Bales understood all too well and removed the hand pinning hers to her chest to bear even more weight down on top of her. Spittle and sweat dripped down onto her cheek. He let out a strained little laugh. Under his weight and talent, her field was beginning to falter.

Behind Bales, Pare struggled to his feet before Colton, his arms held to his side with unnatural stiffness. Colton had leaned in close and was whispering something in his ear. Every muscle in Pare's body vibrated and Eriane saw he was openly crying through gritted teeth, his tears cutting streams through the blood on his face. Colton was going to make Pare watch her die.

Eriane brought her gaze back to meet Bales's eyes. She stared right into them as she shifted her free hand away from the field and rolled her hips. Bales's full weight dropped down onto the knife. At first, Eriane felt only pressure, the weight of him coming down on her abdomen. Her muscles froze. Then there was heat. An excruciating fire bloomed in her belly that overtook all her senses. Her eyes rolled back; Bales's face slid out of her vision.

Her muscles unlocked, and her hand fumbled around underneath her, groping to find the lump that dug into her thigh. Bales grunted and twisted the knife. Shockwaves of heat and pain threatened to wash away her thoughts, but she fought against it to keep herself focused. Her fingers found the worked-metal buttcap of a pistol handle, but under her weight she couldn't pull it into her grip. Agony threatened to overtake consciousness as the knife dug into her gut, and the killer leaned his head beside hers to whisper in her ear.

"Can you feel it? Your life, slipping away?" he said. "It's all about to be over."

The slight shift in his weight was all she needed. His sickening voice snapped her back to her senses as the gun came free in her hand. Bales lifted his head to smile down at her, but his expression changed to one of confusion.

"You're right, it is over," Eriane said, and pulled the trigger. She felt the muffled concussion against her chest, the heat of the blast. Something warm washed over her hand and Bales's expression went blank. He convulsed once and a small trickle of blood dripped from his lower lip before he fell to the side onto the cobblestones, still staring at Eriane with unseeing eyes.

The emotion struck her like a hammer. Terror, elation, regret, and confusion twisting her features and clawing at her focus. Her eyelids fluttered and she lay back, wanting nothing more than to close her eyes and wake from her nightmare. The world was deathly quiet, and every ounce of her being slipped toward sleep. A strangled grunt and pained sobs floated through her stupor. At first she thought it was her own, but the voice was not hers. It belonged to Pare.

Her will came tumbling back, the crashing awareness of her surroundings also sharpening the burn of her injuries. She reached back again, the knife sliding loosely in her belly. The roll put strain on her leg and the pieces of her broken thighbone ground together, a blazing spear of agony that pierced through her hip and side and brought with it a prodding rush of adrenaline. Her second pistol came free in her blood-soaked hand and she rolled, dropping her wrist across Bales's lifeless body.

She shook, from head to toe, her effort at odds with her injuries and loss of blood, her body telling her it was time to shut down. Focus gathered around her like a swarm, pushing away the shock and exhaustion, stilling her hand and sharpening her vision. Colton's dumbfounded stare bolstered her, filling her with satisfaction. His fist closed and Pare slammed to his knees. Confusion was replaced by shock, shock then by anger, and the silver-eyed man took a step toward her.

At this distance, her pistol's accuracy would have been suspect in the hands of any other. But every intricacy of the action was known to her. Every interaction from the trigger's pull to the hammer's fall to the ignition of the powder to the propulsion of the lead ball was known to her. Every wisp of breeze and change in air density was known to her. She adjusted her aim to compensate for the inadequacies of the imperfect weapon, and bent her talent into funneling the projectile to its target. She pulled the trigger.

In that moment, that fraction of a second, Colton's confusion turned to abject fear. A ripple of cold light wavered in front of him as the bullet passed through a hasty construction of *khet*, but his effort could not slow the projectile nor shift it from its path.

Colton's left eye exploded sideways and tore away his temple, spinning him around on his feet and showering Pare in a spray of blood. The silver-eyed killer landed hard on the cobblestone street. Pare's muscles went limp and he dropped to his knees next to Colton's twisted form. Blood began to fill the spaces between the stones, expanding outward from where Colton had fallen.

The world crashed back together. Eriane took a deep, painful breath. Through the smoke from the muzzle of her pistol Pare stared, his expression unreadable. The mob outside the dome dropped into a delirious frenzy, throwing themselves against the barrier with renewed vehemence, the release of Colton's control leaving them locked in mindless bloodlust. The clatter of their attacks didn't seem to register with Pare, whose eyes never left Eriane and the pistol in her hand. His jaw and lower lip began to shake.

Eriane dropped the gun when she saw Samuel begin to stir. Every breath was agony, Bales's knife still buried in her abdomen. She held Pare's gaze and mustered the strength to speak. "Pare?" was all she could say.

Pare didn't respond. He struggled to his feet, never turning his head or moving his eyes. With a breath, he steadied his expression, and whatever emotion had been there before was gone. Backing away, he held Eriane in his now blank stare.

"Pare, no," Eriane said, fresh tears of her own welling up. "Please, no." If he heard her, he made no indication. Pare tore his eyes away from her, taking halting steps toward the edge of the dome. His movement stuttered when Samuel said something Eriane couldn't hear, but he kept walking. When he reached the edge of the circle he raised a hand to rest on the bump field.

On the other side, the people of the Grotto struck the barrier where Pare stood, like wild dogs trying to get at prey behind a fence. Pare lowered his head and begin gathering *khet*; but for what, she couldn't fathom. "Pare!" she yelled, but he did not turn. "Pariadnus, please!"

What Eriane saw next stripped her of her breath. The throng outside the barrier slowly shifted their attention away from Pare. Their bloodshot eyes, once fixed on the closest prey, now turned toward Eriane and Samuel, ignoring Pare as though he didn't exist. Outside the bubble they separated to either side, just like they had for Colton.

"Pare?" Eriane said, so weak she couldn't even yell, barely getting the word out as she began to cry.

The bump field wavered, a shimmering disruption that rolled

outward from Pare's outstretched hand. He raised his head in silence and, without looking back, stepped through the bump field, out into the lane that had opened for him in the Grotto and walked away.

Eriane wailed, an incoherent sound that rose above the din in the square as the mass of people closed down until she could no longer see any trace of Pare amongst them. She rolled onto her back and cried as the world faded away to blackness.

Chapter Forty-Seven

The echo of the shot was the first thing Samuel heard as his hearing returned. Colton's body dropped to the street and Pare slumped. Samuel tried to speak but couldn't. He was only just beginning to move. Pare's expression had gone from rage to confusion to sadness and back, and as the boy stood Samuel saw nothing behind his eyes; a blank stare stripped of all emotion.

Unable to turn, Samuel couldn't see if Eriane was all right. Pare's feet backed away from him, and he heard her voice carry weakly through the noise in the Grotto, crying Pare's name. Regaining some small amount of mobility, Samuel planted the palm of his hand on the street so he could move to see where Pare was going.

"Pare, wait," he said, surprising himself that his voice had returned. Pare didn't respond. The boy's hand moved against the bump field, and once again Samuel felt the gathering power. The mob outside had turned their attentions away, and Samuel had never been more afraid of, and afraid for, Pare before. "Pare, don't go. Eriane and I need you."

Samuel, strength rolling back into his frame, pushed himself up onto his hands. "Pare?" He said, one last time, before the boy pushed through the barrier without a word and vanished into the crowd beyond. Samuel stared at the spot where Pare had just been, unable to process what had just happened. A rising wail pierced the air of the Grotto, snapping Samuel back to reality.

Bales lay on his side next to Eriane, whose body convulsed as she sobbed. He willed his legs to work, getting to his feet and stumbling to her side. As his line of sight cleared Bales's body her twisted leg came into view and he saw a knife handle protruding from her belly. Time stopped for him as she lost consciousness and he scrambled to his knees at her side.

"No, no, no, no, no. Don't do this, Eri, don't die on me." He lifted her shoulders and her head lolled to one side, but when he leaned down he could still hear her breathing. "Come on, Eri, come back to me, okay?" He shook her face and tapped her cheeks as lightly as he could manage, but she didn't respond. Laying her back on the ground he leaned over her face. "I don't know what to do, Eriane. I don't know how to help. Please wake up."

Panic overtook him. Eriane had stuck by his side through everything. She'd had no reason to follow him or to trust him, and yet she poured herself into helping him, and now he was about to lose her. She wasn't responding to his calls. Her breathing began to slow as the blood poured around the knife in her abdomen. Without thinking, Samuel tore a section of fabric from the edge of Bales's cloak and balled it up. He pulled the knife out of Eriane's belly to a torrent of fresh blood and pressed the wad of fabric into the wound.

Eriane screamed and opened her eyes. With one hand, Samuel kept the fabric pressed to the wound, and with the other, pulled her shoulders up onto his lap and supported her head. Her breathing was thin and her eyes glazed over her as she looked up at him.

"I don't know what to do, Eriane," he said. "I need you to stay awake. I need your help."

Eriane made a weak attempt to shake her head. "No... no way... out," she whispered.

Samuel froze, but then nodded. "I know," was all he could say. There was no way out of the bump field now. They were unable to break through the mob even when Pare was with them. With him gone and Eriane injured, Samuel wouldn't be able to hold them off by himself, even if he could bring down the dome. Hopelessness took hold as he realized there was nothing he could do for her. He would sit here, helpless, and watch this brave girl die in his arms.

"There has to be some way," he said, to no one in particular.

"It's okay, S…Samuel," Eriane said. "They can't…get you now." Her whispers were growing quieter with each word. Samuel's insides felt like they were being torn apart, and all he wanted to do was scream. She closed her eyes and drifted back into unconsciousness.

Samuel just looked down at her and held her, shaking his head. "No, Eri."

"Samuel."

The whispered word found its way past Samuel's grief, but he couldn't find its origin. Eriane was unconscious, still slipping away.

"Samuel!"

It was louder this time, but Samuel shrugged it away as he looked down upon Eriane. Whatever he was hearing, he was convinced it couldn't be real.

"SAMUEL!"

This time, he recognized the voice. The noise drew the attention of the people outside the barrier, some of whom began splitting off toward one of the buildings at the edge of the square, confirming the voice was not, in fact, in Samuel's head.

"Samuel, up here!" Jacob looked down on him from the top of the building where he'd been thrown. The side of his head was caked in blood, one of his eyes was swollen shut, and he cradled one of his arms. Injured though he was, he was alive.

"Samuel, you have to drop the field," Jacob said.

Was this some sort of trick? "The field is the only thing protecting us!" he said.

"Samuel, I can get us out of here, but I can't translocate through the field," Jacob said. "What's holding it up?"

"Eriane has a guilestone." Samuel replied. "I can't drop the field without her."

"You can. You have to destroy the guilestone." There was a crash inside the building at one of the lower levels. "Look, Samuel, you have plenty of reason to distrust me, but if there's any chance at all of saving Eriane, you have to do this quick. They're coming for me, and I don't have much time left up here!"

Samuel didn't have the time to be torn. Jacob was right: this was Eriane's only chance, and Samuel wasn't about to be the one to squander it. He knelt down and gently picked her up, her broken leg dangling at a sickening angle, and rushed over to where the guilestone lay between the cobblestones.

Another crash. "Just smash it, Samuel. That's all you need to do."

Samuel took one last look down at the small polished stone, then looked back up at Jacob, still unsure of whether or not he could trust the man who'd already betrayed his confidence, but his indecision was inconsequential. Samuel crushed the guilestone under his heel.

At first, the bump field seemed like it would hold, but then it flickered and dissipated into the musty air of the Grotto. It took a moment for the mob outside to realize the barrier was gone. Just as they rushed in, Samuel once again felt the horrible falling sensation as Jacob slipped them away.

Chapter Forty-Eight

Samuel's gaze rose from the slab on which he sat as the door to the back room opened. Much to his chagrin only Jacob emerged, his movements slowed by a distinct limp. The blood had been cleaned from his face and he'd been given some fresh clothes, a merchant's smock that made him look enough like Sorrell to make Samuel a little uncomfortable. Jacob's hand gripped his injured shoulder, his left arm pressed against his abdomen by a tight sling. Their eyes met and Jacob returned the look with a shrug and a shake of his head.

He hadn't spoken much to Jacob since their escape from the Grotto. A mix of emotions Samuel wasn't used to dealing with seized his voice every time he thought to speak. It was Jacob who had effected their escape and found them refuge at the home of Jo Tellis, the woman whom they'd been tasked to find by Mane in the first place. How he'd known where to find her was a mystery to Samuel, but he wasn't going to fret over their good fortune.

Jacob slid down next to Samuel on the bench. Neither of them spoke. Jacob's breathing was irregular, punctuated by stoppages and deep inhalations every time he moved a certain way. Phrase after phrase danced across Samuel's mind, from admonitions to questions to statements having little or nothing to do with their relationship or predicament. As the words swung by his emotions caught onto them, eliciting everything from gratitude to rage, and none of it felt quite right. After what felt like hours, Jacob spoke first.

"Who were they?" he asked.

The question seemed strange to Samuel, but at least it was an opening. "Killers," was all he said.

Jacob nodded. "That's the obvious point. Why were they after us?"

"They weren't after *us*," Samuel said. "They were after *me*. Something I'd seen; another construct's memories."

"So it's true, then?" Jacob asked. "You're a Chronicler?"

Samuel nodded.

"Your memories?" Jacob asked. "Did Acthemenius…?"

Samuel shook his head.

Jacob ran his fingers through his hair and rested his hand on the back of his neck. "And what was it they were after you for having seen?"

"Bales killed the Queen Consort." Samuel said.

Jacob whistled a note of surprise. "So they weren't just trying to cover for someone else. But now that Bales is dead, it's over. Isn't it?"

"Bales may have killed her," Samuel said. "But that doesn't mean he's *responsible*. I know there's more to this. There's still a lot to sort out."

Jacob just nodded, massaging his neck. His discomfort had become palpable, as though he were wrestling with an internal struggle. Minutes ticked away without either saying another word until Jacob finally stood. "I need some sleep," he said. "You'll…you'll let me know if…?"

Samuel didn't move or look up, and couldn't bring himself to respond. He had no right or reason to expect Jacob's help, but knowing he likely wouldn't see Jacob again didn't make it any easier to accept. Footsteps and a closing door indicated Jacob had retired to his room, leaving Samuel alone in the hall, with nothing to do but wait.

Jo Tellis was a bit on the frumpy side, favoring comfortable clothes over fashionable. She kept her hair in a ponytail to the middle of her back, the graying strands not easily distinguishable from the bright blonde of its nature. Her jovial smile was motherly and wise, and it remained the predominant image of her in Samuel's mind even though it had only lasted a few seconds upon their first meeting. During the chaos of their arrival he had relayed Mane's fate to her, but there hadn't yet been time for the whole story, nor any time for her to express the sadness that had crossed her face at the hearing.

Samuel had yet to move from the slab-bench in the entry since they had arrived. He had no concept of how long he'd been there when Jo emerged from the room at the back of her house, removing her thin-rimmed glasses for just enough time to wipe her brow and stretch her back. Samuel rose, and Jacob had emerged from his room without prompting; it was obvious sleep had evaded him. Neither of them spoke while they waited for Jo's verdict.

"Have a seat, you two," Jo said, replacing her glasses near the end of her nose. The two of them obeyed, claiming the same seats they'd used before, and Jo sat down beneath a wall filled with needlepoint pictures in worn wooden frames. A tired smile came to her face. "She'll be all right."

Jacob blew out the breath he'd been holding and slumped back onto the bench, and Samuel, buried for so long under the darkness of the last few days, felt as though he'd seen a tiny break of light.

"Now, there's still some danger here," Jo said. "She hasn't woken up yet, and I'm not sure when she will. Only time will tell if it's just her body taking time to recuperate or—"

"If she's in a coma," Jacob finished. Jo just nodded.

"Her injuries?" Samuel asked, not entirely sure what he was asking.

"Her leg will be fine," Jo said. "She'll have a limp for a while, but I was able to get it straightened out and set right, so even that should go away. Her gut was the harder of the two to work out. That stab is gonna keep hurting her, in some way or another, for the rest of her life. But it's closed and it'll heal, with time."

"I...I don't know what to say," Samuel said.

"There's nothing to be said," Jo replied with her matriarchal smile. "You three have a place to stay safe and warm as long as you need it. I can keep the guard at bay, and once this blows over, you all can find your way again."

"Thank you," Jacob said.

The sadness crept out from behind Jo's eyes again. "Mane always had a habit of taking in strays. I guess I picked it up from him." Her voice caught in her throat and she nodded again, giving them one more strained smile before patting them both on the knees. "You can go in and see her, but try not to disturb her, okay?" She nodded again before padding off to the front of the house.

Samuel was standing before the door before he even knew he'd stood. He hesitated and looked over his shoulder to find Jacob still halfway back down the hallway.

"You go on ahead," Jacob said, without prompting. "I don't think..." he trailed off, never finishing his sentence, then stepped down the side hall and into his room.

Judging by the number of times Jo came into the room for routine checks, Samuel figured he had spent at least three days at Eriane's bedside. She tended to leave Samuel to his thoughts, but every so often would ask something of their journey, or of the fight in the Grotto, or of his time with Mane. Samuel was never forced to answer the same question twice, and felt he had recounted his entire waking life to her in a short amount of time, which was a stark reminder of how short his time had been.

As Eriane lay in her bed she looked as beautiful and untouched as when they had first met, save the long splint around her leg and the hefty bandages around her midsection, which Jo changed regularly. Her sleep was not peaceful, often interrupted by weak moans and the thrashing of her head against her pillow, her mind replaying untold nightmares from which she was unable to defend herself. Still, she did not wake, and Samuel worried.

It was on the morning of the fourth day that Jacob had come to the room. His entrance was tentative and at first he wouldn't approach Eriane's bed, but Samuel kept quiet and let him move at his own pace. Jacob crossed the room and tilted his head to look down on her, taking up her hand in his own for the briefest of moments before his jaw trembled and he let her go. He took a deep breath, and walked over to Samuel.

"Can we talk?"

They sat in the parlor, silent longer than Samuel had expected. Jacob almost spoke three times, but seemed to think better of it, and now Samuel was beginning to grow impatient. He quelled his agitation by studying a shelf filled with dolls in hand-crocheted gowns, and waited for Jacob to make the first move.

"In the past," Jacob said, "I would have just left a note."

Samuel was confused, but waited for Jacob to continue.

"I've made some pretty big mistakes since you and I met, Samuel," he said. "I have a lot to make up for, but there's one thing I want both you and Eri to understand above all else: I never led them to you. I wouldn't do that."

Samuel leaned back and Jacob took a deep breath. "I know how it looks," he said, "especially here in Kelef. You have to believe I was trying to help."

Samuel mulled over how to respond. "There's a difference between trying to help us and just not trying to screw us over, Jacob."

Jacob lowered his eyes and nodded.

"So," Samuel said. "What happens now? Now that I'm not so...interesting anymore?"

Jacob ran a hand over his mouth. "It's not like that anymore, Samuel."

"Oh?" Samuel said.

"Yeah," Jacob said, meeting Samuel's gaze for the first time. "Look... When I first met you, I knew there was something different about you. Something that put you above the rest of the constructs I'd known. I was intrigued. In the past, that would be enough for me – it was all I'd ever sought. In the past, once the intrigue ran out, or things got a little too hairy, I'd be smoke in the breeze."

"So what's stopping you?" Samuel said. "It's not like you owe me any kind of debt."

"No, I don't," Jacob replied. "But something in me wants you and Eriane to know that...that I'm not just in this for the intrigue anymore. That the two of you...you matter to me."

Something about Jacob's demeanor told Samuel this might be the most genuine thing he'd said since they met. "You have a long road ahead of you, then."

"I know," Jacob said with a nod. "Which is why I'm leaving."

Samuel shook his head. "I know I'm not very old, Jacob, but that doesn't make any sense."

"I have some loose ends to tie up. If I'm going to throw in with you for the long haul, I have to…put a few things away."

"How long?" Samuel asked, reeling in genuine surprise at Jacob's admission he intended to stay with them.

"I don't honestly know," Jacob said, crossing the room to lay a hand on Samuel's shoulder. "Not long, I hope. I know trust isn't something that has ever, or ever likely will, come easy between us, Samuel. I promise, though, I'm not just stepping out on you like Pare did."

Anger and regret stabbed through Samuel at the mention of Pare. It was beyond Samuel's imagination that someone as close to a brother as Eriane had ever known could see her, in her state back in the Grotto, and turn his back. Of all that had happened to them, that was the one thing for which Samuel was least prepared.

He felt a squeeze on his shoulder. "This will not be the last time you see me," Jacob said. Samuel knew he meant it. Jacob handed him a folded letter. "You'll probably head there anyway, but if you need me you can find me in Balefor. There's a moneylender there named Jenner. Give him that. He'll know how to get in touch." There was an uncomfortable pause. Jacob nodded and left the room, leaving Samuel unsure of whether anything had been resolved between them. The next morning Jacob was gone.

Chapter Forty-Nine

Samuel spent his time by Eriane's bedside doing his best to sift through what images Acthemenius had pushed to him. Like all the memories he had received, they were incomplete, but now covered a span of time so much longer he couldn't discern a starting point. There were more points of reference, but his fragmentation was not repaired, so it was still a mess.

And perhaps that was the key. As far as he knew, Acthemenius had survived the attack. Colton never made it into his hideout, and Bales didn't seem to be doing the destruction himself, so maybe he could take a moment and pay the old construct another visit. Who knows what kind of mood he would be in after the attack, but it was Samuel's only chance at sorting things out. He gave Eriane's hand a pat and she stirred but did not wake, so he made his way out into the hall.

Firelight flickered into the entryway from the parlor, and Samuel found Jo there with her feet pulled under her on one of the large couches, knitting something out of smooth, cream colored yarn. She raised her eyes above her glasses as he entered.

"Is everything all right?" she asked.

Samuel nodded. "Everything's fine. At least, there's no change, that is."

Jo set her project aside on the couch, giving Samuel her full attention. "What do you need?"

"I need to know what it's like out there," Samuel said, "if you take my meaning. If it would be safe for me to go out into the city."

Jo tipped her head back and forth above a curt shrug. "Maybe, maybe not," she said. "The fervor has died down some, but some very public murders and what appeared to be a riot have the guard clenched up pretty tight right now. Especially since there were guns involved."

"I need to see if I can get back to Acthemenius," Samuel said. "He's the only one, right now, who might be able to help me sort all of this out."

Samuel's hopes sank with a quick shake of Jo's head. "Oh, that's not going to happen, Samuel."

"What happened?" he asked, unsure whether he wanted to hear the answer.

"You see, after you all escaped down there, the Guard came in. Most of the people, the ones who were still alive, that is, had come back to their senses, and didn't remember a damned thing. That wasn't all of them, though. The few who did remember described an ancient-looking, battered old construct right in the middle of all the strife."

"And they all thought it was Acthemenius," Samuel concluded.

Jo nodded. "He's long gone. The guard's been looking for a reason to douse him for a while. Word is they finally rounded him up and tossed him in the canner bin."

"Canner bin?" Samuel asked.

A wry grin crossed Jo's face. "I forget how young you are. It's a construct prison," she said, her smile fading. "And Kelef's bin is one of the deepest in the world, bored right out of the mountain under the backside of the Keep. Sorry, Samuel, but there's no way anyone, especially you, is setting foot in there. Acthemenius is gone."

As lost as ever, Samuel sat by Eriane's bedside mulling over what to do next, but his lack of experience left him floundering. The more he brooded, the more defeated he felt. He had no leads, no direction, and the only people who could have provided any for him were dead or locked away in an inaccessible dungeon. Pacing back and forth in the room, all his pent up frustration boiled to the top and he slammed his hand down on the closest surface.

"Damnit!" The small side table he struck clattered broken to the floor.

Eriane stirred again, in the midst of another nightmare. Her head rolled toward him and a dry noise escaped her throat that might have been a word. She had cried out in her sleep before, but something about her movements drew Samuel's attention and he rushed back to her side. A bead of sweat rolled down her forehead and Samuel took her hand in his, and his frustration melted into a brief hope as he watched her wrestle with some unseen aggressor. The hope was quick to fade; he knew better than to get himself worked up, and in his sadness he wished he could cry for her.

Eriane settled, appearing to have defeated whatever disquiet had roused her in the first place. She lay back into her pillow, took a deep breath, and opened her eyes.

After Eriane awoke, Jo hustled Samuel out of her room and would only let him back in at prescribed times to visit while she recovered. Over the weeks while she regained her strength, their time together was limited. Eriane spoke very little, answering any questions with curt phrases just informative enough to get her point across. The subject of the Grotto was rarely broached, and Samuel couldn't bring himself to speak of Pare. Eriane never mentioned him.

After a while, they fell into a routine. Samuel helped around the house while Jo tended to Eriane's recovery. After she'd found the strength to stand, Samuel would spot her as she learned to navigate with crutches. He sat to the side while Jo and Eriane took meals together, and watched over her while she spent her days by the window in Jo's parlor. Eriane was distant, entangled in her own mind and blocking out the rest. It seemed to Samuel, all her effort focused on getting healthy again and avoiding any real outside engagement.

Something was different, and always would be. Even Samuel knew that no person of any age could go through what Eriane had experienced and come out the other side unchanged. Still, there were moments where the old Eriane would shine through, and in the past week or two she'd even smiled and allowed herself to laugh. After an amusing conversation with Jo during supper one dark winter night, Eriane stood from her empty plate, walked over to Samuel, threw her arms around his neck and hugged him tight, then slid away to bed without saying a word.

The gesture froze him in place, and even Jo had stopped in her tracks. "I think that girl's going to be all right," she said.

For the first time in weeks, Samuel thought so too.

Eriane wasn't back to her old self. She was something new now, different, and Mane's apprentice was gone forever. Her demeanor was more serious and, in spite of the occasional smile or sly remark, she was anything but jovial. She'd begun to take walks in the morning and had denied Samuel's company, noting he still couldn't be seen in public for fear of being recognized, and Jo agreed. A young girl, bundled up and out for a walk in the snow, wouldn't draw attention, but an ancient and very unique construct would.

Eriane spoke one evening of having visited the city library several times. When Samuel pressed about what she was looking for, she would shrug off the question and explain that she loved libraries, especially after living with Mane. Although she rarely spoke after returning from her walks, she would sometimes draw Jo aside and engage in short, low conversations Samuel wasn't able to overhear. The conversations felt like preparations, and Samuel was beginning to go stir-crazy at not being included.

As safe as he was here, the time for him to leave was approaching, and he needed to address it with Eriane and Jo sooner or later. The conversation wouldn't be comfortable, but he couldn't avoid it forever. Samuel approached her one afternoon as she returned from another outing, shaking fresh snow from her hood and dropping her book-laden pack by the door.

"Eri, can we talk?"

Eriane shot him a look of concern, like she was about to get in some kind of trouble. "Um...sure, Samuel." She led them into the parlor.

"I need to do something," Samuel said.

Eriane furrowed her brow. "Like what?"

"I don't know," Samuel replied. "But I can't just sit around here anymore, now that you're back on your feet. I feel like you're safe here. You have a place where you can make a life for yourself, and I think it's time for me to be on my way. I have so much to figure out, and so many things—"

"Wait a minute," Eriane interrupted him, holding up her hand. "What do you mean, time for *you* to be on *your* way?"

"Well...Eri..." Samuel stammered. "You seem to have found some comfort here, and you get along well with Jo. I just assumed—"

"You assumed wrong," she said, flashing genuine irritation.

"I..."

"Samuel," Eriane said. "The only thing I have in common with Jo is Mane. She's been asking me for weeks to tell her stories of his life, of mine and...my life with him." Maybe the quiet conversations weren't what Samuel thought they were. "She's a wonderful woman and she's done so much for me, but if you think I'm going to let you set out on your own after everything we've been through, you're insane."

"I can't put you in any more danger, Eriane," Samuel said. "You were almost killed, and I don't know what I would've done if you'd died."

Eriane's face was unsympathetic. "Well how about you let me be responsible for me, then?" she said. "Samuel, you still don't get it. My decisions are my own. Mine. And my decision is that I need to help you figure out whatever it is we're in the middle of now. Not you. WE."

"But—"

"Ah-ah..." she said, waggling her finger. "No *but!*"

It was apparent Samuel had no room to argue this point, and he wasn't sure that displeased him. "Okay, then." He paused. "Where do we start?"

Eriane smiled, an unfamiliar expression playing across an all too familiar face. She unshouldered her pack and moved to sit in the parlor, waving for him to come over. When Samuel caught up her eyes were closed, her breath uneven, obviously fighting with words that needed to be said but wanted to be buried.

"When Pare and—" her words caught, and it took her a moment to recover. "When we were at the library, we found a passage in a book, a really obscure book of myths and legends. It was...It was about you." She pulled a book from her bag and set it on the table in front of her.

"What do you mean?" Samuel asked.

"There was a picture," she continued. "Four constructs, laid out on tables in a cross, with four artificers standing over them with their hands on the construct's chests. The passage around the picture spoke of the early days of constructs and their makers, and of...and of the creation of the Chroniclers."

"Didn't you say this was a book of myth?" Samuel asked.

"Yes, but it was the next part of the passage that caught our attention. Mane used to say every myth has its roots buried somewhere in truth. The passage named the four artificers: Solmenius, Dracanthus," she hesitated, "Acthemenius, and Aesamaelus."

Samuel's head swam at the implication. "Let me see."

Eriane's face scrunched. "That's the problem." She split the book at a bookmark and when she laid it flat, Samuel could see there were several pages missing, the ragged remnants of their bound edge slipping up between the others. "At the time, we didn't think we could get the book out of the Library, so Pare tore out the pages and we were bringing them to you in the Grotto. They're... They were still in his pack."

Samuel sank to a knee beside the table, his fingers resting on the bits of torn parchment. "Are there other copies?"

"Only four are known, only two anywhere we could get to." She scrunched up her face again, as if preparing for an admonition. "The first was housed in the Library of Kelef," she gestured to the book in front of them. "The other is in the great Artificer's Guildhouse in Balefor."

"And I take it that's not an option?" Samuel asked. Eriane just shook her head, downtrodden. He watched her expression transform before his eyes, though, replaced by the same sly grin she wore whenever she had an idea. "What?" he asked. "I think I know where to find Dracanthus."

In a few weeks they would set off, as the onset of spring curtailed any new snowfall, and the workers in Kelef would begin clearing the roads to the city. Jo's maps showed them all the routes out of Kelef. There was another road into the city from the west, the route Colton and Bales must have used after the rockslide had destroyed the road from Morrelton. How the two of them could've made the roundabout journey so fast was a mystery, and one Samuel would likely never solve. Eriane's findings would lead them east, over the rest of the pass through the high mountains and into the open plain that ran all the way to the eastern oceans.

Her route took them through a large area marked on the map only as The Drain. Jo explained the inhospitability of the place, a dead expanse that would threaten both Eriane and Samuel's safety. A place so bereft of life it was rumored its center was devoid even of *khet*. Their destination lay far to the southeast of the expanse. Samuel suggested they circumnavigate the desert, but Eriane was insistent, eyeballing Samuel in a way that urged him not to further the discussion in front of Jo.

After Jo had retired for the evening, Samuel rekindled the subject. "So what's in The Drain that's so important?"

"Samuel..." She hesitated, taking a deep breath. "There's someone I need to see there." She unrolled one of Jo's maps of the eastern expanse, pointing to a small settlement near the southwestern edge of The Drain. "We'll stop here, in Porral. It's a small village, so you should be safe there while I go take care of this."

"How do you know this place?" Samuel asked.

"It's... It's where I'm from," Eriane said. That's where I grew up. Before Mane took me in."

Samuel nodded. "Ah. Well, you're mistaken if you think you're leaving me there while you go off on your own."

Eriane lowered her eyes and rubbed her forehead. "Samuel, it's too dangerous."

"That's your argument for me staying behind?" Samuel said. "You speak to me of the danger of what you're about do and expect that to convince me to let you do it alone?"

361

"I can't ask you to come with me," Eriane said.

"Then don't ask. I'm coming with you," Samuel said.

Eriane allowed a smile to emerge. She reached out and squeezed Samuel's hand.

"It wasn't too long ago you yourself said 'Not you. WE'." Samuel said. "So. Where are *we* going?"

Eriane chewed her lip, as though indecisive about what to tell him. The young face that regarded Samuel was at once the face of the girl he'd met in Mane's cabin not too long ago and the face of someone altogether different. She settled her resolve and looked Samuel in the eyes.

"I'm going to see a man about a gun."

Epilogue

As winter melted into spring, the southern valley was pelted with the constant rainfall that made the little farming villages in the area so prosperous. Taeman detested travelling under these conditions, but the caravan with whom he traveled made some of their best money helping these farming communities prepare for the coming year. If the previous year's crops had been fruitful, the farmers would have plenty of stores left by the end of winter to fund their trade with the caravan, who would provide them with all manner of alchemical solutions, traps for predators, building materials, and repair services for everything from fences to scarecrows to wagons to constructs.

Taeman had to admit business was good. He'd sold almost all his stock, and was now enjoying a steady stream of new income from repairing and replacing farming constructs, many of which he'd provided to these same farmers in the first place. It was times like this, however, when he was forced to work out in the rain and muck and directing his small crew of constructs on stabilizing his wagon against the driving wind, he almost felt like it wasn't worth it.

The caravan had stopped just outside a small village that could barely be called such, a smattering of low huts surrounded by sheep pens and containing one large, barn-like building that housed their constructs and equipment for farming as well as a small slaughterhouse. The visit hadn't been entirely lucrative, and the village wasn't large enough to have an inn or even a hospitable tavern. There were at least three more stops like this in the coming weeks before they would approach a reasonable town, and even then Flagonstave—the all-too-clever name of a collection of ramshackle buildings that had sprung up around a dirty roadside inn called *The Flagon & Stave*—barely qualified.

At least they have an inn, Taeman thought. *And ale. And maybe even a real bed.* He checked the sturdiness of the braces to ensure his wagon wouldn't blow over in the night, his feet sloshing in the muddy ground. All the caravan's horses were huddled on the leeward side of the wagons, taking advantage of what little shelter they offered from the wind. Satisfied everything was in place, Taeman clomped his way up the steps on the rear of the wagon, knocking his boots along the sides to clear as much mud away as possible.

As he reached the top of the stairs, a glint of light caught his eye, the flickering of a candle flame from within the wagon. Taeman didn't remember lighting a candle or a lamp. By reflex, his hand dropped to the hilt of the dagger at his waist, a weapon rarely drawn and never used, but comforting nonetheless. With his free hand he pulled his hood away from his bald head and pushed open the door, taking the top step and leaning into the small space to see.

Everything was as he had left it, except for two candles now burning on his workbench. A figure stirred in the shadows to the back, amorphous in the dim light. "Who goes there?" Taeman said, failing to infuse his voice with the confidence he felt the increased volume would portray.

The figure moved, a cloaked shape in the darkness. Candlelight revealed gloved hands that moved to draw back a hood and revealed long, dark hair framing a slender face of coffee or olive, a face Taeman knew all too well. His heart thudded in his chest and his voice failed him. The cloaked man leaned forward into the light and looked Taeman in the eyes, pulling at the fingers of one of his gloves to remove it. He rubbed his bare fingers together and there was a crackle of energy to them, a deeper black even than the shadow from which he'd emerged. Taeman felt a wet warmth creeping down his thighs.

"Hello, Taeman," Jacob said. "We have a lot to discuss, you and I."

Author's Note

Let's start with the obvious: You bought my book. However you discovered it: thank you.

I write, and will continue to write, because I have stories in my head that I want to share. A perpetual bit of writing advice is "write the stories that you want to read", and that's exactly what I did. Not living in under a rock, I assume that there are at least a few people out there with the same tastes in stories as me. Hopefully that's you.

So here's where I shamelessly ask for something in return.

Discovery for self-published fiction being what it is, you likely picked this book up due to word-of-mouth, or perhaps a reader review. If you enjoyed it, please take a moment to rate and/or review it at your storefront of choice, or on your favorite bookish social site like GoodReads or LibraryThing. Reviews translate into publicity, which doesn't just feed my ego, but gives me the ability to keep on writing stories. I cannot stress enough the importance of reader reviews to authors like me.

You already have my utmost gratitude just for purchasing my book in the first place. A review or rating would just be the cherry on top.

I'd love to hear what brought you to my writing. I am always available online at **geekelite.geekerific.com** or **www.chroniclersaga.com**. You can also find me occasionally tooling around the comments on Chuck Wendig's **www.terribleminds.com**, or on my author page over at GoodReads. Social media-wise, you can find me at the Chronicler Saga group on Facebook, or on Twitter @GeekElite. I always look forward to hearing from fans, and I try to reply as often as I can.

Ignoring all that shilling, my biggest hope is just that you enjoyed what you read here. Those hours of escapism we can find in our favorite prose are some of the most precious in life, and I hope that I was able to contribute a few hours to yours.

Thank you. No, really: THANK YOU

Acknowledgments

Some think it cliché of authors to thank their spouses for the support they offer. This is not a cliché – many of us rely on the support of our significant others in order to partake in our craft. I am no different. At a time in our life when we'd built a comfortably worryless existence, my wife agreed to give that up so I could leave my well-paying day job and write full-time. Well... write, and do chores.

Christina's support is the foundation upon which this book is built. Without her by my side, I realistically never would've finished it, much less followed through on the heaps of work required to publish it. There are innumerable things about my marriage for which I am eternally grateful. Add this one to the pile.

I love you, Christina.

Although I wrote the text, Construct was not a one-person job.

My developmental editor, Annetta Ribken, was instrumental in honing this manuscript into the story you hold in your hands,. She pushed me to flesh out those pieces I'd left too vague, and to re-write weaknesses I otherwise would've left alone. The key? She didn't let me be lazy, and it shows in the finished work. You can find her at www.wordwebbing.com.

My copy editor, Jennifer Wingard, took that "finished" manuscript and tightened all the bolts and cinched down all the straps. Her work is the life-raft that elevates this text above a sea of unedited dreck. Her influence can be felt on every single page. She can be found at www.theindependentpen.com.

My cover artist, Carmen Sinek, was a delight to work with. Her dedication to the beautiful piece that graces this book's cover was inspiring. She was laid back and understanding, even as I nitpicked and vetoed my way through our collaboration. The finished product so far exceeds my vision and expectations that I fear I'll start to gush if I continue typing. Oh, wait... I already have. See more of Carmen's work at www.toomanylayers.com.

Together, these three women elevated my cobbled-together manuscript into a real, live, marketable novel. Thank you, one and all, for your contributions.

There are a few more people I have to thank, starting with Jon Schindihette. I worked with Jon at Wizards of the Coast (by "worked with", I mean "worked in the same building as") in the early 2000's, when he was a Creative Director and I was a flunky. I contacted him on Facebook when I was in the market for a cover artist within my price range, and he was able to give me the names of several artists I could try. Without Jon's help, I never would've found Carmen, and for that, I can't thank him enough.

After my third draft, Jared Carew did a copy-edit pass on the book before I sent it to beta readers. That pass taught me more about my writing than almost anything that had come before. Even though it was probably a bit early in the process, it made a readable beta out of a pretty big mess, and I have Jared to thank.

And, speaking of beta readers, it's time to thank the brave souls who provided feedback for one of my early drafts: Chelsea Hallenbeck, Dave McGee, Sam Beavin, and Chris Evans. Thank you guys for enduring a manuscript that likely bears little resemblance to the finished product, in large part because of your feedback.

An unabashed geek, Luke Matthews is a fervent reader, cinephile, gamer, and comic book fan, and he has been an avid poker player since his early twenties. A life filled with so many hobbies doesn't lend itself to easy devotion to a craft, but when the beginnings of *CONSTRUCT* found the page, those words pulled him inexorably toward writing, now the primary passion in his life.

Luke lives in the Pacific Northwest with his wife, three cats, and a rambunctious German wirehaired pointer.